For Alik

Enjoy the story!

OPUS

ALEX

OPUS

Edward Alexander

Library of Congress Number: 00-192450
ISBN #: Hardcover 0-7388-4228-1
Softcover 0-7388-4229-X

This is a work of fiction. Names, characters, places and incidents either are the product of the author's imagination or are used fictitiously, and any resemblance to any actual persons, living or dead, events, or locales is entirely coincidental.

This book was printed in the United States of America.

To order additional copies of this book, contact:
Xlibris Corporation
1-888-7-XLIBRIS
www.Xlibris.com
Orders@Xlibris.com

Contents

To my three sons
Mark, Scott and Christian,
each of whom, in his own way,
has inspired the writing of this novel

"Take one hundred century-old oak trees and write his name with them in giant letters on a plain . . . carve his likeness in colossal proportions that he may gaze above the mountains as he did when living, and when foreigners ask the name of that giant, every child may answer—It is Beethoven."

Robert Schumann

"If I had been there when Beethoven was alive, I would have terrorized him until he wrote at least three concertos for the cello."

Mstislav Rostropovich

PROLOGUE

Bad Nauheim

Germany

1945

-ALEX

PROLOGUE

Until the four firm knocks on the door, it had been a quiet morning.

There had been the usual batch of intelligence reports from each of defeated Germany's four military zones, dealing with some old and some new problems. The new problems were accounts of Soviet political cadres rounding up thousands of Red Army prisoners of war and re-indoctrinating them, in the American Zone itself. But most of the reports were primarily de-briefings of former SS personnel from the concentration camps whose barbarism destroyed all illusions of a sane world. Then, there were the scores of files of Germans whose dubious pasts made them high risks for the administrative positions they sought in the Military Occupation

He sighed, shook his head, despairing that there should be such continuing problems every day even though the most destructive war in history was but three months over. Then came the four raps. 'Fate knocking on my door,' he said to himself.

He looked up at the imposing figure standing in the doorway. He had not expected anyone and was looking forward to catching up with the reports which seemed to cascade onto his desk every morning. He nodded and beckoned the visitor to enter.

The gentleman was clearly German, about 50 years of age, with silver hair, strong features, and an aristocratic bearing. He strode in purposefully, bent his head abruptly in a formal bow, and said—

"*Entschuldigen Sie, bitte, aber ich suche Herr Philip Faljian.*"

"I am Faljian and I am a corporal," came the reply in German, and then— "May I ask who you are?"

"Please excuse my unannounced visit to your office, Corporal Faljian, but it is an urgent matter that brings me here. I am Dr. Hellmuth von Hase, and you have undoubtedly never heard of me, but until very recently, by which I mean until the end of the war, I was the head of the Leipzig musical publishing firm of *Breitkopf und Härtel*."

He paused to study the effect of his remarks but seeing no reaction, he continued—

"It is perhaps not known to you that—and if I am making a false assumption, I apologize—but in any case, that your military authorities have determined that I cannot continue in my former capacity in the American Zone and have denied me a license to pursue the work of my firm."

Faljian felt a slight surge of pleasure within him as the purpose of the visit became evident. Of the multifarious functions he had to perform, sitting in this old German villa commandeered for his office, none was so satisfying as the process which was known as de-nazification. In contrast to the grisly reports he had to read and summarize of concentration camp horrors, or of the brutality practiced by Soviet 're-education commissars' on their own citizens in American camps, groping through the dark maze of convoluted Nazi pasts was almost a game.

"So, you have come to me in the hope that I can perhaps persuade my superiors to overturn the decision. But *Herr Doktor*, I am only a corporal and they are colonels."

Surely, a German, and such a Prussian-looking German at that, would understand the difference, even though Faljian, as he had to admit to himself, was being disingenuous, for he knew very well that in matters such as these, the higher the military rank, the more remote the knowledge and the interest.

Von Hase smiled, a sad smile, but also a wise smile.

"To be sure, *Herr Gefreite*, I am aware of that, but I have come to you not because of your rank but because . . ." he paused for a second . . ." because it is already known throughout the Frankfurt area that there is an American soldier in our midst who comprehends the deeper cultural problems which we, the defeated, are facing, and that this same American has an influence which far exceeds his military rank."

Faljian was not a vain person but he could not avoid an inner sense of satisfaction at hearing this description of his de-nazification efforts. Writers, poets, artists of all kinds had paraded through his small office as he sifted through their lives and degrees of involvement with the Third Reich.

His commanding officers, mostly former executives from the newspaper world holding high rank, were largely ignorant of German culture and had funneled the entire de-nazification process to his office. On the one hand, he was not grateful for the massive overload of work, but he did enjoy the responsibility of being in a position to guide post-nazi cultural life.

"Be that as it may, *Herr Doktor*, what is it you wish of me?"

Realizing his visitor was standing virtually at attention, he gestured toward a chair. Now seated, but clearly not at ease, von Hase began—"With your permission, *Herr Gefreite*, please allow me to provide some background first. The firm of *Breitkopf und Härtel* was founded in 1719 by Bernhard Christoph Breitkopf. His successor, Gottlieb Immanuel Breitkopf, invented the printing of music and then soon thereafter the firm was sold to my great-grandfather, Gottfried Härtel, who was—and this is important to know—a friend of Beethoven, whose music was published by our firm. Since then, which was 1795, the firm began the publication of a series of the complete works of many composers, and has remained in the family, one of Härtel's grandsons being my father, Dr. Oskar von Hase. I hope this is not too ponderous and that you will excuse the genealogy."

Faljian beckoned for him to continue.

"I need perhaps not describe to you the importance of *Breitkopf und Härtel* in the musical life of my country, and if I may go so far without seeming arrogant, in the musical life of the world. In 1903, for instance, we issued a catalogue of all our publications which alone consisted of 1200 closely-printed pages. I am speaking, as I am certain you know, not just of musical scores but of every kind of musical publication. I need only mention the 65-volume 'Monuments of German Music,' the Köchel Catalogue of Mozart's music, and just about everything concerning the music of Bach. I do not wish to overstate the issue, *Herr* Faljian, but as you can see, my firm has been in the very vortex of German musical life."

Von Hase's reversion to civilian address did not displease Faljian who preferred to be called by his surname anyway rather than as 'Mr. Corporal.' He said—"It is not an overstatement, Dr. von Hase. I am aware of the importance of your firm."

"On December 4, 1943," von Hase continued, "during a massive American air raid on Leipzig, your bombers destroyed many parts of the city including the Leipzig Conservatory, the famous *Gewandhaus* and 80% of my firm, *Breitkopf und Härtel.* Of course, less important than the building were the original manuscripts, the treasury of music, by which I mean the plates of music, books, and countless invaluable publications, including—and again this is important to stress—the irreplaceable correspondence between *Breitkopf und Härtel* and all the famous composers, especially Beethoven, whose music the firm published."

"May I interrupt you for a small correction, *Herr Doktor*? The air raid you speak of was fully reported in the American press and was not directed at your famous musical institutions. I am sure you can appreciate the importance at the time of Leipzig as the rail center of Germany. And incidentally, it was a British and not American raid, not that it matters. Please go on."

Von Hase continued as though there had been no

interruption—"In the remaining year and a half before war's end, I gathered as much as I could and bided my time. When the American Army approached Leipzig I was able to find my way westward and settled in Wiesbaden. There, I planned to somehow collect what I could and resume once again the great tradition of my firm.

"And now, the problem. *Herr* Faljian, the United States Military authorities have denied me a license. I am unable to continue the work of my forebears which means not only the end of a tradition dating back 226 years, but a major blow to the renaissance of Germany's musical culture. *Breitkopf und Härtel*, represented by me, would be the only major music publisher in the American Zone. The others are all still in the Russian Zone.

"This is why I have come to you, in the knowledge that you have the depth of understanding and the foresight to comprehend the significance of a refusal by the American authorities to resume the work of my firm."

Faljian gazed at his visitor, studying his intense demeanor, his general aura of sincerity tinged with a degree of haughtiness. The summer was slowly coming to an end but the outside heat even at this late morning hour was beginning to infiltrate the high-ceilinged, panelled office he occupied and he didn't want to prolong this visit. But there were still a number of gaps, pro and con von Hase, to bridge.

"Dr. von Hase, I cannot believe that my superiors would have made such a decision purely on the basis of what you have just told me. Let us have an understanding right now. If you wish my help, I must know absolutely everything. Everything."

Von Hase crossed and uncrossed his legs, wiped his forehead with a clean white handkerchief, then said—"*Herr* Faljian, I did not have the intention of omitting vital information. I must tell you that I have already admitted to things in my past which, I presume, have already hurt me. But there are other things which

I hope will impress you more than they appear to have impressed your superiors."

"Let me make clear what I mean, Dr. von Hase," Phil interjected. "It is difficult for me to believe that the head of such an important enterprise as *Breitkopf und Härtel* can spend between 1933 and 1945 in Hitler's Germany and not be associated, affiliated, or be in some kind of even benign relationship with the National Socialists."

Von Hase nodded quickly—"Of course, of course, *Herr* Faljian, and I shall not spare myself. First, some positive things. While head of my firm, I was also President of the German Music Publishers Association and President of the Leipzig *Gewandhaus* Board of Directors. All of these were, as I am certain you appreciate, very prominent and demanding positions.

"From the time the Nazis came to power, I was in constant conflict with them, not only because I never showed any interest in National Socialism, but more importantly, because I was publishing music and literature by Jewish and so-called undesirable musicians and scholars, and exporting them. I know you will recognize some names, even if your superiors do not—Paul Hindemith, Curt Sachs, Adolph Busch, Felix Weingartner. I was under constant attack by Nazi cultural organs, such as *Die Musik* which published insulting comments about me by the Propaganda Ministry. That is a matter of record and easily verified.

"In 1934 I was relieved of my post at the German Music Publishers Association, but struggled to keep my firm on its feet. The next open clash with the Nazis came two years later when they removed the statue of Felix Mendelssohn from in front of the *Gewandhaus* where it had stood for a century—the same *Gewandhaus* where he had conducted his famous concerts and the *St.Matthew Passion* of Bach for the first time in one hundred years. I resisted the removal of the statue with every means at my disposal, especially as head of the *Gewandhaus*.

"The Nazis didn't know how to handle my resistance until, in reply to an inquiry I received from Switzerland, I described in a letter why and by whom the Mendelssohn statue had been removed. The repercussions were immediate. I was denounced as a traitor to National Socialism, and my firm was deprived of long-standing municipal business, such as the publication of the Leipzig city map. Then it was made public that I was residing in the home of a well-known Jewish merchant, as a consequence of which my name was added by the SS to its black list.

"I feared for myself and my post at the *Gewandhaus* but, at the same time, my inner resistance to the barbarians who were ruining our culture prodded me to an even more dangerous venture. In 1937, I infuriated the Nazi functionaries in Leipzig and Berlin when I published one of the greatest scholarly works in the field of musicology: the Third Edition—the first since 1905—of the Köchel Catalogue of Mozart's Works, the fruit of years of research and preparation by the famed musicologist Alfred Einstein. This was the only work by a Jewish author to appear in the Third Reich, complete with the author's name."

Faljian was impressed. He leaned forward and asked the consequence of such a bold act.

"I lost my post as president of the *Gewandhaus*, and major publishing contracts were cancelled, such as the 'Monuments of German Music.' Somehow, we struggled to keep the firm going but things were indeed looking very bleak. Then the war came and I was drafted into the *Wehrmacht*, but members of the firm kept in touch with me and I found out that a formal boycott was in the making and would soon be followed by the total closing down of the firm. I was advised to forget all of my principles and to take the only course which—Nazi officials in Leipzig told me—might alleviate the situation. This I did, with heavy heart, when I joined the Nazi Party in 1940 while still in the army. But even this step, which I took to insure the continued employment of 500 people and to carry over the irreplaceable cultural values of the old publishing house through the war, did not help.

"Nazi rivals in the publishing field in Leipzig saw to it that my two-centuries old firm—the first great name in German music publishing—was closed down in September 1943. The official reason given me was that *Breitkopf und Härtel* 'has not been active in the sense desired by the NSDAP.' Then, three months later, the air raid transformed our printing presses into molten metal. We saved only some plates and some volumes.

"Immediately after the bombing, I submitted my resignation from the Nazi Party and although I was warned by friends of how dangerous, even fatal, this could be, I had decided to make a clean sweep of everything and to renounce all association with the Nazis."

Faljian warmed to the subject—"But your friends were absolutely right. Wasn't it a foolish thing to do? I presume you were out of the army by then"—von Hase nodded—"and knowing the war was going badly for Germany, why weren't you planning your next course of action for the firm?"

"Because," von Hase replied, "something entirely new intervened, something I had a distant knowledge of but which I never expected would touch me."

He looked at Faljian silently for a moment and then asked almost timidly—"Does the name Goerdeler mean anything to you?"

*

Von Hase had spoken the name barely audibly, but its very utterance transformed and electrified the atmosphere of the musty, humid office. The name his guest had evoked had been unknown to Faljian until his recent interrogations of prominent German political figures, many with implicit Nazi affiliations who were anxious to identify with it.

Faljian sat upright and looked fixedly into von Hase's eyes.

"Would you like a cup of coffee, *Herr Doktor*?" he asked and when the German, astonished at the sudden hospitality, nodded murmuring "Bitte," Faljian requested two from his German secretary. He could hear the beating of his heart as he said, his voice taut—"I assume you are referring to Carl Goerdeler, the former Mayor of Leipzig, who was a leader in the resistance movement against the Nazis. Yes, the name certainly means something to me, Dr. von Hase. But are you going to tell me now that you were part of *Walküre*—the plot to kill Hitler?"

The details of the July 20 assassination attempt on Hitler's life were only recently emerging as more and more German political figures, some former Nazis, were being questioned and it was not improbable that von Hase, living in Leipzig, might have had some connection with the leaders of the plot.

Von Hase's response displayed greater assurance—"Carl and I had known each other for many years. We were contemporaries. You should understand that in Leipzig, he as Mayor since 1930 and I in my various music posts, would have had frequent contact. But we had something else in common—a loathing of Hitler and National Socialism. Carl had objected early to the Nazi persecution of the Jews and in fact he resigned as Mayor when the Mendelssohn statue was taken down. Thereafter, we often exchanged our private rebellious thoughts about Hitler and the future of Germany."

"And you were involved with the resistance movement against the Nazis?"

"Only in my heart, *Herr* Faljian, not as a plotter. I never went that far, although Carl would have been happy to add my name to the long list of civilian and military people he had recruited. Oh, thank you, *Fräulein*, no milk or sugar, please."

As both men sipped their coffee, Faljian waited for the rest of the story, which von Hase was eager to relate.

"No, it was not I who became involved, but a relative, about whom you probably have not as yet heard. He was Lt. General Paul von Hase, military commander of the Berlin Garrison, who became one of the leaders of the resistance, directly involved in the July 20 plot to assassinate Hitler. Had the plot succeeded, it was Paul's mission to take charge of the entire city of Berlin."

He stopped briefly, intending for Faljian to absorb the full import of his words.

"Between the six months of my resignation from the party and the attempt on Hitler's life, there was something of a void. Then, after July 20, the *Gestapo* suddenly took an enormous interest in me. *Gestapo* agents pursued me constantly, seeking to find some connection between my voluntary resignation from the NSDAP and the coup against Hitler in which Paul had been involved."

"Since there was no connection, what finally happened?"

"Fully aware of the nature of such investigations and knowing the fate of many who might even have been innocent, I decided to escape into the countryside. Fortunately, the *Gestapo* lost track of me. But Carl and Paul, tragically, did not escape. Both were hanged, Paul three weeks after the bombing and Carl a few months later. Actually in February of this year. *Imagine*, *Herr* Faljian, just seven months ago. What a great chancellor of Germany Carl would have made!"

Overcome for the moment with these thoughts, von Hase stared silently at the floor, then continued—"But then came April 1945, when the American soldiers entered Leipzig. Oh, what a beautiful sight that was, a wonderful day for all of us in the city, that is, until we learned that Leipzig was destined to be in the Russian Zone of Occupation!

"I immediately appealed to the American authorities to permit me and essential members of my firm to flee to the American Zone. Permission was granted and we arrived eventually in Wiesbaden, bringing samples of our most important publications which we could reproduce through photographic processes."

"*Herr Doktor*, excuse me, but I fail to see why you have brought Goerdeler's name to my attention. The fact is, your connection with one of the leaders of the anti-Nazi resistance was, to put it gently, quite peripheral. One might even say you had virtually nothing to do with it at all."

Von Hase displayed a contrite face, nodding and looking down. "Please excuse my obviously feeble attempt to gain your respect. I thought that perhaps my association with Goerdeler, which incidentally was very real and very close, might arouse sympathy in you for my plight."

Faljian decided to bring the interview to a rapid end. He asked if everything that he had just heard was known to the military authorities.

Von Hase placed his empty cup and saucer on the desk. "I applied for a license at the Military Government office in Wiesbaden to continue the publication activities of *Breitkopf und Härtel*. I was interrogated and asked to fill out the *Fragebogen*."

"Filling out the Questionnaire is normal in such requests," Phil pointed out.

"Yes, yes, I know. But then I was interrogated a second time, and then a third. The pressure on me was enormous, the suspicions of the interrogators were very tangible. I don't know if my story received a full hearing. In fact, I was beginning to fear the worst, and, as matters turned out, my fears were well-founded. I was informed by the License and Publications Section of the Information Control Detachment that on the basis of my membership in the NSDAP, I was being denied licensing privileges, and that the decision would stand indefinitely.

"My dear *Herr* Faljian, that is how things stand at present. I had hoped that there would be more understanding by your authorities. My four years in the party should not be considered such a crime. I was never active, never held office, never performed a party function and, except for compulsory dues, never donated money to the National Socialist cause.

"Now, I appeal to you, to your understanding of the need to continue the work of *Breitkopf und Härtel* and by doing so, continuing the great current of the German cultural heritage."

Von Hase was exhausted, and to a lesser degree, so was Faljian. This recital of the many aspects of von Hase's background was indeed filled with a number of plusses, but there were still those four years in the party and Faljian knew how strictly his superiors viewed Nazi party membership. Only a week before, one of them, Col. Silverstein, a former New York publishing executive, had stopped by and described a gruesome incident at the Belsen Concentration Camp. The SS guards had organized an orchestra of Jewish prisoners from seven countries who had been forced to perform while hundreds of women stood naked for hours awaiting the gas chamber. He had said that if Faljian ever came across any of those SS guards, he should immediately let him know."Even music, Corporal, even music!"

Faljian couldn't blame him for his fury.

Von Hase, on the other hand, was something else. Faljian was impressed with his sincerity, and despite the air of haughtiness, even admitted to himself that he liked the man. It was true that his superiors often viewed de-nazification in black and white terms. Captains, majors, colonels, and one general—they had been drawn largely from the media, serving at first in Psychological Warfare, where they were comfortable, and now in the immediate post-war period, in Military Intelligence and de-nazification, where they weren't. As for knowledge of cultural matters, they were totally at sea. In their eyes, membership in the NSDAP spelled pure and unadulterated guilt, canceling out any professional qualifications. For them, there was no absolution for the sin of party membership.

But when interrogations brought cultural pasts and cultural problems to the surface, they always turned to Faljian, respecting his fluency in German, which none of them could equal, and his knowledge of German culture, especially music, in which his expertise was unchallenged.

It was this reputation which had drawn von Hase to his office. This time, perhaps, there just might be an outside chance. In any case, it was worth a try. After a silence of several minutes in which he mulled over the facts as von Hase had presented them, Faljian said—"*Herr Doktor*, I fully appreciate the importance of *Breitkopf und Härtel*, whose historical role has long since been known to me from my studies in musicology. I agree with you about the necessity of continuing its work. I also appreciate that you are best qualified to perform that function. I cannot give you any guarantee that my efforts will be successful, but I do believe that there are mitigating circumstances in your case. Consequently, I shall raise it with my superiors and ask for an appeal and review."

Von Hase rose from his chair, his face flushed, and bowed with great solemnity. Assuming there was no more to be said, Faljian extended his hand, but von Hase suddenly sat down and spoke again.

"*Herr* Faljian, you cannot know what this means to me. In fact, it is of such importance that I . . . I . . ."

"Yes, *Herr Doktor*, I can understand your gratitude, but let us first await the outcome."

"No, *Herr* Faljian, you do not understand. It is simply that I . . . ," he hesitated, swallowed hard, then continued—"With your permission, *Herr* Faljian, may I return tomorrow morning? I wish a little more time to be absolutely certain of my decision before I speak to you again . . . about one more thing . . . which I have reason to believe you will find of considerable importance. Please do not deny me this privilege. I am certain you will not regret it."

When the German had left, Phil remained seated, staring at the closed door and mused—What was he talking about? What decision? Had he omitted some very vital bit of information which he had kept from all his previous interrogators? That would be stupid. On the other hand, perhaps it was something that only he could appreciate—and act on. It sounded intriguing . . . or was it yet another ploy to gain his sympathy?

Turning once again to the reports on his desk, Faljian tried to concentrate on the problems they posed, but for the rest of the day, von Hase's promise of 'one more thing' lurked at the back of his mind.

*

Punctual and looking alert the next morning, von Hase knocked, entered and sat down when Faljian gestured toward a chair. He exuded a sense of confidence which Faljian construed to mean that von Hase had made his decision to talk about whatever it was that he considered so important.

Displaying a small smile, his eyes sparkling, he said—"I do very much appreciate this opportunity to see you again, *Herr* Faljian, and I expect that when we have finished, you will feel the very same. I should now like to ask you a question."

Then, scrutinizing Faljian closely, he asked—"What do you know about Beethoven's Cello Concerto?"

Completely taken aback by what seemed a total *non sequitur*, but recovering quickly, Faljian shot back—

"Is this a rather transparent attempt to test my knowledge, *Herr Doktor*? If so, I resent it."

"Please do not be offended, *Herr* Faljian. I repeat the question—Beethoven's Cello Concerto?"

Still annoyed, Faljian replied—"You know as well as I that Beethoven never wrote a Cello Concerto!"

"Excellent! Excellent!" Von Hase now moved forward to the edge of his chair, his voice tinged with excitement.

"I should have expected no less from you. Good, very good. Now, please listen to me. I told you before that my great-grandfather, Gottfried von Härtel, had been a friend of Beethoven. In fact, Beethoven often confided in him, corresponded frequently. You know, old Ludwig was a great writer of letters. Well, one day, he wrote that he was planning a work for Cello and Orchestra, had already made some sketches, and would let my great-grandfather know of its further progress. He asked also that all this be kept secret. Ah, I see that you are incredulous."

Anticipating what he thought von Hase was about to say, Faljian smiled and said dismissively—"Oh come now, Dr.von Hase. The Nazis are defeated and suddenly we discover a new work by Beethoven of which, as far as musicology knows, there has never been any evidence. Please . . ."

Von Hase, his hands clenched together, his voice jubilant, continued—"I am delighted that you appreciate the value of my revelation. But I beg you to be patient and allow me to continue. Beethoven's letter—the only one, by the way, on this subject—had apparently been put by my great-grandfather in a drawer in a locked file in an old part of our building. He hadn't told anyone of it, as Beethoven had requested, and it had remained there for more than a century.

"Then, one day in 1934, in searching for a Bach manuscript and having gone through a number of old files, I came across this drawer. It didn't open readily and I had to pull hard on it. Once opened, I took out the thick cluster of manuscripts mostly from long forgotten composers of the 18th century. I searched through them but could not find the Bach. Disappointed, I started to put them back when I saw that at the very rear of the drawer there was a large packet. Hoping it might be what I had been searching for, I reached in and brought it out. It was tied with very old string but rather well preserved. On its face were the handwritten words 'Do not open,' followed by the initials 'GvH.'

"Those words, in my great-grandfather's handwriting, as well as his initials, sent a shiver down my spine. What was I about to discover? I do not hesitate to tell you my hands were trembling as I untied the string and opened the envelope. Please believe me, *Herr* Faljian, when I tell you that the sight of the topmost sheet made my hair stand on end.

"It was the Beethoven letter I just mentioned, in his own execrable handwriting, which with some difficulty I set about reading. Then, very carefully, I laid the letter, which was on one side of a sheet of paper, aside and beheld the first page of a manuscript in the unmistakable musical notation of the Master himself. On it was written—'*Konzert für Violoncello und Orchester*.' Even to the red pencil! You know, of course, that Beethoven always used red pencil for his titles. I fell back in a state of such turbulence, you cannot imagine."

Faljian himself now experienced the same excitement. His mind raced back to his days as a student of musicology when he had often wondered why it was that Beethoven—and Mozart too, for that matter—had never composed a concerto for the cello. It hardly made any sense. Beethoven had written a violin concerto, five piano concertos, as well as a Triple Concerto for violin, piano and cello. If he had written all of those, why not one also for the cello alone?

"I have so many questions, *Herr Doktor*, I don't know where to start," Faljian blurted out, the climate of the interview now having completely changed. "First of all, if you have known this since 1934, why have you kept it a secret?"

"A totally understandable question, *Herr* Faljian, but again it goes back to my inner feelings about the National Socialists. At that time, in the early years of the Third Reich, the Nazis were seeking international approval. They seemed to have had the consent of the German people in the election, and now they looked to Europe and the world, and I needn't remind you of the role that culture played in their politics. I knew that if I revealed the existence of this letter and manuscript, it would not be *Breitkopf und Härtel* but the Propaganda Ministry which would take credit. Goebbels would have seen to that, and by doing so, bolster the image of a culture-loving ideology. Therefore, I kept the secret.

"I did, however, do one thing in recognition of the huge value of my discovery. Instead of returning the manuscript and letter to the old drawer, I put both into the private steel safe in my office."

Faljian could not restrain his bursting curiosity—"And you have brought them with you?"

Von Hase frowned, shaking his head from side to side—"If I had them still, I would be showing them to you at this moment. No, unfortunately, they disappeared."

Faljian studied the Prussian features of the dignified gentleman sitting opposite him, then asked—"One of the employees? Perhaps someone untrustworthy who might have wanted to curry favor with Leipzig party officials?"

Von Hase waved his hands impatiently, as though to dispel such a supposition. "None of my employees. Our firm, our building, was a treasure house of manuscripts, letters, notes, sketches of every kind from every famous musician we represented, and nothing was ever missing. No, not them. And most of all not Scheidemann."

Seeing Faljian's raised eyebrows, he explained—"Scheidemann was my most trusted employee, a kind of personal aide. But I do have a theory, in my view a very sound theory, and that is why I tell all this to you, in the hope you can pursue it, no matter what the outcome of my case.

"In the middle of 1943 I was visited by a Hungarian musicologist named Ferenc Fekete. I had heard of him in the late thirties, a second-rate scholar specializing in the transition from musical classicism to romanticism. When he arrived he made no secret of his admiration for National Socialism and in conversations with him it emerged that he was a member of the Hungarian Arrow Cross Party.

"*Herr* Faljian, I don't know how familiar you are with Hungarian politics . . ."

Faljian shook his head.

"Well, the Arrow Cross was a fascist party in close affiliation with the Nazis. As an example, Fekete, not to my surprise, was a vicious anti-Semite and a believer in the purity of blood. He himself, by the way, was hardly an example of purity. I disliked him for a number of reasons, one of which was that he was so obese that he sweated profusely and reeked odiously.

"In any case, I knew that he often entered my office without my permission. My secretary told me of frequent such violations of privacy when I was absent. She also told me that she had once found him kneeling at my safe. He had quickly arisen, kissed her hand—something he was always doing with women—and left. For the remainder of his stay with us I tolerated him. That is the only word I can think of to describe how I felt about his presence in our hallowed building. I couldn't ask him to leave without incurring the further displeasure of the Party. But then, events brought about a resolution.

"On the first day of December I had to go to Dresden for a series of consultations which were to last all week. Late in the morning of December 4 I received a frantic phone call from Scheidemann telling me—his voice trembling with grief—that most of *Breitkopf und Härtel* had been destroyed only hours before in a massive air raid and that I should return immediately. I did, of course, and rushed to *Nürnberger Strasse* where the sight of the terrible destruction made me ill. Then, I stood in front of what was left of our two-hundred year old firm and wept. *Herr* Faljian, I asked the good Lord—Why us, dear God, why us? Fortunately, still intact was Bach's St. Thomas Church, but gone were the Conservatory, the *Gewandhaus* . . . and most of *Breitkopf und Härtel*.

"I worked my way through the still smoldering rubble, firemen shouting at me to be cautious. I learned that no one had been hurt. Eventually, I found my office, which was completely in shambles. I looked around, feeling totally helpless, and then my eyes fell on the safe. It had been blown apart, its heavy door blasted off its hinges. I looked inside and saw that apart from charred scraps of paper it was empty. And then, I suddenly remembered the Beethoven!

"Now with Scheidemann's help, I began frantically searching through the papers strewn around the floor, some scorched but some intact. I told myself that whatever else I had had in the safe, nothing could possibly match the value of that score. We searched for almost two hours, but in vain. Neither the score nor the letter were to be found. Despondent beyond description, I now turned to the welfare of my employees."

Faljian listened with undisguised interest, his mind buzzing with the kaleidoscopic images of the dramatic episodes von Hase had described. Both men were hunched forward on opposite sides of Faljian's desk, the silence in the room interrupted only by the chirping of birds outside in the summer air. Finally, it was the American who spoke—"And you have told me all this, *Herr Doktor*, because . . ."

". . . because . . ." von Hase went on, "I am grateful to you for your sympathetic understanding of my situation. At the same time, I fully realize that all I have done is to reveal to you the existence of an incomplete composition by the greatest of all composers, the evidence of which remains elusive."

He hesitated for a moment—"There is something else as well, but," he looked fleetingly out the window, "perhaps it is no longer important. In any case, the few clues I have given you are vague, I know, and it remains for you to pursue them, track them down. But please consider what I have told you, *Herr* Faljian, as my gift to you. In my present circumstances, it is the most valuable gift I could possibly offer."

Von Hase sat still, his eyes closed, only his head moving, nodding repeatedly, his thoughts apparently distant. Then, abruptly, he stood up, bowed formally and appeared pleased when Faljian also arose to accompany him to the door. There, they shook hands and Faljian said he would do his best on the appeal.

Alone now in his office, he looked out of his open windows at the greenery of the gentle German town which he knew he would always associate not with the sights of Nature but with the events described in the reports on his desk of concentration camp atrocities beyond the comprehension of civilized minds. Close by was Frankfurt, the city of Goethe's birth. To the north Bonn, where Beethoven had been born. But to the east, Dachau . . . He shook his head. And now, von Hase and his strange but intriguing story.

Yes, the Colonel had been right—"Even music, Corporal, even music!"

Only yesterday, he had had to review the file of the great

German pianist Walter Gieseking, and that had been a dismal experience. Why had he remained in Germany throughout the war, played countless concerts for the Nazis, lent them the prestige of his name?

Even worse, the greatest living German composer, Richard Strauss, who in the first days of Nazi power had accepted the post of President of the Reich Music Council, had personally met with Hitler, Goebbels and Goering, had approved of the denunciation of fellow composer Paul Hindemith, and finally, had agreed to replace Bruno Walter when he was denied permission to conduct the Berlin Philharmonic because he was a Jew. Then in 1935, Strauss had broken with the Nazis but remained in Germany. Faljian was scheduled to interrogate the famous man, now 85, in his Bavarian villa in Garmisch. His file, too, lay on Faljian's desk.

Strauss the composer, Gieseking the pianist, von Hase the publisher—all purveyors of German musical culture.

Faljian held his head in his hands wondering how he, a native New Yorker of 22, had gotten into a situation where his word could engineer the destinies of three prominent personalities in the world of music. But as he sat still, mulling over the implications of such a huge responsibility, von Hase's astonishing revelation flashed through his mind. A Cello Concerto by the Master himself!

During his musicological studies, Faljian had been aware of Beethoven's plans for a Tenth Symphony when he had been invited to England by the Philharmonic Society. For the occasion, he had promised two symphonies which were to be the Ninth and Tenth. He had already been working on the Ninth and, of course, completed it. The trip to England never materialized and death overtook him before he could work any further. A Tenth Symphony never got beyond those staves and notes in his tattered sketchbook.

Von Hase, however, was not speaking of sketches but of an entire movement. Even if not a traditional three movement concerto, the one movement would be enough to cause a cultural tremor of international proportions. If Schubert could write a great symphony of only *two* movements, why not Beethoven with a

Cello Concerto of only *one* movement. In his later years, his iconoclasm had known no bounds, even to writing a string quartet in *seven* movements.

Faljian fantasized about the great cellists vying for its first performance amid the excitement of the music world, the recording world. And there was also the world of rare manuscripts. This score would be virtually priceless and every collector would be after it.

He sank back in his chair, aware now of the beating of his heart. The Leipzig raid had taken place in December 1943 and the manuscript was missed immediately thereafter. That was only two years ago, he realized. If von Hase's theory were close to the mark, and Fekete had indeed stolen the manuscript, it might still be in Hungary. Fekete himself could perhaps still be alive!

That prospect excited him even more as a riot of images raced through his mind—of secret compartments, bundled manuscripts, yellowing scores, hand-kissing Hungarians, bombs bursting savagely, safes blown apart, and a bent, white-haired figure weeping in the midst of smoking debris. If von Hase was to be believed, only four people in the world knew of such a manuscript—von Hase, his aide in Leipzig, Fekete, and now he, an unproven musicologist still in uniform. Von Hase had abdicated the search, and the aide was by now either dead or inaccessible. That left only Fekete.

Faljian stared out the window, his eyes narrowed, his chin set. "If he's alive, I'll find him—and the Beethoven," he muttered. "But when will I ever get to Hungary?"

***

BUDAPEST

Hungary

1966

-ALEX

One

Jim Garland was standing in the doorway of his residence in Buda, gulping down the last drops of coffee and impatiently watching for the car to come up the driveway.

The phone call had been brief and urgent. "Wait for me and we'll drive to the Embassy together," Phil Faljian had said in clipped tones, very unlike the cordial manner the Public Affairs Officer normally adopted when speaking to the Deputy Chief of Mission. Clearly, something was up, Garland concluded, because on any normal morning, they drove down in their own cars across the Danube into Pest and met only after they were inside the Embassy.

He saw the black station wagon turn into the gate and watched it drive up into the small parking area where Faljian got out.

They greeted each other curtly and after Jim kissed his wife and gave her the empty cup, he turned and, still in the driveway, asked—

"OK, what's up?"

"Anti-Vietnam demonstration today at 1500 hours, a big one."

Garland's face grew grim. The bane of every Embassy, he thought. The cables reporting demonstrations against American Embassies elsewhere in East Europe had made for very disturbing reading.

"On a scale of one to five, how good is your source?"

"Four plus," came the terse reply, as they entered the DCM's car.

Garland drove slowly down the winding driveway and turned onto the street before he spoke."Can you tell me anything more about it, Phil?"

Phil Faljian shook his head quickly and muttered—"At the Embassy."

Garland knew what that meant. The place to talk about it was in the 'tank,' the glass-encased secure room in the Embassy. Hungarian and Soviet electronic ingenuity had penetrated every American structure and car which periodic electronic sweeps by regional specialists from Frankfurt were continually discovering—tiny microphones planted in homes, cars and the Embassy.

They drove the twenty minutes to the Embassy in silence, only the radio interrupting their thoughts with the monotone voice of a Hungarian announcer reporting heavy American losses to the Viet Cong.

They reached the square called *Moskva tér*, then drove across the *Margit híd*, which bridged the Danube, turned right past the Party Central Committee Headquarters, finally reaching the American Embassy situated on *Szabadság tér*, where Jim parked. They walked past the five-man uniformed and civilian police that 'guarded' the Embassy, but more accurately merely waited for the improbable day when they would arrest the Embassy's illustrious inhabitant, Joseph Cardinal Mindszenty, were he to walk out.

They entered the building, greeted Annie the cheerful Hungarian receptionist, and rode up in the elevator to the third floor. Garland said he would get the key while Phil waited at the secure room. Other Embassy officers began arriving and one of them, noticing Phil standing at the tank's door, asked if there was to be an unscheduled staff meeting, just as Garland approached. The DCM's untypically gruff response of "I'll let you know" raised a few eyebrows but also suggested that something unusual was up.

When they were inside and the electronic noise scrambler was turned on, the DCM said—"Alright, Phil, let's have it."

"At 1500 hours today, there's going to be a mass demonstration against the Embassy. They're calling it a student demonstration. Lots of young people. It's all about Vietnam. I guess our time has come. Moscow, Warsaw, Prague and Bucharest had theirs and now Budapest has to show its colors."

Garland's lips tightened. He nodded, then asked—"And you're sure of your source?"

"Absolutely."

"OK, I'll tell the Old Man when he arrives in . . ." looking at his watch . . . "in, dammit, in forty minutes. We can't lose any time but we've got to wait for him. OK, Phil, not a word to the others. Just go about your business until we assemble again. I'll spread the word about a staff meeting."

Phil went to the Communications Room and read the incoming cables from Washington and European posts. Everything was virtually the same as the day before and the day before that. As for the daily situation report from Saigon, the cable was permeated with gloom.

He went to his office and began to read *Népszabadság*. The Party daily was filled with more speeches, more polemics against the United States, more encomiums to 'Soviet peace policies.' He desperately wanted a cup of coffee but the trip to the basement kitchen would take too long. He sat back facing the barred windows which looked out on a courtyard. The bars looked so firm, so unyielding, so secure. He indulged in a half smile.

Only one month before, the security specialists had discovered that three of the bars had been sawed with such a fine and delicate blade as to be unnoticeable. This meant that the Embassy had been penetrated by the Hungarian Secret Police, the dreaded AVO, but for what purpose?

Certainly not to harm the Cardinal. That they could do almost daily as he took his evening walk in the courtyard. No, it was in all probability to implant more listening devices in the Embassy. With Marines not yet assigned, Embassy officers took turns sleeping in the building overnight, taking the Cardinal on his nightly walk, bringing him his dinner from the kitchen, and after that, making a security tour of the entire building, from the basement to the attic.

The Embassy officers who performed this function all agreed that the most disquieting part of the exercise was going into the dark attic close to midnight with a flashlight. A few admitted—very privately to each other—that after one trip up there, they had never gone again. Phil agreed with one colleague who had said—"That's the spookiest place I've ever seen."

Phil was awakened from his reverie when Garland stuck his head into the office and said—"The Ambassador's here. But before we go, Phil, there's something I must ask you. I feel I've gotten to know you very well and this demonstration somehow doesn't strike me as the kind of thing that would throw you into such a doldrum. There's something else, isn't there?"

Phil studied his friend, a fellow officer with whom, in the short time they had come to know each other, he had developed great rapport, but to whom he had not as yet confided his secret passion. A Deputy Chief of Mission served often as a kind of First Sergeant in a platoon, someone who was supposed to know not only every aspect of the Embassy's operations but every facet of an officer's motives. And yet, Phil had never sat down with Garland and laid it all out: Bad Nauheim, von Hase, Beethoven, the air raid, the missing score, Fekete, and now, searching in Hungary. But this was still not the right time.

'Yes, Jim, you're right. There *is* something else, and I do want you to know about it. But in the broader scheme of the Embassy's work, it's secondary, so please have patience with me for now. You'll know everything soon."

Garland shook his head, his features firm—"But obviously not so secondary for you. That's not good enough, Phil. What's going on that I don't know?"

As Phil began to speak, the Ambassador walked past his office and barked impatiently to both—"Come on, let's go."

Garland looked abruptly at Phil and beckoned with his head in the direction of the door.

"You owe me an explanation, Phil, and I'm not letting you off the hook."

When both walked into the Secure Room, every chair was filled. At the DCM's suggestion, the Ambassador had ordered that the entire staff attend, where normally it was only the Country Team—the heads of the various sections. But now, the usual attendees numbering ten had swollen to twenty. Once the door was shut, the scrambler sound was dimmer, and Ambassador George Quigley, a portly man in his fifties, began, almost resentfully, as though his day had been ruined.

"Good morning. Today, Friday, is not a staff meeting day, as you all know, but something of a very urgent nature has come up which I want everyone in this Embassy to know about and to be prepared for. The DCM will now continue. Jim . . ."

Jim Garland cleared his throat—"We have it on the best advice that a large-scale anti-American demonstration by so-called 'students' will take place this afternoon at about three o'clock in front of the Embassy."

The sounds of groans, shifting feet and rustling papers filled the compact room and the Military Attache muttered an obscenity.

The DCM continued—"The subject, as those of you who have been reading the cables from other posts suspect, is Vietnam. We don't know what will happen or how violent it will be. Only that it will take place.

"I don't know how many of you have ever witnessed an anti-American demonstration in your careers, but I can tell you it is a harrowing experience. There isn't much we can do in the way of preparation, and we certainly aren't going to board up the building. We do not want to give the impression of fear. But there are a few things to be done.

"The Ambassador and I want those of you who are married to inform your wives not to come to the Embassy at any time today and to make certain all the children are home from school. Do this not by phone but personally in about an hour, and not all at once. I also recommend that all cars be moved several blocks from the Embassy by one o'clock. Further . . ."

"Excuse me for interrupting, Jim, but how sure are we that this will happen. I mean, has the Foreign Ministry informed us?"

All heads turned toward Eric Hager, who had been the Embassy's Political Officer for the last two years and was due for a transfer. A tall, lanky, sallow and humorless officer, Hager was always suspicious of outside sources of information, trusting no one and depending for his reporting only on the Foreign Ministry officials he occasionally saw and the Hungarian press. His distrust even extended to political officers from friendly embassies whom he viewed as dupes of 'Hungarian trained seals,' his term for all private contacts.

The DCM hesitated for a moment, as though reluctant to divulge the source of his information, but then said—"No, the Foreign Ministry has not been in touch with us. Not yet, anyway. We are expecting this demonstration because one of our own Embassy officers was alerted to it."

Garland had long known of the animosity which Hager harbored against Phil Faljian. It was Hager's view that the Embassy's Public Affairs Officer should confine his work to press and cultural matters and had no business meddling in political affairs which Hager jealously felt was his domain. Time and again, because of his unique network of contacts, Faljian had come up with information that no one else in the Embassy had seemed to be privy to and which had infuriated Hager. The Ambassador and DCM were delighted with Faljian's harvest of data for which the Embassy had several times been commended by Washington.

But now, the DCM thought, if this turns out to be disinformation, Hager will have a field day. He turned to the Ambassador, his face a question mark. George Quigley said—"The bearer of this information is our Public Affairs Officer."

Hager snorted loudly and, with sarcasm dripping from his voice, asked of Faljian—"Pray tell us, if you are at liberty to do so, who this untainted source is in whom you obviously have so much confidence."

Ignoring the tone of his questioner, Faljian looked at the Ambassador and said "Sir, with your permission, I should like to protect my source even in this room, but I have no problem in identifying him privately to you and the DCM."

Hager turned white, whispering, "Always protecting his red-feathered friends," and sank lower in his seat, conceding the loss of yet another battle.

"Now let's all get to it and without letting on to the local Hungarian employees," the Ambassador said, dismissing everyone but Faljian and Garland. When the door was shut again, he said—"Allright, Phil, Jim and I want to know everything you know. And don't pay attention to Hager. We all know how vitriolic he can be."

"Thank you, Sir. I hope you understand, both of you, that my sources are your sources, but if they become common knowledge in this Embassy, they will dry up."

"We do know that, Phil," Quigley said as he looked pointedly at his wristwatch. "We've got four hours before the explosion and I've got to make certain Grace stays home today."

"Right, Sir. OK. My source is a *Magyar Nemzet* journalist named Tibor Hegedus. He is a Party member but a Hungarian first, and he has no love for the Soviets. As you may recall, Sir, he served in Washington as a foreign correspondent for three years, and that is where we first met. I think a great deal has rubbed off on him. Tibor and I are such good friends that we decided some time ago that if he ever had something urgent to tell me, he should phone me at night. When I answered, he would say 'Mr. Varga?' and I would reply 'I think you have the wrong number'—all of this in Hungarian of course, and then hang up. With this exchange we would both know that within one hour we should meet in the corner of a park on the Buda side. But if I were unable to meet him, my response was to be—'No one by that name lives here.'

"Well, last night Tibor phoned and we met. He told me that the word has spread to the editorial offices of all newspapers that a demonstration would take place today at 3. But he had more to tell me.

"It turns out his girl friend, or mistress—but that's irrelevant now, except that she's quite young—works at the Hungarian Chamber of Commerce, and shares his political feelings. She was telephoned yesterday morning by the local secretary of KISZ, the Hungarian Young Communist League, and instructed to leave her job this afternoon and participate in a two-hour demonstration in front of the American Embassy. When she argued that she had a cold—which apparently she doesn't but she didn't want to demonstrate against Americans—he insisted and said she would be paid for two hours of lost work for just standing in front of the Embassy and shouting 'Johnson-Murderer' over and over again. She told Tibor she had no choice. She also found out that other colleagues had received the same order."

After a moment of silence, Ambassador Quigley asked—"Is there any more, Phil?"

"Yes Sir, but only some collaborative color. One of Tibor's Party colleagues from *Népszabadság* told him yesterday afternoon a rather depressing thing. As I recall it, he said: 'Somewhere in Moscow there is a building, and in that building there is an office, and in that office there is a desk, and in that desk there is a drawer, and in that drawer there is a book with the title 'Hungary.' And whatever the Soviets write in that book is our fate. We are a satellite and there is nothing we can do about it. This time, the Soviets want a demonstration and that's what we'll give them.'"

"That *is* very depressing," the DCM said, shaking his head, "but nothing we didn't suspect. Only, when it comes so directly from a Hungarian communist source . . ."

As the Ambassador arose to leave, Phil said—"Sir, one request. Do I have your permission to tell the Security Officer to lower the steel shutters in our display windows? They are on street level and I'm sure the pictures of the President and the other photographs will be inviting targets."

"Of course. Tell Frascatti to take care of that. He heard everything that was said at the meeting. And keep me informed if anything new turns up."

When they departed from the tank, Phil returned to his office, sat at his desk and held his head in his hands. Shaking it slowly from side to side, he mused—More delays, more distractions, although this is a major one. Here I am in Hungary where I never thought I'd be, but how much progress have I made searching for that manuscript? Not very much. And now this—plus the mistrust of the DCM!

He checked the time on his wristwatch and went to the forward section of the building. Standing outside the Ambassador's office, he looked down from the third floor onto *Szabadság tér*. Freedom Square. What a farce, he thought, so named by the Soviets when they entered Budapest in 1945.

"Is it going to be very rough, Phil?" It was the Ambassador's secretary, now standing beside him.

"Well, Kiki, our other embassies in the area have had a rough time of it. I suppose we can expect the worst. I was just looking to see if the so-called students were already gathering. We've got an hour and a half to go."

"Yes, the Ambassador told me. Phil, I'm scared."

He put his arm around her shoulders—"Don't be, darling, You'll be allright, but the building might suffer some broken windows," and seeing no one around, gave her a quick peck on the cheek.

Leaving the third floor, he went down in the elevator to the Embassy Security Officer. Salvatore Frascatti had been a Marine in the Pacific during World War II and had killed a score of Japanese for which he had been decorated. Now, in his new career as General Services Officer, responsible also for Embassy Security, Frascatti always seemed frustrated when confronted by the many dangers threatening the Embassy. At staff meetings, he always made ominous mention of cleaning his gun and once said that during night duty, if he ever encountered an AVO in the attic, he would use it. The Ambassador had admonished him to keep his gun out of sight.

"Sal," Phil said, "the Ambassador authorized me to ask you to start lowering the steel shutters around two o'clock. You were very quiet at the staff meeting, but you heard it all. And, of course, Sal, you'll be sure to keep your gun in its holster."

Frascatti grimaced, his head bobbing like a toy on a spring.

At two o'clock, Faljian heard Kiki's voice up the hall—"They're starting to come!"

Phil ran up the long corridor to the front windows and confirmed that the throng was beginning to collect. Suddenly, he wondered if anyone had told the Cardinal. His quarters were only five feet away, opposite the Ambassador's office. Entering, he approached the legendary recluse.

"Your Eminence," he said in Hungarian on seeing the Cardinal standing at his own window and looking down on *Szabadság tér*—"You should not be endangering yourself like that. Has anyone told you what is happening?"

Cardinal Mindszenty bowed his head, with its small red skullcap, gently to one side, clasped his hands and said—"Yes, Mr. Secretary, I am aware that the Bolsheviks are up to their usual tricks. But don't worry about me. I have faced graver dangers."

Reassured, Phil closed the door behind him. He stood at the window overlooking the square as other officers began to join him: the Consuls from the first floor, the Budget and Fiscal and Military Attaches from the second. Hager remained in his office as though in protest against a demonstration whose coming he should have been the one to report. What an idiot, Phil thought. How would he be able to write a report on something he isn't even witnessing, knowing that the Ambassador would want a summary cable with the impressions of every officer.

At two-fifteen, the DCM came into his office and said with a bitter smile—"I've got a real big scoop, Phil. The American Desk of the Foreign Ministry just phoned to say they had heard there might be a demonstration this afternoon in front of our Embassy. Nice of them to let us know, don't you think?"

Thirty minutes later, *Szabadság tér* was teeming with people and the air was thick with the buzz of voices, laughter and occasional shouts of recognition as friends greeted each other. Phil began to make out some of the signs which had been passed onto those standing nearer to the sidewalk directly in front of the building.

One read—"*Él a kezekkél vietnamtól!*" and to make certain the Embassy understood, it was accompanied by an English translation—"Hands off Vietnam!"

Others read "Johnson *gyilkos*" repeating what Tibor's girlfriend had been told to shout; some were only in English, such as "How many children did you kill today?" "Our hearts are with Vietnam" and "We accuse you of imperialism!" and "Death to the aggressors!"

Two young men held high a tall poster depicting a human figure in agony, his head lifted to the sky, a dead child at his feet and on either side the divided words "Viet Nam."

Sal shouted—"Hey everybody, look at this."

On the street only a few feet from the building was the replica of an airplane, with a fifteen foot fuselage and a wingspan of ten, on which was painted—"USA Air Force 1207."

By now, the roar of the crowd was stentorian. Phil could barely hear what his colleagues were saying. The Ambassador kept shouting for everyone to stay away from the windows, for it became almost a ritual that every time an Embassy member was seen at a window, the din of the crowd would increase ten-fold. The street was littered with small leaflets which were too distant to be read. Suddenly, someone rang the front door bell of the Embassy, which was wired to also ring upstairs. Frascatti looked questioningly at the Ambassador, who said—"Sal, better see who that is," and when Sal became tense, the Ambassador, reading the ex-Marine's mind, said—

"No, Sal. No gun."

Frascatti went to the front door and saw a delegation of four young men and women. When he opened the grilled door a few inches, they presented him with a sheet of paper. Once the door was shut, a large rock shattered the glass just missing an enraged Frascatti, who rushed the document upstairs where the Ambassador asked Phil to read it. It was a petition demanding that the United States pull its troops out of Vietnam, stop the war, and recognize the victory of Ho Chi Minh.

As Phil ended his translation, Kiki suddenly began to sob loudly and ran towards them. "Something's burning down there," she shouted hysterically. Phil walked cautiously to the window and peered down. In the middle of the street, a few feet from the building, the demonstrators had set fire to a fifteen foot effigy of President Johnson and its full length was ablaze, the flames soaring almost to the third floor where Phil was standing.

As he stared down at the mad scene below, rocks began to strike the panes, showering him with glass splinters. He held up his hands to protect himself and heard the DCM shout—"Phil, get the hell away from there!"

At that exact moment, he felt a violent blow to the side of his head and as he fell, the last thing he heard before losing consciousness was Kiki's scream when—as she told him later—she beheld the blood gushing from his temple.

Two

When Phil came to, he was lying on the sofa in Jim Garland's office and his head was throbbing. Putting his hand to his temple, he felt a soggy bandage and saw that it had stained his fingers with streaks of blood.

"The bleeding has stopped," he heard the DCM say as he entered the room and sat on the edge of the sofa. "Why did you take such a risk? Going to the window like that?"

Phil cleared his throat but could only get out the words—"Kiki . . . said . . ."

"Yeah, I know. Kiki said something was burning. It was the biggest God-damned effigy I've ever seen. Burned like a torch. The smoke is still in the front rooms. Anyway, it's over now."

"Is it really over?

"Almost. Those phony students are beginning to disband. Good thing we have that First Aid room."

"How did I get here?"

"You may not believe this, but Eric Hager helped me carry you in here. I think he was shook up."

"Will wonders never cease. Tell me, how bad is it?"

"Actually, not bad at all. You know, scalp wounds bleed profusely even if the cut is superficial. This is what did it."

He held up a dark object for Phil to see. It was an orange-sized rock, embedded in jagged cement. "The Old Man wants me to take this to the Foreign Ministry and register an official protest. I want very much to do that. The bastards! Another half inch and you might have been killed."

"It's a good thing I wasn't," Phil said, his eyebrows arching, as they both smiled.

"Well, at least your sense of humor is still intact. Except for your injury, Phil, these demonstrations verge on the absurd. A Roman circus over and over again. Take it easy for now and get some rest. I'll close the door behind me."

*

Alone now, Phil looked around the DCM's office, noting once again, as he had so often, the bust of Thomas Jefferson, Garland's idol; the reproduction of Grant Wood's "American Gothic;" the photographs of Garland's parents in Montana, of his wife Sarah, her parents in Iowa; the poster of a Chicago exhibit of Frank Lloyd Wright's later architecture.

Garland's career had begun in obscure posts in Southeast Asia and Africa, but his innate abilities had been recognized early and he had risen rapidly in the Foreign Service, serving later in Prague as Political Officer and eventually in more important European embassies, such as London and Paris, as Political Counselor. Budapest was yet another promotion—his first assignment as Deputy Chief of Mission. It had come so unexpectedly that he had had little time to study the language or the country's history, so that his new duties and the learning process had coincided.

Garland had arrived in Budapest six months after Phil and had soon recognized that their ethnic difference—Phil the Armenian, Garland the Irish-Welshman—fed and nourished whatever lagunae existed in their respective makeups, and this, plus an unusual compatibility of personality and intellect, had drawn the two officers to each other.

Phil liked Jim Garland's outgoing personality, his decency and honesty, the way he put tribulation into perspective. He was, as Phil had realized, after groping for the right word, just plainly and simply, very American.

For his part, Phil liked to think that his own gift for reaching into the inner spirit of people, his dedication to his work, and his generosity in sharing the fruits of his toil in the vineyards of Hungarian society, were what Garland found attractive in him. Phil was not wrong, and had also sensed that yet another feature which Garland found appealing was a certain devil-may-care attitude toward life, an insouciance born not so much of cynicism as of a resignation to adversity, which had been the lot of Armenians. In fact, for Garland, Phil's ethnic heritage was itself an attraction. Having grown up in the West, Garland had for many years never even heard of Armenians, and after he had, still had not met one—until Phil Faljian.

Within months of serving together, enduring the frustrations of an Iron Curtain assignment and sensing in each other a complement to their respective spirits, the two men had become fast friends.

They bonded even more one long evening when in a lengthy exploration by Garland of his Public Affairs Officers early life, Phil spoke of his troubled childhood on the East side of New York, and of the problems he and his parents faced because of their ethnic origin. As a family Phil's parents, isolated in the neighborhood, mingled only with other Armenians, primarily at the Armenian Church, where he had been baptised. In late afternoons, however, during the week when he came home from school, it was a daily certainty that he be confronted by the Italian and Irish bullies waiting for him at his door. To them, he was a 'foreigner' whom they jeered and pushed around until, spurred on by his observable fear, they resorted to physical assault, so that his parents, coming home from work, often found him bloodied and crying on the apartment doorstep. It reached such a crisis that even on just seeing slovenly dressed classmates at school in caps and knickers, like the neighborhood toughs, young Phil was panic-stricken. The psychic injury of those terrifying months left their mark on him, long after he was sent away to live with his Grandmother and continue his schooling in a suburban and more tolerant borough of the city.

The Garlands were astonished to hear that such ethnically-motivated brutality existed in as cosmopolitan a city as New York. But when Phil described the more subtle taunts he had been subjected to in the Foreign Service, where he had once overheard himself described as 'our token starving Armenian,' they registered shock. It had brought home to him, as Phil observed to Garland wryly, the true meaning of the phrase 'second-class citizen.' The Foreign Service immediately after the war, he told Jim and Sarah, was a white male Americans' club and Blacks, Hispanics, Jews, 'and this Armenian,' were looked upon by some WASP members of that club as pariahs who had to be tolerated for the sake of image.

Phil noted that it was his total immersion in his work and whatever diplomatic skills he displayed to appreciative superiors that facilitated gradual advancement. His experiences in childhood and in the Foreign Service developed in Phil a shyness and, he had to admit, even an ambivalence, about being Armenian, especially in a career where the few Armenians he knew were consigned to non-diplomatic, mostly secretarial, duties.

Garland had listened with dismay and had pledged that nothing of this nature would happen in Embassy Budapest. On another occasion, in response to Garland's query about Phil's father and his reaction to such disagreeable experiences, Phil said his father had been outraged that after fleeing his own persecution in Turkey, his son should be undergoing new terrors in the land of the free for being Armenian. As though to fight back in his own way, his father, Phil explained, made him speak only Armenian at home and filled his son with stories of Armenian history and heroism. Thus, despite the torments of his earlier years, Phil always retained the pride of his ethnic identity, even as he suffered its consequences.

It was his father, Phil remarked, who encouraged him to

pursue music, for which the youth showed a marked affinity. But later in college, his father was disappointed to discover that Phil's interest had deviated from performance into music criticism and musicology. Phil smiled as he described his father's confusion at not knowing what musicology was.

At this point, Phil had inexplicably paused, as Garland and his wife exchanged glances, unaware that Phil was silently debating whether he should relate or suppress the true reason for eventually forsaking musicology, But then, resolving to do so on another occasion, Phil resumed his early history. When the war broke out in 1941, thereby interrupting his budding career, and ended in 1945 with his entrance into the Foreign Service months later, his father was pleased to have, as he had expressed it with pride, 'the first diplomat in our Armenian family tree.'

It was on that night after this second recital of his troubled past that Jim Garland, his new-found friend and colleague, gave him the reassuring words he had always hoped to hear—"Phil, the Foreign Service has changed in the last two decades. It's no longer the kind of club you recalled. Sure, you'll encounter prejudices here and there, but by and large, its strength is in its diversity, and that diversity lies in ethnicity. In your case, it's being Armenian, which gives you insights into other nations' problems and helps the rest of us understand them better. That's why you are such a success here in Hungary. Your Armenian heritage is your strength, not your weakness."

*

Phil slept for almost an hour and was awakened by a kiss. It was Kiki, her face wet with tears, and as he stroked her black hair, she murmured—"Oh, Phil, I feel so responsible."

"But why, Kiki? You didn't throw the rock."

"No, but I became hysterical and you tried to find out why. My darling, can you forgive me?"

He smiled lovingly, kissed her and walked over to his office.

As he sank onto the sofa, Eric Hager appeared at the door. He took a step in and said—"I'm sorry about what happened, Phil. Really sorry. Can I do anything?"

"Thanks, Eric, nothing now. And thanks for before, too."

Alone again, he closed his eyes, the throbbing less pronounced. A soft rustling sound close by prompted him to open his eyes. The Cardinal was bending over him and looking anxious.

"Faljian *úr*, I was informed of your injury. I am deeply sorry."

"Oh, Your Eminence, please do not concern yourself. I am told it is not dangerous. But I appreciate your concern."

"I shall pray for you."

Phil closed his eyes once more and felt a warm glow as he realized that the Cardinal, who always addressed him by his diplomatic title, had used his name for the very first time.

Interrupted again by a soft knock, Phil opened his eyes to see Ambassador Quigley standing over him."Phil, I want you to go home. Imre my driver will take you. I also want you to know how much I appreciate what you found out, which prepared us for this . . . this . . . stupid thing. Jim's already got an appointment for tomorrow morning to protest. I've been on the phone with Washington and the Secretary was informed immediately. You are a valuable officer, Phil. I'm proud to have you on my staff. and will so inform the Director of your Agency. Now let's get you home."

Phil wondered if the Director of the United States Information Agency even remembered who the Public Affairs Officer in Budapest was. In fact, many American diplomats often thought of Washington as the center of navel-contemplation, its denizens unable to see beyond the banks of the Potomac.

Garland accompanied him to the elevator and then down to the street. As they emerged, the civilian 'guards' looked sheepishly at them and Phil could not contain his irritation and called out sardonically in Hungarian—"We thank you for protecting us from the students."

They turned their backs on the two Americans as the Ambassador's Lincoln pulled up and Imre quickly jumped out and helped Phil into the back seat. As always, Imre, middle-aged and ruddy, looked dapper in his gray chauffeur's uniform and cap. He was a handsome man with a kind face and Phil had always liked him. Certainly an AVO plant, he had thought, but Hell, who on the staff wasn't? Some were decent, some weren't.

Phil looked at the window displays and saw that the steel shutters had not been pulled completely down so that red ink was smeared all over the glass and posters containing President Johnson's picture and the words "*Gyilkos*—Murderer" written across them were stuck to the building. The DCM waved as they drove away.

Phil saw Imre's eyes on him in the rearview mirror.

"How are you, Imre?"

"Thank you, Faljian *úr*, I am well but the question is, how are *you*? I am very distressed to see you like that. These things, well, they get out of hand. I think you understand, there is nothing personal in it. If you will allow me to say so, Faljian *úr*, it is well-known that you are a friend of Hungary."

"Thank you, Imre. I do understand."

At his residence, he was helped upstairs by Erzsébet, his stocky housekeeper, and then in to bed. When she was about to leave the room, she said—"The *nyúl* called and wanted to know when you arrive. Shall I let her know?"

Erzsébet looked grim. She always referred to Grace Quigley as The Rabbit because, Phil had long since realized, Erzsébet had seen through the Ambassador's wife. Phil signaled with an emphatic downward thrust of his thumb as Erzsébet exited, a small smile of satisfaction on her lips. The peasant woman was a good conservative Catholic and frowned on the antics of women such as the one she had dubbed The Rabbit.

He took off his shoes and lay back on the large bed. The curse of living next door to the Ambassador! It had been an arrangement made soon after the war when a State Department team had been dispatched to Hungary to purchase the Embassy, a number of residences for the officers, and two apartment buildings to house the staffs. It had been a very good deal at the time, especially because some of the homes were in the wooded hills of Buda, but two of them—the residences of the Ambassador and the Public Affairs Officer—were only 100 feet apart.

The Residence had been the home of Jenö Hubay, the great 19th century Hungarian violinist and friend of Johannes Brahms. Hubay had erected a guest house next door, which became the PAO's residence. Phil had been stunned by the grandeur of the 'guesthouse' the first time he had walked in—the chandeliers and the spacious rooms where he could entertain and show films to Hungarian guests—and in time became intrigued by the walnut paneling, housing, he was certain, ultramodern electronic gadgetry.

The major drawback had been the proximity of the Residence. Not because of the Ambassador, whom Phil liked. George Quigley was an amiable, mild-mannered human being who clearly looked with favor on Phil and had him over to dinner often, for the Quigleys entertained frequently and lavishly. That was how Phil got to know Grace Quigley. She was the major drawback.

*

It had begun one night a year ago soon after the Quigleys had arrived when they had had their first dinner party. The table was sumptuous, the newly polished silver and crystal sparkled, and the white-gloved waiters were elegant and attentive to the twenty guests, some from other embassies, and a sprinkling from the various Hungarian ministries with which the Embassy dealt. Every time Phil, who was seated near the middle of the long table, had looked at Grace Quigley, seated at the end of the table, he found her looking at him. Phil found her not unattractive. He figured her to be about fifty, some ten years older than he, with wavy brown hair, restless eyes, a pouting mouth that rarely smiled, and a face that seemed frozen in a perpetual sulk. He also noticed that she drained her wineglass three times.

Later, as the women withdrew to the sitting room and the men had their brandy and cigars in the library, Phil saw her throw him what he considered an unusually long parting glance as she closed the French doors. 'It's surely my imagination,' he muttered to himself as he turned to the Ambassador's male guests and engaged them for the next thirty minutes in trite conversation about events of the day.

After the third dinner party, however, he knew that something was indeed in the air, especially when, after all the guests had left and he was bidding his hosts goodnight, her hand had lingered in his a few seconds too long. The Ambassador had already turned away and was walking toward the stairs. Grace Quigley, standing close, had looked into his eyes and murmured—"I particularly enjoyed having you here, Phil, and hope you will come again, and often. After all, you are our neighbor."

Phil thanked her and fled next door. But the very next day, in one of her infrequent visits to the Embassy, she arrived late in the morning, and getting off at the third floor, came directly to his office. Looking around the room, she said—"So this is where you work."

Phil watched as she frowned at the Beethoven death mask on one wall, and peered stony-faced at the large ink profile of Bach on the opposite wall.

"You'll notice, Mrs. Quigley, that his hair consists entirely of notes in his own musical handwriting. I acquired it in Germany. Unusual, don't you think?"

She didn't react to his comments, but suddenly brightened, pointing with obvious approval to a Matisse reprint which seemed to radiate its brilliant seaside hues into the otherwise sombre office. "Now, that is nice!"

"In fact, ma'm, it is Nice," he said with a smile, but she did not react to his wordplay.

"Have you read all these books?" she asked, approaching his heavily-lined shelves.

"Not all of the new acquisitions, ma'm. Some of the others are from my previous posts, and I did read all of them."

Then, to his astonishment and consternation, she suddenly bent over, raised her skirt to her thigh, and as he watched, his mouth agape, adjusted one stocking, and then the other, walked to the door, and with an airy—"See you soon, neighbor," proceeded up the corridor to her husband's office.

She was wearing a particularly pungent perfume and long after she had gone, its aroma remained like an invisible cloud in his ill-ventilated office. Garland, walking in a few minutes later, demonstratively sniffed the air and said—"Had a visitor, I see—or rather, smell."

He said nothing more but had looked with amusement at Phil, who was staring at the door, still stunned by the encounter. When Grace Quigley's visits to his office and phone calls to his residence persisted, Phil knew he had to inform Garland who, as it turned out, had already sensed the truth. He was no longer amused but appreciated Phil's candor.

"What you've got to do, Phil," he counseled one day over lunch, "is to keep her at bay. If you know she's coming to the Embassy, plan to have an outside appointment. At home, tell your maid you are not in to Grace. Maybe in time, she'll get the point."

"Yeah sure, and what if she gets her revenge through him?"

"George Quigley has the highest regard for you, Phil. Don't worry about that."

There were occasions, however, when he invited them to dinner parties for his many Hungarian contacts in the press and cultural world, who were delighted also to be meeting the Ambassador and his wife, Phil would screen a recent Hollywood film, at which point Ambassador Quigley, no fan of the movies, would leave. Grace would then move to a seat nearer to him, but Phil would fiddle with the projector, change the reels, and avoid her by seeing to the Hungarian guests. He also would find someone to escort her across the way to the Residence. One night when he couldn't, he took her arm and led her on the gravel path. At the side door, she turned and said—"Don't think you're off the hook, young fellah. I don't give up easily, and I always get my way."

*

The throbbing in his head returned and he tried to get some sleep. He saw that it was already eight o'clock. He heard a footstep. It was Erzsébet.

"Faljian *úr*," she said gently, "a little soup will do you good. It will also help you fall asleep."

"Allright, Erzsi, bring some up."

Twenty minutes later, she brought him a delicious *gyulás* soup which he put away with relish, but it made him drowsy and as Erzsébet took the tray away, he asked not to be disturbed, to which came the protective reply as she closed the door—"I'll take care of the Rabbit myself."

Phil fell into a fitful sleep, with troubling dreams peopled by faceless secret police, a frowning Ambassador, the DCM smiling but shaking his head, a handsome white-haired Teutonic gentleman whom he could not identify, followed by a leering Grace. Then, suddenly, in the dream, there loomed before him the anxious face of Erzsébet who was saying something to him that he couldn't understand, but when she began repeating one word over and over again, it emerged clearly from all the rest—"*Nyúl, nyúl, nyúl.*"

Phil awoke abruptly. His underclothes were drenched with sweat and clung uncomfortably to his body. But the throbbing had stopped, his head seemed clear, and he suddenly knew, in a moment of illumination, why Erzsébet's repetition of *nyúl* had awakened him. It *could* have meant Grace Quigley, but it also could have been a subconscious reference to the patrician and courtly Prussian whom he had met twenty years before.

For just as the Hungarian word *nyúl* translated into English as "rabbit," it also translated into German as "Hase."

"Hellmuth von Hase!" Phil said out loud, his words echoing in the empty bedroom, "Well . . . I'll . . . be . . . damned!"

'Father Freud,' he reflected with awe, 'what tricks you play on us in our dreams! Through my housekeeper, of all people, who knows nothing about Beethoven or manuscripts or concertos, you prod me in a dream. Or were you scolding me about Grace?'

Highly pleased at his interpretation and that it could go both ways, he crawled back into the cocoon of a deep sleep.

Three

A bright warm sun penetrated the drapes and awakened him. Looking at his night table he saw that it was eleven o'clock. Erzsébet had allowed him to sleep late. As he lay under the quilt, his gently throbbing head a reminder of the previous day's violence, his thoughts mingled drowsily with the stimulus of his dream, especially with Erzsébet's importunate reminder.

It had been twenty years since he had first learned of the manuscript's possible existence, and while his entry into the Foreign Service had taken him to parts of the world alien to his quest, he had always hoped ultimately for an assignment to Hungary. But he seemed to be cursed with one non-productive assignment after the other, serving in American Embassies in cities where progress on his search was unattainable—Cairo, Ottawa, The Hague, Bonn and one stint in Washington.

While in The Netherlands, he had written to the American cultural officer in Budapest asking him to find out if there was a Ferenc Fekete in the phone book who was a musicologist. After a month, Phil received the reply that five people by that name had been phoned: the first was a steel worker, the second a mechanic, the third a clerk, the fourth's phone had been disconnected, but the fifth—Phil took special notice—had barked incoherently at his caller and abruptly hung up! Phil contemplated following up with a trip to Budapest but dismissed the idea knowing that embassies do not look kindly, in fact even with suspicion, on colleagues from other posts poking around in their own backyards.

He was next assigned to the Embassy in Bonn, where he spent many hours in the *Beethoven Haus*. Even so, these were futile, for he could find no enlightenment in a lock of Beethoven's hair, his last will, his life mask, his last piano, his ear trumpets or the room where he was born. In any case, German-American relations had made great demands on Phil's time, and as the Embassy's Officer for Cultural Affairs, he was constantly on the run, delivering talks on American music, literature and art throughout the Federal Republic.

In his travels throughout Western Germany, he had once lectured in Wiesbaden and thumbing through a telephone book found the number for *Breitkopf und Härtel*, which pleased him for it meant his intervention in 1945 had succeeded. But when he phoned and asked for Helmuth von Hase, intending to invite him that evening, he was told von Hase was in England. Two years later, he tried again and this time was informed that von Hase had died. That saddened him deeply because he had liked the distinguished Prussian; besides, outside of Fekete, if he were still alive, von Hase had been the only other link to the vanished Beethoven score.

There was, however, one other thing he could do while in Germany, he told himself—telephone Dr. Karl-Heinz Keilberth, the prominent Beethoven scholar, in East Berlin. But the more he thought about it, the more he realized that he might be getting Keilberth in trouble, so he abandoned that idea. On the heels of that decision he found himself transferred to Washington for a position on the Policy Staff. Frustrated again, he spent three years of erosive in-fighting among the decision makers at the White House, State and Defense Departments and the United States Information Agency, until the exhilarating day he learned of his next assignment—to Hungary.

At the time, he had recalled the despondency of his words in Bad Nauheim—"But when will I ever get to Hungary?" The assignment seemed to have come out of nowhere—"sheer good fortune," he told some colleagues. Not so, said his Personnel Officer, totally unaware of Phil's objective.

Phil learned that he had been a candidate for an Iron Curtain assignment for over a year, and one of three candidates for Hungary for professional qualifications gleaned from his records: he already spoke two languages other than English—German and Armenian—which indicated an aptitude for learning another—especially one as difficult as Hungarian; he was well-versed in Marxist theory and practice; he was knowledgeable on the Kremlin's policies and attitudes toward its East European satellites, and, in the case of Hungary, vice versa; and he was a bachelor, consequently with no family obligations to curtail extra-curricular activities in Hungary's free-wheeling society. Further, there was the remarkable coincidence of the timing, which had been just right, for after almost a year at the Foreign Service Institute, Phil would be arriving in Hungary just as his predecessor was scheduled to depart. Which is exactly the way it happened. The overlap was painless and, as it emerged, unnecessary because Phil realized immediately that his approach would be totally different from the blandness and superficiality of the colleague he had succeeded.

As Phil settled in, next door to the Ambassador's Residence, he felt a rising excitement within him at the thought that he was now where, for twenty years, he had wanted to be. It was only after his Embassy duties began that his fervor had temporarily diminished when he discovered the overwhelming demands—both official and private—on his time. Beyond several fruitless attempts to phone the various Ferenc Feketes in the telephone directory, and considerable background reading late at night, he had not, after several months in Budapest, made much headway.

Now, as he lay in bed, the dream still fresh in his mind, he felt a resurgence of his earlier passion as fragments of von Hase's narrative came rushing back. He sat up in bed, agitated at all of the obstacles he had faced since his arrival in Hungary—

Embassy projects, protocol matters, reports to Washington, press and cultural contacts, daily briefings of the Ambassador, of the DCM, keeping Grace at bay, entertaining Kiki, and now the demonstration.

His features grim and his fists clenched, he pledged to no longer waste a single day in his search for the manuscript of the Cello Concerto. 'If Beethoven did compose one, and if it is here in Hungary, by God, I will find it, no matter what it takes,' he solemnly swore.

He got up and showered, unwinding the clotted bandage as he stood under the steady spray. Moments later, looking in the mirror he saw that the wound was actually small and could barely be seen through his thick shock of black hair. As he came out wrapped in a terry-cloth robe, Erzsébet knocked lightly, entered and after asking how he was, said that breakfast awaited him downstairs.

Phil put on sport clothes and descended the ornate staircase into the dining room. Erzsébet had brought in some freshly-cut flowers for the table and had laid out the best china. She entered with a tray bearing his favorite breakfast—bacon and eggs.

"*Köszönöm szépen,* Erzsi," he said, adding a warm smile to his expression of thanks, which she returned with the customary "*Szívesen.*" Erzsébet had a deep affection for Phil who treated her like an equal and had been generous to her children at Easter and Christmas.

They also had a quiet understanding. Just as Phil knew that Imre was an AVO plant, he had no reason to think otherwise of Erzsébet. Except that an incident one day clarified her status for him. Every ten days or so, she would arrive late and Phil had noticed that on those particular days, she seemed upset and when she looked at him, she would quickly avert her eyes.

One morning, after this had happened several times and noticing what he interpreted as a reflection of guilt, Phil led her out into the garden and said—"Erzsi, you don't have to answer any question I ask, but I cannot help notice how sometimes, when you come late, you are disturbed. Can I know why?"

Erzsébet started to cry, but she recovered, dried her tears and said—"Faljian *úr*, if you weren't so good to me, I would remain silent, but I think I must tell you something. You perhaps suspect that I work for the AVO, but please believe me, I do not. Nevertheless, they want to see me every fortnight or so. They ask me questions like—Who comes to his house? What do they talk about? What is he especially interested in?—and many, many other things."

"Well, Erzsi, you know that I am not here to do mischief in Hungary. I invite people to my home because I like them, and if they want to tell me things, that's their affair. But all I ask is that you tell the AVO the truth."

Erzsébet nodded, relaxed and relieved, and said—"Faljian *úr*, I tell the AVO only what I feel like telling them. That is true of some of the others who work here and next door. I don't understand English so I cannot truly know what *all* of the conversations are about. I tell the AVO that you are interested primarily in cultural matters and that most of the people who come here—as if they don't already know who they are!—are Hungarian intellectuals. That is all."

"*Kedves* Erzsi, do not trouble yourself any more. Tell the AVO whatever you like, but don't ever be concerned that I will be cross with you. Are we clear on that now?"

Erzsébet was at ease as they re-entered the house. Phil thought to himself—'Why do they persecute this poor woman when they have informers all over the place, including some of the people who come to my dinners.'

Now, on this morning, he went into the warm sun room and looked through the Hungarian newspapers. Erzsi brought him another cup of coffee and said—"Did you hear the phone earlier? It was Garland *úr* asking about you. He said you should call him at the Embassy."

Phil went to the phone, dialed and greeted Jim with a hearty—"My headache's almost gone, Jim. How's yours?"

The DCM laughed—"I was at the Foreign Ministry and met

with Deputy Foreign Minister Kovács. He said the Ministry was shocked to hear of the demonstration. He actually said 'shocked.' Can you believe that kind of bullshit? Just like the police chief being shocked to discover there was gambling in Rick's Cafe."

"And for all you eavesdroppers listening in on this line, let me repeat—pure bullshit!"

Jim laughed again—"You *are* feeling better. Well, take it easy, buddy. Listen to your music, read your books, and stay at home. If you need anything, give me or Sarah a buzz. She's concerned about you. Oh, and let's not forget that other matter you're going to tell me about."

"It's at the top of my agenda, Jim," Phil said and hung up. 'The time is just about here,' he mused, 'when I'll have to tell Jim the whole story. Else, how can I explain the absences which are going to come?'

He returned to his easy chair and soon became drowsy in the warm coziness of the glass-enclosed room. Towards noon, the phone ran again. It was Ambassador Quigley. "How are you, my boy? Feeling any better?"

"Yes Sir, much better. I had a good long sleep. I'm going to take it easy today."

"Good. That's the right thing to do. Look Phil, Grace and I would like to have you over for lunch tomorrow. I don't know how you had planned to spend the day, but Grace tells me your housekeeper doesn't come on Sunday and so we thought you might like to while away a few hours with us."

Phil bit his lip. He noticed Erzsébet looking at him from the kitchen, knowing who was on the phone. He thought—lunch with the Quigleys . . . Grace trying to behave normally . . . but, sure as hell, unable to. Yet, it *was* the Ambassador inviting him . . .

"Thank you, Sir. I'll be delighted to come over tomorrow."

Erzsi came out and asked in her fragmented English—"You go? Eat?"

"I go. Eat." he mimicked, then laughed and embraced her—"Erzsi, *Nem baj*. Don't worry. I'll be allright."

"Not with the Rabbit, you won't," she said sharply, returning to the kitchen.

Phil knew she had his best interests at heart and he never resented her criticisms. And today, he was especially grateful to Erzsébet for that dream.

He went to his library and found the two large frayed volumes of Alexander Wheelock Thayer's "Life of Beethoven," and curled up with them in the sun room. In the absence of any other truly informative research materials at every previous post, he had, of course, gone through the already dog-eared books from beginning to end. Even though having been written a full century ago, Thayer's was still the best biography of the composer, and there was always the chance of having overlooked a vital clue.

*

When Phil had first arrived at the Embassy, he had planned to go about the search in three ways: to determine if Ferenc Fekete, who may have stolen the manuscript after the shattering air raid on Leipzig in December 1943, was still alive, and if so, to locate him; to focus intensively on books like Thayer's—of which there were a few in Hungary—about the possibility of Beethoven ever having conceived of composing a Cello Concerto; and finally, to visit Martonvásár, a small town about forty minutes from Budapest, where there was a Beethoven museum, erected because Beethoven had visited the Brunsvik family there and even worked on some music.

Of these three objectives, the nearest he ever came to any in his first months in Budapest was to randomly collect books and brochures on Beethoven and Hungary, which he put on his bookshelf and seldom got to. For, once ensconced in the Embassy, Phil found himself inundated with work, primarily at the urgent request of the Ambassador and DCM. Because his area of activity, namely the worlds of culture and the media, was yielding so much information about the inner workings of Hungary's political life, he was compelled to give priority to reporting on the bonanza of information which fell into his lap. This earned him the respect and admiration of the Ambassador and the DCM, even as it incurred the bitter envy of Eric Hager. Phil could not help gloat more than a little that 'the token starving Armenian' was supplying the Embassy and Washington with political gold that should normally have been coming from the Political Officer.

A question mark in this equation was the CIA Station Chief, a rotund, genial officer named Carleton Squibb, who at staff meetings was always making veiled references to the 'demands of headquarters.' He had frequently complimented Phil on his scoops, and early on had wondered if he might on occasion join Phil during a lunch with a contact. Phil had agreed to it once ("We all work for the same government, Carl, so why not?"), but at lunch with the Chief Editorial writer of *Népszava,* Squibb had been so tactless and blunt as to make the Hungarian guest nervous.

In fact, that was the last time that Phil invited Squibb and the last time the editor agreed to meet with Phil. Thereafter, the Station Chief was always very proper with Phil but the cordiality was absent. Without Phil's cooperation—and looked upon as anathema by Hager, who recoiled from any CIA business—Squibb operated on his own, and often even the Ambassador had no idea what he did. In time, as Jim once said to Phil, the consensus was that Squibb could do little but wait for that rare phenomenon, a "walk-in"—someone purporting to reveal Hungary's secrets.

Now, alone with his Thayer in the sun room, Phil promised himself that while his obligation to the Ambassador and DCM were paramount, he would devote with a passion all of his otherwise free time to tracking down the manuscript of the Cello Concerto.

Long before, during his Columbia University studies in musicology, Phil had concluded that in the pantheon of great creators of music, Beethoven stood alone. There were those other two giants, Bach and Mozart, certainly, but there was a difference. Bach had brought the baroque in music to its epitome, and Mozart had done the same with the rococo—tinged with romanticism. Beethoven, on the other hand, had built on the orthodox classicism before him and, intellectually restless, had begun to look ahead, to pioneer.

Once his early works had established his mastery of classical forms, Beethoven leaped forward, investing the work of his middle period with an emotional power and turbulent conflict that carried him further and further from classicism. Then, in his final works, especially the piano sonatas and the last quartets, he turned inward, probably because of his deafness, and revealed a higher sphere of musical contemplation that still enthralls—and yet baffles. Bach speaks to the mind, Mozart to the heart, but Beethoven speaks to the mind, the heart—and the soul.

How did the Cello Concerto, if there was one, fit in? Where was it composed? When and for whom? Phil was determined to search for the answers—and for the manuscript itself. This was one of the more exciting aspects of musicology, a discipline that required knowledge not just of music, obviously, but also of history, art, literature and sociology, with dashes of psychology and, on occasion, even of medicine. The professional musicologist had a good grasp of all of these and, in the case at hand, which was in many ways a mystery story, the ability to recognize and integrate clues, like a shrewd detective.

But yet, whenever Phil felt his old ardor begin to return, it was always subdued by the experience at Columbia he had kept that night from the Garlands. Embedded in his psyche was insidious treatment at the hands of one faculty member, a prominent musicologist who had left his native Austria in the early 1930s and was seeking to establish himself in American academic circles with the publication of a ground-breaking book.

Eric Peter Kurz, it seemed to Phil, had taken an instant dislike to him and displayed his hostility often in class. Kurz would harass him with questions such as—"Mr. Faljian, can you name even one contribution by Armenia to western musical thought?" Or, "We have in our midst, ladies and gentlemen, the first Armenian musicologist—if he gets that far—in the history of music." Phil could not understand why his being Armenian was such a persistently disturbing factor in Kurz's often brilliant explorations of musicology. Was it somehow linked, Phil wondered, to Kurz's fervent nationalism which often produced irrelevant outbursts in praise of Austrian musical culture?

"Haydn, Mozart, Schubert," he would cry out, "all Austrians! And where did Beethoven and Brahms live, compose and die—in Vienna, the capital of Austria!" He would strike his desk with his fist, staring down the twenty-two musicology majors he harangued twice a week, but glaring at the one Armenian in the class.

Phil tried to ignore the animosity, gratified to be studying with so eminent an authority, but it was ultimately in vain, just as the reason for it was obscure. Until, that is, one day as he waited outside Kurz's office to discuss a paper on the Dutch composer Obrecht. The professor's door was closed but Phil could hear the muffled but unclear sounds of his voice, and hearing no other, he realized Kurz was probably on the phone. And suddenly, the musicologist's voice burst into a series of invectives that even startled his secretary sitting at her desk near Phil.

But it was what followed that made Phil's blood freeze, for in one final explosion Kurz, inexplicably inflamed, shouted—"Listen, I've just about had it over here. Half my class consists of Jews and we also have one damned Armenian. Don't complain to me about the naiveté of your American students. I'd rather have your ignorant know-nothings than these lower species. Jews and Armenians! One and the same. As far as I'm concerned, the news coming out of Berlin these days is long overdue."

Phil was utterly shaken and had turned so pale that the secretary offered him a glass of water. He walked out, his heart broken at the viciousness of the man who, until a few moments ago, he had continued to grudgingly respect. He realized then and there that he could never advance in musicology or even make it a career, not with the likes of Kurz holding the musicological reins of power.

He also wondered whether Kurz would continue to use his services for the book the musicologist was writing, the first history of music in the western world employing the full panoply of musicological techniques. To earn money towards his tuition, which had put a strain on his parents, Phil had part-time employment typing Kurz's lengthy manuscript. This nightly labor did more than ameliorate the pain of the barbs directed at him in class. But Kurz kept him on, inasmuch as Columbia and not he was paying Phil. When the manuscript was completed, Phil saw in the acknowledgments which the secretary had typed that his name appeared among prominent members of the faculty, which exhilarated him. When the book was published, however, Kurz had excised Phil's name, which was the final blow. Such a minor inclusion would have meant much to the budding musicologist, and he was shattered. After the outbreak of war, and a few days before entering the army, Phil visited some of his favorite professors, especially in the Music Department, and pointedly ignored Kurz who, aware of Phil's slight, turned with a sneer and slammed his office door.

Throughout his four years in the war, Phil had sought to erase those dark days from memory and had vowed to leave musicology forever despite his extensive training and evident talents. And that is the way it had remained until that fateful day in Bad Nauheim when he heard those four knocks on his door and Hellmuth von Hase walked into his life. Phil realized then and there that his musicological past, dormant for so long, was about to be rejuvenated.

*

He read until three o'clock, waving away Erzsébet's repeated admonitions to lunch, unable to tear himself away from descriptions of Beethoven's peripatetic life in Vienna. He finally dined at six, watched some Hungarian television until nine and retired at ten. His head seemed in good shape and his soul less troubled.

Four

Lunch with the Quigleys on Sunday was relaxed, thanks largely to the Ambassador's laid-back manner and his obvious liking for Phil. He was full of praise for his PAO and observed, as he had many times before, that the Embassy's reporting cables attracted Washington's attention primarily because of his input.

Phil always felt uneasy when lauded by the Ambassador, especially in the presence of Grace. He had a genuine liking and respect for the Ambassador and, consequently, found her occasional displays of contempt for her husband distasteful and discomforting.

George Quigley had inherited his father's insurance business in Hartford and his conservative bent revealed itself in contributions to the Republican Party. His magnanimity caught the attention of party leaders and when Eisenhower won the election, the thirty-eight year old insurance executive was asked if he would accept an ambassadorial post. Within three months, the Quigleys were basking in the sun of a Caribbean post. Within three years, they were bored by the sun, the sea and the indolence of life on a semi-tropical island.

Bitten by the diplomatic bug, Quigley decided to remain in government in the hope that another foreign assignment might be forthcoming. Grace too entertained the same hopes, having found the perquisites and privileges of diplomatic life to her liking. Quigley was bounced around the State Department for six years until the Hungarian assignment, a vacancy created through the sudden death of the *chargé d'affaires* in Budapest. Quigley took a crash course in Marxist economics at the Foreign Service Institute, learned some elementary Hungarian, did some reading on Soviet power in East Europe, and thus armed, arrived in Budapest in late 1965 as the Vietnam war cast a pall over American relations with the entire Soviet bloc.

At the luncheon table, Phil sought to avoid Grace Quigley's eyes but realized it would appear rude. He hoped that the Ambassador would not notice her sparkle every time she addressed Phil, which was often. Fortunately, they were never left alone, for which he was grateful, but as he was leaving, she seized a moment alone at the door to whisper that she would phone around ten.

He spent the rest of the day walking in the Buda hills. Spring was in the air and many Hungarians were doing as he was, some of whom even greeted him. At one point he thought an approaching couple looked familiar, and as they neared, he saw that it was indeed the Deputy Foreign Minister and his wife.

"Good afternoon, Mr. Faljian," the Minister said in English, doffing his hat. "I am glad to see you have recovered."

"Thank you, Kovács *úr* ," Phil replied in Hungarian. "I was lucky—by a few millimeters. One of your students had rather good aim."

Kovács sighed—"You know how students are, Faljian *úr*. You have the same problem, as I recall."

Reluctant to let that pass, Phil replied briskly—"Kovács *úr*, we don't order our students to demonstrate. They do so spontaneously."

Kovács spread his hands apart, his smile seeming to ask for understanding.

As Phil continued walking he noticed out of the corner of his eye that Kovács had turned and was watching him. Not a really bad guy, Phil thought, but an ideologically committed organization man. Tired and hungry, he returned home three hours later, warmed up some leftovers which Erzsébet, on her off day, had taken out of the refrigerator, and then settled down again with Thayer, in pursuit this time of Beethoven's connection to the cello. It was astonishing how numerous those connections were.

Interestingly, there were many works written when Beethoven was still in his teens, works without opus numbers, wherein the cello was rarely used. But then, of his first eleven published works, eight included a cello one way or the other: in four trios, a quintet, a serenade and two sonatas.

From that time on, Beethoven not only wrote cello parts for various combinations of chamber music, but his own coterie of friends seemed to be predominantly cellists. In fact, the cello served almost as a link between Beethoven in Vienna and the Brunsvik family in Martonvásár.

"OK, so here we are again in Hungary," Phil said out loud as he sought a more comfortable position and read on.

But Thayer, as he had known for some time, contained actually very little about this period in Beethoven's life. Phil went to his library shelves and took down some of the Hungarian source material he had collected in his browsing through Antiquariats, as Used Book Stores were known in Europe. He wriggled into a comfortable position once again and picked up the family history of the Brunsviks.

They had settled in Martonvásár during the 16th century when the Turks had annexed Central Hungary as a province. After the Turks departed, the Brunsviks turned the barren swampland into a habitable estate, eventually erecting a castle and Anton Brunsvik was made a Count by the Austro-Hungarian Empress, Maria Theresia. His son, also named Anton, married a court attendant of the Empress and had four children, three girls—Marie Therese, Josephine and Charlotte, and a son Franz. Anton had a passion for music, which he passed on to his children, and when he died, his widow cultivated that aspect of their education.

In 1799, she took her three daughters to Vienna for two reasons: to find suitable husbands for them and to study music with the most sought-after teacher in Vienna, the twenty-nine year-old Ludwig van Beethoven. The Brunsviks not only knew who Beethoven was but when his very first published work appeared, Three Trios for Piano, Violin and Cello, the Widow Brunsvik was one of twelve music devotees in Hungary who ordered the scores.

Contact with Beethoven was made very early during this trip, and Therese recorded the following in her diary when she and Charlotte visited the composer in his third-floor apartment on St. Peter's Square—

"*We entered his apartment, I clutching Beethoven's score like a schoolgirl. The immortal dear Louis [*she wrote in French*] van Beethoven was very friendly and so polite . . . I sat at the piano and with both of us singing the violin and cello parts, I played the piano part. Beethoven was enchanted and promised to come to our hotel every day for the remainder of our stay in Vienna . . .*"

He apparently kept his word for of the eighteen days the girls were in Vienna, Therese said Beethoven came on sixteen, often remaining four and five hours. This was the beginning of the Beethoven-Brunsvik connection. No less intimate was Beethoven's relationship with Franz Brunsvik who, as Beethoven discovered, was a good cellist and chamber music player. Beethoven developed a close friendship with Franz, even to addressing him with the informal *Du*, and spoke of him as his brother. Later, he dedicated his *Appassionata* Sonata to Franz.

In Vienna, another close friend of the Brunsviks was Nikolaus Zmeskall, whom Beethoven got to know very well. Zmeskall was known widely in musical Vienna as an outstanding cellist. In addition to him and Franz Brunsvik, others among their friends played the cello, such as Nikolaus Kraft, and they would all gather for weekly concerts in Vienna with Beethoven, the central figure at the piano, playing his music.

'Allright. We've established the connection with the Brunsvik family. Now, how about Beethoven and Hungary?' Phil mused.

He didn't have far to read. In 1800, on the occasion of some festivities connected with the Royal Court, Beethoven was induced by Franz Brunsvik to participate in a concert in the Castle in Buda, at which time the composer played the piano part of his Sonata for Piano and Horn. He stayed in Hungary from late April until early July.

Six years later, Franz invited Beethoven to Hungary again, this time to Martonvásár where he completed his *Appassionata* Sonata, with its dedication to Franz. In 1809 Beethoven went to Hungary a third time, visiting Franz in Buda and also in Martonvásár. There he composed two works for piano, the Opus 77 Fantasy, dedicated to Franz, and the Opus 78 Sonata, dedicated to Therese.

Phil lay back and closed his eyes. It was obvious that Beethoven's connections to Hungary were linked to his friendship with the Brunsvik family, whom he visited in Martonvásár but saw very frequently in Vienna. Therese, living in Martonvásár, would get letters from her two sisters, now living in Vienna, in which they described Beethoven's visits when he sang parts of his opera *Fidelio*, on which he was working, or performed one of his piano sonatas, or how several friends played a string quartet—with Zmeskall on cello.

Phil fell back, thoroughly exhausted by his readings, yet not depressed, in fact somewhat animated. For it was obvious there might be some substance to the idea that Beethoven had more than a composer's normal interest in the cello. Surely, at some point, one or the other of his two closest friends must have made the suggestion to him. Not that he had ever avoided writing for the cello. In fact, he wrote five sonatas for piano and cello, one of which, the Opus 69, had achieved considerable popularity. But it was not a concerto.

"No, it most certainly is not a concerto," he murmured, and just as he did, the phone rang.

'Oh please, not Grace,' he pleaded, noticing that it was still an hour before ten o'clock.

"Yes?" he said into the receiver.

"Hello. Is this Phil Faljian?"

"It is."

"This is Isaac Stern. How about meeting me in the lobby of the Hotel Gellért in an hour for a salami sandwich?"

Five

Leaning casually against a chair in the Gellért Hotel lobby was the familiar figure of Isaac Stern, his ruddy, round face wreathed in a big toothy smile.

"You must be Phil Faljian. I'm really, I mean really, glad to see you. Call me Isaac."

"Thank you, Isaac. You know, we had no idea you were coming."

"Let's grab something to eat and I'll tell you how I got here," Stern said, taking Phil's arm and leading him into the restaurant.

"The Hungarians have been trying to get me here for years, The problem has been that my bookings have not allowed it. Play here, play there, you know. Then suddenly, I saw an opening for a brief, maybe two or three day stopover in Budapest. The money wasn't important. I even cut my fee in half to accommodate them. I know they don't have hard currency. So I wired *Interconcert*, their booking agency, and told them of my availability and they agreed. They didn't tell you about this?"

"Not a word," Phil said flatly, "That's why I'm so astonished to see you."

"Well, I'm here, and nobody met me at the airport. So I called the Embassy and asked for the Cultural Officer and somebody gave me your number. I'm glad you could come down."

"What has *Interconcert* planned for you?"

"Good question. I have no idea. Musically, I'd like to give two performance—a solo recital and a concert with orchestra, free for all the students of the Conservatory. Beyond that, I want to meet with intellectuals and students to find out what they are thinking and doing."

Phil promised to be at the Gellért again in the morning and said Stern had come at a very good time because his involvement with students would be an excellent counterbalance to the so-called 'student' demonstration of two days ago.

The next morning, the DCM was already at the Embassy when Phil strode into his office—"Jim, you aren't going to believe this but listen," and told him of the previous evening's conversation with Stern.

Garland shook his head in disbelief and growled—"Why can't these people get their act straight? *They* arrange directly with Isaac Stern to come to Budapest but don't meet him. They don't tell you, and they leave him in the dark about his program. You'd better get over to the Gellért before he explodes."

"I'm going to drop everything and spend the next three days with him, if that's allright with you and the Old Man. I also think you might want to have a lunch for him tomorrow. I'll get you some good people for that. My apologies to Sarah."

"Will do, and don't worry about anything else. Just take care of him."

Phil called the Director of *Interconcert*, complained bitterly about the agency's indifference, asked caustically if they would dare treat a visiting Soviet artist so disrespectfully, and then wanted to know the plans for Stern. The reaction to Phil's sharp tone was immediate. The Director said the recital was set for the following night at the Academy of Music, but that an orchestral concert at the Conservatory was impossible to arrange.

Phil phoned Zoltán Kodály. The great composer was delighted to know that Isaac Stern was in Budapest and would be performing and agreed immediately to guide him to various music schools. Phil also asked if the composer and his wife were free to come to lunch with the Sterns the next afternoon and Kodály agreed to that as well.

Next, Phil invited two other leading musical figures to the Garlands' luncheon—the conductor of the Budapest Philharmonic, János Ferencsik, and musicologist Bence Szabolcsi, with whom he had long wanted to explore the matter of the Beethoven manuscript. He then picked up the Sterns and escorted them on a day-long sightseeing trip and when they returned to the hotel, Stern said—"Phil, I have a special request. I want you to take us to a place where we can eat good Hungarian food, but more important, where we can hear some good Gypsy violin."

At nine, Phil picked up the Sterns and they drove to the *Mátyás Pince,* the most Hungarian of Budapest's many restaurants. As they descended the steps into the basement, Sándor Lakatos, the band leader, espied Phil and raised his eyebrows questioningly. Lakatos had gotten to know the Embassy's Cultural Officer and aware that the guests he often brought there were very special. When they were seated, Phil beckoned Lakatos to their table and introduced him to Isaac Stern. Lakatos was beside himself for joy, and for the next ninety minutes Isaac Stern was treated to Hungarian and Gypsy music played with a passion that even Phil himself had never heard before.

At the hotel, Phil said—"Isaac, I've known many musicians and, quite frankly, most can't bear to hear *any* kind of music during their leisure hours. Can you tell me why you wanted to hear Gypsy music tonight?"

Stern laughed—"I know what you mean, Phil, but it's really quite simple. I'm a fiddler and Lakatos is a fiddler. But I'll tell you a secret. He can do things with his fiddle that I can't."

The luncheon at the Garlands' residence the following day was a great success. Stern told his distinguished dinner companions of the failings of the concert agency and the Hungarians present nodded knowingly, Kodály commenting that, given the slipshod state of cultural bureaucracy in Hungary, he was not surprised.

The 83-year old composer, his white, Liszt-like hair almost

touching his shoulders, apologized for *Interconcert*'s ill manners and told Stern that the reactions of the audience at his recital would represent the true feelings of Hungary for him and, he stressed, for the United States. Kodály later said he wished to escort the Sterns to various schools to hear the richness and variety of Hungary's children choruses—"Our musical future," he added.

After dessert, Phil took Bence Szabolcsi aside for his long anticipated chat. The musicologist, a short, stocky figure with tortoise-shell glasses, was diffident and self-effacing, with a reputation that went far beyond Hungary's borders. Phil had met him by chance one afternoon at the Béla Bartók Archives in Buda where they had had a brief conversation, and Szabolcsi had invited Phil to spend an evening with him sometime. This had not yet happened so Phil took advantage of the present occasion to further explore new avenues in his search.

"Dr. Szabolcsi, what can you tell me about a Beethoven manuscript that might possibly be a movement, or perhaps all, of a Cello Concerto?"

The musicologist, looking owlish, peered at him through his thick lenses—"What makes you think such a manuscript exists?"

"I have reason to believe that a Hungarian musicologist is somehow connected to such a manuscript, although I cannot prove that it exists."

"And who might this Hungarian musicologist be?"

"His name is Ferenc Fekete," Phil almost whispered the name.

A fleeting moment of exultation overcame him at seeing Szabolcsi frown with displeasure—to Phil a clear sign of recognition.

"This is a small country, Dr. Szabolcsi. Surely you must know this Ferenc Fekete, a fellow musicologist?"

Szabolcsi wet his lips, stroked his mustache with a forefinger and said—"Of course I know Fekete, Faljian *úr*. Unfortunately."

"You used the present tense. That means, he is alive?"

"Very much alive." Szabolcsi looked pensively at Phil—"I have heard good things about you, my young friend, and Kodály, whom you have gotten to know, tells me he likes you. He does not take to people so readily. Consequently, may I advise you to stay away from Fekete, as I do. His kind brings only trouble."

Undaunted, Phil continued his questioning—"Please excuse my insistence, Dr. Szabolcsi, but it is a matter I have vowed to pursue. This is neither the time nor place to do so. Can we meet elsewhere?"

Szabolcsi thought for a moment then said—"I intend to conduct some research at the Archives on Bartók's use of Central European melodies in his string quartets. As you may know, I have written a small book on melody."

Phil smiled indulgently. Szabolcsi, the author of many tomes, was known to always refer to his output as "small books."

"I shall be at the Bartók Archives every Friday next month. Why don't you meet me there around three on the last Friday in June, and we can talk some more," Szabolcsi suggested.

They rejoined the others in time to hear Kodåly tell of the visit a few years earlier of the great cellist Pablo Casals, and how both enjoyed sharing the fact that they had married their former students. The most silent guest of the afternoon was Ferencsik who, emptying his glass all too frequently, seemed to be more interested in one of the waiters than in the illustrious American seated close to him.

The next day Zoltán Kodály and his wife took the Sterns to a number of schools and the great violinist spent most of his time talking music with students and illustrating on his Stradivarius.

That night, he gave his solo recital at the Academy of Music which, despite the short notice, was packed. There were so many seated on the stage that Stern had difficulty winding his way through them to the center.

After the official part of the program, Stern performed encores for forty-five minutes, one of the encores being an arrangement by Kodály who, when he appeared on the stage to take a bow with Stern, unleashed yet another storm of applause and thunderous stamping of feet. When, finally, Isaac Stern took his concluding bow, a woman ran to the edge of the stage and kissed his shoes.

Driving to the airport the following day, Stern asked Phil to review for him what the Hungarian press had said about his recital. Phil said he would gladly send the articles on to Stern's New York address.

"You're hiding something from me, Phil. I'm a big boy, so give it to me straight."

"Allright, Isaac, but I'm enormously embarrassed. In the notices of the recital, all of them very brief, you are referred to as 'the world-famous Russian violinist living in New York.'"

Stern burst out laughing. "Thank you very much, Hungary," he said, but without bitterness.

"Isaac, please forget the negative things that happened and take away with you the memory of that woman kissing your shoes. That should tell you all."

Six

Phil returned from the airport in time to hear that the Ambassador had called a staff meeting in the 'bubble,' another euphemism for the Secure Room. Most of the Country Team was already assembled when Phil entered: Garland was whispering to the Ambassador, Hager was scowling as usual, Squibb was fingering the pipe clenched between his teeth, Dudley Watson, the Economics Officer, a pale, blonde newcomer, was looking nervously about him, and an uptight Frascatti was shuffling papers spread in front of him on the table.

"Good morning, gentlemen," the Ambassador began. "We've had a bad experience and . . ." looking at Phil, "a near fatality. But we've all survived. I've called this meeting to get reactions and assessments of the physical and psychological damage to this Embassy. Let's start with the DCM."

"Thank you, Sir. I'm certain we are all gratified that the Foreign Ministry has conveyed its regrets on the student demonstration."

Everyone guffawed at Garland's irony. He then went on to describe his protest on Saturday morning and the outrage of the United States at the inability of the Hungarian police to protect the Embassy. He had also shown the rock that had knocked Phil unconscious.

"What did they say?" Hager asked.

"They were very sorry. Deputy Foreign Minister Kovács said that students in any country are difficult to control, as the United States should know. I responded that in the United States, student demonstrations are not state-instigated riots against foreign embassies. Kovács didn't like that, but he can PNG me if he wants."

Ambassador Quigley shot him an alarmed look. He would not tolerate any Hungarian move to declare his DCM *persona non grata.*

Garland said he wanted to send Washington a cable on the demonstration with input from everyone and asked Frascatti for a brief rundown on the damage. Actually, outside of much broken glass and gallons of red ink, simulating blood, thrown on the windows and walls, the building had not sustained much physical damage.

"I don't suppose, Sal, that we got much help from the goons outside on the sidewalk?" the Ambassador inquired.

"As usual, Sir, they stood by and looked amused. I don't think they expected the Cardinal to walk out at that time, either."

"Speaking of the Cardinal, I talked to him yesterday and he seems to have taken all this rather well. Brave soul."

Phil was aware that the Ambassador was not a Catholic but Quigley respected Cardinal Mindszenty's courage and adherence to principle. Once every five or six weeks he and his wife would attend the Cardinal's Sunday morning service for Embassy staff members. On very rare occasions, Quigley would invite a friendly Ambassador, from Italy or France or England to the service. The Garlands, on the other hand, who were Catholic, attended the Cardinal's mass every Sunday, out of religious devotion and for His Eminence's morale.

"Allright, that's enough on the demonstration. Let's move on. In the last three days, we've had a surprise visit by a prominent cultural personality. Phil, perhaps you can brighten our day with a summary of what happened."

None of the staff appeared to know of the visit so that when Phil mentioned Isaac Stern's phone call late Sunday night, everyone was astonished The Ambassador had learned of it the next morning, having been informed by Garland of the visit and the luncheon. The Quigleys were not culturally oriented and always deferred to the Garlands for entertainment in that area. Phil described the infelicity and discourtesy of the Hungarian side in virtually ignoring the great artist, despite having sought for years to invite him.

"How did Stern take it?" Ambassador Quigley asked.

"With remarkable equanimity, Sir. Although understandably put out at times, he plunged into whatever could be arranged with enthusiasm, especially when visiting schools. If it hadn't been for Zoltán Kodály, who made all those arrangements and accompanied them, I don't know how the Sterns would have spent their time."

"Sir," the DCM interjected, "Phil is being too modest. He improvised constantly, and despite his injury, spent all his time with the Sterns. He filled in the gaps and made the luncheon at my home a big success by inviting just the right people on the shortest possible notice."

Phil always felt uneasy at such times and was relieved when the Ambassador looked at his pocket watch, said there was lots to do, thanked everyone and specifically Phil, and said the meeting was over.

Returning to his office, Faljian found an envelope on his desk. The note inside read—"Where were you Sunday night?" No signature, but it was a feminine handwriting. Phil sat down for a minute looking at the note, then walked over to the DCM's office.

"Jim, I need your help. Look at this."

Garland read the note, looked up at Phil and silently mouthed the name 'Grace' questioningly. Phil nodded. Garland arose and taking Phil's arm, walked him outside and to the elevator, suggesting they have a coffee in the basement kitchen. Once there, he asked—"Is she getting out of hand, Phil?"

"You know, Jim, I really don't know. They had me to lunch on Sunday and I felt very awkward. The way she looks at me! How can the Old Man not see, or suspect?"

"I don't think he does, Phil, else he'd indicate it in someway. He's really a very good guy, and he thinks the world of you. But God knows, he deserves better than Grace. Look, I'll have Sarah inform Grace about Isaac Stern and mention that you were occupied with him from Sunday to Wednesday morning."

A moment later, Garland said—"Phil, as they say in omnibus cables—New Subject. I've noticed lately that you've been doing a lot of reading about Beethoven. There are two books in German I saw on your desk, a map of Hungary with Martonvásár encircled in red, a place that I happen to know has a Beethoven museum, and a Hungarian newspaper feature about the Beethoven piano in the National Museum. As you know, I'm not much for music, but you've told me about your earlier preoccupation with musicology. And frankly, I can't help wonder whether all of this doesn't have something to do with what we talked about—or *didn't* talk about—the other day just before the demonstration. I should think this is as good a time and place to fill me in. What do you say, Phil?"

Phil sighed and nodded. "Yes, it is, Jim. But I wouldn't want you to think that somehow I've been holding out on you. Your friendship means a great deal to me and I've felt a deep sense of guilt about this. This private mission of mine was so personal and so removed from the American national interest we are here to promote that I considered it almost profane to mention it. But now, because you are so perceptive and have raised it with me, I feel not only grateful but relieved. So here it is, everything out on the table.

"This very special compulsion of mine concerns a stolen, perhaps lost, manuscript of a composition by Beethoven that the world of musicology knows nothing about.The few facts surrounding it that are known indicate that Beethoven may, I stress, *may* have composed such a work, a Cello Concerto, but these too are problematical. In any case, it is a fascinating mystery which if solved will most certainly not change the course of history nor have any impact on American foreign policy. But if discovered, the concerto will cause a considerable ripple in the cultural world and—please excuse the seeming vanity—bring renown to the musicologist who reveals it. Here are the relevant background facts."

Phil now related the entire episode with von Hase in Bad Nauheim, omitting nothing, and when he had finished, Garland, who had sat transfixed by the graphic details, exclaimed—"My God, what a story! I can well understand why you are so obsessed. Tell me, have you been to Martonvásár yet?"

"No," Phil replied, "but I've already done so much research that going there will be only to get a feel for the place. Like those inns back home that advertise—George Washington slept here. So, if I happen to see the room in the Brunsvik Castle where Beethoven laid down his head, it won't help me very much with the manuscript. Right?"

"Of course. I understand. By the way, have you made contact with Fekete yet?"

Phil shook his head—"No. In fact, I didn't know until my conversation with Szabolcsi at your house that he was still alive. But Szabolcsi will tell me more when I meet him in a few weeks. I already know he dislikes Fekete."

Garland's silence for a few moments led Phil to ask—"Jim, you aren't upset with me, are you?"

"Hell, no! It's OK to have a diversion on the side. Our work is trying enough. And I'm really glad that it's out in the open, at least between us. I ask only that you keep me informed, Phil. While it is all very intriguing, let's understand one another. I'll tolerate occasional absences during the day from the Embassy but I will not condone undue emphasis on this matter at the expense of our mission here. Embassy business comes first, always. Understood?"

"Understood, Jim. Trust me."

"Good. Oh, and Phil, one thing before we go back up. Could you start working on the names of your press and cultural people for the Fourth of July party? The Ambassador wants every officer's list by the end of the week."

"Of course, Jim, it's that time again."

Phil appeared to be suppressing a smile.

"Did I say something funny?"

"I'm sorry, Jim. No, it's nothing you said. It's just that whenever the Fourth of July comes up, I can't help remembering something that happened at the first Fourth I celebrated here only weeks after I arrived. Our *chargé d'affaires,* Elim O'Shaughnessy, called us together in this same tank for a *post mortem* on the party, and looking at me with a twinkle in his eye observed that an honored poet I had invited had been dead for several years. O'Shaughnessy said, to general laughter—'Young man, you invited someone to my Independence Day celebration who was once a prominent poet but is now a prominent boulevard.' You can imagine my chagrin."

Garland laughed loudly—"Yes, I certainly can. So, make sure you separate the was-es from the is-es this time."

"I'll try. No avenues, squares or statues. It's a promise."

Seven

On the last Friday in June, Phil drove across the *Lánc híd* and up the hills to *Országház utca* No. 9 where the Bartók Archives had recently been established under the aegis of the Hungarian Academy of Sciences. Entering, he was overwhelmed, as he had been on his first visit, at the large photographs of Béla Bartók and the many showcases displaying manuscripts and memorabilia of the brilliant Hungarian composer. Bartók was an especial favorite of Phil's because, without resorting to the new but bland idiom of atonal or twelvetone music, Bartók had employed the time-honored diatonic scale to create a body of work of originality, excitement and style—music that was remarkably inventive and communicative. Not the least of his techniques was to employ Hungarian folk songs or to create melodies with a Hungarian emphasis and mode. Taken all in all, Bartók was as much an innovator of the art of music today as Beethoven had been one hundred and fifty years before.

Phil asked a young man whether Dr. Szabolcsi was in the Archives and was led to a small office. Szabolcsi looked up, smiled and greeted his American visitor warmly. He suggested they take a walk. Outside, Phil almost felt like he was in Vienna at the time of his musical idol: the winding, cobblestoned streets, the old rococo buildings, and his walking companion, who held him amicably by the arm, a figure very much of the previous century.

"Tell me about your interest in musicology," Szabolcsi urged.

Phil described his early love of music and his intention to

become a music critic, which evolved later into a deeper interest in the collateral elements and personal factors influencing musical composition—in a word, musicology. At Szabolcsi's prompting, he named the prominent teachers with whom he had studied and explained how each had opened new horizons of research to him in the symphony, the opera, chamber music, and especially the string quartet.

"They are musical scientists with formidable reputations, but apparently you were not sufficiently convinced to follow in their paths, for now you are a diplomat. What happened?"

Phil sighed, slowing his gait, hesitant to reveal his experience at Columbia. He began—"Several things. First, the war. It took four years out of my life. Then, when I came out, I went to see some of my mentors. I was distressed to find them professionally dowdy, intellectually sedentary, and, perhaps most disturbing, cutting each other down. All had published books and all were sardonically critical of each other's writings. I had considered working toward a doctorate in musicology after the war, but now I wondered if this were the life I wanted. Would I become like them?"

Phil paused for a moment and perceived that Szabolcsi was watching him acutely. He continued—"Of course, I know that all musicologists aren't like that . I have met some who are humble, modest, and even generous. But diplomacy with its broad scope, its involvement with other cultures and potential for personal development attracted me immensely. And on top of all that, let me add, my musicological training has been a cogent factor and frequently served me well. For one thing, it has led me to you."

Szabolcsi looked kindly at his younger companion. "It pleases me that you find at least one musicologist who does not repeat your unhappy experience with our colleagues. But let me assure you, my young friend, even here in our so-called 'socialist fraternity,' there is intense jealousy—the Russians, the Romanians, the Czechs, and even some Hungarians. May I say something which might pain you, dear colleague? When you were telling me of your training, I sensed some . . . what shall I call it? . . . some problem, some anguish. It was written all over your face. Something bad happened, didn't it?"

Phil smiled sheepishly—"You are very observant, dear Dr. Szabolcsi. Yes it did. I must confess that when I mentioned the faculty at Columbia University where I studied music and musicology, I omitted one name."

"Eric Peter Kurz."

Phil was completely taken aback. "How do you know that?"

"Well, dear colleague, he too was at Columbia and has made a tremendous name for himself in America with his book. He is considered now the dean of American musicologists. And don't think we, who have labored behind the lines, as it were, don't wonder how someone with such . . ." he hesitated, ". . . such uncivilized views, could have established himself in your country. For all our intra-mural conflicts, we musicologists try to remain above the political fray. How did he hurt you? You are not a Jew."

"You know about that too! Well, in his eyes, I might as well be. For him, apparently, there is no difference."

The elderly musicologist showed no emotion and continued walking. "Tell me," he asked, "what Kurz did to you."

Phil described the humiliation he suffered in Kurz's class and how he hadn't understood the motivation until overhearing the phone conversation, which he related in detail.

Szabolcsi stopped walking and for a full minute peered down at the cobblestones. Phil could see that the old man was deeply affected by the story. Dr. Szabolcsi then said gently—"And yet, after this terrible person appears to have shaken your faith in a scholarly career, you now seem determined in your present career, to pursue what you might have before. Tell my why?"

"I'm not entirely sure myself why," Phil said, stopping now and facing his Hungarian friend. "Is it to prove something to my father, who frowned on musicology? Is it to get back at Kurz, by proving that a member of the 'lower species' can make a remarkable discovery that the great musicologist himself couldn't? Then there are other scores to settle, which I won't go into.

"I have got to find that Beethoven manuscript, Dr. Szabolcsi. It was once a dream that has since become an obsession. Those may be *my* reasons. But surely, *you* understand the impact on the world of music, the world of culture, of such a discovery?"

"Of course, of course," the elderly scholar replied, nodding vigorously. "I understand your zeal much better now. We shall solve this mystery together. Come, let us walk on."

Szabolcsi spoke glowingly of Isaac Stern, of his genuine interest in Hungarian music education, particularly of the Kodály method of teaching music to the young, and of his performance at the Academy of Music. He then came to the subject about which they were meeting.

"My friend, since I cannot seem to dissuade you from avoiding the general subject of Fekete, the next best thing I can do is to give you some background so that you will, I hope, eventually realize on your own what you are dealing with."

Walking slowly, the venerable musicologist went back in time to the early-forties when Hungary was ruled by a Regent named Miklos Horthy and Hitler sought to influence his policies. Hitler succeeded, up to a point, but Horthy harbored a secret conviction that the Allies would eventually win the war, and found ways to diminish the authority of Hungarian elements sympathetic to the Nazis, such as a political party which had arisen ten years before called the Arrow Cross. At that time, Horthy sought to protect Hungarian Jews and even came to a secret agreement with the Allies that he would surrender unconditionally when their troops reached Hungary.

Szabolcsi cleared his throat and continued: Hitler obviously could not countenance any of this, called Horthy to Berchtesgaden and offered him the choice of either full cooperation with Germany's war effort or total occupation of Hungary, as though it were a conquered enemy country. Horthy went along with Hitler and almost half a million Jews from outside Budapest were deported, largely to the gas chambers of Auschwitz.

Szabolcsi looked up as they entered Holy Trinity Square and stood in front of the *Mátyás templom*—"A truly beautiful church, don't you think?" he said as they studied the St. Matthew Church's ornate facade and tall spire. Szabolcsi then resumed his narrative:

When Horthy felt German influence on the wane in 1944, he halted the Jewish deportations before they reached Budapest and sought again to open contact with the West, but the Allies insisted he talk to the Soviet Union, whose Red Army was already at the border. When he did, the Germans forced him to abdicate and installed in his place the pro-Nazi head of the Arrow Cross Party, Ferencz Szálasi.

"That happened on October 15 in 1944," Szabolcsi said, "and from that date until April 4 in 1945, the so-called liberation by the Red Army, we suffered as never before."

They were now at the curious turrets and crenelations known as the *Halász bástya*—the Fishermen's Bastion. They mounted the steps and stood at its midway point, looking down at the Danube. Across the river they could see far into Pest and beyond, while to their left stood the splendid Gothic Hungarian Parliament. It was a sunny warm Summer day and the uncommonly blue sky was reflected in the waters of the renowned river that flowed through the capital.

"What a magnificent sight, don't you agree?" Phil said, looking down at the river. Szabolcsi was silent, and when Phil turned to look at him, he saw that his companion's lips were trembling, and a tear was running down his wrinkled cheek.

"My God, Dr. Szabolcsi! What did I say to upset you?"

The musicologist dried his eyes, and when he had recovered, said—"My dear friend, it is nothing you have said. It is only my memory. You must understand that when *you* look at the Danube, you see a beautiful river and perhaps even hear a famous melody. But when *I* look at the Danube . . ." he hesitated, his lips tightened, ". . . when *I* look at the Danube . . ." his voice now became hushed, "I see men lined up, their hands tied behind their backs, blindfolded, Hungarian soldiers standing behind them, firing bullets into their heads, and shoving them into the river. I can see the ice floes carrying the bodies down the river and the so-called beautiful blue Danube red with blood. Those were my fellow Jews, Faljian *úr*, executed by Szálasi's Arrow Cross fascist criminals. And if that weren't enough, as they withdrew, the Germans and their Arrow Cross allies blew up all the bridges and dismantled the city, leaving behind nothing but rubble and corpses of every kind, human and animal."

Phil refrained from speaking, not wishing to add to Szabolcsi's sudden grief, but put his arm around the other's shoulders and held him for a minute. Szabolcsi brightened and said—"Well, my young friend, you are perhaps thinking—what has any of this to do with my interests, namely a missing Beethoven manuscript? Has old Szabolcsi become a victim of his memories?"

"To tell you the truth, I *have* been wondering."

"Let's find a small cafe and have some coffee. Do you have any views on *fekete*?"

"It's kind of strong," Phil said laughing, and quickly caught himself as he realized that *fekete*, meaning black and the term used popularly for Hungarian coffee, was also the name of the man for whom he was searching.

"Dr. Szabolcsi, I strongly suspect you are teasing me."

"Yes, I am," he said, shyfully tilting his head. "Here's a nice little place. Let's sit down."

They ordered and when the coffee came, Szabolcsi continued—

"I first met Ferenc Fekete at the Hungarian Academy of Sciences in the thirties. The Music Division was a lively place then with two already famous composers—Bartók and Kodály. We all got to know this weasel Fekete. He was a master of intrigue and none of us trusted him. The main reason for *my* distrust was that he was a vicious anti-Semite and aligned with Szálasi and the Arrow Cross. He knew I was a Jew and he made disparaging comments about me always. Neither Bartók nor Kodály paid him any attention and were both very friendly and helpful to me, then a budding musicologist. Because I was in the capital I survived the deportations forced on Horthy. Mind you, I do not defend Horthy but history cannot be changed.

"Then, one day in 1943, Fekete disappeared and didn't show up again until Christmas of that year. When he did, he seemed even more arrogant and outspoken than before. He obviously sensed that his friend and protector Szálasi would soon be in power. What Fekete wanted, I have no idea. Maybe to be the Director of the Academy of Music? Liszt would have turned in his grave."

Szabolcsi sipped his coffee and looked absently across the street at nothing at all. Then he continued—"When we got the news of the July 20 attempt on Hitler's life in 1944 and how he had survived, Fekete was jubilant, told everyone that Fate had saved Hitler for greater things. Bartók had been so repelled by the Germans and the Hungarian fascists that he had already emigrated to the United States four years before. That left only Kodály to protect me from Fekete's diatribes and intrigues, but I felt safe. Until, of course, those final days I described a moment ago to you. I kept listening for knocks on my door and lived in fear . . . until the arrival of the Red Army. That was when we learned that liberation is a double-edged sword. What happened to us, to our women . . . But that is another story."

Phil ordered two more coffees and then gently asked—"Dr. Szabolcsi, is that the end of *this* story?"

"No, it is not, Faljian *úr*. When the 'Muscovites'—you know, the Hungarian Communists who had spent the war in Moscow—returned to Budapest, led by Mátyás Rákosi, who was a Jew, Fekete for the first time felt himself to be in peril. Will you be as amazed as I was when I tell you that he then turned . . . to me?"

"After persecuting you? What gall! What did he want?"

"He visited me one night. He looked pitiful, and for an hour or so I forgot his insults and humiliations and listened. In brief, this is what he told me. He said that he had discovered a manuscript, that he had acquired it legally, and that it was a genuine Beethoven score—one that he had authenticated—of the first movement of a Cello Concerto."

Phil's pulse quickened. This was not only the very first mention of the manuscript since von Hase's revelation, but also a confirmation of its existence by someone who had actually seen it.

"I'm almost afraid to ask, but . . . did he show it to you?"

"Yes. He had brought it with him. When I examined it, there was no question in my mind of its authenticity—the dreadful musical handwriting, the coffee stains on the paper, the red pencil, the yellowness of the manuscript. I feel certain it was genuine."

Phil could not suppress his excitement. He leaned over and seized Szabolcsi's arm—"Tell me, what did it look like? The music, I mean."

"Fekete showed me only the title page and the first page of the score, and from what I could see, it began with a long cello solo of about twenty or so measures before the orchestra came in. And when I reached for the next page, Fekete snatched the two pages from my hand and turned the entire manuscript face down. He stared at me with those pig eyes of his and said his plan was as follows:

"He intended to announce to the music world that while conducting research in Martonvásár, he had found this manuscript hidden away in the former bedroom closet of Therese von Brunsvik. He planned to show that the Concerto was of Hungarian origin because, not only had it been conceived in Hungary but was inspired by Beethoven's Hungarian cellist friends. Further, he would provide evidence, although he was vague about this, that he had discovered references to the Concerto in the diaries of Therese von Brunsvik. Finally, he said to me, he was preparing a monograph which would analyse all of these sources and, in the long run, bring credit to Hungary."

"He's a real patriot," Phil said caustically. "How much of this did you believe?"

"Well, consider that bedroom closet of Therese von Brunsvik, for instance. Now, you may or may not know that the Brunsvik castle, which was built in the late 18th century, was completely renovated 100 years later in the English new Gothic style. When the Brunsvik family died out, a Hapsburg archduke took over the castle, and after that the Dreher beer manufacturing family bought it. Since the end of World War II it has been an agricultural research center.

"What could possibly be left of Therese's bedroom and closet? But, who knows, manuscripts have been found in stranger places, and Beethoven and Therese had a very special bond, as we know from her diaries, which are filled with references to 'dear Louis,' as she called him in French. The intrigue had an aura of plausibility about it. Fekete went on to propose that if I intervened and protected him from charges of anti-Semitism, he would make me the joint-discoverer of the Concerto.

"You can imagine how I felt. This monster who had vilified me beyond belief was now asking for my protection. As I sat opposite him and looked at that revolting creature, I said to myself—What would Beethoven have done, that noble, tortured spirit who had himself suffered so much? Would he have sold his soul for the sake of fame? I was faced with a Faustian dilemma, but not for long.

"I stood up and told Fekete I could not help him and that he should leave my home at once. Fekete was incredulous and stared at me, so certain had he been that I would be enticed by his offer. That was the last time I saw him."

Phil sat back and digested the details of Szabolcsi's narrative for a few moments, then said—"Dr. Szabolcsi, please allow me to tell you that Ferenc Fekete is an outright liar and a thief. He may possibly have the Beethoven manuscript, but by no manner or means did he find it in Martonvásár. He stole it in Leipzig. Does the name Hellmuth von Hase mean anything to you?"

Szabolcsi took his glasses off and wiped them slowly and thoughtfully—"Yes, it does. If I am not mistaken, he was the Director of *Breitkopf und Härtel* in Leipzig. I heard the Russians captured him."

"On the contrary, he escaped to the American Zone in the closing days of the war and I met him and helped him in his attempt to start his publishing house in West Germany."

Phil then related the entire episode relative to the Beethoven manuscript—the Leipzig air raid, the great damage to the publishing house and the simultaneous disappearance of the manuscript and Fekete.

Szabolcsi's face was flushed with anger when Phil finished.

"Not only a liar and a thief but a charlatan as well," he said, his voice rising, "How could I have been taken in by his story!"

He sat in inconsolable silence under Phil's gaze, then asked—"How can you want to deal with this . . . this . . . swindler . . . this hypocrite?" He seemed to be utterly shaken by Phil's story. "This fraud is a blight on the honorable science of musicology."

"There are five people listed under that name in the telephone book," Phil said. "Three can be eliminated, the fourth has been disconnected, but the fifth . . . I have tried calling many times but the minute I start speaking, he hangs up Despite your strong feelings about him, Dr. Szabolcsi, I simply must see that man. It is a matter of the utmost importance to me. It is . . . personal. Please give me Fekete's address."

Szabolcsi looked sternly at Faljian—"After all that I have told you and all that you have told me, you still wish to meet with him?"

"Please, Dr. Szabolcsi."

The musicologist took out a pen and slowly shook his head as he reluctantly wrote an address on his napkin.

"I only hope, my friend, that you will not regret this. He is not your kind. He is evil . . . and dangerous."

Eight

Phil smiled as he walked away, went down in the elevator, and drove off to the address Szabolcsi had written on the napkin. It was centrally located, about fifteen minutes from the Embassy and just off *Rákóczi út*, one of Budapest's busiest main streets. Ironically, it was on *Dohány utca,* close to the Synagogue, the largest in Europe. Phil wondered how such a rabid anti-Semite could stomach that.

He parked, walked through a large gate and entered a courtyard. Walking around to the various doors, he finally found the name and rang the bell. There was no sound for almost a minute, then a light came on at the end of what seemed to be a long corridor. Finally, the door opened slightly but not enough for Phil to see anyone clearly.

"*Tessék?*" a voice asked.

"Fekete *úr*?"

"*Igen.*"

"My name is Philip Faljian. I would like to speak with you," he continued in Hungarian.

The door opened wider and Phil looked down at a much shorter figure who looked uncomfortably stout. 'My God,' he thought,' Peter Lorre has returned to Budapest.' A raspy voice conveyed deep irritation—"I have nothing to say to you. I know who you are, the American who is nosing into affairs that are none of your business. Go away."

As he tried to close the door, Phil pressed against it firmly and said—"Fekete *úr*, I am not hostile to you. I think it would do us both good if we could talk. Please. Just for a few minutes."

Fekete looked suspiciously at him, then grunted and opened the door wider. Phil followed him into a dimly lit parlor with huge stuffed chairs. Fekete waddled in his slippered feet ahead of Phil, who figured him to be about five feet in both height and width. He wore baggy pants and a very wrinkled shirt open at the collar.

Seated, they faced each other; Phil tried to be cordial, but Fekete with a scowl on his face, said—"I still do not see what we have to talk about."

"Please allow me to tell you, Fekete *úr*."

He explained that in all probability he and Fekete had been trained in the same disciplines since he too had wanted to enter musicology but the war had intervened. He then cautiously broached the subject of de-nazification and of the complex problems that posed and eventually got to the subject he knew would raise Fekete's hackles.

"Into my office walked a tall, distinguished German who needed my help. I liked him and agreed to intervene on his behalf. In gratitude, he told me something which at first I found it hard to believe, but since then, there is little doubt in my mind that it is true. The German was Hellmuth von Hase, and he . . ."

Fekete leaped to his feet and began to shout hysterically—

"Get out, get out of my house. Why are you persecuting me like this? You damned Americans are always making trouble!"

He seized Faljian by the arm and pushed him to the door, opened it and as he forced him out, shouted—"I don't want to see you again," and slammed the door.

Phil stood outside the door in a rage at such treatment, but he pulled himself together, drove to the Embassy and went directly to the DCM's office, and told Garland what had just happened.

"It was a disaster," he told Garland, "but I don't think it was a mistake. He's a deeply troubled man with a powerful guilt complex. Normal civility would have called for at least a courteous confrontation. But he obviously doesn't trust me. There's no question he knows something because I no sooner mentioned von Hase's name than he exploded and pushed me out of his apartment."

Garland listened to Phil's recital of the visit and said—"It sounds to me like this guy is not only uncivilized but an emotional wreck. You'd better stay away from him."

"But, Jim, he's got the secret and I've got to find out more."

Nine

Summer had arrived, the blue skies and clean air—devoid of the haze and the pervasive odor of lignite—lifted spirits, and the ubiquitous leafy green trees gave to the city a freshness and lustre that reminded many of the Budapest of pre-war days.

The Fourth of July party had brought together the usual mix of several hundred diplomats and Hungarian government and party officials, as well as a large contingent from the press and cultural communities. For many of the Western ambassadors present, this was the only opportunity they had to converse freely with knowledgeable Hungarians, and as Phil walked around to make certain no one was standing alone or unattended, as did all other American Embassy members, he enjoyed hearing the snippets of dialogue which he knew would constitute the kernel of cables to many capitals the next day.

The following morning Phil prepared for three weeks' leave, regrettably alone, because he knew the Ambassador could not spare Kiki for so long a period. He decided to spend it in Crete where he could swim and sightsee the island's many archeological sites. He settled whatever outstanding business he had, informed the DCM and Ambassador of his plans and then proceeded to the task he knew would be unpleasant—telling Kiki. He was not wrong.

"I don't believe it!" she cried out. "Going to *Greece* of all places, to *Greece!* My own native country, *without me!* Well, thank you very much. Oh, you . . . you . . . you Armenian!"

Phil explained softly that the Ambassador couldn't spare her for that long, but Kiki would not be assuaged. Fleeing her wrath, he took a flight to Athens, and then to Heraklion.

Crete was the ideal retreat, the perfect Greek island for rest and meditation. Once, lying on the beach, his body permeated by the heat from the sand, and his eyes fixed on a barely visible crescent in the shimmering Greek sky, he sought to assess his status.

Professionally, he assured himself, he was secure. His work was of value, and appreciated. Working not only days but long into the nights, his contacts had become so widespread that he could service any reasonable request made by the Ambassador, the Deputy Chief of Mission, or Washington. Emotionally, he knew that what he felt for Kiki was more than passing affection or the mere gratification of appetites born of isolation. Surely, he convinced himself, it was love. There was Grace, of course, and the distant sense of guilt he felt at being the object of her desire—strictly a one-way street, he told himself.

Then, almost magically, there tumbled into his head a rapid succession of images—of Beethoven, the Brunsviks, Szabolcsi, Fekete, Martonvásár, the manuscript. 'God,' he thought, 'it all seems so far away. And so does Hungary,' and he felt a compulsion to get back to Budapest, to the mystery of its political intrigues, the verbal duels with its cultural and journalistic intellectuals, the festering frustration of its populace. But perhaps overridingly, he was anxious to pick up whatever leads he could in pursuit of his private mission, aided wittingly and unwittingly by two musicologists, one of whom was almost saintly, while the other seemed satanic.

On August 30 he made the short flight to Athens, spent a sunny afternoon on the Acropolis, walking around and into the Parthenon, and examining other remnants of Greece's golden age. The next morning he boarded a Hungarian Malev plane and was flown back to Budapest.

Erzsébet was overjoyed to see him and commented on his

deep suntan. He changed his clothes and drove to the Embassy. Annie greeted him cheerily at the Reception Desk, as did all the Hungarian employees he ran into. Upstairs, the DCM came into his office and shook his hand. "We missed you, Phil. I mean that. The Ambassador will be very pleased to see you. He keeps asking when you'll be back."

Phil walked up to the Ambassador's office and noticed that Kiki, fortunately, was absent.

George Quigley rose from his chair, a very big smile on his face—"Wonderful to have you back, my boy. We might be having a busy Autumn and Winter, so it's good you had a restful time. Oh, and Grace asked me to convey her own pleasure that, as she put it, 'our neighbor has returned.'"

Back in his office, Phil looked at his calendar, and swore. That very afternoon there was a reception at the National Gallery, which was re-opening an old wing filled with Hungarian masters. He knew he had to attend because if he didn't, his absence would be noted. It was part of the burden of being a super-power. That's why he was certain that his Soviet counterpart would be there.

Ten

Phil could not say he really knew Gregor Adamov. They had met casually at a number of receptions and engaged in light conversation. Phil found him pleasant and quite unlike some of the other officers of the Soviet Embassy in Budapest, or for that matter in any other capital. Adamov was not heavy-handed, did not go out of his way to defend the policies of his government, nor to go beyond a laughing, gentle rebuke of U.S. policy in Vietnam. Adamov didn't look very Russian. He had a dark complexion, dark hair and dark expressive eyes in a face that was personable and pleasing. He was always uncommonly cordial to Phil in the several times they had run into each other, working arduously through crowds at packed receptions for a face-to-face exchange of greetings.

Their relationship bordered on the superficial, and Phil saw no reason to intensify it, viewing the brief contact they occasionally made as adequate and, he had decided, irrelevant.

Phil raced through his paperwork, checked with the DCM for any special assignments or requests from Washington which the Embassy would want him to explore, and informed him of his attendance at the reception. He then drove to the National Gallery.

It was jammed with Hungarian artists, officials and diplomats. Phil was the only American there and after dutifully listening to three speeches, he circulated and had chats with the Minister of Culture, two painters and a sculptor. As he was about to leave, he spotted Lili Ország across the large foyer. He owned several of her evocative, Hebrew-oriented paintings and considered her among the finest painters in all of East Europe. They spoke for ten minutes and agreed to meet at her studio soon. Then, just as he was preparing to depart, someone touched his arm. Turning, he saw the smiling face of Adamov.

"Good evening, Mr. Faljian," he said in English, the language he used with Phil.

"Good evening, Mr. Adamov. I kind of expected to see you here."

"My Embassy would not want the Hungarians to think we had lost interest in them," he said and Phil acknowledged Adamov's irony with a low chuckle.

They talked about the re-opened wing and some of the paintings and when Phil sneaked a look at his watch, Adamov said—"Got another appointment?"

"Oh, no, just that it's already six and I've got lots of paperwork that must get done."

"I was wondering," Adamov began hesitantly, "whether you would consider having dinner with me or must you really rush off?"

The invitation took Phil by surprise. It was not only gently made, but struck him as being extended so timorously as though Adamov fully expected a rebuff. There was nothing back at the Embassy that warranted his attention and besides, most everyone had already left. Killing two hours to dine with Adamov might be a suitable alternative to one of Erzsébet's rich Hungarian dinners.

He accepted and then, with Adamov within earshot, phoned her to say he wouldn't be eating at home that night.

Adamov asked if Phil knew the *Kiskakukk* Restaurant on *Pozsonyi út* and when Phil nodded, they hailed a cab and were there within twenty minutes.

Both ordered the apricot brandy known as *barackpálinka*, Adamov lit a cigarette after Phil had declined one, inhaled deeply, and when the smoke had left his lungs, said—"I've seen you at a number of functions but we've never really talked. I hope you won't think me forward in initiating this today. We are, after all, in the same business and represent the two countries that Hungary, one way or the other, must pay heed to. Or do you consider that an overstatement?"

"Not at all, Mr. Adamov . . ."

"My first name is Gregor and I would be pleased if you addressed me that way. May I call you Philip?"

"Phil will do."

The drinks came after which Adamov said—"You had a huge success with Isaac Stern. I was in the audience. It's not every day I can hear one of the world's greatest violinists."

"Oh, you mean the Russian who lives in New York?"

Adamov laughed—"That *was* stupid, wasn't it? Hungarian editors seem to think we will take offense if they say nice things about an American."

"They didn't have to say anything nice, but merely to acknowledge that Stern is an American," Phil insisted.

"Of course he is and everybody in this country knows it. Everybody in *my* country, too. When Stern performed in the Soviet Union, he was acclaimed as an American. Even my Ambassador thought it was a dumb thing for the Hungarians to say."

They sipped their drinks, the silence broken by Adamov a minute later—"Are you expecting any more cultural figures like Stern?"

"There's nothing on the horizon right now."

"Well, I'm certain your East European staffs in Washington are planning something, wouldn't you say?"

Is he fishing for information, Phil mused?

"I wouldn't know. They don't tell me their plans."

He almost used Adamov's first name but felt awkward about doing so. American diplomats did not get that chummy with their Soviet counterparts.

As though reading his mind, Adamov said—"I believe very

strongly, Phil, that we in the lower ranks should not behave with each other as our leaders do. Oh, here's the waiter. May I do this for both of us? Thank you."

He then proceeded to order a variety of dishes in excellent Hungarian, which aroused Phil's admiration. When Adamov had finished, Phil asked him how he had developed such fluency.

"One of my colleagues who was in the Soviet UN Delegation told me a joke he had heard in New York. A tourist asks someone—'How do you get to Carnegie Hall?' and gets the reply—'Practice, practice, practice.' I've always found that very funny. But that is the answer to your question. And here in Hungary, one's opportunity for practice is immeasurable."

It was an old joke and Phil laughed at it out of courtesy, but set him to thinking whether anyone in Moscow, an Uzbek visitor, for instance, might ever ask 'How do you get to the Bolshoi?' and get the same reply. It just didn't have the same punch.

Adamov appeared so anxious to light up a cigarette that he wolfed his food down and finished well before Phil. His exhaled smoke enveloped them both, almost choking Phil, but he didn't complain. When the thick, black coffee arrived, Adamov was expatiating on the paintings both had seen at the National Gallery opening, finding them lacking in originality.

"I saw you chatting with some of the Hungarian artists there," he said. "Frankly, I find their literature more daring than their painting."

Phil agreed, but had no desire to get any of his friends in trouble. Instead, he asked if Adamov had much contact with Hungarian intellectuals.

"Yes, quite often we get together and discuss Hungarian and Soviet literature, but I must tell you, Phil, that on occasion, your name comes up."

Ah, now perhaps we are getting closer to the purpose of this invitation, Phil mused. He looked questioningly at his luncheon partner, who continued—"Don't be alarmed. It is not negative. You are held in high esteem by the intellectual elite here. For one thing, you are helpful to them, with books, magazines and information they might need. We know you do these things. You are also very active in getting around, visiting and advising. *You* may not be aware of your talent for communication or of your own effectiveness, but *they* are."

Phil was taken aback by the flattery and sensed he had reddened some. "It's nice of you to say so, Gregor, but I'm sure you are just as active."

"But not as effective. I know very well how Hungarians look at the Soviet Union and how they perceive the United States. The balance weighs heavily on your side."

Phil tried not to show his astonishment at such frank talk from a Soviet diplomat. But even as he suppressed his own feelings, he began to observe a slight sense of restlessness in Adamov, who chain-lit another cigarette and seemed ill at ease. He blinked several times, wet his lips, and took extra long drags on his cigarette. He then said something, but so inaudibly that the din of the restaurant obliterated it completely. Phil bent forward and said—"I'm sorry but I didn't understand you."

"What I said was—You will have difficulty believing this, I know, but . . . and I really mean this . . . the way you conduct your affairs fills me with admiration, and . . . pride."

As he spoke the last word, he looked up at Phil, who, on hearing it stared at him in perplexity. He saw that Adamov was dead serious.

"Really, Gregor, I don't know what to say. Pride? Coming from the Soviet Embassy? I have the feeling you are about to tell me something more. Are you?"

It was a risk, a big risk which could backfire, but there was something in Adamov's demeanor which impelled Phil to take it.

And Adamov responded. He leaned closer, and as though having made a sudden decision, his voice trembling slightly, he said—

"What I want to say, Phil, is—*Menk hayrenagits enk.*"

Phil's eyes and mouth opened wide, his knife and fork in

mid-air. Slowly and incredulously, he repeated the Armenian phrase in English as a question—"We are compatriots? You, Gregor Adamov, are Armenian?"

"Yes, one hundred percent Armenian," Adamov replied in Armenian. "From your name, I have always known you were too. I assume, since you understood what I said, that you speak our language."

Phil, still stunned, responded by continuing in Armenian—"This is unbelievable. I mean, I've seen your name in the Diplomatic List and never suspected . . ."

"You couldn't because my name has been Russianized. Many do that for more rapid advancement in our Foreign Service. But my real name is Krikor Movsesovich Adamyants. My colleagues call me Gregor, but with you I much prefer Krikor."

Phil sat back and looked long at the Soviet diplomat. There could not be, he thought to himself, another situation like this in the entire diplomatic world. The United States Foreign Service had barely a handful of officers who were ethnically Armenian, whereas he had heard that the Soviet Foreign Service had more. And he was now face-to-face with one of them. He tried to look into Adamov's eyes but the Soviet kept shifting his gaze. Phil felt a degree of pleasure, of connection, at this unusual revelation, but he was not unaware also of an inner ambivalence. Being Armenian had not been all to his advantage, neither to his childhood, nor his musicological potential, nor to his Foreign Service career. Would this turn of events with a Soviet Embassy officer lead to yet another setback?

"I don't quite know what to say, Gregor, uh, excuse me, Krikor. You were a Soviet diplomat to me, and now I learn, to my astonishment, that you are also Armenian, just as I am an American diplomat but also Armenian. What does it mean, in this situation here in Budapest, that we are both Armenian? I hope that you will not exploit this for any nefarious purposes."

"I can understand that you could have doubts, Phil, but you shouldn't. There are some in my Embassy who know I am

Armenian, just as they know, from your name, that you are, too. I can assure you, however, that no one on my side will exploit this. Why don't we just agree that we have something in common, and let it go at that for now?"

His gaze was piercingly sincere and gave Phil some assurance. Then he extended his hand, and looked expectantly at Phil. They clasped hands, as though sealing some secret bond. Moments later, they arose and at Adamyants' suggestion, agreed to walk along the Danube and continue talking.

It was some ten minutes before Adamyants broke the silence.

"I would really like to get to know you better. I hope you will not think I'm prying. If you ever do, tell me so, but I hope you will appreciate that our blood ties go back at least 2000 years."

"I do, Krikor," Phil replied, continuing to wonder at his Soviet colleague's pursuit of their ethnic link.

"I'm curious about your spare time. I mean, what do you do for leisure. Do you read? Listen to music? Save stamps? Hungary is great for stamps. For instance, *I* study languages. I'm now into very advanced German."

"Maybe I can help you, Krikor. I'm fluent in German. As to your question, well, I read alot. Lately, I've been reading in German, English and Hungarian more than I usually do."

"What, for instance? Novels? History?"

"No, musicology. I'm interested in the various influences on musical creation. Do you like serious music? Classical music?"

Adamyants tilted his head tentatively and shrugged his shoulders—"Actually, I came to the Isaac Stern concert out of regard for the event, and not particularly for the music."

"Well, music is my passion. I studied to be a musicologist and here in Hungary, besides my various duties, I'm on a somewhat personal mission. In fact, it's become an obsession."

Adamyants nodded with interest and encouraged Phil to continue.

"If music is not something that moves you, Krikor, then perhaps you won't appreciate my obsession."

"Well, I will admit that classical music is not my forte, but out of sheer curiosity, what is this personal mission of yours?"

"I'll tell you because it seems to me, whether you are into music or not, your diplomatic title identifies you as a Cultural Officer, and therefore you should have some understanding of my mission. I am searching for a manuscript."

"A manuscript? Any manuscript, or one in particular?"

"One in particular. The manuscript of a work by Beethoven."

Adamyants stopped walking, turned and looked at Phil, his eyes narrowed. His smile and show of sympathetic interest had vanished so quickly that Phil, his brow furrowed, stared back in bewilderment.

"Can you tell me what this is a manuscript of?"

"Yes, of course. It is possibly a Cello Concerto."

Adamyants lit a cigarette very slowly, exhaled noisily, and, looking down at his cigarette, asked in a manner which struck Phil as overly casual—"Why is this particular manuscript of such interest to you?"

"*You,* a Cultural Officer, don't understand why? Well, since you don't seem to know music, let me explain something. There has never been any evidence of a Cello Concerto by Beethoven, and in all my studies and research, I never came across a note, letter or sketch by Beethoven indicating he even contemplated writing one. But twenty years ago, I was told, unequivocally, that such a concerto existed."

Phil then related the long story of his encounter with Hellmuth von Hase and the mystery of the missing manuscript. As Adamyants stood stiffly and watched him, Phil described von Hase's suspicions about the Hungarian musicologist, whom he did not name. When he had finished, he asked—"Do you now begin to understand? This is like a detective story for me. You asked what I do in my leisure time. Well, now you know."

Adamyants' features remained immobile. Fingering his cigarette, he said—"Phil, this is something we're going to have to discuss in greater detail. I don't know exactly when, but I can assure you, very soon."

"That's allright by me, Krikor, but I really fail to see why this seems to have thrown a pall over our first get-together. It was such a nice occasion, but now . . ."

"It was indeed a nice occasion, Phil, and I truly apologize for my reaction. But I ask you to trust me. I promise you that this will be cleared up shortly."

Driving back to the Embassy, Phil weighed the pros and cons of the dinner. The revelation of a common Armenian heritage was certainly remarkable and something that lent spice to his relationship with a Soviet Embassy officer. But Adamyants' transformation at mention of the Beethoven manuscript and his enigmatic comments were striking.

Phil juggled these two very different facets of the conversation in his mind: stimulated at the first, baffled by the second.

After he parked at the Embassy, however, he sat for a few moments in his car and wondered: 'Could these matters be in some way connected? I don't see how. Impossible!'

Eleven

Phil checked in at the Embassy for any late messages and almost immediately regretted that he had. Kiki was leaning against his door, a wry smile on her olive-hued face.

"I see my wonderful Greek sun shone brightly on you. Was it fun without Kiki? I still can't believe you went to Greece without me. Is this some Armenian game you are playing?"

"Can I make it up to you this weekend? Tennis at the Club?"

Kiki hesitated tauntingly, gave him a long skeptical look, then broke out in a wide smile, agreed and left just as Jim Garland walked in clutching a cable—"Read this. It just came in—an IMMEDIATE from the White House."

It was a cable announcing the arrival in November of a White House official named Garrison Portland and requesting the Embassy to set up a series of appointments with senior functionaries at the Foreign Ministry, the Economics Ministry, and any officials of the Hungarian Socialist Workers Party—the local name for the Communist Party—with whom the Embassy had contact.

"My, my! Doesn't want much, does he? What the hell is *this* all about, Jim?"

The DCM's grave expression seemed a harbinger of the answer to Phil as he pointed in the direction of the 'tank.' Once inside, he said—"Portland is a former analyst of Soviet and East European affairs who after twenty years of research has come to believe that in time our world and the communist world will somehow come to terms. Not co-existence. He means *real* terms, like adopting some elements of each others' systems—distribution of wealth, health care, price regulation, grass roots representation in government, enforcement of legislation against bigotry, things like that, and much more."

"Of course! Now I remember. Portland is the advocate of the Convergence Theory. Geez, Jim, is that what the White House is pushing now?"

"I can't believe it, but Portland is highly respected in Washington and this may be nothing more than just a feeler to get a sense of how the Soviets would react. Portland knows that Hungary would not volunteer an opinion without approval from the East, and that is probably what this trip is all about. From here he goes only to Yugoslavia, which means that he is focusing more on the creative and malleable Hungarians for reactions than any other bloc country."

"I guess this means a chaotic week in November."

"More for me than you. The Ambassador has designated me the Escort Officer and I'll soon be requesting the appointments Portland wants."

"So, if it's in your hands, does that leave me out, for a change?"

"You haven't read the last paragraph on page two."

Phil had not gotten that far and turned the page. The cable concluded by pointing out that Portland would be accompanied by his wife who spoke Hungarian and was especially interested in visiting some of the cultural museums and monuments in Budapest.

"OK, I get it. So that means me," Phil said with a grimace

"Correct, so forget Szabolcsi, forget Fekete, forget Beethoven—for the time being, anyway. The whole visit will be kicked off with a reception by the Quigleys, and then the ball gets rolling."

As Phil got up to open the door, Garland said—"By the way, how was your lunch? What happened?"

Phil got right to the point—"Turns out Adamov's name is really Adamyants. In other words, he's Armenian."

"The saints preserve us," Garland said in mock horror, "an Armenian in each camp."

Phil considered Garland to be perhaps the only one in the Embassy who might have an appreciation of ethnic relationships, of understanding for the mystic ties which Armenians from all corners of the globe experienced on contact. But he hesitated to elaborate or even mention the other surprise at lunch, largely because he himself was in the dark.

"Did you converse in Armenian?" Garland asked.

"Absolutely, that's why it might even turn out to be fun. Why are you looking at me like that?"

"Fun, eh? It sounds to me like something quite different. Like . . ." and he spoke the next word slowly and with emphasis on each of its three syllables ". . . re-cruit-ment."

The two men looked at each other without expression and when Garland raised an eyebrow, as though waiting for a reaction, Phil shook his head, but his eyes reflected doubt.

"Yes, he could be KGB. The thought has crossed my mind. They utilize everyone in their Foreign Service, even Cultural Officers, to try and turn us into spies, and they think we do too. But you and I know we got out of that business years ago. No, I think he's pretty much on the level. But I'll be careful."

On Saturday morning after breakfast and the morning papers, Phil put on his tennis togs and drove to the Club higher up in the Buda hills. The oddly-named American Air Free Club was a weekend sanctuary for all the western diplomats in Budapest and during good weather it was packed with families—the children in the swimming pool or playground, and the adults either playing tennis on the one court or golf on the four-hole course.

Kiki was already there and she greeted Phil with a hearty—"*Ya sou!*"

He kissed her on the cheek and she whispered—"*S'agapo.*"

"Kiki, behave yourself. From 'Hello' to 'I love you' is a big leap, even for a Greek."

"Not for a Greek like me," she laughed and said she had

found another couple to play with them. It was the Turkish Ambassador and his secretary. "I thought you would appreciate an Armenian and a Greek playing against two Turks."

Phil frowned. He had nothing against the ethnic mix of the match, merely that the Turk had a sadistic streak and seemed to enjoy hitting balls hard at any woman on the opposite side of the net.

They shook hands with the Turks and began to play. After losing the first set, Phil and Kiki took the second, but only after she was struck twice in the legs by the Turk's bullet-like volleys. Inasmuch as others were waiting for the court, they retired to a table for a cool drink. Kiki looked more charming than ever despite the fatigue and perspiration. She was almost a poster-perfect model of a young Greek woman—dark eyes, dark hair, fleshy nose, sensual lips, and moderately hirsute.

Ekaterina—trimmed at an early age to Kiki—Boutos was 28 when, after five years as a State Department secretary, she put in for Foreign Service, certain that her Greek heritage would ensure an assignment to Athens. But Washington's perverse personnel procedures endured, and instead, she was disappointed to find herself in widely divergent posts, ranging from Latin America and Africa to the Middle East and West Europe, and now communist Hungary. Her life was one of solitude; not enjoying diplomatic status, she was seldom invited to diplomatic functions; going to occasional staff parties, she always arrived alone and went home alone, except from the Greek Embassy whence, in tribute to the Embassy she represented, she was always driven back in the Ambassador's car.

As she confided one night to Phil, like most other Embassy single females, she always had her eye out for the one man who would change her life, but until Budapest, that had not happened. She confessed to attractions, but never love. "You are my one and only love," she had whispered to him during a concert and kissed his ear. For his part, Phil had been attracted to her from the start. Although he had always hoped to marry an Armenian, the Foreign Service did not offer much opportunity. If not an Armenian, he had rationalized, perhaps a Greek. Two months after she had arrived in Budapest, they became intimate.

After George Quigley's arrival. Kiki, with her unfailing Mediterranean instinct in matters of the heart, took one look at Grace Quigley and had a suspicion. And when one day she walked into Phil's office and almost collided with a smiling Grace Quigley, it was for Kiki a confirmation of her worst fears.

Until the student demonstration, she and Phil had dated less often, but the shock of seeing him unconscious near her desk, his head in a pool of blood, eradicated all the reserve within her. His invitation to tennis made it all right again.

Noticing his admiring gaze, she smiled and said in a low seductive voice—"I hope this means that you'll have some time for me—tonight."

"How about nine?"

"*En taksi,*" she said.

He heard her car come up the driveway that night. Kiki was so completely different from the few women he had become involved with—all passion and drama. Electra and Medea. Phil had already decided that was why Greek men looked so much older than their years, or why the women they had married appeared to be so much younger than their husbands.

Kiki insisted on staying over and the night passed with the lustful turbulence that Phil had grown accustomed to, and enjoyed. After breakfast, they lounged in each others' arms in the sunroom, Kiki's affection soon intensifying. Phil cautioned that they could be seen by anyone walking past the glass-enclosed room. She responded by flinging her robe aside, and yet another hour passed in lubricious engagement.

Kiki left shortly after noon, and as Phil was making a sandwich, he heard the phone. He let it ring once, twice, three times, then it stopped. As he bit into the sandwich, it rang again. This time he picked up the receiver.

"Nice to know you're still alive." The voice was frosty but the words were slurred. "If you think you can find the time today, perhaps you might want to walk the great distance between us. After all, I'm a bit nearer than the God-damned Aegean Sea."

He mumbled something and abruptly hung up. If she remonstrated, he would tell her the connection was interrupted—something that did happen, and often.

Phil spent the rest of the day and evening reading his Beethoven materials, with occasional flights of reverie involving Fekete, Martonvásár, and the widening mystery about the manuscript. One aspect of Beethoven's musical creation impressed him particularly, namely that the year 1817 was a barren period. For such a prolific composer, this was astonishing. Could this have been the time when he was considering the Cello Concerto? His deafness had now become total and he was seldom without his Conversation Books, in which people wrote down their questions, but Beethoven's replies are not recorded anywhere. This was once described by the great Beethoven authority in East Berlin, Dr. Karl-Heinz Keilbert, as "like hearing only one end of a phone conversation."

Phil wondered whether Dr. Keilbert would be able to tell him anything about the existence of the Cello Concerto. Face-to-face contact was virtually impossible inasmuch as the United States had no diplomatic relations with the German Democratic Republic. But perhaps . . . Phil looked up from his book, then shook his head, rejecting for the moment the fleeting thought that flew through his mind.

He recalled what Szabolcsi had said about the opening measures—a long cello solo. Not the way most cello concertos begin. But 1817 was already the beginning of Beethoven's third period when his music became contemplative and philosophical. It was also the beginning of the last ten years of his life. Perhaps he had begun the Concerto and then abandoned it, inspired to work on something else. Most composers set aside works they had started, sometimes permanently. Perhaps that was what happened here.

Phil fell asleep, mesmerised by the mystery.

Twelve

Two months went by and Phil found himself involved mostly with the journalistic side of his two-pronged function as Press and Cultural Officer. Some of the newsmen were from Moscow and had come to Budapest not only for stories but for R & R—Foreign Service abbreviation for Rest and Rehabilitation from tension-filled posts. They looked to Phil for special angles to explore—ideological vagaries among the satellites or major differences with the Soviet Union—but when these gave out, they always fell back on the standard theme that their editors back home played up, namely women's styles as exemplified by Hungarian chic, which was famous throughout the communist world.

But much of Phil's time was taken up with trying to steer Hungarian journalists and editors down paths friendlier to the United States. Journalists such as *Magyar Nemzet's* Tibor Hegedus, who had tipped off Phil to the student demonstration, were beyond the need for such corrective behaviour, long since having been convinced of the bankruptcy of Marxist theory and practice.

This was not the case, however, with some editors. Phil invited one such editor to lunch after having read his editorial that same day which denounced the United States as a "fascist, imperialistic aggressor" because of the war in Vietnam. At lunch Phil lectured the editor and gave him background on the conflict wondering to himself as he did how he could argue so vehemently in favor of a cause he had long privately opposed.

Three days later, another editorial appeared in the same paper along the same lines. Phil went to the editor's office and complained, asking whether his earlier arguments had made no impression. The editor looked perplexed and asked—"But, surely, you couldn't have read my editorial very carefully, else you would have noticed that I dropped the word 'fascist.'"

Phil burst out laughing.

"So we are no longer fascists but merely imperialistic aggressors! And for you, that is a concession? Is that what you're saying? My God, how do you people think?"

He knew the answer to his question, rhetorical as it was, very well. He walked back to the Embassy through depressing streets, and looked up at the deteriorating apartment houses on either side of him. Except for an occasional flower-pot on the window sill, everything was drab, totally devoid of color or life, and many of the outer walls of the buildings were pockmarked—scars of either the bitter final 'liberation' of 1945 or of the fierce revolution of 1956. In either case, no effort seemed to have been made to repair them.

These communist regimes had money for Olympic sports and armaments—where their presence had an international prestige, but none for sandblasting and a coat of paint. The fear of the secret police apparently exercised such a domestic force that the leadership throughout Eastern Europe had no concerns about the depressed spirits of its minions, which made for rockbottom morale and, consequently, an absence of resistance. Phil looked at the many men and women who passed by. What a handsome people these Hungarians are, he thought, and, as he had gathered from his many contacts, what a proud people. In their creative talents that transcended borders and languages, such as mathematics, chemistry and the nuclear sciences, they had been instrumental in the production of nuclear energy and bombs.

It was no different in music, he thought, remembering the composers, conductors and soloists whose names graced concert programs in many countries. It was only the unique Hungarian language and its linguistic isolation which acted as an impediment to this country's penetration of the world's literary consciousness.

All of this had been going on for more than a century, and even now, despite the veneer of communism with its absurd principles of 'socialist realism' and cultural and scientific strictures. Of course, here and there, especially in corners of the literary and journalistic world, there were the hangers-on, the lackeys, those whose sycophancy earned them material benefits, entry into higher circles and, perhaps the most coveted perquisite of all—travel to the West.

Most of those whom Phil knew were cynical of the regime. In the beginning some had embraced the new approach to the human condition, not unlike gifted poets to the East, such as Mayakovsky in Russia and Charents in Armenia. And why not? In so many of its doctrines, communism preached the same tenets as Christianity; in fact, as most religions. But after that, they parted company. Religious faith and economics went their separate ways, especially when the economics, which had sounded so attractive initially—'the means of production belong to the people,' 'to each according to his needs'—had to be enforced by terror. But by then, for the intellectual elite, it was almost too late. Join or be crushed. The Hungarians *he* knew had taken a third course—create on the fringe, live, and hope.

Phil neared the Embassy now and went to his office. On the cultural side of his agenda, the scene was calm except for a few art openings and two operatic premiers at the Erkel Theatre. Phil called Szabolcsi but the musicologist said he had not come up with any new information on the manuscript. He suggested that Phil visit Martonvásár, more to absorb the climate of the Beethoven Museum and its artifacts than for any concrete data. Phil planned trips, once in September and another in October, but the weather changed and he canceled.

In fact, the increasingly cold weather found Hungarians bundled up in heavy coats and the city slowly overcome with the haze and smog of brown coal whose acrid smell burned one's nostrils. In consequence, tennis and golf at the Club on weekends became increasingly rare, especially as the days became shorter. Instead, Phil took to entertaining more frequently, his Hungarian guests pleased as much with the warmth of his residence as with the food, drink and the always popular American film showing.

Both in sports and at dinner parties, Kiki was frequently his companion. Phil knew that Grace would eventually find that out. He tried to avoid her, often didn't return her phone calls, which were taken by Erzsébet and dutifully, if soberly, reported to him. But somehow, by chance and good luck, he had managed to keep contact with her to a minimum; however, it couldn't last.

Before anyone realized it, November arrived, bringing with it the realization that the Garrison Portland visit was finally imminent. Phil had been through more stressful occasions. The epitome, of course, was a Presidential visit, of which he had had two—Kennedy and Johnson. Nothing compared with such occasions as armies of security people, communication specialists, White House aides and planeloads of journalists descended on hapless posts throwing everything into such disarray that it took months for a return to normalcy. Next came Congressional Delegations, known for short as Codels, as otherwise obscure members of Congress suddenly appeared in embassies and made all kinds of preposterous demands on cowed Foreign Service officers.

The Portland visit would have less of an impact on the Embassy's routine, but a misstep could have dire consequences. Passing by Eric Hager's office one afternoon, Phil overheard the Political Officer warning his economic colleague Dudley Watson—

"Something you do or say in his presence can make or break you. Watch your step. Your entire career can be at stake."

There was considerable truth to that, but Phil knew that Hager would go to some lengths to impress the high-level visitor. Once, a week before the visit, he entered Hager's office and found him studying a promotion list from the previous year. He looked up sheepishly when he saw Phil and quickly covered the list, but realizing Phil had seen it, said—"Just looking ahead. I would expect a promotion in two years and a DCM-ship in four. Careers must be planned. Not in your agency though. Everybody gets promoted regularly."

"Only if it's deserved, Eric. USIA is just as strict with laggards as your agency. And just as prone to select out the bad guys."

Hager frowned as Phil walked out. Even his closest friend in the Embassy seemed to be affected by the pending visit. Phil stopped by and found the DCM looking haggard, his manner surly, his temperament cranky. He had been working the phone with the Foreign Ministry seeking appointments and drawing up schedules, and the week-long effort seemed to have gotten to him. Phil warily backed out of Garland's office.

Finally, the unwanted day came. On a Monday morning, Ambassador Quigley was all nerves as the hour for the Portlands' arrival neared. He made excessive demands of the staff and Kiki was a virtual blur as she ran up and down the corridor and in and out of offices with memoranda and schedules. Once, she ran into Phil's office for a quick kiss and ran out just before Hager looked in—"Well, I guess, for once, this will not be your show. I see Jim is very uptight. You must feel fortunate."

Phil didn't know whether that was said in irony or envy, but he acknowledged it with an ambiguous smile and a wave of his hand.

The Ambassador and DCM finally went down in the elevator shortly after noon. Grace Quigley was waiting in the Lincoln Continental, Imre standing sharply at attention and holding the door. Garland sat up front while a second car followed them to *Ferihegy* Airport.

While Phil was waiting in his office, Sarah Garland phoned—

"Oh Phil, have they left already? They have? I see. Allright. I'm to meet them at the Residence and see if Mrs. Portland needs anything. If not, I guess she'll want to rest up before tonight's reception."

Wonderful woman, Sarah, he thought. Jim is so fortunate. I should be so lucky.

Kiki tiptoed in for another kiss.

"Kee-keeeee, you've got to control yourself!"

"You're mine, all mine. You are my very own Filippos, and that's all I care about."

At four o'clock the DCM returned to the Embassy, stuck his head in Phil's doorway and said—"They're here, tired but in good spirits, and for some reason so am I. Portland's quite excited. I think he's expecting some kind of breakthrough. I didn't want to deflate him. As for *Mrs.* Portland, all I can say is—Wow, what a dish!"

Phil went home at five, rested, and as was required of all staff members, arrived a half hour before the seven o'clock reception began. He engaged in light banter with his colleagues and the Garlands. Sarah, a jovial reddish-blonde, chatted flirtatiously with Phil, whose attentions she always enjoyed.

"Anytime Jim drops you, let me know and I'll be there," he said, making certain the DCM heard him. Garland waved a forefinger at him in mock reproach—"Don't get greedy. I would imagine your hands are pretty full right now."

Sarah said that Mrs.Portland had asked to be driven to a special hairdresser off Lenin Boulevard—"She sure knows her way around Budapest, but that'll delay her coming down."

It did. Meanwhile, the DCM introduced Garrison Portland to the Embassy staff just before the guests began arriving and were then greeted at the receiving line by the Quigleys and Portland. Mrs.Portland was apparently still upstairs. Within thirty minutes the Residence was jammed with Hungarians and Ambassadors from most of the other embassies in Budapest.

Phil avoided Grace's eyes and Grace herself, always grateful as she began to approach when a guest joined him in the nick of time for a chat. Phil was especially popular with the Ambassadors and DCMs of non-communist embassies because of his intimate familiarity with internal Hungarian developments.

Someone touched his arm and a familiar voice said—"*Jó estét*, Faljian *úr*."

He turned and greeted Deputy Foreign Minister Kovács cordially—"And good evening to you too, Sir."

They carried on a brief conversation, at the end of which Kovács said—"I am looking forward to greeting Mr. Portland tomorrow at the Ministry. As for Mrs. Portland, I find her most charming, but I suppose that is my pro-Hungarian prejudice showing."

"You've already met her?" Phil asked in surprise.

"Why yes, just ten minutes ago. She's over there talking to my wife."

Phil looked around, his curiosity peaking, and saw Mrs. Kovács across the packed room, and as he did, the blonde woman she was speaking with turned, beamed at him, excused herself and worked her way through the throng. Standing now only inches away, she looked into his disbelieving eyes and, with a mocking smile, asked—"And how's my Philly doing in Budapest?"

Thirteen

The tremor of pleasure that swept through him was followed immediately by a sense of apprehension, as though his past had been revealed and he was standing naked before everyone.

"Ilona! I don't believe this. What in hell are you doing here?"

"Why, Philly, I am Garrison Portland's wife. I have every reason to be here."

He looked into her hazel eyes and saw sheer joy. 'God,' he thought, 'she is as ravishing as ever.'

"And you are here to help him explore this theory of his?"

"Well, maybe a little. But mostly, Philly, because you are here and I wanted to see you."

Phil saw out of the corner of his eye that Grace Quigley, although pretending to converse with the British Ambassador, was firing scorching looks in their direction, and knew that he would hear about his display of cordiality to the stunning blonde.

Just as he was about to tell her that she had become even more beautiful since he had last seen her, Jim Garland interrupted—

"I see you two have met. Well, you certainly have one thing in common—the Hungarian language."

As Ilona laughed, a little too self-consciously, Phil thought—'If you only knew, Jim, how very much more we have in common.'

Ambassador Quigley beckoned to Phil to join him and Garrison Portland, and as Phil walked away, Ilona winked slyly at him.

"Mr. Portland, this is Phil Faljian. I guess he probably knows more influential Hungarians than all of us put together. Anything you want, just let him know through Jim Garland, who will be at your side always."

Portland shook Phil's hand. He was an arresting figure—tall, erect, with greying hair and mustache, a handsome man, healthy, in peak condition, in his fifties. Quigley walked away leaving them alone to chat about life in Budapest, then returned bringing over Deputy Foreign Minister Kovács.

"Mr. Minister, this is Garrison Portland from the White House who has an appointment with you tomorrow morning. I thought you might like to get acquainted before then. Mr. Faljian you already know."

"Delighted to meet you, Mr. Portland, and of course I know Mr.Faljian. I am glad to see you have completely recovered from your injury."

"Thank you, Mr. Minister. I'm still alive."

Portland looked to one and the other questioningly, but Phil had no desire to explain and left that to Kovács, excused himself and turned around just in time to bump into Grace Quigley.

She was not happy, as her cutting voice let him know—"No time for a stupid little phone call?"

"Mrs. Quigley please . . ." he began, and looking over her shoulder saw Ilona watching them with a knowing smile. That woman, he thought, just doesn't miss a trick.

"Don't *Mrs. Quigley* me, and don't think I didn't notice your infatuation with that slut. That's all she is, just a slut. Gets in late, runs to the hairdresser, comes back looking like a sex bomb, turning everyone's head. And I mean *everybody*," looking sharply at Phil.

Phil felt the perspiration run down his back. He was becoming very uncomfortable and hoping others hadn't noticed Grace's demeanor. Again, it was the DCM who rescued him.

"Oh, Grace, may I borrow Phil for a moment? Thank you."

Grace turned sharply and walked towards a waiter who was carrying a trayful of drinks. Phil wondered how many she had already had.

"Thanks, Jim, she's going out of her mind. On top of the alcohol, we now have jealousy, sheer, naked jealousy. And all because of . . . guess who?"

"I know damned well who. That's why I came over to get you, and in the nick of time, it looks like. But it may get worse, because Mrs. Portland has a special request. She wants to visit the museums and art galleries in town and asked if the Embassy Cultural Officer could escort her. Why do you always get the whipped cream and I get the crumbs? By the way, would you know when she left Budapest? She sure knows a lot of our guests."

Phil feigned innocence, even though he knew every detail of Ilona's earlier life.

"Why not ask her? Nothing wrong with it."

They reached Ilona Portland who was just saying to the Turkish Ambassador—"No, I'm afraid tennis is not my game. I used to be a fencer. You know, Hungarian women had championship fencing teams at the Olympics. Oh here are Mr. Garland and Mr. Faljian. Of course you know both of them."

The Turk shook hands jovially and said Phil was always a worthy tennis opponent as he walked away.

Ilona turned to Phil—"Mr. Faljian, I understand from Mr. Garland here that you are familiar with every cultural institution in Budapest. Could I prevail upon you to take me around tomorrow?"

"Of course, Mrs. Portland," he said. Garland left them and lowering her voice, Ilona said—"The culture is only a ruse to spend time with you. I'm sure you know that."

"Ilona, remember this is Budapest, not Washington. We live in a fishbowl here. The AVO sees all, hears all. Probably listening in to us right now."

"Not with all this chatter and noise going on," she said, sipping her drink. "You forget that I grew up in this environment. Pick me up tomorrow morning here at the Residence. I believe you live next door, don't you? How convenient. Anyway, pick me up and we'll drive to the National Gallery, then have lunch, and part ways, but only for an hour. I'll give you the address of an old schoolmate of mine who has a modest little apartment. I know that *I'm* looking forward to it. I hope that *you* are too. And keep the afternoon free. We've got a lot of catching up to do. Agreed?"

"Nine-thirty tomorrow morning."

Phil circulated among some of the Hungarian intellectuals who were also his friends. He listened in on the novelist Tibor Déry, who was holding court with a group of East European ambassadors, telling them about the very personal, erotic memoirs he was writing. Moving on, Phil waved to the historian István Gál in another corner, his arthritis requiring him to sit, as he expounded on nineteenth century ties between Hungary and the United States to Eric Hager and Dudley Watson. Off in a corner he momentarily joined Sándor Weores who was informing the Hungarian Minister of Culture of his latest book of Chinese-inspired poetry.

'Too bad Szabolcsi isn't here,' Phil thought, 'we could have at least chatted about our favorite subject.' But the Ambassador had asked only for a few prominent intellectuals for his party, and preferably English speakers.

Phil sought to work his way through the buzzing throng in the hope of reaching a Party official he recognized who was engaged in intense conversation with the Soviet Ambassador. He barely got to within ten feet of his quarry when he heard the Oxford intonations of the British Ambassador—"Oh, here's Faljian, Pierre, perhaps he can throw some light on it for us."

Phil knew he was hooked for another ten minutes. Roger Mandrake, elegant in his British cut dark suit, and his French counterpart, Pierre Fauquier, were forever snagging Phil at receptions to ask him the same old questions, as Mandrake did now—"Can you tell us what Kádár meant in that third paragraph of the speech he gave at Debrecen yesterday? We assume you read your *Népszabadság* this morning."

Mandrake, a moderately good tennis player, would pull the same stunt on the court, usually when they were changing sides, and Phil would have to hold up the game to clarify an editorial or speech. At diplomatic receptions, it was less obtrusive, but equally irritating. Phil concluded that his analyses were sprung by Mandrake on his staff as his own to display his political acumen, which, Phil knew, never fooled the highly capable officers of the British Embassy. Nevertheless, Ambassador Quigley had instructed him to always cooperate with Allied ambassadors, especially the British ("Special relationship, you know").

Phil described the circumstances which had led to Kádár's visit to the University of Debrecen—a dispute concerning the teaching of certain aspects of Western literature at the university which conflicted with Marxist doctrine. Ambassador Fauquier followed up with a few questions about French authors available in Budapest book stores, prompting Phil to wonder why Fauquier couldn't find out such things from his own Cultural Officer, and then speculating that it was probably for the very same reason as Mandrake's. Both Ambassadors expressed their gratitude and promptly resumed talking to each other.

Phil saw that the Party official he wished to converse with was edging toward the door and about to leave. He sneaked a look at his watch. An hour had gone by. Soon, the reception would be thinning out, but he knew that Grace would catch him again before it was over. He hadn't long to wait.

"Hello there, good looking." Grace was standing behind him and when he turned to her, he saw that she was unsteady.

"Well, this is a truly successful party, Mrs. Quigley."

Still smiling, she said between clenched teeth—"That's a lotta crap, and you know it."

Her eyes were bleary and her hair was no longer in array. He guided her to the long, richly-laden table, filled a dish with fingerfood and helped her sit down.

Grace asked what the program was for the next day and he told her of Ilona Portland's wish to visit cultural sites. Grace snorted with derision."She'd be more at home visiting the bordello she worked in."

Many guests had left and Phil caught first the DCM's eye then the Ambassador's, both indicating with brief nods that he should help see the guests out. Within another thirty minutes everyone had gone, including the American staff, except for the Garlands, the Portlands and Phil, who had been kept back by the Ambassador.

"How about a nightcap before retiring?" Quigley asked. Everyone helped themselves, Phil reluctantly serving Grace as Ilona looked on with amusement, and after some chitchat, the Garlands departed, the Portlands and Quigleys retired and Phil walked back to his residence.

*

As he lay in bed, a distant time and place floated into his mind. Washington. October 1956. The Hungarian Revolt against the communist regime was dominating the newspapers, television and the radio. Every day brought new images of buildings pitted by gunfire, rubble everywhere and weary Hungarians with rifles, firing at Soviet tanks. Hungary was in chaos and it was happening before the eyes of a watching but otherwise un-involved world.

Phil had just returned from a four-year posting in Ottawa and had been assigned to the Bureau for Cultural Affairs. One day, late in December, during his lunch hour, he had walked over to Stanley Kramer's Book Store where, because of its proximity to USIA headquarters on Pennsylvania Avenue, he often went to browse. While searching for literature on the Dutch painter Vermeer, he heard a female voice ask at the desk for a book on English. The accent was distinctly Hungarian, the question poorly enunciated. He turned and saw a stunning blonde woman of about 30 who seemed very self-assured. She saw him looking, smiled, and turned politely away. When the clerk brought a grammar for her inspection, Phil saw that it was very complicated, as she did too when she examined some pages. She shook her head and left.

When Phil emerged from the book store moments later, she was standing on the corner of 18th Street studying a map of Washington. He walked uncertainly toward her, hesitated, aware that his good intentions might be misconstrued, but then made up his mind and asked—"Miss, can I possibly help you?"

She looked up, thanked him, and explained that she was searching for a good primer in English and was trying to locate the bookstores whose addresses she had found in the telephone directory.

"I am Hungarian," she said, to him an unnecessary admission, adding—"I come only now here and must learn language."

Phil suggested they have a cup of coffee and he would tell her of the best course she could take.

Once they were seated, he described the USIA course called "Teaching of English as a Foreign Language" and said that he would get her the textbooks and all the tape materials, even though he was aware they were for use only in foreign countries.

That was the beginning of the love affair between Phil Faljian and Ilona Harsányi, a refugee from communist Hungary who had wangled her way from Budapest to the camps of Austria and then to Washington.

It lasted for the three years that Phil was stationed in Washington. Through Ilona, he learned some Hungarian, but between the course materials, which she studied assiduously, and the intimacy with Phil, she soon became adept in speaking English. When the time came for his next assignment, to The Hague, Ilona wept for days, ran the gamut of sorrow and anger, even proposed they get married, but Phil said he wasn't ready for that yet. She accused him of wanting The Netherlands more so he could live there with his beloved Vermeers. He told her they had very few of them in Holland, but it didn't pacify her. The parting was agonizing.

In preparing for his Hungarian assignment five years later, he preferred not to attend the Foreign Service Institute in Washington because it would entangle him again with Ilona Harsányi, the Hungarians in Washington being a tight ethnic community. He chose instead the Army Language School in Garmisch, in distant West Germany, and a private tutor. When he finally arrived in Budapest in 1965, he was virtually fluent, and Ilona Harsányi a lovely but remote memory.

But here she was again, married to an influential Washingtonian working in the White House, and as dazzling as she had been a decade ago.

'Wait 'til Erzsi finds out about *this*,' he thought, chuckling.

Fourteen

Phil arose early and drove to the Embassy, arriving shortly after the DCM, in whose office they chatted.

"Portland is coming down with the Ambassador around nine-thirty and I'll take him to his first appointment with Kovács. And as I recall, you'll be taking Mrs. Portland around to various museums. Lucky guy."

Phil nodded solemnly.

"What's wrong, Phil? She's lively, vivacious and a doll, to boot."

"Oh, it's not her. It's Grace. She's having fits, convinced I've already got something going with her guest."

"Is Grace crazy? With Garrison Portland's wife? In Budapest?"

"The answers to your questions are—Yes, Yes and Yes."

He walked into the Communications Room and picked up the incoming cable traffic, reading everything that he found relevant, then went to his office and scanned the Hungarian press. *Népszabadság* had a brief item on the arrival of the Portlands from Washington, as did several other papers; it was standard procedure to repeat verbatim and without comment what MTI—the Hungarian News Agency—distributed internally to the media throughout the country.

A knock on the door made him look up. It was the Cardinal, standing slightly stooped over, hands clasped. Phil stood up.

"May I molest you, Faljian *úr*?"

The Cardinal's quaint English was often a literal translation of the Latin he knew well.

"Your Eminence, you never molest me. What can I do for you?"

"There is a book I need and I thought perhaps you could get it for me. It is Edward Crankshaw's 'Fall of the House of Habsburg.'I read about it in an Austrian newspaper."

"Consider it done, Your Eminence."

"Shall we be talking soon?" the lonely recluse inquired.

"I believe tomorrow night, Your Eminence," Phil assured him.

The Cardinal was referring to the rotating nightly duty of the Embassy officers who escorted him to the courtyard for his thirty-minute walk and brought him his dinner. With those few who spoke Hungarian, essentially Consul Harold Fillmore and Phil, it was more congenial to the Embassy's famous shut-in. With Phil, the discussions were always political and interesting, and although he didn't look forward to Embassy overnight duty, conversations with the Cardinal more than compensated for the discomfort of sleeping at the Embassy.

At nine o'clock sharp he drove back to his residence in the Buda hills. Erzsébet was already dusting and about to vacuum when he walked in. He told her of the Portlands and what the schedule was and that he would be out all day with Mrs. Portland, but have dinner at home in the evening.

"Is the Rabbit going too?"

"I hope not," he said, his brow puckering. He hadn't thought of that. What if she insisted?

"You're not telling me everything," she said sternly.

Phil looked at her and burst out laughing—"Oh my God. You too, Erzsi? What is it about you Hungarian women? Are we men all so transparent to you?"

He checked his watch and walked over to the Residence, where a second Embassy car was waiting, Béla, its driver, standing by the open door. Phil greeted him and entered the Residence.

Grace Quigley was pacing up and down the living room,

nervously puffing on a cigarette in which she wasn't taking any pleasure. When she heard him she turned her head, her stare even icier than her body language.

"The slut is still upstairs, getting ready—for you."

"Good Lord, Grace, she's the wife of a distinguished White House official. Why are you behaving in this way?"

"Phil, spare me the bullshit. I could see what was going on here last night. I can't believe it was love at first sight. Almost as though you two knew each other before. Well, for your information, I've decided to go along. Maybe *she* can instruct me in some Hungarian culture. *You* sure as hell haven't."

"I didn't know you were interested."

"Listen, young man, just remember I'm the Ambassador's wife."

Phil sighed—"Oh Grace, you should be reminding *yourself* of that every day. So please, spare *me* the bull."

Before she could respond, Ilona Portland descended the long winding staircase, looking resplendent. Phil almost gasped at the lovely sight and heard Grace's low snort behind him.

"Good morning, Mr. Faljian, you are very punctual. I'm all ready for our morning jaunt through Budapest's treasures."

Her smile, her voice and her manner were overwhelming. She shook hands with him and greeted Grace cordially. Grace nodded, still puffing furiously on her cigarette.

"I'm thinking of joining you," she said in a shrill, tense voice.

Ilona took this bit of unwelcome information in stride—"As you wish, Mrs. Quigley, but it is an overcast day, and the radio is predicting rain. We're going to do a lot of walking, through museums and galleries. Those heels will kill your feet very quickly, that's why I'm wearing flats. Why don't you save yourself from an arduous experience. What time is lunch, by the way?"

Grace spat out—"One-thirty."

"We'll be back on time. I'll see to that."

Phil was afraid to look back at Grace as they walked out. Once in the car, Béla drove down the hill to *Moskva tér*, across the *Margit híd* and towards the center of town where they picked up the tree-lined avenue leading directly to *Hösök tere* and the Museum of Fine Arts.

Once, Ilona turned her head abruptly to look at a building they were passing but straightened herself and sat back. She said—"Are you aware, Philly, that this lovely road we are on, which goes directly to Heroes Square, has a special aura? It's because it has undergone a number of name changes, and those changes are almost a record of Hungarian history. In the olden days, it was known as *Sugár út*, because it's straight as a beam, as the word *sugár* means. During the Habsburgs, it was changed to *Andrássy út,* named after Emperor Franz Joseph's favorite Hungarian Foreign Minister. During the 1956 Revolution, for a few days anyway, we changed it to *Magyarifjúság út,* in honor of Hungarian youth. But when the Soviet tanks came rolling back in on November 4, the name was changed to what it is today, *Népköztársaság utja*."

"People's Republic Avenue," Phil translated. "What a horror of a name. I like *Andrássy út* the best."

"So does everyone in Budapest. If you get into a cab now and tell the driver *Andrássy út*, he knows exactly where to go. For example," she leaned forward and asked in Hungarian—"Béla, what street are we on now?"

"*Andrássy*, Portland *né*," Béla replied, looking at her curiously in the rearview mirror, obviously wondering why she would ask a question to which she well knew the answer.

They arrived at the Museum entrance on Heroes Square and when they were out of the car and walking up the steps of the museum, Ilona said—"What a bitch! I have no intention of returning for lunch. I'll tell Béla to deliver that message. You kept your afternoon free, I hope?"

"As you said I should."

They spent an hour in the Museum. Ilona seemed transported.

"I always loved this Museum. Can you imagine a small country like this having all these marvelous things—from El

Grecos and Dürers and Titians and Giorgiones, right up to the modern French like the Impressionists and Utrillo."

"But no Vermeers, Ilona, and I hunger to see one."

"You're asking too much, Philly. You've been to the Netherlands for that. Weren't they enough?"

"Not for me. But there are a few in this part of Europe."

"If I know you, you'll get to see those too," she laughed and hugged his arm.

They returned to the car and she told Béla to drive to Buda and the Hungarian National Gallery where they immersed themselves in the fascinating Hungarian artists who filled the walls of the building—Csontváry, Barabás, Munkácsy and many, many others.

It was now almost one o'clock. As they walked to the car, she gave Phil the address of her schoolmate's apartment in Pest and told him to meet her there at two. Once inside the car, she told Béla to drop her off at the apartment and when that was done, Béla took Phil back to the Embassy and then drove to the Residence conveying Ilona's regrets for lunch.

At two o'clock Phil parked near the address she had given him and rang the bell of an apartment in the rear of an old building. Ilona opened the door and held out her arms to him. Phil stood motionless, nervous and uncertain, but she grabbed his arm and pulled him in.

"I've missed you so much, Philly," she said and embraced him tightly.

"Ilona, please, just wait, please. Let's talk."

She drew back, hearing the edge in his voice, and looked into his eyes.

"The past is already forgotten, is it?"

"The past can never be forgotten, Ilona. It is the present we must think of."

He led her to the sofa, and sitting close to her, said—

"Ilona, darling, you are as stunning as ever. The years have been wonderful to you, but you must realize that we cannot pick up where we left off."

"I see. Is it the prima donna in the Residence?"

"Hell, no! She's got nothing to do with this. It's other things—where we are, who you are, who I am. You simply must understand."

Ilona fell back against the sofa and emitted a long disappointed sigh. "I guess I do, but there was always the hope . . ." her voice trailed off. She arose, lit a cigarette, exhaled noisily and said—"Allright, Philly, allright. You're right. I know deep down that you are. Tell me, where are you parked?"

"About three blocks from here."

"Look, let's not prolong this today. Leave first and drive to the next corner on *Pozsonyi út*. I'll meet you there and you can drop me at the Embassy and Béla can take me home, unless Garry has already finished his appointments, in which case, he and I can drive back with the Ambassador. Meanwhile, Philly, now that we know where we stand, can we meet again tomorrow, here, for oldtime's sake? Please say Yes, Philly. I just enjoy so much being alone with you, even if it leads to . . . nothing."

He saw that she was in earnest, and agreed.

"Wonderful!" she exclaimed. "I do appreciate that, Philly. Until then, I'll keep myself busy with that vulture at the Residence. I guess I'd better make up for today's missed lunch."

There were no messages when he returned to the Embassy so he busied himself with some paperwork, distracted not a little by the clinging aroma of Ilona and her perfume .

"Nice to see you back," the DCM said, sticking his head in the doorway. "Dispensed with a lot of culture?"

Phil felt a flush in his cheeks.

"She's got a fabulous appetite for the things she grew up with in Budapest. She knows her stuff, Jim. It was very enjoyable."

Garland gave him a knowing smile—"I'll bet."

Then, with a grimace, he added—"And I also bet that a certain lady has been stewing in her juice all day. I don't know,

Phil. I just don't like that whole thing. The more it progresses, the worse it gets, and the darker the clouds that I foresee on the horizon."

"I know you're right, Jim. I've got to find a way to resolve it."

Garland nodded and left. Phil worked late, more to divert his own concern over his friend's anxiety than to accomplish any Embassy business. Around eight, he arrived home to a supper that Erzsébet had left for him in the oven. She had also left a note saying that the Rabbit phoned three times.

He knew the Quigleys and the Portlands were going to the opera so Grace wouldn't be home. Anyway, he had no intention of returning the calls even if she were.

Retiring early, he resumed his musicological readings but realized after an hour that none of the journals could help pinpoint a time and place where Beethoven might have begun composing a Cello Concerto; nor could they help in finding the manuscript. That secret lay elsewhere, possibly right here in Budapest.

As he often did in trying to solve the mystery, Phil briefly reviewed the parts of the puzzle which were known to him. But it always came down to the one central figure—Ferenc Fekete.

There was Fekete's disappearance from Leipzig with the manuscript; Fekete's complicity with the Hungarian fascists; Fekete's approach to Szabolcsi with the manuscript, exploiting it as an instrument to clear his name.

But now, there was a new factor . . . something . . . what exactly, it was hard to say, but . . . something, which had to do with the Soviet Embassy.

'And all because of a few pages of music,' he thought, 'whose location is known to but one obnoxious man, who hates me.'

Fifteen

The next afternoon at two o'clock, Phil rang the doorbell and a glowing Ilona opened the door.

She kissed him lightly on the cheek, and looked up at him mischievously.

"Ilona . . ." he began.

"Yes?" she responded hopefully.

"Nothing," he said abruptly, put his arms around her and kissed her as of old.

"Yesterday, Ilona, you said today would be for old times' sake. That kiss was for old times' sake. You have got to simply understand, in this situation, I just cannot . . . you cannot . . ."

She put her fingers to his lips, silencing him, and said softly—"Philly, Philly, I *do* understand. When I told you that I had come to Budapest just to see *you*, I was not lying. *You* may have forgotten what we had in Washington, but *I* have not. You don't know how much I've missed you . . . even after the cruel way you . . ." her voice trailed off.

Phil led her to the sofa, put his arm around her, and murmured—"I know. I've never felt good about what I did, leaving you like that and going off to The Netherlands. Just mark it down to . . . immaturity."

"Philly, since you, I've met a few more Armenians, and immaturity is not the trait common to you all. It's a kind of impetuousness mixed with inner confusion."

"Call it whatever you want, Ilona, but you have got to know

that I am deeply, deeply sorry. I don't know how I'm ever going to make it up to you."

They sat without speaking for a few moments, then she arose and went to the refrigerator and took out several sandwiches. She had brewed some American coffee—"I brought it myself"—and they sat at a small table by the window overlooking the Danube.

Their eyes met several times as they ate and after they had finished, he said—"Can I ask you something about your life in Washington?"

"Anything at all, Philly. Ask me what you want."

"Are you in the White House often?"

"Very often. Garry is in the Oval Office frequently and very much in the President's circle. As a consequence, we are invited to White House functions—you know, dinners for heads of state, awards ceremonies, governors' receptions,—things like that."

"That means you see the President often?"

"Of course. He knows me personally, calls me by my name. I like that because I happen to like him. I think he is one damned good President. Strong. Forceful. A real leader."

"The rumor is that he's got a wicked eye for the ladies."

Ilona giggled. "You know, Philly, only a very priggish woman would take offense at an affectionate pat on her ass by the President of the United States, and you know that this gal from Budapest is certainly no prig.

"Now, it's my turn," she said, looking at him impishly—

"Tell me about the Ambassador's wife."

"Oh Ilona, must I?"

"Well, anyone with an eye for such things can see how she feels about you. Does *he* know?"

"Certainly not."

"Really, Philly! The *Ambassador's* wife. I mean . . . whew!"

"No, no, no, Ilona. I'm not out of my mind. Believe me, it's *all Grace's doing.* But to tell her the brutal truth will turn into a scene of such hysteria that . . ." Phil closed his eyes.

She placed a sympathetic hand on his cheek and

murmured—"Allright, Philly, let's drop the subject." Then, cheerily, she asked—"Tell me, what do you do in your spare time? I mean, do you travel, go to the political cabaret, the theatre? What?"

"Well, only because you ask, yes, all of those and . . . something else. You know that I'm a romantic through and through. Maybe that's why I spend my time searching for something that may not be accessible to me."

"Here in Budapest?" Ilona asked, her curiosity aroused. "Tell me about it."

He then repeated—for the nth time, he told himself—the story of his meeting in Bad Nauheim in 1945 with Hellmuth von Hase. He went through every phase of it, and again, as with Adamyants, omitted the name of the suspected thief.

"The manuscript, I have reason to believe, is here in Hungary. No need to go into every particular of what I know so far, but there are some very strange aspects to the whole thing.."

"Like what?"

"Well, for instance. I happened to mention this the other day to my colleague from the Soviet Embassy. He handles cultural affairs as I do. He's a rather nice fellow."

"What's his name?"

Phil was surprised by the question—

"You wouldn't know him after only three days here, Ilona, but since you ask, his name is Adamov."

"I *do* know him, Philly. He was here in 1956. I met him at a youth rally at *Eötvös Loránd* University. He was speaking Hungarian with some of us and so well that we didn't realize what he was. Then, suddenly, one of the goons from the Soviet Embassy shouted something at him in Russian. It was a stupid thing to do because it gave him away. However, I saw him again in the Gorki Book Store, and recognized him. I spoke to him, he was very pleasant, and I thought, rather handsome. It was the great week of Hungarian freedom, just days before the Soviet tanks returned. He invited me to have a *fekete* and I accepted. He apologized for the course of events, said that some of the Embassy staff was sympathetic to the Hungarians, but that there were elements in Moscow which could not permit any loosening of the bonds, and, believe it or not, he advised me to leave Hungary before chaos returned."

Ilona looked blankly out the window, her thoughts back to the grim days of 1956. "So, he's back now, is he? And you like him?"

"Actually, I do."

"Why did he come up now? I forgot."

"Because when I mentioned to him that I was searching for that particular manuscript—strangely, he had asked me the very same question you did about my leisure time—his reaction was unusual. His manner changed completely, he became almost like another person."

Ilona arose and almost absent-mindedly lit a cigarette, her eyes looking at the Danube. After several puffs, she turned and asked—"Tell me, Philly, is the Hungarian musicologist, the Leipzig thief you have told me about, by any chance Ferenc Fekete?"

Phil gave a hoot of astonishment—"Ilona, you are without doubt the most amazing woman I have ever known. Yes, that is the bastard's name. But how in hell would you know him?"

"What time is it? Mmm. Almost three. I'm supposed to meet Garry at four-thirty at the Embassy, then to the Residence for an early drink, after which we apparently have a dinner engagement with someone in the Party. Look, Phil, I want to fill you in on Fekete. I'll have to speak fast. You called him a bastard. He is worse, far worse. Let me try in twenty minutes to tell you what I know.

"When I was about ten, my father, one of Hungary's finest philosophers and a close friend but not a disciple of the Marxist György Lukács, was a senior member of the Hungarian Academy of Sciences. He had known Fekete as a young musicologist, and although he didn't particularly like him, he would sometimes bring him home. I took an instant dislike to Fekete. I found him repulsive. He also stank. I wondered if he ever bathed. Whenever my father would leave us alone he would stare at me, and smile, showing his small yellow teeth.

"Then, one afternoon, my father brought him home again. My mother had passed away five years before and Father and I lived alone. At one point, Father said he would bring in some Tokay wine. Fekete watched him intently as he left, and as soon as we were alone, he arose, came to where I was sitting, placed me between his legs and slid his hand under my dress. I started to protest but he whispered that I would be punished if I cried out. Then he began to caress my legs and finally put his hand under my panties. I don't have to draw you pictures as to what he did but I tried to struggle. He put his other hand over my mouth, held me very tight against him, and began to tremble. I remember it all as though it were yesterday. His foul breath nauseated me, he was sweating and making hoarse sounds, and he didn't let me go until we heard Father's footsteps.

"I fled the room, didn't tell my father. I felt so ashamed, defiled by that pig. As I grew older, whenever I knew he was coming over, I made certain to be out. I later heard that the other members of the Academy's Music Division loathed him, mostly for his fascist and Nazi ties. But my father was a dear, forgiving man who always said we should not hold the past against anyone because we could never know his reasons.

"Here in Budapest, Philly, there is a wonderful, sweet man, a musicologist also, who was like an uncle to me. In fact, I called him that, Bence *bácsi*. Szabolcsi is his name. Have you met him?"

"Oh yes, I have, Ilona, and grown very fond of him. He has told me about Fekete's fascist ties. Actually, Fekete approached him with the manuscript itself, and tried to bribe him."

Ilona snuffed out her cigarette—"That doesn't surprise me. Philly, tomorrow I will call on the bastard. I'd like that."

"Ilona, you mustn't. I didn't mean for you . . ."

"I've made up my mind," she said, "and you know how stubborn I can be."

She looked at her wristwatch, pressed her lips together and said—"It really is time for me to go. Now, how about one for the road."

He put his arms around her and they kissed. She caressed the nape of his neck, and he felt himself weakening, but then, she broke away.

"Remember, new relationship," she said with a gently sardonic laugh, "besides, there's no time," and left.

Béla was waiting and drove her to the Embassy. Fifteen minutes later, Phil picked up his car three blocks away and drove to the Embassy, in time to see Imre driving the Ambassador and the Portlands towards Buda, the large black Lincoln proudly displaying the American flag from its fender stanchion.

Upstairs he found a message to call Adamyants. Krikor was very cordial on the phone and asked if Phil could have a drink with him at six. Phil agreed and they met at a small cafe near the Parliament.

Adamyants didn't lose any time and spoke in Armenian. "I'm under some pressure, Phil, to find out more about why Portland is in Budapest. I realize our understanding is not to probe each other's minds. Let's leave that to those who enjoy such games. But, could we possibly make an exception this once? It's simply that the Hungarians aren't telling us and Moscow is edgy. Portland is known for his theory. You know what I'm talking about, don't you?"

"Yes, I do. OK, I don't think I'm telling you anything that would compromise me. Yes, he is here to test his theory, and that is really all I know, because I'm not in on any of the discussions."

Adamyants seemed satisfied with that, smiled and said—"Not in any of the discussions with *Mr.* Portland, but *Mrs.* Portland is quite another matter, eh Phil?"

"You scoundrel," Phil blurted and they both laughed.

"Ah, these Hungarian women, even the emigrés."

Phil looked at his luncheon partner warily—"You wouldn't happen to remember her, would you, Krikor?"

"Should I? She's been in your country for something like ten years."

"I ask because *she* remembers *you.* You didn't tell me, Krikor, that you were here during the Hungarian Revolt in 1956. Mrs. Portland was a student then and you invited her for a coffee."

"I did? Well, perhaps. Of course, we have known she was a Hungarian refugee. I guess we probably did meet because, quite truthfully, Phil, I did what many of us were doing at that time, you know, trying to get information. I didn't tell you about 1956 because I didn't think it was relevant."

The two diplomats looked at each other, each waiting for the other to speak.

"Krikor, when I told you last time about the Hungarian musicologist and the missing manuscript, you knew then it was Fekete I was talking about, didn't you, even though I didn't name him?"

"Yes, I knew you meant Fekete, because I know him in a different, although related context, which I will be able to describe to you, very soon, I hope."

"I visited him."

"Phil, why would you involve yourself with such scum? It could not have been pleasant."

"It wasn't. I was so damned curious about him. But he threw me out of his apartment. I've been hearing about him for so long that I just had to see for myself. I don't intend to return."

Phil wondered why Adamyants took the news of his visit to Fekete so casually, almost as though it were known to the Soviet diplomat all along.

"I'm glad to hear that. Now please listen carefully to me. The time has come for an important phase in your mission, a mission which, as you seemed surprised to discover, interests us as well. No, please, no questions—yet. But there is one condition: what I am going to propose must remain an absolute secret. When I say that, Phil, I am not implying that you *might*, if you wish, tell your DCM or Ambassador or your station chief. I am saying to you unequivocally—*no one must know.*"

"And what is it that I am sworn to keep secret?"

"A meeting that I will arrange within two weeks."

Sixteen

Two days before the Portlands' departure, late in the afternoon, Ilona sent a hurriedly scribbled note to Phil through Béla. She must have figured that Béla suspected their secret, Phil surmised, therefore she had no qualms about using that channel. The note asked him to be home at six sharp and to meet her in the garden between his place and the Residence. She wrote 'Urgent' and underscored it.

He got home at five-thirty, had a drink, told Erzsébet he would be nearby and to hold dinner until 7:30. She made a face and he told her it had nothing to do with the Rabbit.

He phoned Harold Fillmore and asked if the Consul could take over his night duty at the Embassy and apologized for the short notice. Another conversation with the Cardinal would have to wait until after the Portlands left.

At six, he went out. It grew dark every day by four so he had no fear of discovery. He stood under a tree and waited. He saw a sudden gleam of light from the Residence porch as a door opened and shut, heard footsteps, and within seconds, Ilona stood before him.

They embraced briefly, and then, slightly breathless, she said—"Philly, I don't have much time. Now listen carefully. I've been busy today—for you. First, I went to Fekete's flat. I rang, he opened the door, his jaw dropped, not because he recognized me, but, I imagine, because he didn't expect to see a good-looking blonde at his door. He invited me in, still obsequious and oily. I mentioned Professor Harsányi as a mutual friend. He nodded, said he remembered him well, and asked what relationship I had to him. I told him that Harsányi was my father. We were seated opposite each other, and when he heard what I said, beads of sweat appeared on his brow.

"He became agitated, asked what I wanted. I leaned forward, put my hand on his knee and said—'Just a little bit of information. For the sake of the past, if you can remember, Ferenc *bácsi.* 'What do you mean by that?' he asked, his face kind of twisted. I stood up, my voice changed, I became aggressive—'For the sake of a ten year-old innocent!'

"'What information do you want?' he asked, a bundle of stinking sweat. So I briefly repeated the Leipzig story and the theft of the manuscript together with his disappearance. I left out the Szabolcsi part to protect that dear man. Fekete is capable of everything. Finally, I asked for the whereabouts of the manuscript.

"And what do you think he said to me? He said—'You've been talking to that American at the Embassy, who is spreading lies about me.' So I said—'Well and good, Fekete *úr*. When I spread the story about your filthy ways with little girls and how many you have corrupted, you will regret this.' He reacted to that by swallowing hard, wiping his brow, then his glasses, all the time staring at the ceiling, and when he put them back on, obviously stalling for time to prepare an adequate response, he said—

"'Perhaps I can help you. I repeat, only perhaps. You should know that I myself have no direct knowledge of this manuscript. Let me make that very clear to you. But there is a rumor that the document you seek might, I stress, might be in a vault of the *Magyar Nemzeti Bank*—if, in fact, the manuscript is even in Hungary.'

"I stood up and shouted at him—'You know, you are no different than when you put your filthy hands under the dress of a child. You are disgusting,' and I stormed out."

Phil embraced her, caressed her cheek and murmured—"You put yourself through all that just for me?"

"I did more, my darling. Now listen. Somehow, in this whole thing, I smell AVO."

"The Hungarian Secret Police? But why?"

"How else would he know that you were, as he put it, 'spreading lies about him?' He mentioned no one other than you. It is the AVO which listens and knows everything—except when we're here in the garden. It's got to be the answer. Unless . . . could it be your new Soviet friend?"

"No. Strangely, I would vouch for him."

"OK. Now, I don't want you to get uppity with me when I tell you this. Promise? Good. I used to have a boyfriend in the AVO. He was young and low level. He was in love with me, wanted to marry me. My father was bitterly opposed, said he would never allow a daughter of his to marry into the AVO. Oh, don't look so morose. That was all of fifteen years ago. Since then, Jenö—Jenö Polgár—has moved up. I phoned AVO headquarters and asked for him. He is a Colonel, and he almost flipped, wanted me to come over right away.

"Do you remember the other day when we were driving to the Museum, you saw me turn and look at a building on *Andrássy út*? It was No. 60—AVO headquarters. Well, I refused to go there. I told him he surely knew who my husband was and of course he did. So we met for a cognac nearby. It was fascinating. Jenö is in charge of Intelligence gathered from Western diplomatic channels, which means he knows almost everything. By the way Phil, who is Kiki? Jenö said you have something going with her and, at the same time, resisting the advances of the Ambassador's wife."

Ilona laughed low but heartily—"You're a very busy fellow, Philly, but I am a European, and what is more, a Hungarian, darling. Things like that do not trouble me, not here anyway. OK. Jenö said the AVO is very interested in Fekete with whom they *have* been in contact. The manuscript is definitely not in the *Magyar Nemzeti Bank*, which he would certainly know."

Phil looked at her quizically—"I don't understand why the AVO, or your friend, cannot interrogate Fekete more fully."

"Good point, which I raised also, the answer to which was that Fekete has a close friendship with a top Party figure in the Hungarian Politburo who protects him. Consequently, Jenö said they must rely on the surfacing of chance information, through the normal ways they find things out. You know what that means, Philly, you can't be indiscreet in the Embassy, even in the toilets.

"Now, here's the main thing. The AVO wants the manuscript, but doesn't know why, only that the AVO knows that the KGB wants it too, which to them is reason enough. But why does the KGB want it? How can there be a secret, Jenö asked, in music which Beethoven composed a century and a half ago, that is of interest to the KGB? Big mystery.

"I've got to hurry back, darling, but Jenö said another thing to me. 'Ilona,' he said, 'Intelligence is one thing, sexual filth is quite another. This Fekete you are interested in is a walking cesspool and I can assure you there are quite a few Hungarian mothers who would like nothing better than to squelch him like a roach. Stay away from him.'

"Oh yes, and one final thing that I must tell you. Jenö said something odd. He raised the possibility that the manuscript might be a forgery. Had you considered that?"

She kissed him quickly and walked rapidly to the porch entrance of the Residence and disappeared inside. Phil stood in the cool of the evening, reflecting on all this new information. After a few moments, he gave up. It was becoming ever more complicated. He walked back and sat at his table, served silently by Erzsébet, and wondered what it was that Adamyants had in store for him that he couldn't even confide to his closest colleague in the Embassy.

Seventeen

Ambassador Quigley called Faljian into his office the following morning.

"Phil, I know how busy you are and that if there is anything you don't need, it's another dinner party. But this is not my doing. You are invited tonight to a farewell for the Portlands. You seem to have made a big hit with Mrs. Portland."

"It's kind of you to tell me that, Sir. Of course I accept the invitation. May I ask who is coming?"

"Well, for sure the Deputy Foreign Minister."

"Kovács has been the Hungarian point man for this whole thing, so that makes sense. May I ask who else?"

"I've invited István Szirmai from the Politburo. That might be of special interest, don't you think?"

"He's accepted? That's wonderful! As the Politburo's ideological chief, Szirmai should certainly be interested in Portland's Convergence Theory. How come Portland didn't make a call on him?"

"We tried but Szirmai was in Moscow and is returning only this afternoon. I imagine you will enjoy a conversation with him as well."

Phil felt elated at the thought of spending an evening with Szirmai, a key figure in the regime yet rarely in the public eye, and completely outside Phil's circle of activity.

"This is a very special time to be associating with him. Do you know that, Sir?"

"What do you mean, Phil?"

"Well, he has just published an article in *Tårsadålmi Szemle* which . . ."

"What is *that*, Phil?"

"Sir, it's a very important theoretical magazine meaning *Social Review* and the article has attracted very wide interest among the intellectuals because of what Szirmai is saying."

"Give me some examples. This might be good preparation for the dinner."

"For one thing, Szirmai calls for a new constitution which encourages freedom of speech and criticism. He wants more candidates in elections rather than a single slate. He is worried about the loss of Soviet prestige. And for the first time that I can remember, he raises the question of defectors. Real good stuff, and quite incredible, coming from the man they refer to as Hungary's Suslov, although he's clearly more liberal."

Quigley was delighted and adjusted his stocky frame in the high-backed office chair—

"I see there'll be much to talk about tonight."

"Sir, it's not up to me to tell you what to say at your own dinner party, but if I may, I would suggest not touching on any of those subjects unless he does first. I believe he'll be hyper-sensitive on all those issues."

Quigley accepted Phil's suggestion, nodding glumly.

"Who else, Sir?" he asked, although now that he knew that the Politburo's top idea man would be there, he had minimal interest in the other guests.

"Roger Mandrake, of course, and the Garlands. That makes it eleven plus you and whomever you would like to invite. Someone in the diplomatic community who will understand being asked on such short notice."

"Well, Sir, if she is available, I will ask Helga Kirsch. We have talked at several diplomatic functions recently. She is very relaxed and a highly presentable member of the West German Permanent Mission. She also speaks excellent English."

"Sounds good to me, my boy. May we see you at 7:30 PM?"

"We'll be there, Mr. Ambassador."

Phil returned to his office and immediately put in a call to the German Mission. Helga Kirsch was delighted at the invitation and said she did not mind the short notice.

He spent the rest of the day cleaning up odds and ends on his desk, and sending a message back to Washington requesting three sets of encyclopaedias which he wanted to donate to two universities and a cultural institute. He also discovered a three-page airgram, which had been buried among many other messages, announcing a State Department-sponsored visit by film star Kirk Douglas. Phil groaned at the prospect of the work such visits entailed, ran his eyes quickly through the first page, and groaned again when he saw Douglas' special request. He set the message aside, deciding he would focus on it when the visit grew near.

The enigma of the Beethoven manuscript passed through his mind but he decided to pursue that only after the Portlands had departed the next morning.

At seven that night, dressed in a dark suit, he picked up Helga Kirsch at her apartment and they drove to *Zugligeti út* in the Buda hills. He and Helga had met casually at receptions and beyond observing that she was attractive, had paid little attention to her. She was about 30, with blonde hair and a clear white complexion. As they drove, he looked at her approvingly and she responded with a grateful smile, aware she had made a hit. He drove to his residence, parked, and said—

"Let me explain what this dinner party is all about."

He then described the Portlands and their mission, the presence of both a major Hungarian Government and Party figure, and the other guests.

"I apologize again for the short notice, but by way of compensation, you will be in the company of Tivadar Kovács, the Deputy Foreign Minister and István Szirmai, the top Party ideologist. I don't imagine you meet with them very often."

"In fact, never, Mr. Faljian," she laughed.

"How's your Hungarian?"

"Nothing like yours, but I'll do my best."

"Don't worry. Your English will get you by famously. And by the way, let's make it Phil. May I call you Helga?"

"But of course . . . Phil."

He helped her out of the car and said they could walk over to the Residence. He wondered what impact she would have on Grace and Ilona, and then predicted that Ilona would be amused, but Grace would seethe.

They entered from the side porch at 7:30 sharp. The Garlands and Mandrakes were already there and the Kovácses were just arriving. The Quigleys met the Deputy Foreign Minister and his wife at the door and everyone gathered in the large living room as the white-gloved, black-jacketed waiters walked around with trays of drinks. Phil caught a look from Grace, who pointedly stared quickly at Helga, then back at Phil, then again at Helga. Clearly, she was unhappy at his choice of a party mate.

Five minutes later, the Portlands came down the stairs. He was distinguished as ever with his full crop of white hair and poised elegance, while Ilona radiated an aura of stardom, with a bouffant hair-do and a rather risque black and white gown whose cleavage raised every eyebrow in the room.

Once the introductions were made, they broke into small conversation groups. Phil found himself face to face with Grace, who with her coiffed hair and still trim figure looked very chic, and he told her so. His words softened the expression in her eyes.

"What a sweet thing to say," she responded, then, lowering her voice she asked—"And where, may I ask, did you find that *Fräulein?*"

Without waiting for his answer, she looked over at Ilona, busy talking in Hungarian with Mrs. Kovács, and said, her voice now sharp-edged—"Mrs. Portland tells me you know a great deal about the museums here. She mentioned the Beethoven piano in the National Museum. Why haven't you taken me there?"

"Whenever you say, Mrs. Quigley."

"Don't give me that garbage," she spat at him. "And remember I'm the wife of the Ambassador."

Both of them were late in seeing Jim Garland only a foot away, so absorbed were they in their give and take. He gave Phil a stern look and tactfully turned away.

"Grace," Phil pleaded softly, "why can't you control yourself? Enjoy the party, for Heaven's sake, and circulate among our guests, can't you?"

She answered with her eyes, which became steely, and walked over to Tivadar Kovács.

"Well, well, I see Madame is raging mad," said the mellifluous voice of Ilona Portland, who now joined Phil.

"She's very difficult, in fact impossible. I'm going to miss you, Ilona."

"And I you. By the way, did I understand correctly that the remaining guest is István Szirmai?"

"That is my understanding, but he seems to be delayed. Don't tell me you know him too?"

"No, I don't, and it doesn't matter if he is late, so long as he comes. This should be exceptionally interesting."

It was almost an hour later that the doorbell rang and everyone faced the two late arrivals—unmistakably the corpulent István Szirmai of the Hungarian Politburo, and a diffident young man who, according to Quigley, would act as his interpreter, since Szirmai spoke no English.

Ambassador Quigley had met Szirmai only once at a Hungarian National Day reception, but beyond the amenities had never held a conversation with him. He took Szirmai around the room and introduced everyone. The only crack in the bulky official's stolid exterior came when he was introduced to Ilona, whereupon he bent over and kissed her hand and hearing her speak Hungarian, engaged her in conversation while Grace and Sarah Garland waited patiently. It was somewhat rude, Phil thought, but Szirmai was known for his lack of manners.

Phil wondered if the evening would produce any reaction. Szirmai had just returned from Moscow that day and in all probability had conferred with Mikhail Suslov, the Kremlin's top ideologist. They must have discussed the Portland approach, he surmised. After all, the Soviets knew that Portland was in Budapest and Szirmai knew that he would be spending an evening with the White House official at the American Ambassador's Residence.

When the introductions were over, Portland, Quigley, Szirmai and the interpreter grouped together to one side. Kovács, having shaken Szirmai's hand briefly when he arrived, seemed to be keeping his distance from him, engaging the DCM and the British Ambassador in conversation. Consequently, Phil was disappointed to find himself left with the ladies, all six of them, and while he enjoyed their attention, he was painfully aware that his hostess did not. She bit her lip, drank in quick sips, lit a cigarette which she put out after three puffs, and shifted her weight from one foot to the other.

It was, therefore, a relief to everyone in that circle when one of the waiters whispered in Grace's ear and she announced that dinner was being served. Phil found his place card and saw that he was seated between Mrs. Kovács and Mrs. Mandrake. He smiled inwardly. This was surely Grace's doing, for Ilona was on the same side of the table and to Ambassador Quigley's right, which meant they couldn't even have eye contact.

Dinner was uneventful and the conversation with his two table partners went quite smoothly. He and Mrs. Mandrake spoke about British films and gossiped about some of the other diplomats they knew, while Mrs. Kovács revealed that she was the editor of a popular women's program on Hungarian Television. Phil had never watched the program, which was on in the afternoons, but with discreet questions was able to keep her occupied with table talk.

He beheld Grace attempting to balance conversation with Szirmai sitting on her right and Portland to her left. The interpreter was kept so busy that he was unable to eat, his eyes darting nervously from one to the other. Phil pitied him. Szirmai, as though eager to trumpet his lack of table manners, slurped his soup, spoke with seeming disrespect to his hostess, and cleared his throat noisily a number of times. Phil wondered whether these were not symptoms of his failing health. Szirmai, he knew, had a serious heart condition which sent the 58-year old ideologist often to the hospital.

Finally, after dessert, the men withdrew into the library. Phil saw that Ilona seemed reluctant to join the women but winked at her as he followed the male entourage.

Szirmai, Portland and the interpreter were seated in a corner, already deep in conversation, as Quigley, Garland, Kovács, Mandrake and Phil went to the opposite corner, out of earshot, and were offered cognac and cigars. All of them knew that anything worthwhile happening was taking place at the other end of the library, but they pretended interest in each other's contributions to a bland recapitulation of the week's events in Hungary and East Europe, and hoping, fruitlessly as it emerged, for some edification from Kovács.

It was another thirty minutes before Szirmai stood up, bade Portland farewell, thanked Ambassador Quigley—and Grace who hurried in from the porch where the women had congregated—and went to the coatroom. At that moment, Ilona broke away from the others and disappeared in the foyer. Phil could hear their voices but not the words. Szirmai seemed surprised and sounded jocular. Everyone stood almost transfixed and expressionless, except for Grace who had lit yet another cigarette. Her irritation was transparent. Finally, Szirmai and his aide left and Ilona returned, went directly to her husband and said something softly to him. He kissed her cheek in approval.

Kovács looked at his watch and said he had a busy day the next morning and hoped Portland would excuse him. Phil sensed a certain disgruntlement in the Deputy Foreign Minister, who had clearly been upstaged by the Politburo official. When he and his wife had departed, Quigley drew Phil to one side—

"The Portlands leave on a noon flight tomorrow, Phil. In the morning, I want to meet in the bubble with him, Garland and you. Let's make that at nine, which will give us enough time to talk and then drive to *Ferihegy* Airport. I want you to be briefed by Portland on his visit here in case there are press inquiries."

He went over to Helga Kirsch and thanked her for accepting on such short notice. It was his fault, he explained, not Phil's. She graciously thanked him and said it had been a memorable evening. Grace shook her hand silently and gave Phil a venomous look as he thanked her for the evening. He waved to the Garlands, told Portland he would see him in the morning and as he escorted the German woman out and passed Ilona, she whispered—

"I must talk to you at the airport."

Phil and Helga Kirsch walked across the garden and, standing by his car, he said in German—

"Helga, this is where I live. If you like, we can have a nightcap."

"Allright," she said with a smile, pleased to hear his German.

Inside, he fixed a whiskey and soda for each and took her to the glass-enclosed porch, which was warm. He asked about her work in the German Mission, her contacts with Hungarians, and the extent of her travels in the country. Helga Kirsch said she had served in the German Embassy in Vienna, her first post, and had come a number of times to Hungary. Meeting Hungarians was always a problem, but essential for a Political Officer, otherwise one had to rely exclusively on the press. As for travel, she had yet to visit cities outside the capital.

Their conversation had been in progress for half an hour, when she said—"We have always been a small diplomatic entity, no more than four or five. But last week, we were joined by a new officer. His name is Christian Sommer and one of the first things he asked me was whether I knew you."

Phil wrinkled his brow—"I don't know a Christian Sommer. In my years in Bonn, I don't ever recall meeting anyone named Sommer. What else did he want to know?"

"Nothing more, but I had the impression he will be in touch with you."

"Anytime he wants. I'll take you home now."

Phil drove to her apartment in Pest, saw her to the door and kissed her lightly on the cheek. He liked her, but, as he told himself, in a strictly collegial way.

Once in bed, he reviewed the evening and dismissed most of the banter during and after dinner as superficial and unworthy of any attention. It was only later, at the time of the farewells, that two significant things had happened which lingered now in his mind: Ilona's private, somewhat ostentatious chat with Szirmai, followed shortly by her whispered desire to talk at the airport.

Ilona had obviously discovered something that she had to tell him before leaving Budapest.

Eighteen

Phil arrived at the Embassy at eight in the morning, got a cup of coffee in the snack bar and went up to his office. On his desk was a handwritten note from the Cardinal reminding him to get the Crankshaw book on the Habsburgs. Phil had indeed forgotten it and quickly wrote out a cable asking the Embassy in Vienna to acquire a copy.

Three messages were passed on to him from the Reception Desk downstairs, all of them from the media: NBC from Paris, The New York Times from Rome, The Christian Science Monitor from Vienna. Phil knew they concerned Garrison Portland's visit.

The DCM looked in on him briefly. "Good show last night, but too bad you couldn't talk to that boor from the Politburo."

"I know. A rare opportunity lost. At my diplomatic level, I'm not in his league. Let's hope it was worthwhile for Portland."

"We'll know in half an hour," Garland said as he walked out.

At five minutes to nine, the elevator brought Ambassador Quigley and Garrison Portland to the third floor and within ten minutes, they, the DCM and Phil were securely locked in the bubble, with the noise generator going full blast.

"Mr. Portland," Ambassador Quigley began, "this is the only place we can discuss what happened last night. I don't know if the conversation you held with Szirmai was productive, but I'd like to suggest two things. First, with your permission, I will have Jim Garland, our DCM, summarize what you are about to tell us in a cable to Washington. EYES ONLY FOR THE WHITE HOUSE.

Second, I'd like to work out with you some talking points that Phil Faljian, our Public Affairs Officer, can use with the press. Are you agreed?"

Crossing his legs and becoming comfortable, Portland replied—"That's fine with me, Mr. Ambassador. Well, let me begin by saying that Mr. Szirmai was not the least impressed with my approach to his system. He pointed out that he had discussed my theory with the Soviet Politburo, especially its chief ideologist, whose name is, I believe, Suslov. What my theory fails to do, according to him, is to recognize that the most fundamental difference between the two systems is, generally speaking, economic, and more specifically, the means of production.

"He accused me of not knowing my Karl Marx, and even said he might know more than I about the bases of our capitalist system, since every good Marxist was duty-bound to know the enemy so as to better destroy it. He said we in the capitalist world, especially in the United States, delude ourselves into thinking we have introduced democracy into our economic system when we distribute shares in large corporations and call it popular investment. He said there was a puerile attempt only a decade or so ago by the 'Voice of America' to make our system more palatable by labelling it 'peoples' capitalism.' He then became very sarcastic and asked if we were going to also inflict 'peoples' imperialism' on the world.

"He asked me what aspect of a Marxist society did I think might be acceptable to the Western world, and when I mentioned low-cost health care, he laughed, and said the American people seemed frightened of what they called 'socialized medicine.'

"I told him his attitude verged on the offensive, and that I had not come this distance because I was some Utopian dreamer, but because I was close enough to the President to convince him that he could ease tensions in the world by considering aspects of my theory. In fact, I asserted, my theory transcended the Soviet campaign of peaceful co-existence, because that is a static idea whereas my theory represents movement and progress, recognizing that seemingly opposing, even contradictory societal systems can find a mutuality of interests."

Portland sat back and looked at the other three in the bubble. Quigley was silent for a few moments while Garland took notes, but then said—

"Mr. Portland, Phil Faljian here is our resident scholar of Hungarian communist ideology. Would you like to hear any views he might have on your meeting with Szirmai?"

"Of course I would. I need some perspective on all this, something concrete I can tell the President."

Garland stopped writing and all three now looked at Phil, who began—"With all due respect, Mr. Portland, allow me to say that Szirmai's reaction comes as no surprise. You already know that he is the leading formulator of ideology in Hungary. You must also realize that he is the Central Committee's Chief of Agitation and Propaganda. In that capacity, he cannot for one moment tolerate any deviation from Marxist doctrine. What you are proposing is reasonable, logical, humane, and even generous—but only when viewed through *our* eyes. Through the eyes of a Szirmai, or Suslov, his boss in Moscow, any concession to your theory is plain and simple heresy. In other words, it is intolerable. Even so, I think it was worth a try and I will support it in every conversation I have with Hungarian intellectuals.

"I appreciate your candor, Mr. Faljian, and I understand what you have said. What can you tell me about this fellow Szirmai?"

"I would say that there are two or three things worth knowing about him. First, that he enjoys the full confidence of Party Secretary János Kádár, his boss in Budapest. Second, that he is an intellectual, by which I mean a creative thinker, even within the strict confines of Marxist ideology. And third, that he is a Jew. I mention that because being Jewish is a factor in Hungarian politics, but Szirmai does not hide his origins, and in fact was once the editor of a Zionist magazine. Kádár himself entertains no anti-Semitic attitudes, and holds intellectuals in high regard. Consequently, Szirmai is both professionally and personally close to him. In the polycentrist communist world that is evolving now, Kådár turns always to Szirmai for advice, which has aroused resentment and jealousy—and even some of the latent anti-Semitism—in some Party circles. You may have noticed a certain coolness last night between Szirmai and Kovács. But I would be hard-pressed to determine what proportion of that is attributable to Szirmai's heritage."

Portland, who was listening intently and occasionally nodding his head, said—"I know from my wife that several hundred thousand Hungarian Jews were deported to Auschwitz during the war and that anti-Semitism exists here and elswhere in Eastern Europe. Would you say that Szirmai might be a token Jew in the Politburo?"

"No, not at all. I think he is there because Kádár, who is performing the most dangerous high-wire act in East Europe, believes Szirmai can supply the ideological ballast to keep him going."

"That's a curious way to put it, if I may say so," Portland observed, looking slightly amused. "It almost sounds as though Kádár is flirting with western liberalism and this fellow Szirmai is supporting him. Yet, you tell me he cannot deviate from Marxist ideology because he is the top AgitProp man, and close to Suslov. Or am I missing something?"

Phil laughed—"No Sir, you aren't missing anything, and I admit that it does sound almost contradictory." He looked quickly at Ambassador Quigley, who signaled for him to continue—

"First of all, Kádár has gone from being the most hated communist in Hungary, as he was in 1956, to becoming the most acceptable leader the country has had. Why? Because he has adopted a policy of 'small steps,' which means that he is granting the public some of the things they miss most and has done this by ideological deviations of such low profile that Moscow is not concerned. Yesterday, I told the Ambassador about an article just published in which Szirmai calls for reforms which, while not undermining the system, would certainly modify it. Kádár, and Szirmai too, are about as liberal as communists can get. But in standing up to an American senior official, and one who is close to the President, Szirmai could perform no differently than he has."

Portland sighed, folded his arms and shook his head.

"Is there no hope, then?"

"In your place, Sir, I would never give up."

Portland liked that and smiled appreciately at Phil. "Do you think there will be press inquiries?"

"Absolutely, there are three already. But I would like to suggest a standard press release, with your permission."

Portland nodded and waited.

"I will say that you, Sir, accompanied by your wife, spent several days in Budapest as the guest of the American Ambasssador, during the course of which you met with officials at the Foreign Ministry, headed by Deputy Foreign Minister Kovács, and some Central Committee personnel. You could not meet with Szirmai because he was in Moscow but returned in time for a working dinner at the Residence. At that meeting, there was a frank exchange of views concerning the positions of both sides in the area of improving relations. It was agreed that the discussions would continue at other levels."

Phil looked at Portland and then at Quigley, both of whom then looked at each other and nodded.

"I've got no problem with that," Portland said, "and when asked, as I surely will be in Washington, I will respond no differently."

Ambassador Quigley arose and Phil unlocked the door of the Secure Room to let everyone out. Thirty minutes later, they all descended in the elevator to the street where Imre had driven Ilona Portland down from the Residence. Phil wondered where Grace was.

Garrison Portland turned to Phil and said—"Come to the airport with us. I believe Ilona wants to talk to you."

Phil looked at Jim Garland who waved him into his car. Soon

they were driving through the late morning traffic behind the official car carrying Quigley and the Portlands.

The weather had turned chilly as Autumn approached and the smell of brown coal was already in the air. It was the smell of East Europe, to Phil a communist smell that he associated with the neighboring countries in which he had traveled.

Garland drove mostly in silence, except for occasionally swearing at the slowness of Hungarian drivers, to whose caution Phil had long since become accustomed. Hungarians sometimes went to extremes to avoid accidents because spare parts for their cars were almost impossible to acquire.

At *Ferihegy* Airport, everyone got out, Garland and Phil saw to it that the Portlands and Quigley went through Customs without a hitch and then escorted them to the VIP Room. There, Ilona said something to her husband who nodded and looked at Phil. She walked over and asked Phil to join her in a corner.

"Ilona, won't your husband . . . ?"

She interrupted him—"Darling, Garry knows. I've already told him about you and me, and that it was over ten years ago. He understands, but he also knows that this conversation is about something else. Can we get a coffee? We still have half an hour."

Phil put in orders for everyone, then re-joined her.

"Now listen, Philly. I'm sure you were astonished at my move last night in collaring Szirmai as he left. Well, he was just as surprised. He asked when I had left Hungary. I told him in 1956 soon after my father passed away. He asked my father's name and when I said Béla Harsányi, he stopped putting on his coat and asked—'The head of the Philosophy Division of the Academy? I don't believe it. Then, you must be the little girl who always ran out of the room.' He asked if I had visited with anyone. I said György Lukács of course in his sixth floor apartment, and a few others, and then—holding my breath, because of what I was about to say—I mentioned several names and threw in the name of Ferenc Fekete. Philly, you should have seen his reaction.

"'You visited Fekete?' He was aghast. 'But why?'

"I said he and Father had known each other quite well. Szirmai looked at me strangely, then asked if Fekete had ever spent time with me when I was young. I lied and said not at all, and I asked him how *he* knew Fekete. That is what I was getting at, and to my amazement and utter joy, he replied—'Fekete is a nephew of my wife's.'

"Philly, do you realize what he told me? *Szirmai is Fekete's protector!* I wonder if even my AVO friend Jenö knows that."

"Wait a minute, Ilona. There's something wrong here. Everything I know about Szirmai tells me that although a communist ideologue and rather coarse in his ways, he has streaks of decency, even having saved some Freedom Fighters from imprisonment and exile. But any semblance of loyalty to his wife could not possibly outweigh the viciousness of Fekete's anti-Semitism, especially to someone as committed to his Jewishness as Szirmai. How do you reconcile all of that?"

"Very simply," Ilona said with a big smile. "Szirmai's wife is a Jew, which means that her nephew is also. Ferenc Fekete is that most obnoxious of all anti-Semites—a Jew-hating Jew."

Phil picked up the train of thought from that point—"So, he joined in with the general chorus, first with Szálasi then with the Nazis, all for personal gain. It actually got him a tremendous prize, the Beethoven manuscript. To the list of things that he is—thief, liar, charlatan, child molester, sexual deviant, we can now add racist and hypocrite. No wonder Szirmai was astonished when you mentioned visiting Fekete."

"Astonished and openly contemptuous. Szirmai has a generally good reputation, and I don't think he would want his name sullied by being publicly associated with the likes of Fekete. He despises him, yet, for his wife';s sake, intervenes on his behalf. So, Philly, I did it for you, and it is what I leave you with. I really wanted to find the damned manuscript for you but a few days just weren't enough. You'll let me know what happens, won't you?

"And, oh yes, about Grace. I told her to stay home. I wanted to see you alone today and she sensed it. She's bad news, Philly. Maybe that other one—was it Kiki?—is better for you."

The flight was announced, final farewells made, and as Quigley was getting into his car, he said to Phil—"That was a good job this morning, my boy. I'm proud of you. And you should know also that Portland had nothing but high praise for you, too. That's the way careers are made, you know."

Nineteen

"Faljian *úr*, can you meet me at the *Széchényi* Library in the main lobby sometime today?"

Bence Szabolcsi's voice on the phone seemed anxious. It had to be important for him to be calling at nine in the morning.

"How about two this afternoon?" Phil proposed.

"I'll be waiting for you."

Phil finished reading the morning Hungarian press, went to the Embassy translator's office downstairs and identified the pieces to be summarized into English for the Ambassador and DCM. He then looked at his schedule and saw that he had no appointments, but realized he had to start planning for the Kirk Douglas visit in three months.

Douglas' visit had been announced in a circular airgram sent to four embassies: Warsaw, Prague, Bucharest and Budapest. The message read that in all four posts Douglas wanted, among other things, to meet with the chief of the Communist Party in the country. Two of his colleagues in the other posts had already phoned him, wondering how Phil was going to handle the request.

Phil said it did appear to be hopeless, but he advised his colleagues to put in an official request. "You never know," he pointed out, "your principals might be intrigued by the idea of chatting with an American movie star. I've heard that when Douglas was in Yugolsavia a few years back, Tito, a movie fan, invited him to Brioni. That may have put the thought in Douglas' mind that any Communist Party chief is accessible. In any case, we've got to make the effort."

At the other end of the line, his colleagues groaned.

Phil made a few calls to official contacts in the Hungarian film industry and was told that Kirk Douglas was a known commodity in Hungary and that film directors and actors would welcome an exchange of views with him about Hollywood.

Phil walked across the corridor to the DCM's office. Garland was busy writing a cable about renovations to the Communications Room, which was sadly in need of refurbishing, including a decent bed for night-duty officers to sleep on.

"You look distraught, Phil. I can't believe there's anything wrong. We've got a war going on in Southeast Asia that the local government violently objects to; we've got the Cardinal in political asylum, which the local government finds a thorn in its side; we've got the crown of St. Stephen in a vault in Fort Knox which the local government wants back before we can discuss improved relations; we are refusing to grant Most Favored Nation treatment which the local government desperately wants; and we've got Kirk Douglas who wants to have a friendly chat with the local government's boss. So, tell me, which is it?"

"All of the above," Phil blurted out, plunking himself down into the leather sofa, as both of them grimaced.

"Well, at least we've gotten through the Portland visit without any flaps. Now," he continued, his eyes riveted to Phil's, "do we still have a problem *here*?"

"What does that mean, Jim?"

Phil did know what Garland was referring to—Grace Quigley's behaviour at the dinner party.

"Let's go out to the corridor," Garland said as he arose from his desk. Once there, he continued—"Look, Phil. A man's personal life is nobody's business. Except, dammit, we live and work in a place where it is very much *my* business. And . . . the Ambassador's."

"Has he said something to you?" Phil barely got the words out.

"No, he hasn't. But Phil, you've got to control this thing. You are an outstanding officer with a great future ahead of you. So, why are you skating on such thin ice. If you sink, you squander everything, and she's the kind, believe me, who'll let you drown."

"Jim, I can't tell you how often I wish somehow she would realize that this is totally unthinkable. But for me to take the bull by the horns . . . surely, you know my chief concern, my great fear."

"I do—your fear that she might find some way to retaliate against an outright rejection. But," Garland continued more aggressively, "you've got to take that risk."

Phil slumped against the wall, morose and cowed by his friend's censorious tone. He said—"I keep wondering what capricious trick of Fate brought her and me to the same embassy. I've served in embassies where the Ambassador's wife is the very model of decorum and dignity, the First Lady in every sense."

"Well, this one's different. And the time is well past when you've got to confront her with the hard truth. By which, Phil, I mean *very soon.*"

"I know, Jim, and believe me, I don't resent your raising it. What pains me so deeply is that I cause you any anxiety. Let me pledge to you, here and now, that I will set her straight. I don't know how or when. She's a very difficult and high-strung woman, but I promise you that I will. Can we shake on it?"

Garland looked at his Public Affairs Officer benignly and extended his hand, saying—"You son of a bitch! You know, Phil, I had never met an Armenian before. But now that I've met you, I know that, even though I may get to know others, you are one Armenian I will never forget. Let's get a cup of coffee."

They rode down in the elevator and in the canteen ran into Eric Hager just getting a sandwich. When Garland greeted him, Hager replied—"Sorry I can't join you, Jim. I've got two political science professors upstairs from Columbia and Yale. They want a briefing on the internal workings of the party here and how it affects the political life of the country. I'm already late."

"Well, good luck, Eric. That's a tall order. By the way, when you go on leave next week, where will you be?"

"In Zakopane. Skiing. Since my last assignment in Poland, I'm forgetting the language and this'll help me brush up on it. Gotta prepare for the future, you know."

Garland and Faljian exchanged looks. They had heard Hager refer more than once to his hopes for becoming DCM in Warsaw. 'Not if I have anything to do with it,' Garland had grumbled.

Phil told him of his appointment with Szabolcsi and when they finished lunch, drove toward the *Lánc híd.* From the bridge he could see the brown rushing waters of the Danube below, and wondered wondered whether the Vienna stretch of the river that had so inspired Johann Strauss was really ever blue. He parked his car and walked up the stairs of the *Széchényi* Library.

Szabolcsi was seated on a bench in the lobby, watching the main entry as Phil walked in. He arose immediately and, holding Phil by the arm, said with a broad smile—"I believe I have found something which will please you, as it pleases me, very much, *kedves kartárs.*" Szabolcsi frequently addressed Phil as 'dear colleague,' in deference to his earlier calling as a budding musicologist. "Let us proceed to the third floor where I have a small office for my private use."

Once there, Szabolcsi asked a young secretary to fetch a box from the vault. When it arrived, they sat facing each other on opposite sides of the desk. Szabolcsi opened the box and took out a musty, loosely-bound album. Holding it still in his hand, he peered at Phil through his thick lenses and said softly—"Therese von Brunsvik's diary."

Phil's eyes widened as Szabolcsi, pleased at his friend's reaction, continued—"Do you know how many times I have read this diary, looking for, I really don't know what. Just clues to . . . something, anything. But it wasn't until you and I met and we talked about the manuscript and Fekete's lies about finding it in

Martonvásár that I began to wonder whether there might not be some truth to it. Not, of course, that Fekete had found the manuscript in Martonvásár. You have cleared that up once and for all with the sad history of von Hase, the Leipzig air raid and the sudden disappearance of both Fekete and the manuscript.

"No, none of that. What I began to think about were clues to the origin of the concerto—its time, its inspiration. I went back to my Beethoven sources, for which I am grateful to you, *kedves kartárs,* because so much came back to me from my youthful days at the academy when I was deep into musicology.

"First of all, it is important to realize that Beethoven had the incomparable ability to be working on several things at one time. And what things! As you know quite well, in one year alone, he composed the three Rasoumovsky quartets, the Fourth Symphony, the Fourth Piano Concerto and the Violin Concerto. True genius, indeed.

"Allright, that was in 1806. Then came something of a drought. Between 1812 and 1824 there were no symphonies. Also, his last public performance as a pianist—something which he enjoyed and did often—took place in 1815. What was happening?

"You and I know only too well what it was. Beethoven was slowly growing deaf. He was depending more and more on his Conversation Books and withdrawing more and more into himself. This was the time of what we refer to as his Third Style, when his later works revealed a vastly different Beethoven than we had known. Now we come to the year 1817."

Phil sat transfixed by Szabolcsi's narrative, wondering where it was leading, and eager to know what Therese's diaries had revealed.

"The year 1817 was a singularly unproductive year. For a genius who could compose those six towering masterpieces in one year, now all he could do was begin a piano sonata and produce some sketches which would eventually become the Ninth Symphony. You will recall that the London Philharmonic Society had invited him to England and commissioned two symphonies.

He never got to England. He finished the Ninth six years later and planned a Tenth, which he never wrote, but for which there are sketches. This did not mean he was a total recluse. We know that he attended musicales at the homes of friends in Vienna."

Szabolcsi now smiled broadly at Phil, tapped the frazzled diary before him and said—"And thanks to Therese von Brunsvik, we now know more. I really am deeply indebted to you, my young colleague, for having sent me back to this source and for having revived in me that instinct for detection which is at the heart of musicology. The Bible tells us—'Seek and ye shall find.' But first, one must know what he is seeking. How is your French?"

"Very, very rusty, Dr. Szabolcsi."

"Very well. I shall translate for you. Let me turn in Therese's diary to the summer of 1817. One moment please. I have marked it, yes, here it is. Now please listen—'My dear and ill friend Louis had visited the baths in Buda and Franz prevailed on him to come to Martonvásár. Oh, what a pitiful sight it was to see him. How he had aged, only 47 years old, but looking much older. We spent the evening talking, I sometimes having to shout but more often writing down what I was saying on a sheet of paper. He told us that he had left his Conversation Book in Vienna. Louis stayed with us several days, and we left him in peace to enjoy the beautiful Hungarian summer. We knew he was working, for his lamps were lit late into the night. Then he left. It was to be the last time I saw him. Three days after Louis returned to Vienna, I sat at his desk to write my sister a letter and couldn't find any writing paper. I looked in the drawers and then, by chance, looked in one of the pigeonholes of the desk. Curled up and tucked away was a page of manuscript.'"

Phil was on the edge of his seat and Szabolcsi, noticing his excitement, calmed him down by gesturing with his palm, and continued—"'I pulled the page out. It was covered with music. It was not the first page nor the last and must have gotten misplaced. I took it to Franz and asked if he would take it to Vienna, because I wouldn't want to entrust it to the mails. Franz looked at it. He smiled and said he would deliver it by hand because Louis had told him that *he* had inspired a new work and was dedicating it to him. This was obviously it and Franz wanted to thank Louis personally.'"

Szabolcsi looked up, tilted his balding head and asked—"Do you know, I have seen this many times, in fact every time I have read through Therese's diary. But it never meant very much to me. After all, the work is unidentified, and even if it were dedicated to Franz, it could have been anything, something Beethoven perhaps did not consider worth publishing. But now, we know a little more, and we owe it to Therese.

"Could this page she found be part of a Cello Concerto? Inspired by Franz, dedicated to him, a known cellist? Did von Hase ever give you a date for the letter that his great-grandfather received from Beethoven?"

"No, he did not and the letter seems to have been destroyed in the raid. Fekete has not mentioned it to you or to me, although it is unlikely he would have to me. Surely, he does not have it."

"Well, actually," Szabolcsi went on, adjusting his eyeglasses, "I have one other piece of independent information which might help us. Only two years before, in other words in 1815, Beethoven again became interested in the instrument and wrote two sonatas for cello and piano, which were published in 1817. The year of mystery—1817. But these two cello sonatas are unlike the others the Master had composed, and unlike the cello part in the Triple Concerto. These are musically much more advanced, and much closer to what we normally call his Third Style—philosophical, ruminative, meditative, and revealing Beethoven's preoccupation with counterpoint. There is also something else: one of those sonatas is not unlike that one page of the concerto that I briefly looked at."

He paused and looked up at Phil. Neither spoke for a few moments, both meditating on Szabolcsi's latest findings, who then continued—"One more thing. Both these cello sonatas are dedicated to Countess Erdödy, the wife of a Hungarian nobleman living on the outskirts of Vienna. You know, my young friend, this entire involvement of Beethoven with Hungarians, with Hungarian cellists, with Martonvásár—it makes me almost envious of Fekete. Just think what an honest, intelligent musicologist could make of all this. What a shame he is such a charlatan."

"Dr. Szabolcsi, something occurred to me recently. Beethoven always worked out his ideas in his Sketch Books. Have you ever seen anything that might suggest he was thinking of a Cello Concerto?"

"No, I never have, but that is far from conclusive, for the simple reason that through carelessness, misplacement and thievery, many sketches have been lost. Just as we know about lost or unfinished works from sketches Beethoven made which have been preserved, we also have completed works, some of them masterpieces, for which no sketches have ever been found. No, my friend, we cannot consider that as a valid argument against the existence of a Cello Concerto."

Phil thanked Szabolcsi profusely and offered to drive him home but the elderly musicologist said he wished to remain at the *Széchényi* Library to continue his other researches.

'So what do I have?' Phil asked himself as he slowly drove back to the Embassy. 'Thanks to Szabolcsi, there is now some confirmation that the manuscript may exist, that it was in Fekete's hands in Budapest after the war, and that it could have been composed in 1817, as implied by Therese's diary, and inspired by her brother Franz, Beethoven's very close friend.'

This last fact was in and by itself far less important because it was only helpful in establishing the when and the why. The manuscript itself, he considered, might provide enough clues to settle those questions.

At that moment, as though triggered by the afternoon's findings, something Ilona had said almost as a throwaway line materialized in his mind. Her AVO friend had raised the possibility that the manuscript might be a forgery. No one had even suggested such a possibility before.

There were, then, two questions which could only be resolved when the manuscript was found: was it a genuine piece of music by Beethoven, and, what mystery lurked in its pages that so intrigued the secret police of a major communist country, and was possibly involving a second?

'Obviously, I need the help of my Soviet Armenian friend,' he said to himself.

Twenty

"*Jó napot, kivannok. Szeretnék Adamov ürral beszélni.*"

Phil purposely made the phone request to the Soviet Embassy in Hungarian, knowing that it would throw whomever was at the other end of the line into a tizzy. Soviet embassies had so little trust in local populations, even in Eastern Europe, that they staffed their missions only with Soviet employees.

There was a long pause, after which a male voice muttered something incomprehensible. Phil smirked, visualizing a goon running around in the Soviet Embassy looking for a Hungarian-speaker. Another long pause, then a familiar voice—

"Adamov. *Tessék.*"

"Krikor, this is Phil. I've been incredibly busy, that's why I haven't been in touch."

"Oh, it's you, Phil. I'm very glad you phoned because I was going to call *you.* Are you free for lunch tomorrow?"

"Yes I am. Name the place."

"Do you know a restaurant called *Hüvös Völgy*?"

"No, but I'll find it. One o'clock allright?"

"Perfect. See you there."

Phil spent most of the day cleaning out his In-Box. It had accumulated a small mountain of paper and as he went through it item by item, he smiled, and sat back. Yet another recollection crossed his mind of something told to him once by Elim O'Shaughnessy, George Quigley's predecessor. Although they had spent barely a year together before O'Shaughnessy's sudden demise, Phil had developed a deep attachment to the austere-looking but warm-hearted career diplomat who lived and comported himself like an aristocrat.

Passing Phil's office one late afternoon, O'Shaughnessy had stopped to watch his PAO struggling with cables, airgrams and memoranda, whereupon he said—"A word of advice. Tend to the urgent things right away, but at the end of the year, take your entire In-Box and dump it into your Burn Bag. That's what a British Ambassador recommended to me years ago and I've followed his advice for two decades. I might add, without *any* repercussions."

Phil laughed quietly at this reminiscence, but noted that it was far from the end of the year. In any case, it might be unwise to burn all the information coming in on the Kirk Douglas visit in the Spring. He extracted a number of messages related to the visit, not only from Washington but from the three other East European posts the film star would visit, and put them in a separate folder. He was amused to see his colleagues attempting to circumvent their frustration by the use of euphemistic language, but the message was clear: this visit was going to be a massive headache.

Sal Frascatti looked in on him and said—"You haven't forgotten that you swapped with Fillmore for the duty tonight, have you?"

"No, I haven't, Sal," he lied.

He phoned Erzsébet and told her she could leave early and why.

At five o'clock, he began the first of the many routines obligatory to performing night duty at the Embassy, specifically, going down to the Reception Desk and relieving Annie at the switchboard. In the next forty-five minutes, the duty officer would bid "Goodnight" to all the departing personnel, including the Ambassador and DCM. At six, he would lock the front door, go up to the third floor and take in the American flag that hung from the Embassy flagpole. He would then escort the Cardinal down to the courtyard for his nightly walk, which lasted about twenty minutes, depending on the length of the conversation with the duty officer.

With Phil and Harold Fillmore, it was usually half an hour because the Cardinal enjoyed their conversation. Then, back up to the third floor and the Cardinal's quarters and picking up the Cardinal's dinner, which Julishka, the cook, put on the elevator. Then, Julishka was let out, and the only two people in the Embassy would be the duty officer, who would go to the Communications Room, and the Cardinal, who remained in his quarters.

Until November 4, 1956, the large room with adjoining bedroom, small kitchen and bath, had been the office of the Chief of Mission. But on that day, when Soviet tanks re-entered Budapest and crushed the Revolt once and for all, the Cardinal, who had sought safety in the nearby Parliament building, fled to the nearest place of refuge, which was then still the American Legation. The only convenient place for him in the building was the American Minister's quarters, which is where he settled, while everyone else moved to the next descending order of office. The Cardinal and Ambassador—the Legation having been raised to an Embassy meanwhile, thereby elevating the Principal Officer to Ambassador—now were on opposite sides of a large foyer, in the middle of which sat the Ambassador's and DCM's secretaries.

On this night, the Cardinal greeted Phil warmly in Hungarian and said he was looking forward to a good conversation. They walked the long corridor leading out to the elevator. It was a small conveyance, able to hold no more than four people, with a small bench to sit on, although no one ever used it. As it turned out, however, it did have a useful purpose. On occasion, the ancient elevator would get stuck in transit, which happened for the first time in Phil's experience one night when he was taking the Cardinal down for his walk. He became concerned and totally at a loss as to how to proceed with the motionless contraption, when to his astonishment, the Cardinal suddenly leaped up on the bench and jumped on it several times with considerable force, whereupon the elevator resumed its downward movement.

In the courtyard, they emerged into the biting, wintry air and began a brisk walk around its four corners. Phil wondered what themes would preoccupy the Cardinal tonight on his half-hour constitutional. Previous themes had been: his arrest and trial; his confinement in prison; his release in 1956 by the Freedom Fighters; his hatred of János Kádár and everything he stood for; listening to the radio, which he refused to do, condemning every station, including the Vatican Radio, as broadcasting 'Bolshevik propaganda;' and visits by Vatican emissaries, such as Cardinal Casaroli from Rome and Cardinal Koenig from Vienna to convince him to give up his asylum and leave the Embassy.

It had been on one of those visits that Phil had encountered a memorable episode, which he had related at one of the Ambassador's staff meetings in the 'bubble,' and everyone, including even Hager, had greeted it with hearty laughter.

Phil had been the Duty Officer when Cardinal Koenig had arrived late one afternoon from Vienna. After having taken dinner to the two prelates, Phil had re-entered the room to remove the dishes, interrupting their colloquy in Latin, the language the two Cardinals employed for communication, and learned that because the discussion was still underway, Cardinal Koenig had decided to spend the night in the Embassy. Phil had made up a cot for him and when the Cardinal retired, so did Phil. An hour later, the phone rang.

"*Amerikai Nagykövetség*," he responded, assuming the caller was Hungarian.

"What did you say?" an aggressive male American voice asked.

"I'm sorry, sir, but I was simply saying in Hungarian that this is the American Embassy."

"Oh, I see. Are you an American?"

"Yes, sir, I am."

"That's good. OK. Now tell me how the Cardinals are making out?"

Phil had been taken aback. The visits of Cardinals were always kept secret, and certainly beyond the purview of American tourists.

"Sir, with all due respect, that is not a subject I can comment on."

There was a silence at the other end, and then a remark made apparently to someone else standing nearby—"Can you believe this? The God-damned Embassy can't talk about the Cardinals. Wait'll I get back home."

Then, to Phil—"You know, fellah, this beats the hell out of me. I'm an American far from home trying to find out how the Cardinals are making out, and you can't talk about that?"

It was an odd formulation and spurred Phil into asking—"Sir, could you be more specific? What exactly did you want to know?"

The voice snorted loudly into the mouthpiece and then bellowed—

"Great balls of fire, man, I'm from St. Louis and only trying to find out how our baseball team made out yesterday."

Phil was deeply chagrined, apologized profusely and explained that the Embassy had not yet received the Paris Herald-Tribune where the day-old baseball scores would be listed. The tourist had banged down the receiver testily without further word, leaving Phil to speculate on how this telephonic exchange would be reported back home.

As he and Cardinal Mindszenty began the walk on this evening, His Eminence asked if Phil could bring back some chocolate bars on his next trip to Vienna. Phil agreed to do so, knowing the Cardinal's great affection for children and how much he enjoyed giving them the chocolate when they came to his Sunday Mass with their parents.

Phil spoke of an article in a Vienna newspaper about the

helplessness and hunger of children in the world, and thought the Cardinal might have seen it too.

"I am deeply aware of the problem, Mr. Secretary. I have read about the desperate plight of children in the Third World. Populations are growing and children are suffering. The rich nations and the poor nations . . ."

His voice trailed off as he looked down sadly at the cement ground and adjusted his small red skull-cap, referred to by some of the more irreverent staff members as the Cardinal's 'beanie.'

"You know, Your Eminence, there is a way to ease that problem."

"Are you going to suggest birth control?" He turned and looked at Phil with the piercing eyes that always betokened dissent.

"With all due respect, Your Eminence, I am."

"What does the Armenian Church say about that?"

When they had had their first conversation over a year ago, the Cardinal had been delighted to learn that Phil was Armenian, even as Phil learned that the Cardinal knew more about Armenian Church history than he.

Although not well-versed in all the tenets of the Armenian Church, once some years ago, Phil had discussed birth control with an Armenian Archbishop and he drew on that conversation now.

"According to my information, Your Eminence, the Armenian Church asks every parishioner to act with the knowledge of God and to follow his own conscience."

The Cardinal asked—"So, what is it you wish to say to me about birth control?"

"Your Eminence, you love children so very much. Does it not cause you anguish to see them suffer when, in fact, their numbers could be controlled?"

The Cardinal stopped, looked up aimlessly at the surrounding apartments where, as Sal had discovered, the AVO had posted guards to observe the Cardinal during his walks, and said—"The Holy Father has spoken out against birth control."

Phil swallowed hard, wondering if he wouldn't be pushing matters too far, but because of his cordial relationship with the Cardinal, decided to take the chance—"Your Eminence, please do not misunderstand me. I venerate the Pope even though I am not Catholic. I wish only to point out that . . . he is a human being, a man like you and I. And as we know so well, human beings sometimes err."

Phil felt his mouth go dry. Was this blasphemy? Would he be denounced? But when he looked again at the Cardinal, who now resumed walking, he saw that his demeanor was calm and that the remarks had not perturbed him. His response was stated with simplicity but firmness—"The Holy Book says it is wrong."

Phil dropped the subject. The rest of the conversation was devoted to the Cardinal's favorite theme—the Treaty of Trianon, which had ceded parts of Hungary to neighboring countries, mostly, Transylvania to Romania. He not only raised this in conversations with other Embassy officers as well but even in his Sunday sermons, especially when ambassadors from friendly countries attended mass.

Finally, the walk was over and Phil took the Cardinal back to his quarters. He checked a few new cables that had come in late in the afternoon and then went into the Communications Room, where he would sleep. But first, as he well knew, he had to check the upstairs attic. This was the one part of night duty which every officer spoke of with apprehension.

The attic had no light, was mostly unfinished, treacherous to walk around in, and filled with many dark corners in which, surely, there lurked every monster the human imagination could conjure up. The duty officer's flashlight would knife through the blackness of the vast space looking for . . . no one knew exactly what. It had been the routine to inspect the attic and every duty officer was obliged to do it, although a few confessed—but only to each other—that they had done so only the first time.

Sal Frascatti, the Security Officer and intrepid former Marine, was the only Embassy staffer to maintain that the attic held no terrors for him. "If I ever catch an AVO bastard up there," he would bellow, "I'll make him a soprano for life!"

Jim Garland had once confided to Phil that he too felt a chill around his heart when he had once examined the attic, but observed that an even spookier experience was checking the upper reaches of the American Embassy in Prague, which had once been a castle.

Duty bound, Phil knew he had to make the dreaded 'attic check,' and did, returning eventually to the Communications Room where he spent most of a sleepless night trying to sort out the various threads of the increasingly complex Beethoven tapestry.

Twenty-One

The *Hüvös Völgy* Restaurant was located in the Buda hills and was appropriately named after the wooded area in which it was found—Cool Valley. Phil had no difficulty finding it and when he parked, he saw the Soviet Embassy license plate and knew Adamyants was already there.

He greeted Phil, rising from the table and extending his hand.

"I am particularly pleased to see you," he said in Armenian, in which language Phil continued—"My pleasure as well."

They chatted amiably about the delightful ambience of the restaurant and Adamyants said he came there sometimes with Hungarian intellectuals, who had introduced him to it, because the atmosphere of the surrounding forest, so different from the smog and traffic of the city, somehow lent itself to freer discussion.

After they had ordered, Admayants said—"You looked tired. Did the Portlands wear you out? I had the impression that your DCM was handling that project."

"Not the Portlands, Krikor. Night duty. I was on last night and you can never get a good night's rest when you sleep in the Embassy."

He snickered. Adamyants looked questioningly at him.

"It's your people, Krikor. They make it difficult for us to relax."

"Quite the contrary, Phil. My people stay out of things like that. It's the Hungarians who keep you awake, and they tell us as little as possible."

"I always thought you guys pulled together."

Adamyants sighed—"Unfortunately, that is not the case. But let's save that for another time. I wanted you here today for a very specific reason."

The waiter brought their drinks and entrees, and Adamyants waited until he had left before continuing—"Phil, the matter of your manuscript has preoccupied me in the last week and I've had to do some . . . communicating on it."

"Communicating? With whom?"

"I'm coming to that. To you, it is a manuscript by a famous composer, a great musical find, a cultural treasure. I don't take anything away from it or you when I say that. But . . . there are certain ramifications which, in my view, you must be made aware of. Consequently, there is something I would like you to do. Provided, of course, that you trust me, and I sincerely hope that you do."

He looked intently at Phil for a reaction, who then said—"Is it that we are of the same blood? I don't know, but, yes, I guess I do trust you."

Adamyants looked pleased—"Good, very good. Are you free to come to my apartment next Tuesday at three in the afternoon?"

Phil consulted a little memorandum book he kept in his breast pocket and saw that he had a lunch with a Hungarian journalist at one but could leave in time to make it by three.

"Yes, I can be there. I believe you live on *Népköztársaság utja.*"

"Yes, 104. Then, you'll be there. That's wonderful."

They ate silently for five minutes, then Phil said—"You know, Krikor, since knowing that you are an Armenian, I have wondered how interested you really are in anything pertaining to Armenia. For instance, something I came across recently—can you ever imagine that Beethoven would have been aware of Armenia?"

Adamyants' brow furrowed with curiosity—"I know hardly anything about Beethoven, Phil, and very little about Armenia, but it *is* the source of our ancestry. I cannot imagine that a German composer a century-and-a-half ago would know anything about our tiny homeland. Tell me about it."

"So you are as surprised as I was. Listen. In 1821, he wrote a letter to a friend in which he said that Europe was suffering from severe inflation, and cited Spain as an extreme example where the poor received no wages. Beethoven then suggested that these Spaniards go to Armenia to fight, in order to gain their back wages, as he put it."

"In 1821? I'm weak on Armenian history. What was going on that prompted him to say that?"

"Good question. I looked it up and it still wasn't clear to me. In 1821, Armenia, in fact the entire Transcaucasus, was dominated by a Russian viceroy named Yermolov who was apparently ruthless, and the Armenians fought back fiercely. I don't know from whom Beethoven thought Spanish workers could receive mercenary money, but it was one of the most startling things I came across in my research. I still can't believe it—Beethoven and Armenia!"

They spent the next hour talking about Vietnam and the huge demonstration against the American Embassy, but found little common ground. Adamyants finally said—"Phil, I refuse to believe that your heart's in that whole damned war. If Vietnam were Armenia, would you feel the same?"

"Not the same thing, Krikor, and you know it. That's a low blow."

They got nowhere, but the confrontation was amicable. They finished, and as they were about leave, Adamyants leaned forward and said—"Do you remember a promise you made to me last time? I'll remind you. No one in the Embassy must know of . . ." he hesitated for a few seconds, ". . . of . . . your coming to my place. And Phil, when I say no one, you understand who I mean."

Phil nodded. The station chief. Adamyants couldn't know that he wouldn't consider giving Carleton Squibb the time of day. They shook hands and parted.

In the forty minutes it took Phil to drive back, and throughout the entire weekend, he felt himself becoming uncomfortable by the mystery of Adamyants' invitation. True to his pledge, he kept it to himself, although that too was a source of discomfort. He was, as he observed to himself, being more loyal to the enemy than he was to his own people. On Saturday and Sunday, he took his frustration out on tennis balls, which ignited Kiki's volatile Greek temperament.

"For Heaven's sake," she complained, "if you don't want to play with me, just say so."

"Kiki, it has nothing, absolutely nothing, to do with you. Believe me."

On Tuesday, Phil's discomposure was replaced by a nervousness which stayed with him from the moment he arrived at the Embassy through his entire luncheon appointment. The Hungarian journalist had just returned from a trip to Albania and was eager to tell Phil about the fervent hopes of Albanian journalists there that the United States would recognize Albania and in that way insinuate itself into the fabric of political life in the tiny Balkan country.

Phil pointed out that whenever he addressed Albanian diplomats at receptions in Budapest in the hope of initiating a conversation, they would turn their backs on him and walk away.

"That is the regime reacting to you," his luncheon partner explained. "The intellectuals, the journalists, the artists, know better."

Phil sneaked a look at his wristwatch under the table. He had forty-five minutes still. He killed some time with questions about Albanian attitudes toward Greece and Yugoslavia and eventually brought the discussion to an end. They shook hands and Phil went to his car and drove through the mid-afternoon traffic towards *Népköztársaság utja,* the broad tree-lined avenue that, as he remembered from Ilona's description, had had so many different names, but which everyone still referred to as *Andrássy.* He parked one block away from No.104, to avoid being spotted by a passing American officer, and entered the Soviet housing compound. He found Adamyants' bell, under Adamov, and rang.

Five minutes later, he stood in front of the apartment door and was greeted by Adamyants with considerable warmth.

"I cannot tell you how very pleased I am to see you, Phil."

"And I cannot tell you on what tenterhooks I've been all weekend. I hope this is not a game."

"It certainly is not, Phil. In fact, as of now, it becomes . . ."he hesitated again, as he had the other day, ". . . it becomes deadly serious. Please don't be alarmed by that. Simply, have patience. Come in and take a seat."

Phil entered the apartment which was appointed with nouveau East European beige-colored furniture—sleek but without character. Soviet Embassy issue, he told himself. He sat down, Adamyants poured two drinks, and as he handed Phil his glass, the sound of running water came from another room. Phil looked in its direction. A door opened, and a tall but slightly stooped man in his early fifties entered the room, extended his hand, and said in heavily Russian-accented English—"I am glad to meet you."

Automatically, for he was stunned for the moment, Phil shook the extended hand but said nothing.

"You know who I am?"

Phil cleared his throat, saw that Adamyants was smiling broadly at him, and said—"I am not sure but, you look like . . . like . . ."

"Like whom?" Adamyants asked, egging him on.

"Well, difficult as it is for me to believe, like . . . Yuri Andropov."

At mention of the name, the stranger emitted a low laugh, came close to Phil and took him by the arm. "Yes, my friend. I am Andropov."

Phil looked from Andropov to Adamyants. Both were smiling in a friendly manner, which relaxed Phil only slightly. He exclaimed—

"You have to excuse my reaction but . . . Good God! . . . this is something of a shock."

Andropov asked Adamyants something in Russian and Phil's

comment was translated for him, after which Adamyants said in Armenian—"Comrade Andropov does not understand English all that well so I will interpret for him today."

Phil studied the Soviet official closely. He had a scholarly appearance, partly because of his rimless glasses, but his thin lips and cold gray eyes gave him an austere look. His voice was quiet and he exuded an image of calm. The oddest thing about him, Phil thought, was his smile—it was perpetual, yet strangely enigmatic.

The single most important biographical fact that Phil knew about Andropov was that he had been the Soviet Ambassador in Hungary when the Revolt began, and was still there when the Revolt had been crushed. There was nothing enigmatic about that. That had been the exercise of brute force on a helpless people. But what was he doing in Budapest now? And why had Adamyants brought them together?

As though reading his thoughts, Adamyants said—"You may or may not know, Phil, that after Comrade Andropov returned to Moscow, a new post was created just for him, Chief of the Central Committee Department for Foreign Liaison with ruling communist parties. That means, Comrade Andropov visits all the East European countries, and especially Hungary."

He asked Andropov something, and when given the reply, said—

"Since leaving his post here, this is his fourth visit to Budapest to confer with the Hungarian Politburo. His visits are unreported, of course, and remain secret. You understand now why I asked you to make that pledge, don't you?"

Phil nodded absent-mindedly, still stunned by the presence of the senior Soviet official. All three were now seated, and Adamyants raised the exact question Phil had on his mind—

"Now, of course, you will want to know why you were invited here to meet Comrade Andropov?"

Adamyants repeated the question in Russian for Andropov, who, to Phil's surprise, leaned forward and said to him in Hungarian—

"In other words, why do I want to talk to you. My Hungarian is not all that good, but better than my English. It has been almost ten years since I spoke it here. I would like to discuss something with you and prefer that our mutual friend interpret from my Russian. Is that agreeable to you?"

That strange, inscrutable smile again.

"It is certainly agreeable to me," Phil replied in Hungarian.

Now they all settled back and, with Adamyants interpreting for both, Andropov began—

"Tell me, my American friend, why are you searching for this particular manuscript? What meaning does it have for you?"

"Well, although I am a diplomat, my profession was originally musicology. My interest in the manuscript is purely from a musical, cultural if you will, point of view."

He waited a moment, then continued—"This all began about twenty years ago, when I was in the de-nazification program in Germany . . ."

Andropov interrupted, almost rudely, wagging his hand—"I know all that. Gregor has given me the background. So, you are maintaining that your interest in this manuscript is purely musical?"

"Absolutely, Mr. Andropov. I don't understand what other interest there could possibly be."

Andropov and Adamyants exchanged glances, some Russian was spoken between them, Andropov looked at his watch, and stood up. So did Phil.

"I hope this was not an imposition, but it was important that I meet you. I shall be returning in a few months and hope to see you again. Can I count on that?"

"Most certainly, Mr. Andropov. It was . . . an unusual experience, startling too."

Andropov laughed softly and shook his hand. Adamyants escorted him to the door, his every move solicitous and deferential. When they were alone, Adamyants looked at Phil and let out a long sigh of relief—"Well, my dear colleague, you have just met one of the most powerful figures in the Soviet hierarchy. And believe me, he will continue to go up. I hope you were sufficienctly impressed."

"Krikor, I sit here virtually speechless. But don't think the mystery doesn't linger on. May I ask, what in hell this is all about?"

"You may ask, Phil, but for the present, I am not at liberty to tell you. May I request that you trust me a little longer?"

"Allright, but can't you tell me at least what connection you have with a man so high up? I mean, he obviously likes you, trusts you. How come?"

Adamyants nodded, freshened their drinks and began—"This is my second tour in Budapest, as you discovered from your blonde friend. I first came here in 1952 and was a Vice Consul for one year when Comrade Andropov arrived as Counselor of the Embassy. In 1954 he became *chargé d'affaires* and then Ambassador. He seemed a lonely kind of person, austere, withdrawn, and when I saw that he was feared and isolated by most of the staff, I made a point of being friendly to him without seeming obsequious. He immediately appreciated what I was doing and we became friends, to the envy, I should add, of the other diplomats on the staff.

"I became a kind of protegé; he encouraged me, gave me special assignments well beyond my consular responsibilities, and, in time, the inevitable happened—I became his aide. You can imagine what this meant to a young Foreign Service officer. Then, he was transferred to Moscow, and I was certain my fortunes had changed. That is, until, last year, when he suddenly appeared. I imagine my Ambassador knew he was coming, and certainly our *Rezident*, like your Station Chief, you know. But I as the Cultural Officer would not have been informed.

"When Comrade Andropov arrived, however, he asked for me and insisted I be his escort during his entire stay. That was when I knew I was back in the fold. In fact, since that time last year, everyone in the Embassy, including the

Ambassador, treats me with almost exaggerated respect. In our Foreign Service, Phil, having a protector at the top is the greatest insurance."

"In ours too, Krikor, except that things don't operate the way they do in yours. I mean, people aren't elevated or demoted so rapidly. Nor do people simply vanish."

Adamyants made a face, nodded—"I understand what you are saying, but as time passes, such things will happen less and less. Under Stalin, it was . . ." his voice trailed off. "But let's leave that for another day."

"Frankly, Krikor, I've got lots of questions which I really can't leave for another day. But it's getting late and without a protector, I can't stay away from the Embassy as long as you."

Adamyants laughed. They agreed to lunch the following Tuesday again at the *Hüvös Völgy*.

Twenty-Two

Since he was in Buda and only fifteen minutes from his residence, Phil drove directly home. Erzsébet was surprised to see him so early and asked if he were well. He assured her he was feeling fine but that he wasn't very hungry and that a sandwich for later on would be enough. She obliged, cleaned up and left by six.

At seven, the phone rang.

"Well, it looks like *I'm* the one to make a move if we're ever going to see each other again. Are you home tonight?

"Yes," Phil replied with a sinking heart.

"I'll be over at nine."

Phil wished for some emergency—an electrical blackout, another demonstration at the Embassy—anything to avoid the scene he knew would take place. But by nine, no rescue was at hand and when the doorbell rang and he opened the door, a distraught Grace Quigley stood in the entrance.

"Hi, Grace," he said without much enthusiasm, as she walked in.

"Is that the best you can do?"

"Grace, please, pull yourself together"

He guided her into the study and sat down beside her on the sofa.

"You see what's become of me?"

"I don't know why you blame *me*, Grace. What did you expect in the circumstances? I mean, for Heavens sake, you're the wife of the Ambassador, as you've reminded me."

"Everything was, well, sort of fine until that slut showed up, and suddenly, so much changed. I know you spent lots of time with her."

"She wanted to be escorted around Budapest's cultural sites by an Embassy officer. That's me, the Cultural Officer."

"Phil, Phil, Phil, don't hand me any of that. I'm not a fool."

"Of course you're not, Grace, but you invest too much emotion into such passing situations."

"Is my husband's secretary a passing situation too?"

Phil stood up abruptly. "I'll get you a drink."

"You didn't answer me. My husband's secretary . . ."

"I heard you, Grace. Just leave her out of it."

"Why should I? She's part of it, too, isn't she?"

He handed her the drink, sat down and said calmly—"Listen to me. She is part of a normal social life that I lead in Budapest. If you could reason things out, Grace, you would understand that since I can't fraternize with local women, I've got to pass the time *publicly* with someone. I am single and Kiki is single. You, on the other hand, are very much married—to the personal representative of the President of the United States, for Christ's sake. Why can't you understand that?"

"What in hell makes you think I don't?"

"Well then, why do you behave in this way?"

"Because, dammit all, I'm just plain jealous!"

Phil didn't quite know what to make of this open admission, but before he could even absorb it, she murmured—"Are you taking up with that German woman?"

He burst into laughter—"Grace, you're really something, you know? That German woman and I have been together just once, at your dinner party. There is nothing between us. Grace, these outbursts must stop. You know, certain eavesdroppers have probably heard everything we've ever said. Do you ever think of that?"

"No, not at all. They can go shit in their hats, for all I care."

Phil laughed again, sipped his drink, and asked—

"By the way, won't you be missed next door?"

"No, he's at the British Ambassador's stag dinner."

"Well, you'd better be going, Grace, just to be safe. After all, the servants . . . Let me walk you over."

She lingered at the Residence side door but he hurried back, angry at himself for another lost opportunity to put an end to it.

On Tuesday he drove to the *Hüvös Völgy* Restaurant. Adamyants had already arrived and waved to him from his corner table. After exchanging warm greetings and ordering lunch, Phil said—"I still can't get over what happened last week, Krikor. I admit to being very impressed, but can't help wondering what the hell it was all about."

"I agree it was not something that happens every day, but why wonder about it?"

"*Why wonder about it?* For Christ sake, Krikor, one of the top men in the Soviet Union meets with me in your apartment, talks to me for some twenty minutes and then cuts it off without further explanation, and I shouldn't wonder what it was all about?"

"I suppose you have that right, Phil, but let me put your mind at ease. At this stage it is still quite simple. You have stumbled onto something which is of interest to . . . let us say for now . . . to Comrade Andropov, and he was curious about you, wanted an opportunity to judge you personally with a face-to-face meeting. Size you up. That's all."

"The way you phrased that fascinates me. You said that whatever this is about is simple *at this stage* and that it is of interest to Andropov, although you also said *for now*. Krikor, I don't know what to make of any of this. Surely you can understand my confusion?"

"I can, Phil, but believe me, you will learn more in time. I implore you to have patience."

Phil sighed, opened his napkin as the lunch arrived, and agreed not to pursue the matter further for the time being.

"Can I ask some questions about Andropov, or is that also off limits?"

"Not if it's about him personally, his background, career, and so forth."

"Good. Last week you told me how you had met here in Budapest and became his aide. Can you talk about his role in crushing the Hungarian Revolt in 1956?"

"You use rather harsh terms, Phil. We didn't crush a revolt. We prevented a Counter-Revolution from restoring fascism in this country."

Phil looked sternly at his luncheon partner—"Frankly, Krikor, I don't give a damn how you characterize what happened here in 1956. All I'm asking is how Andropov fits into the picture. I get the impression I'm going to be involved with him and I'd simply like to know what kind of guy he is."

"Sorry, Phil. I didn't mean to sound ideological, and I do understand why you ask. We could probably talk about that period for days, but briefly, for your purposes, let me tell you the main things.

"Andropov spent five years in Hungary, four of them as Ambassador. He liked the Hungarians, studied their language, knew their history gave lavish parties with gypsy orchestras. In the critical year of 1956, we in the Embassy knew that something was brewing. Khrushchev had made his famous anti-Stalin speech, the Poles had begun stirring things up and the Hungarians supported them with public demonstrations. When the Revolt, as you call it, came, it shook Moscow. That was when two emissaries came, the ideological chief, Mikhail Suslov, and our own compatriot, Anastas Mikoyan, one of the original Bolsheviks from 1917.

"I was in on all the discussions and heard Mikoyan favor letting the Hungarians alone to solve their problems. Suslov wanted Soviet intervention. As you know, Moscow agreed with Suslov. That guy is a tough, humorless son-of-a-bitch."

"What was Andropov's position?"

"I'm afraid it was more in line with Suslov, not because he believed it to be the best road to take, but because Khrushchev had already agreed, despite Mikoyan's pleading, to intervene, and Andropov simply went along with it."

"That doesn't speak all that well of Andropov," Phil observed wryly.

"I guess not, but he had little choice. In any case, it was Andropov who prevailed on János Kádár to take over as Party chief. They became close allies. Andropov had traveled the country from one end to the other and liked what he saw. When Andropov finally left Hungary in December of 1957, Kádár knew he had a highly-placed friend in Moscow. For his part, Andropov had the same kind of secure feeling. After all, he now had caught the eye of Suslov, Mikoyan and Khrushchev, and was given the new post I told you of last week. Then in 1961, he was elected to the Central Committee.

"Of course, to the rank and file, Andropov was still an unknown, but that changed last year. You may not have noticed it but on April 22, which is Lenin's birthday, Khrushchev chose Andropov to make the ceremonial speech, and his picture and speech were reproduced in every newspaper in the Soviet Union. I think it can be said that on that date, Andropov arrived."

"Incidentally," Phil interjected, "is there something wrong with him? I mean, although the light wasn't too good, he seemed, somehow . . . I don't know . . . not in the best of health."

"That's quite perceptive of you, Phil. Yes, it is true, Yuri Vladimirovich has been suffering from diabetes for some time. In fact, that's also why he comes to Hungary. For treatment, I mean. He also goes for treatment to Stavropol. Do you know where that is?"

"Somewhere in the south, isn't it? In the Caucasus?"

"In the Northern Caucasus. He was born there. But more important, there is a sanatorium in Kislovodsk for senior Party people called *Krasnye Kamni*, which means Red Stones, whose mineral waters seem to ease the problems from which he suffers. I think that's why he gave up tennis."

"He plays tennis? Jesus, imagine me playing with Yuri Andropov!"

Adamyants laughed—"Yes, I'm sure you wouldn't forget that. He used to play with a few Hungarian Politburo members at the courts on *Margit sziget,* you know, that island in the Danube."

"This is really intriguing, Krikor. Tell me more."

"You mean, tell you things like his listening to the English lessons on the 'Voice of America.' Ah, that surprises you? The rest of the staff couldn't listen but the Ambassador, well, he can call his own shots."

"Does he have children?"

"Yes, two, and their early years were not too easy for him. His son Igor was 15 years old when they were in Budapest. He always wanted to be in the theatre, but Yuri Vladimirovich wanted a political career for him. His daughter Irina was also a teenager here in Budapest. She had studied music but wanted to be in the theatre, too. I can remember some fiery scenes between father and son and father and daughter, as poor, quiet, Tatyana Filippovna sat patiently by listening to her husband and children rave and rant at each other."

Phil drank the last of his wine and said—"I get the clear impression you really like this man."

"I think I've gotten to know him better than most. Yes, I do like him, Phil. There is a tough streak in him but he is a straight-shooter. He can't stand liars and crooks, and, according to him, Moscow is full of both. If he ever climbs higher, I pity his enemies."

They paid up and as they walked to their respective cars, Adamyants said—"I guess for you and me, there's no rest. I've got an arts and crafts exhibit coming from every republic of the Soviet Union. I'll send you an invitation. You might enjoy the Armenian stuff. How about you?"

"I've got a Hollywood personality."

"Anyone I may have heard of?"

"Kirk Douglas."

"I think you'll be busier than I."

Twenty-Three

When Phil heard that the Quigleys were going on extended leave over the Christmas holidays, he arranged to be called to Vienna two days earlier for a meeting of American Public Affairs Officers from East European embassies. He made sure to unobtrusively depart Budapest before the Quigleys in order to avoid any last-minute confrontations with Grace. It did work out that way, too. One week before Christmas, the Quigleys flew to Rome, but Phil was already luxuriating in the swank Hotel Sacher. He planned for Kiki to follow him, and a day later when he heard her voice outside his room, he was elated as he opened the door and embraced her.

He attended three sessions of the conference with his counterparts, one of which was devoted exclusively to the Kirk Douglas visit. Everyone seemed at a loss on how to program the actor and more than one hoped the visit would be aborted. Phil excused himself from the other discussions, which were primarily about common problems they all faced in communist countries—secret police surveillance, protest demonstrations, official stone-walling, sudden uprooting of sidewalks in front of embassies. He wanted to get away and begin wallowing in the whipped-cream-and-chocolate sensuality of Vienna, and he wanted Kiki to wallow with him. Only on the second day did he wince as he recalled that this was the Austria on which Kurz had showered so many enconiums. Mostly, however, they spent a glorious week exploring the city, going to the *Staatsoper*, having coffee and a *torte* in the Cafe Mozart, and spending endless hours in the room and bed they shared.

But one morning after breakfast, Phil said—"Today, *kukla mu,* we are going to see the one Vermeer in all of Austria. Are you up to it?"

"I am yours to do with as you wish."

"I take that to mean Yes," he said, biting her ear.

When they emerged from the Sacher, Kiki looked for a taxi, but Phil said—"We won't need one, Kiki. The *Kunsthistorisches Museum* is quite near, so, if you have no objection, we'll walk."

"If necessary, I will walk the length of Vienna for you."

"A few blocks will do, Kiki. It's only a stroll down the Vienna Ring."

When they arrived, Phil asked for the Dutch Section and soon found the Vermeer. It was a magnificent canvas called "The Allegory of Painting," rich in color and subject matter, including even Vermeer himself, seen from the rear. In it, Vermeer was paying tribute to a variety of Muses—history, poetry, music and comedy. Phil stood in silent admiration before the painting. 'By now,' he thought, 'I must be getting close to half of his total output.'

After the Vermeer, Phil wanted more than anything else to visit the various Beethoven shrines in the city. Two of them, he was excited to discover, were outlying houses in which the composer had lived in 1817, that one year when he had produced hardly anything. Phil could not help wonder, as he walked through the rustic buildings, whether the Cello Concerto had not been conceived in the mind of the already quite deaf composer in those rooms. Ever anxious to absorb as much as possible of the Master's Vienna, Phil took Kiki twice to the *Griechen Beisl*, a five centuries-old restaurant where Beethoven frequently ate.

When they had exhausted the Beethoven sites, they went to the Haydn Museum, then to the room where Schubert died, and briefly to the Goethe Museum. Finally, Phil decided to include one of the most legendary addresses of all, *Berggasse* 19, where Siegmund Freud pioneered his researches into the human psyche.

Kiki never seemed happier and never left Phil's side, nor did he want her to. She would fall asleep, clutching him, murmuring—"You are mine, all mine."

Once, totally out of the blue, he heard her say—"She's married and I'm single. No Ambassador's wife is ever going to steal you from me."

At that particular moment, Phil did not doubt it.

Their few days together were so exhilarating that Phil phoned the DCM, who in the Ambassador's absence was *chargé*, and asked for an additional three days of leave. Garland replied that things were relatively quiet and approved.

Phil and Kiki rented a car and drove to Salzburg, visiting Mozart's birthplace and museum. Then they drove across the German border to Berchtesgaden and visited Hitler's Eagles Nest, going up on the cable car and then the special elevator built in the rock. Neither of them were skiiers but they enjoyed watching the many who were. Finally, the week ended and, exhausted but feeling fulfilled, they planed back to Hungary, where on Garland's instructions, they were met by Imre at the airport and driven to their respective domiciles.

The city was covered with the heavy smog of brown coal but the air around Phil's residence in the Buda hills was breathable. Erzsébet was overjoyed to see him and quickly pointed out that the Residence next door was still dark. Phil was relieved to hear that. Later, when he phoned Garland, he was even happier to hear that the Quigleys had sent word they planned to spend New Year in the South of France.

The next morning at the Embassy, Phil found more messages requesting whatever programs had been made for the Kirk Douglas visit. He wished it were the end of the year so he could follow Elim O'Shaughnessy's advice. He walked over to Garland's office.

"Has it been quiet here, Jim?"

"Well, while you were away a Codel of senior Congressional types suddenly decided to include Budapest in their East

European tour and I had to do some fancy improvising to accommodate them. Kovács was especially helpful. He's a good guy."

"Any big names?"

"I'll let you be the judge. How about Senators Strom Thurmond and Hugh Scott. Or Ralph Yarborough. And about fifteen others. The *men* weren't so bad. They arrived on a Sunday afternoon and the first thing one young Southern wife says to me is—'Oh, I've simply got to have one of those lovely zither-like things. Today!' 'Madam,' I said, 'nothing is open today. Won't tomorrow do? After all, you'll be here for three days.' 'No, no, I've got to have it today," she demanded. "I was told the Embassy can do anything.'"

"My God, what did you do?" Phil asked, his shoulders shaking with sympathetic laughter.

"Well, fortunately, her husband, who appeared to have more common sense than his very young wife, said to her—'Honey, why don't you just shut up and let the man do his job?' Very loudly too. That did the trick. Sal Frascatti found a *cembalom* on Monday for her. I took them to the Hungarian Parliament and they sat in the same seats as Kádár and other party bigwigs. They enjoyed that. Taken altogether, however, it wasn't so bad, although I sure could have used you, Phil."

"I'm truly sorry I wasn't here, Jim. But Vienna was very fruitful, both work-wise and personally."

He lunched with Bence Szabolcsi and they discussed Phil's Vienna stay and how he had visited some of the apartments where Beethoven had lived.

"Perhaps, dear colleague, you already know that Beethoven may have moved over two dozen times in the thirty-five years he lived in Vienna. Can you imagine what that must have done to his concentration—moving all his personal belongings and piano, his manuscripts, sketchbooks and scraps of paper, every eighteen months or so to another flat? And that is not counting his summer stays in the outskirts of Vienna every year. To me it is unimagineable. But for a genius, well, obviously it did not interfere with his composing very much. Did you realize, incidentally, when he lived in the city, that he was rarely on the main floor, if he could avoid it? You must have noticed he was seldom below the third floor. You know why? The street sounds and noise from horses' hooves and wagon wheels on the cobblestones were too disturbing. There was also the dust and dirt."

Phil described the plaques on the buildings where Beethoven had lived, even what he had composed there. Szabolcsi smiled sadly—

"It has been a good many years since I was able to go to Vienna and visit those sites. But, you know, you have revived the spirit of research, really of the hunt, in me and I don't dwell so much on my own past as on Beethoven's past. I've been digging through my books and came up with minor facts I had long since forgotten, but which suddenly have a new relevance."

"Such as what, Dr. Szabolcsi?"

"Well, for instance, we know that Beethoven played the viola in the Bonn Opera Orchestra when he was seventeen or eighteen. Do you know that the cellist in that orchestra, Bernhard Romberg, with whom Beethoven was very friendly, was the author of the best instruction book on cello playing of the day? Certainly, Romberg must have exerted some influence on the budding young composer."

Phil asked Szabolcsi to accompany him to Martonvásár, but the aging musicologist pleaded ill health. Besides, he observed, it was not the best time of year for such an outing.

If he was not thinking of Szabolcsi and the mystery of the missing manuscript, he was thinking of Adamyants and the mystery of the Soviet interest in the manuscript, now compounded by the involvement—how exactly, he didn't know—of Yuri Andropov.

He phoned Adamyants and arranged a lunch at the *Száz Éves* because it was in the heart of town. After ordering,

Adamyants asked—"How was your vacation in Vienna? Were you alone?"

"Very enlightening, refreshing and thoroughly enjoyable. And I was not alone."

He learned that Adamyants had not ever been to Vienna. Whether he was not permitted to go there or just hadn't was not clear. But he listened attentively, even with care, as Phil described the various Beethoven sites in the city.

"So, even when you're away from here, your mind is still on your private mission. It seems to be an *idée fixe* with you, Phil."

"An obsession perhaps, Krikor, but frankly, your own reaction to all this, plus the entry of your friend Andropov into the picture, turns it into one big mystery. An international mystery. And I suppose it is still too early to tell me more?"

Adamyants nodded solemnly, flicked the ash of his cigarette, and said calmly—"In good time, Phil, which could mean, very soon. But it's still not up to me."

"In other words, I've just got to wait."

There was a long pause, as though neither knew how to proceed. Then, Phil said—"You know, there is something I want very much to do, but I just can't."

Adamyants looked up from his empty plate with interest."Like what, Phil?"

"Like travel to East Berlin. Without American diplomatic relations with East Germany, I can't make that trip directly from here."

"Why would you want to go there to begin with?"

"Because in East Berlin, there is a musicologist who is the foremost Beethoven scholar alive. I have read his articles, speeches and books. He's a walking encyclopaedia on everything known about Beethoven. His name is Dr. Karl-Heinz Keilbert, and he's in charge of the musical manuscripts in the Berlin *Staatsbibliothek*. If anybody can tell me anything about that manuscript, it would be Keilbert. But he is completely out of my reach."

Adamyants took a long final drag on his cigarette, and as he doused it in the ashtray, he looked up at Phil—"Seeing Keilbert means that much to you? I mean, of course, for the purposes of finding your Concerto?"

"Well, look. I don't know if the manuscript is real, I don't know where it is, and I don't know why you people are so uptight about it. I also don't know how much Keilbert could tell me, but right now, he's the only one who might give me a lead or two. You keep holding out on me, which is damned irritating. He might be my only hope, for now anyway."

"I understand your frustration, Phil. Do you think you could get everything done in one day?"

"Probably. But getting to East Berlin . . ."

"When is your movie star coming? You've certainly got to be here for him."

"Not for some weeks yet. Why?"

"No questions for the time being, Phil. We'll talk again. In fact, I'm expecting Yuri Vladimirovich to come back this summer and I know he wants to meet with you again."

"Well, allright, Krikor, even though I don't fully understand this high level interest in me."

"Give it time.

"I've got plenty of that, but less of patience."

Adamyants smiled as they shook hands and parted.

Twenty-Four

The Quigleys returned to Budapest towards the end of January, tanned and rested. The Ambassador greeted everyone jovially on his first day back and told the DCM he was ready for an intense year, then home leave, and return for a second tour, unless the President decided to replace him. George Quigley had always been loyal to the Administration and Jim Garland had no doubt that he would return.

Grace Quigley kept away from the Embassy, but her husband asked Phil over for a drink. For his part, Quigley always enjoyed chatting with Phil because, as he said, he learned so much from him about Hungary and the people he, the Ambassador, had to deal with. That night, he said—"You know, Phil, if I had my way in cutting expenses, I'd eliminate most of the Embassy and keep just you and the administrative staff, the people who take care of our needs. Everybody else would go."

"With all due respect, Sir, much as I find it flattering, your DCM is your key man. I've seen many and he's about the best there is. Keeps things on an even keel."

"Of course you're right, my boy. Quite right."

Grace looked at Phil several times but soon left them alone.

The weeks went by and in late February a cable arrived informing all four relevant East European posts that the Douglas visit had been postponed until late April, and that program changes should be made appropriately. Phil was amused by that, since he knew that neither he nor his colleagues elsewhere had scheduled anything so far. But everyone felt a sense of reprieve.

Having heard nothing from Adamyants, Phil busied himself with literary matters, spent evenings with writers Tibor Déry and Gyula Illyés, with poets Gábor Devecséri and István Vas, with the gifted lexicographer Lászlo Országh, whose two-volume dictionary had achieved in Hungary an almost biblical stature, and with professors of English at *Eötvös Loránd* University—those, that is, such as Lászlo Kéry, who dared to associate with him. Phil's Armenian heritage somehow always crept into every conversation, and several drew parallels between Armenia and Hungary as 'vassals of the Soviet Union.' When Phil asked if they had such frank discussions with Adamov, underlining that he too was Armenian, Déry, for one, said—"Being Armenian is one thing, but what sort you are is quite another. We prefer the non-Soviet kind."

Then, on March 6, a death plunged the entire country into mourning. Although it was a Monday, when there were no morning newspapers, by mid-afternoon, the entire capital seemed to know that Zoltán Kodály had died, hours before the announcement on Radio Budapest. Phil learned the news from Tibor Hegedus who phoned him at 8:30 in the morning. When the afternoon papers finally appeared, and also on Tuesday morning, the passing of Hungary's foremost composer at 84 was treated as a national event, even though Kodály's deep-seated Hungarian nationalism had long been a thorn in the communist government's side.

Phil canceled all his appointments and spent his time visiting with prominent musical personalities, as well as expressing his condolences to Sárolta Kodály, the deceased composer's widow. Six days later, Kodály lay in state in a sealed coffin at the Academy of Science, where thousands lined up to pay their respects. A requiem mass that evening also drew thousands, primarily simple, peasant folk.

The funeral took place on Saturday and although it had been scheduled for eleven o'clock at *Farkasréti* Cemetery, where the prominent Hungarians were buried, at ten o'clock a huge mass of people had already assembled at the site for a religious service that had not even been announced in the press.

Immediately thereafter, the special guests began arriving, led on the Party side by Politburo member István Szirmai, and for the government Premier Gyula Kallai, as well as the elite of Hungarian intellectual life. Guards of honor, in groups of six, took turns standing in silent tribute at the catafalque for several minutes. Phil recognized composers, conductors, musicians from all over Hungary, and some rarely seen, such as Béla Bartók, Jr.,whose famous father had been a close friend and associate of Kodály.

Of the main speakers, Phil was most taken by the low key, modest words of tribute of Bence Szabolcsi, Kodály's closest friend. His eulogy was the most personal and moving of the day.

Finally, everyone walked the long, solemn route to the gravesite where a full and impressive Catholic burial service was conducted with the crowd joining in appropriate prayers. The celebrant's final eulogy praised Kodály's faith in his God, in his work and in the Hungarian people. All reference to socialism was absent, and in a final comment, Kodály was praised as 'the greatest Hungarian,' which, in view of the presence of so many Party and government officials, may have been a gentle affront to the regime.

When Phil had arrived and was standing in the diplomatic section with many ambassadors, his Hungarian intellectual friends had immediately beckoned for him to join them. Thus, he now stood with sculptor Miklós Bórsós, publicist Iván Boldizsár and writer Gyula Illyés, and could sense the suppressed excitement which suffused them as they noted to each other and to Phil the identity of many who were there. Boldizsár said to Phil—"Hungarian funerals bring out everyone, even those whom one never expects to see, and sometimes those we think may have already died."

The significance of this particular funeral was underlined by

Illyés who said—"Today, we have buried the last of the great Hungarians."

But others there did not agree, for great as Kodály was, so too was Illyés, who would now inherit that mantle of greatness.

As the crowds of thousands slowly dispersed, a shriveled little man shuffled off to the gates of the cemetery, a figure who looked familiar to Phil. He went up to him for a closer look, just as the man turned and smiled. It was the almost never-seen 80-year old Marxist philosopher György Lukács, who had recently been visited by Ilona Portland. He had left the seclusion of his books and study to add, by his presence, his own tribute to the deceased patriot, despite their political and philosophical differences.

Phil was deeply affected by the ceremony and by the presence of so many, among whom were some friends and admirers, but also some political enemies. Yet, there appeared to be a communality of esteem for the man many liked to think of as 'the conscience of the Hungarian people.'

Outside the gate, Phil saw the slowly moving figure of Bence Szabolcsi, and quickly overtook him. Szabolcsi looked up at Phil and smiled sadly. His eyes were moist. Phil put his arm around the elderly musicologist guiding him down to his car and drove him home in silence. He realized how deep Szabolcsi's personal loss was and didn't have the heart to raise the matter that consumed them both.

Twenty-Five

Kodály's passing spread a pall over the populace, and especially over Hungary's intellectuals, even some who had accepted the communist regime but always held out hopes for improvement. With the death of Kodály, however, those hopes seemed to have died as well, and Phil found himself spending long hours with his intellectual friends in consolation sessions that went deep into the night.

Then, as March crept inexorably toward April, suddenly the Kirk Douglas visit was only two weeks away, and his focus abruptly changed. The DCM called him into his office—"I assume you've got things under control, Phil. I get the impression from your buddies in Warsaw, Prague and Bucharest that they've been unable to produce the kind of reception Douglas wants. Where do you stand?"

Phil plunked himself down on the large leather sofa and said—"He arrives on a Thursday, Jim, and leaves on Saturday. I've suggested to the Ambassador that he give a small reception at the Residence, inviting some film people I've proposed. After that, if the Douglases are hungry, I'll make reservations for dining. A very small party—the Douglases, Quigleys, you and Sarah and myself. I won't bring a date. For Friday, which is his only full day, I've got some ideas that I think will appeal to him. Sound allright to you so far?"

Garland displayed no reaction. "Yesterday I got a call from the Department. Just a reminder, I was told, that he's got friends in high places, like Jack Valenti, and you know whose aide *he* is."

On a Thursday afternoon late in April, Phil met the Douglases at *Ferihegy* Airport and escorted them to the Gellért Hotel. Douglas had had no luck in Poland, Czechoslovakia or Romania with his request to meet the party chiefs and, as he unpacked, spoke disparagingly of his swing through East Europe. He asked Phil to dispense with formality and to address him as 'Kirk,' but his tone remained abrupt as he inquired about his Budapest program. He listened without comment to Phil's recitation of the details, but his compressed lips and lowered lids expressed his inherent doubts that the program would have any success.

The evening began with a small cocktail at Ambassador Quigley's Residence where an ebullient Grace curried favor with Mrs. Douglas, a chic, reticent woman, while Douglas, now more relaxed, was gracious with the Hungarian film personalities who surrounded him.

Towards nine, Phil whispered to the Ambassador that he had reserved a table at the *Mátyás Pince* and at nine-thirty, the Douglases, Quigleys, Garlands and Phil piled into two cars and drove to the center of town.

The *Mátyás Pince* was packed, as always, but Phil cleared the way through the entrance and signaled the headwaiter, who, recognizing Phil, seated them at an exclusive corner table. Phil then engaged in a hushed conversation with him as the others at the table watched in curiosity. The restaurant was in high gear, packed with late diners whose excited, high voices mixed with the throbbing, sensuous modes of the gypsy musicians' *cembalom* and strings. Sándor Lakatos, aware that Phil had brought a celebrity to the restaurant, was putting on another display of pyrotechnics with his violin.

The conversation with the headwaiter became animated and the guests at the table observed that Phil seemed to be in high spirits. Suddenly, he bent forward between Douglas and the Ambassador and said, his voice carrying above the din—"I picked this restaurant because every once in a while, János Kádár comes here to eat. If you look around, you'll see that there are far more men here than women. They are bodyguards, protecting Kádár, who *is* here tonight. He's over there, Kirk, in that side booth. This will be the only opportunity for you to meet him, if he is willing to talk to you. With your permission, Mr. Ambassador, I'd like to go over and ask him."

George Quigley could barely contain himself for joy as Phil walked over to the booth where János Kádár, seated next to his wife, was brooding over a bowl of *gyulás*, his craggy face cast in stone.

"Mr. Kádár," Phil said in Hungarian, "I am the American Cultural Officer. I hope I am not disturbing you."

A small smile crept over Kádár's face as he shook his head.

"Tonight I have brought to this restaurant a famous American movie star. Kirk Douglas. Would it be possible for him to meet you?"

"Why not. What films has he made?"

Phil remembered that the one film starring Kirk Douglas which had been shown throughout the Soviet Union and the bloc countries was *Spartacus*, and he mentioned it.

"I've seen that film. Bring him over," Kádár said, as both he and Mrs. Kádár shed their gravity and began to whisper to each other.

Phil went back to the table where Douglas was waiting expectantly and said—"Kirk, Mr. Kádár would like to meet you."

Ambassador Quigley almost rose from his seat in excitement—"Mr. Douglas, make the most of it. This is rarer than you'll ever know."

As Douglas and Phil walked over to Kádár's booth, the orchestra stopped playing, the babel of voices decreased sharply, and scores of stern-eyed men in dark suits suddenly stood up at tables all over the restaurant. After they shook hands, Kádár asked Douglas where he had been, what he planned to do in Hungary, all of which Phil translated, much to Kádár's amusement. Finally, Douglas asked Phil to convey to Kádár how much he appreciated his kindness in talking to him. As Douglas walked back to his table, Phil thanked Kádár for his graciousness, who said, on the contrary, he wished to thank Phil.

Seated back at the Embassy table, Douglas was now bubbling with pleasure and said to Ambassador Quigley—"I've been in Hungary less than six hours and already this has got to be the highpoint of my entire trip. You've got a good man here."

Quigley beamed at Phil and Jim Garland winked at him. Lakatos struck up a series of lively Hungarian tunes, the restaurant returned to its previous level of cacophony, and everyone at the table, especially Douglas and his wife, dined in high spirits on native Hungarian dishes.

Most of the next day was spent in sightseeing and visits to theatrical institutes and *Hungaro Film*, where he was shown three short films, one a candidate for an 'Oscar' that year.

In the evening, awaiting him at the Film Actors Club, were fifty-five of Hungary's leading actors and directors. Douglas spoke for half an hour about his experiences in the other East European countries he had visited, but said Hungary had been the highlight because of his meeting the previous night with Kádár.

During the animated reception, in which Phil recognized the many faces familiar to him from Hungarian stage and screen, his eyes kept returning to one which caught his attention not only because it was strange but also because whenever he looked, he found the other watching him. It was a striking face, with high cheekbones suggesting the Central Asian origins of the Magyars, prominently-boned, almost savage, yet, in a curiously masculine way, handsome. When Phil looked for him a third time, the stranger was gone.

Returning to the hotel after the reception, Douglas continually alluded to his meeting with Kádár and said when he returned to Washington he would describe it to Jack Valenti and the President.

The three-day visit ended the next morning when Phil escorted them to the airport, where, after they were interviewed by waiting journalists, he watched their plane take off.

Phil felt a wave of euphoria sweep over him as Imre drove

him back to the Embassy. There, Ambassador Quigley greeted him in his office by standing up when Phil entered, shaking his hand and saying—"Thanks to you, Phil, that turned out splendidly. He is certain to report all this to the White House."

Phil looked in on the DCM, who, grinning broadly, asked—"Well now, was that good planning or just plain dumb luck? As if I didn't know! Tell me candidly, Phil, what's he really like?"

"Everything you can expect from a famous movie star: somewhat imperious, eager to be recognized. Standing once in front of the hotel waiting for me to take him to the Hungarian Film Actors Club, he apparently hadn't been noticed by anyone, so that when I arrived he was visibly annoyed and grumpy until we got to the Club and he was greeted with lengthy applause. After that, he was right on target and spoke about what they were anxious to hear, namely Hollywood and film-making in the United States. But that meeting with Kádár on the first night was the true highlight and left him with a good feeling about his visit here. I liked him best when he was completely relaxed, and in those moments I had the impression of having penetrated the facade of his public persona. He displayed genuine curiosity about Hungary, my work and its role in the Embassy's overall function—good probing questions—and that was when I sensed being with the inner and real Kirk Douglas."

"Hmm. Sounds like a complex guy. And I know how much pressure you were under. Well, now you have the entire weekend to relax."

"I'll try, Jim, but I've lost precious time."

"You mean, that God-damned manuscript? Nothing seems to divert you from that, does it. Well, it's your business."

"It is, Jim, it is," Phil sighed as he walked across the hall to his office and reminded himself that on Monday morning he should phone Adamyants.

Twenty-Six

After a restful weekend of golf, tennis with Kiki and further reading about the last ten years of Beethoven's life, Phil phoned Adamyants at the Soviet Embassy on Monday morning. There was the usual confusion, then a male voice, speaking heavily-accented English, said—

"Good morning. Is this Mr. Faljian of the American Embassy?"

Startled, Phil conceded it was.

"Comrade Adamov asked me to give you a message. He was called to Moscow on short notice. He apologizes."

Phil thanked the voice at the other end and hung up. He was disappointed and knew he would miss his friend. He also hoped there was nothing wrong and that his compatriot was not in trouble.

He picked up a batch of cables and airgrams and read them without much care. His mind was on his absent colleague. ". . . called to Moscow on short notice . . ." had such an ominous ring to it. Was Andropov behind this? Did it mean a transfer, or even a recall? All he could do was wait.

For one thing, he had pretty well come to an impasse in his Beethoven search. His own endeavors, plus Szabolcsi's, had brought neither of them any nearer to success. If there was any light at the end of the tunnel, the hope that the entire tunnel would eventually be illuminated lay, at this stage anyway, only with Adamyants, whose oblique, mysterious comments on the manuscript at least kept the issue alive.

One airgram had caught his eye—a visit to Budapest by Leopold Stokowski. Could the famed conductor help enlighten him? He re-read it and saw that the visit was still several months away.

Phil wrote a detailed cable to Washington on the highlights of the Kirk Douglas visit, which had aroused great interest beyond Hungary because of an Associated Press dispatch reporting that the movie star had met with János Kádár in a Budapest restaurant. Washington had phoned the Embassy Sunday afternoon wanting to know exactly what had occurred, noting that the White House was especially interested.

The next twenty days were spent largely in devising ways to elude Grace, meet secretly with Kiki, continue talking to Szabolcsi and reading materials at the *Széchényi* Library in Hungarian, German and English, concerning Beethoven's contacts with Hungary and the creative musical production of his later years. But every day that passed, he knew, was one day nearer to the return of his friend—if he returned at all. If anyone could move the project forward, Phil strongly suspected, it was Adamyants. Without him, the search would be over.

When the phone call came, it was as though the sun suddenly broke through a dense overcast of clouds—"Phil, this is Krikor. How about the *Apostolok* at 2 today?"

"Krikor! It is *truly* wonderful to hear your voice. Yes, I'll be there."

Phil was seated at one of the striated wooden tables facing the restaurant door when Adamyants entered smiling happily and the two Armenians embraced warmly. Once their orders were taken, Phil leaned forward and said with urgency—

"Is everything allright, Krikor? I mean, associating with me hasn't gotten you into trouble, has it?"

Adamyants laughed—"Not at all, Phil. Everything is fine. I do sincerely apologize for what happened. I know you got my message. You were busy with your movie star when I got a phone call from Moscow to fly home immediately, so I couldn't get to you. Here, let's start on this food and then I'll fill you in."

Minutes later, between mouthfuls, he began—"The phone call was from my Foreign Ministry's Hungarian Desk Officer who said that I should depart immediately for Moscow. I did, on Saturday. In fact, Phil, I saw you at the airport with your Hollywood celebrity and his wife. They were posing for photographs, but I didn't want to intervene. I know him from *Spartacus.* It played in the Soviet Union. Good film. Progressive. Is he progressive, too?"

"I would call him liberal, Krikor. The way you guys use 'progressive' makes someone sound like a communist."

Adamyants grinned, ate some more, then continued—"The Foreign Ministry wanted the answers to some questions concerning cultural treaties that Hungary had made with non-socialist states, especially the status of negotiations with the United States. I knew from my conversations with you that your government does not favor official cultural pacts, that you prefer private ties. That occupied several days of discussion.

"Then, one morning, I was told to go to a specific room in the Kremlin. I did, curious as to who so high up in the Party wanted to talk to me. It turned out, as perhaps I should have expected, to be Comrade Andropov. Yuri Vladimirovich was in very good spirits, greeted me like a son, asked how I was, and so forth. After the amenities, he asked when I had last seen you. I told him, and said I hadn't informed you personally of my departure because you were deeply involved with the visit of an American movie star.

"Yuri Vladimirovich immediately asked which one, and when I mentioned Douglas, he said—'Oh yes, he was in *Spartacus* I know him.' Then we talked about you."

"Me? I don't understand, just like I don't understand so much about all this, I mean, Andropov, Beethoven, and everything else."

"You will, Phil, you will. But let me set your mind at ease. I can tell you now that we are convinced beyond a doubt that you have been honest with us."

Phil feigned dismay—"I didn't think you had any doubts about me."

"Don't be annoyed. We are very careful, especially in some matters. You know, he took a liking to you. He told me that you had some of the ethnic traits I do, but that you were distinctly American, and he told me that Americans have the attractive qualities of openness and candor. What I am here to convey to you is that Yuri Vladimirovich is coming in three months and wants to see you again. Are you willing?"

"I guess so, Krikor, but I am also somewhat overwhelmed by all the attention."

"That's understandable. But the earlier terms still obtain, Phil. By which I mean, no one, and I again mean *no one* in your Embassy must know. Agreed?"

Phil nodded and murmured concurrence.

"This time, it is of even greater importance that you keep this to yourself. I get the impression you don't know what happened to him two days ago?"

"What do you mean? Don't tell me he's been purged, or something like that."

Adamyants chortled—"No, nothing like that. In fact, from now on, *he'll* do the purging, if it has to be done. Well, since you don't know, Phil, brace yourself. Two days ago, Comrade Andropov was appointed Chairman of the Committee for State Security."

Phil stared silently across the table for a long moment, then said in tones of awe, speaking each letter slowly and distinctly—

"The K-G-B?"

"Yes. Later today, I will send him an EYES ONLY cable saying you agree to another meeting. I have a private channel to him now. And, oh yes, I will also have word for you on that trip to the German Democratic Republic."

Phil looked numb and said nothing. Something he could

not fathom was happening and he appeared to be at the center of it.

"Phil? Are you allright?"

"I'm allright, Krikor. Just . . . just . . . stupefied, dumbstruck, I don't know."

"I see. Well, look, I'll let you know when he's here. My apartment, again of course. Now that that's settled, tell me how the visit went?"

Phil spent the rest of their lunch describing the various activities centering around Kirk Douglas and when he told of the meeting with Kádár, Adamyants nodded knowingly, adding—"Quite a coup. None of your colleagues elsewhere were able to do that. You certainly know how to handle these things."

Phil asked quickly how Adamyants would know that, but got no reply.

Returning to the Embassy, he closed the door of his office and lay on the sofa. His mind was buzzing and he felt a sense of guilt that he had pledged silence to Adamyants. The Ambassador? Well, he didn't have to know everything that went on. But the DCM, his closest friend in the Embassy, who trusted him, covered up for him. Shouldn't he be told? Finally, the Station Chief, particularly now with Andropov's new appointment. Andropov's earlier title and function, imposing as they were, had a peripheral interest, but now, as head of the KGB, should meeting with him not be passed on to the CIA?

Phil buried his face in his hands and held them there for several minutes, and then made a vow: he would keep his pledge, but only for the time being; his American oath of loyalty transcended all pledges and disallowed keeping such secrets from fellow officers; therefore, when it was appropriate and safe to do so, he would break his pledge to Adamyants.

Rising, he went down to the snack bar and had a beer. Carleton Squibb was just having a cup of coffee. Phil tried to avoid him but Squibb picked up his mug and sat down at Phil's table.

"That was quite a coup, Phil, I mean setting up the meeting with Kadar. Kirk Douglas must have been very pleased. I know from my colleagues in the other posts that nothing like that happened with them. I truly envy you your know-how."

Phil was struck by the similarity of language between what Squibb had just said and what he had heard from Adamyants. Observing the Station Chief, he saw that he was sincere; naive perhaps, but honest. At that particular moment, Phil felt sorry for Squibb: sorry for his incapacity to engage in productive dialogue, sorry for the loneliness of his secretive task, sorry for his inability to operate in an environment of constant surveillance. He meant well, Phil concluded, but he was out of his element, his task totally alien to his temperament and personality. Phil excused himself and returned to his office.

He had no sooner settled behind his desk when the phone rang. It was Annie to tell him that Dr. Szabolcsi was on the line.

"What a nice surprise, Dr. Szabolcsi. I haven't seen you since Kodály's funeral more than two months ago."

"Yes, it has been awhile, Faljian *úr*. I wondered if you would like to ride down to Martonvásár one day this week. Is Thursday possible for you? Say, about ten in the morning?"

"I'd be utterly delighted," Phil responded, overjoyed to hear that he would be accompanied by the renowned musicologist. "I'll pick you up at your apartment."

He sank back in his large desk chair, a small smile of pleasure playing about his lips.

Martonvásár—at last!

Twenty-Seven

The stocky figure on the sidewalk was peering myopically up and down the street as Phil pulled up in his car and got out.

"Good morning, Dr. Szabolcsi," he called out cheerfully.

The eminent musicologist greeted the American with warmth—"I am very happy to see you, my young friend. What a beautiful day we have for our excursion. Let us hope it will also be enlightening."

They drove through the busy streets of Budapest and Phil sought and found Road Seven, also known as the B to B route—Budapest to Balaton, the beautiful, placid inland lake that was a summer home to many artists. Martonvásár lay about twenty miles south of Budapest along this route, and at this time of day had little traffic. The trees were beginning to fill out and the countryside was slowing turning green.

They chatted amiably about contemporary Hungarian music and Szabolcsi described some recent attempts to introduce twelve-tone music, which had drawn official frowns. Phil asked if politics played any role in such disapproval, noting that in the Soviet Union, aleatory music was virtually banned.

"Politics, without a doubt, does influence these new composers, but, you know, I am not quite so certain that the Hungarian public is prepared to embrace anything new in music. For instance, Kodály, who wrote music in a traditional way, will always be popular here. But Bartók, he was something quite different. What a restless mind he had, always experimenting, always seeking new combinations of sounds, but never traveling outside that same framework which preoccupied Beethoven, for instance. Almost two centuries apart, but how different. Hungarian audiences recognize that Bartók is one of the few geniuses our country has produced, but they are reserved in their reception. Our musical taste is quite conservative."

They drove on for a few minutes in silence, then Phil opened up with questions about art, and soon was asking about a painting in the Old Gallery of the Museum of Fine Arts he had seen which was attributed to Vermeer.

"You know, Dr. Szabolcsi, I have a great fervor for Vermeer, and I've seen most of his thirty-five or so paintings. How certain are we that that woman's portrait is one of his?"

"Not certain at all. What do *you* think? Is it a forgery?"

"I've examined it often. There is no question it *could* be a Vermeer. But I know he has some imitators. Have you heard about that incredible Dutch forger, Van Meegeren? He could imitate Vermeer so precisely as to fool even the experts. He fooled the Nazis, especially that notorious collector of stolen art, Hermann Goering. But this one in the National Gallery, well, who knows?"

Forgery! The word evoked the question raised by Ilona, to whom her AVO friend had implied that possibility concerning the manuscript. Should he ask Szabolcsi about it? Phil decided against introducing such a likelihood at this time. There were so many other factors yet to be explored, plus the whole Soviet syndrome.

They passed a small road sign in the shape of an arrow on which was written "Martonvásár." Phil felt a slightly heightened tension within him as they turned onto a narrower road and drove through a wooded area where they parked. Ahead, he saw a large pond. Szabolcsi led the way to a wooden foot bridge and they crossed over to the island on which the Brunsvik castle stood.

It was an imposing structure, overgrown with ivy. As they neared, Szabolcsi pointed a finger at a sign which identified the building as the Agricultural Research Institute of the Hungarian Academy of Sciences, his face displaying derision.

"As you can see, our socialist planners have determined that this historic place should no longer serve only the interests of musicology but figure out how to grow better wheat. I suppose that is not unimportant, but could they not have found another place for their agrarian experiments? *Szegény* Beethoven."

Poor Beethoven is right, Phil thought, as they entered the castle. Szabolcsi initiated a running commentary as they began their tour:

"It was in 1870, on the 100th anniversary of Beethoven's birth, that a Hungarian magazine first took note of the connection between Beethoven and the Brunsviks in Martonvásár. Then in 1927, on the 100th anniversary of his death, some good research uncovered much information about these connections, as well as Therese's diaries.

"Following the war, the socialist regime converted the castle into the research institute you see now, but in 1956 the Vienna Beethoven Society and the Budapest Philharmonic Orchestra held a joint celebration, dedicating a concert to the Master's music.

"That led in the following year to an agreement by the Academy of Sciences to provide two rooms of the castle for a small Beethoven Museum, and in 1959 the Beethoven Museum was officially opened. Since 1960, there have been Beethoven concerts in the park behind the castle. If you look through these windows you will see that huge bust of Beethoven, which is where the orchestra performs."

They entered the first of the two rooms. In the middle was a statue of the composer—the first of four in the museum—and Phil studied the showcases which contained parts of letters, notes, and programs, plus the score of the King Stefan Overture, which Beethoven had composed, at the request of Franz Brunsvik, for the opening of a theatre in Pest.

The second room displayed copies of letters written to Josephine Brunsvik, Therese's sister, who, some have believed, was Beethoven's mysterious Immortal Beloved. In a medallion was a lock of his hair. The room also contained the Brunsvik family piano.

"For musicologists, this piano does not compare in value or interest to the Beethoven piano in the National Museum in Budapest," Szabolcsi said, wiping his glasses. "You have seen it, of course."

"Yes, I have," Phil replied, "the piano made by Thomas Broadwood of London in 1818 especially for the deaf composer."

"Correct," Szabolcsi said, nodding approvingly. "It is slightly smaller than today's pianos, only six octaves, and made of mahogany. The Broadwood firm was especially proud of its client and put Beethoven's name on a plaque on the piano. After he died, it was bought by a music publisher who gave it to Ferenc—you say Franz—Liszt in Weimar."

They walked out of the castle into a serene and cool park. After they had sat on a bench for a few moments, Phil broke the silence—

"So this is Martonvásár. Is everything that connects Beethoven to Hungary here?"

"No, not completely. There are a few things elsewhere—a letter in the Esztergom archives, another in Szombathély. But, my dear young colleague, I know them and they will not be helpful. The fact is, we are no nearer to solving our problem than before. For you, this is a first exposure to this place. I have been here many, many times, especially to the concerts. It is inspiring to sit here on a warm summer evening and hear the familiar music. Today, I have accompanied you for reasons of friendship and not because I thought there was anything here to enlighten us. As for Fekete's claim of having found the manuscript in a closet of Therese's bedroom, well, now that you have been here, you can see how improbable that is. Besides, you have good reason to believe otherwise, and you have convinced me too."

They crossed over the pond on the narrow bridge and drove back to Budapest. The answer, if there was one, Phil thought, had to be coming from the Soviet sources he had been cultivating. He might know more in two weeks, but he was growing increasingly impatient.

Twenty-Eight

Ambassador Quigley's second Fourth of July outdoor party was well-attended and Phil observed that his own contacts showed up in even greater force than the previous year. Everyone arrived early and the Quigleys, standing on the receiving line in the expansive garden, were unable to keep up with the guests as they flowed past and rapidly made for the refreshment tables.

Phil was standing next to the Garlands on the receiving line and after ten minutes and almost one hundred guests, the DCM leaned across Sarah and said to him—"Any future boulevards yet?"

Phil laughed—"Only some side-alleys."

Just as Sarah asked what *that* was about, István Szirmai entered the Residence to the amazement of Ambassador Quigley, the DCM and the PAO. They acknowledged this to be a first, inasmuch as the entire Politburo was invited to the Fourth of July party every year, but since 1956, not one had ever come.

After Szirmai had shaken their hands and vanished into the crowd, the DCM asked Phil—"What's your guess? When his time comes, what'll they name after him?"

"Unless he's authored some poetry we don't know about, my guess is—nothing. The Hungarians—communists and non-communists—all idolize poets. Old political figures, however, like Rákóczi, stand a better chance. Then, of course, there's Lenin . . ."

From the moment of Szirmai's entrance, Phil watched him out of the corner of his eye, hoping at some opportune moment for a conversation.

Phil was also watching for his Soviet counterpart. When drawing up his list of invitations, Phil had asked Garland if he might add Adamyants' name, and Garland had consented. When the receiving line finally broke up and the American staff dispersed, Phil was disappointed that his Armenian colleague had not come. Ten minutes later, as he walked around to make certain no guests were unattended, he felt a tap on his shoulder.

"Hello, Phil. Very kind of you to invite me. I'm sure it was your doing."

Phil beamed as he recognized the voice, turned and greeted Adamyants cordially. He apologized for being late and said—"Coming here today saves me a phone call, Phil. I was wondering if you are free for lunch tomorrow."

"Yes I am. Usual place?"

"*Hüvös Völgy*? One o'clock?"

"Suits me fine. See you then."

Spotting Szirmai, who was busily engaged with the Soviet Ambassador only ten feet away, Phil loitered close by until he saw them part. He ambled up to Szirmai and greeted him in Hungarian.

"We are honored to have you here, Szirmai *úr*. Thank you also for coming to the Ambassador's dinner for Garrison Portland."

Szirmai grunted—"It was an opportunity to explore your government's thinking about the larger issues."

"I hope your discussions were fruitful."

Szirmai eyed him silently as he sipped his drink, and replied—"You are assuming that the Politburo's great liberal might find common ground with Mr. Portland," he said with the suggestion of a smile, underlining the words 'great liberal' by a change of intonation. "Do not be too taken by an article I have just published. I know you follow such things, and your Hungarian is more than adequate. Let me give you a word of advice. When such things appear in print in our publications, they are for

Hungarian consumption, and must be read through Hungarian eyes, not through yours. Do not be misled."

Phil sensed having broken through a barrier that always existed in discussions with Party officials, and was delighted to hear these words from so senior a Hungarian communist.

"But reading your article even through American eyes, you must admit, Szirmai *úr,* could stir some interest in our Embassy and our government."

"I repeat—do not be misled. Tell me, did that charming woman enjoy her return to Budapest?"

Szirmai clearly did not wish his political views to be explored further.

"Yes, very much. I also learned some history, such as the various previous names for *Népköztársaság utja.*"

"You mean, of course, *Andrássy út,*" Szirmai laughed loudly at his own little joke. Turning serious, he continued—"Her father was a man I revered, even though I was already a young communist and he would point out our philosophical differences. But there was something else about Harsányi that endeared me to him—the fact that my being a Jew never seemed to matter."

Phil was at first surprised by this open admission, but realized a moment later that Szirmai must be aware how widely his heritage was known. What followed, however, astonished him even more.

"It is a matter of concern to us that anti-Semitism is ingrained in our society, even after the horrors of the Nazis and the Arrow Cross. You know what I am talking about?" Szirmai asked.

Phil nodded, incredulous at this turn of the conversation.

"But what is particularly offensive—no, even worse, outrageous, obscene—is the existence of anti-Semitism among some Hungarian Jews. I caution you to beware of it. *Tsudesutyun,*" he concluded, and turned abruptly to chat with Tibor Déry.

Phil was astounded and stared in astonishment at the bulky figure, not only because of Szirmai's candor but also for his parting "Farewell"—*in Armenian!*

He quickly walked over to Garland, led him by the arm to a secluded corner of the Residence garden and related what had happened.

"That can only mean he knows exactly who you are. Is it from the AVO, do you think?"

"I have no idea. He never addressed me by name."

"But he sure as hell knows some things about you. What's all this about anti-Semitism and Hungarian Jews?"

"I meant to tell you about that," Phil said, reproaching himself that he already hadn't. By the time he had finished repeating what Ilona had told him of her conversation with Szirmai, Phil was flushed and perspiring. Garland laid a hand on his shoulder and said—"Phil, I must say, I may've misjudged the relevance to our Embassy of your manuscript search, but it certainly has led you into some of the more obscure corners of Hungarian life."

Phil was still suffused with excitement the next day when he drove to the wooded spot, parked and entered the *Hüvös Völgy*. Adamyants was already there and waved him to the corner table where he was seated. He seemed very relaxed and in high spirits and moments later revealed why.

"Phil, I have reason to believe that very soon, some of the mystery of this entire business with the Beethoven manuscript will be cleared up for you. I know it has been difficult, and often frustrating. But the reason for seeing you today is to ask that you keep next Friday afternoon free."

Phil raised his eyebrows—"Does that mean what I think it means?"

"It does. Can you make it then?"

"Nothing would deter me, Krikor. I can't wait to find out more."

"Well, I can't guarantee anything but I do know that if Yuri Vladimirovich wants to see you again, it is another step forward."

"Sounds Leninesque, Krikor—one step forward but, and I hate to say it, two steps back?"

Krikor laughed heartily—"Nothing ideological about this, dear friend. I am delighted that you can be there."

Phil studied Adamyants for a few moments, the previous day's event still very much on his mind, and asked—"Krikor, how well do you know Szirmai?"

"Oh. the official you were talking to at your party . . . for quite some time, I noted. Yes, we've met, but I don't know him well. I've been present when Szirmai has come to our Embassy to meet with Comrade Andropov. Nice man, don't you think?"

It was the kind of question to which he obviously didn't expect a reply as he beckoned for the check. Phil also knew at that moment that he would not get a straight answer to *any* question about Szirmai.

On Friday afternoon at three, Phil rang the bell of Adamyants' apartment. His friend opened the door with a big smile. Once inside, Phil beheld the gaunt figure of Yuri Vladimirovich Andropov standing by the window.

"Good afternoon, Mr. Faljian," he said in accented English. "I am pleased to see you again."

"And I am pleased to be here, Mr. Andropov. I wonder if it is appropriate that I congratulate you on your appointment."

Andropov didn't catch the meaning of the last part and looked questioningly at Adamyants. A quick translation into Russian brought a smile to his lips. He now continued in Russian—

"Some might think twice before offering me congratulations. I mean not only in Washington but in Moscow."

Adamyants translated simultaneously as Phil continued in English—"I don't understand. Surely, it is a major step up the Soviet ladder, if you don't mind my saying so."

"Certainly I do not mind, and you are right, it is a move up. But a move to a position that seems to be anathema to many. The chief of the KGB is some kind of devil. Haven't you been trained to think so?"

Phil looked at Andropov and was struck by that strange enigmatic smile, which seemed to have no meaning and yet conveyed a sense of something that was undecipherable and disconcerting.

"Well, I would be disingenuous to deny that when we speak of the KGB, we think of unpleasant things, like kidnaping, terrorism, murder."

Andropov's smile disappeared abruptly and he replied—"Those will be things of the past," and sat down. "Now, let me proceed with the matter which preoccupies you and, I might add, us as well, namely the manuscript. Up until a short while ago, I seriously suspected that you were the Station Chief of the American Embassy."

Phil looked with alarm at Andropov and sat down, listening intently.

"I see that that surprises you. In your shoes, I would react the same way. But if you were in our shoes and observed an American diplomat running all over town meeting people of influence and position in the Party, in journalistic and cultural life, wouldn't you wonder what this fellow was up to?"

"Perhaps," Phil agreed, then added defensively, "but what if he was simply trying to learn as much as he could about the country and what intelligent people were thinking and how they felt about the government and the system?"

"Ah, that is what *you* say. But what if his role was not that at all but simply to recruit a staff for an American intelligence network in Hungary? What do you say to that?"

The enigmatic smile returned.

"I would say, that is sheer nonsense. No offense, Mr. Andropov. We are having a frank talk and I hope you will permit me candid comments."

"Of course, of course. Absolutely no offense taken."

"But you implied before that that is what you believed until recently. What changed your mind?"

Andropov seemed in thought for a moment before he replied—"My new post. When I assumed it, one of the first things I did was to review the files of American Embassy personnel in Moscow and throughout East Europe. Hungary was high on my list. I am certain it is no secret to you that all of you in your Embassy are under constant surveillance. Your FBI does the same to us in Washington."

"So, what you are saying is that you are convinced that I am not the Station Chief. Are you that certain?"

"Yes, absolutely certain, because I now know who the Station Chief is."

Phil avoided probing further, fearful that by some facial reaction he might confirm what Andropov seemed already to know. Instead, he joked—"Maybe we have two."

Andropov laughed—"No, my friend, you have only one. With the small staff of your Embassy, you cannot afford more than one. But that too is not why I wanted to talk to you today."

Phil looked at him expectantly and waited.

"I now know for a fact that your interest in this manuscript is genuine. Your focus is on the music and its inherent value as music and on its worth as a cultural treasure."

The smile was gone and Andropov was speaking earnestly. Peering at Phil through the thick lenses of his rimless glasses, he said—"We, more specifically I, no longer object to your search for this manuscript. In fact, I'm going to facilitate your search. Comrade Adamov informs me that you wish to consult a Dr. Keilbert in Berlin, in *our* part of Berlin. I encourage you to do so. And when you return, I hope you will share what you learn there with us. Because if you do, *all* of us will benefit, especially you. It may very well be the information we all seek. In other words, my Armenian friend, the key to it all."

To Phil, that was as enigmatic as the smile that accompanied it. Andropov then said something in Russian to Adamov, and turned to Phil again—"I must leave you now, but you should know that I have authorized Comrade Adamov to help you. He believes in you and that is good enough for me. I know that both of you are Armenian. I happen to like Armenians, and that is another reason I agreed to this meeting. Besides . . ." he paused and smiled inscrutably again, ". . . being Armenian is very relevant to this matter. Please excuse me if I must go. Good luck."

He arose, shook hands and was escorted out by Adamyants, who returned and looked long at Phil.

"Krikor, may I ask what that was all about? Especially the business about the relevance of being Armenian?"

"In good time, Phil. Patience."

"No, dammit, I have no patience left. Can't you tell me anything?" Adamyants frowned, sat down and lit a cigarette.

"Phil, I can well understand your irritation, and I sympathise fully with you. But believe me, the time is very, very near when I can let it all out. By the way, you have kept your promise not to reveal these meetings, I hope."

"Yes, yes, yes, Krikor. I have kept my word. And I sure as hell won't divulge that the head of the Soviet Secret Police and I have been meeting in the apartment of a Soviet diplomat in Budapest. Everyone in my Embassy would consider me some kind of traitor. By the way, Krikor, now that you guys are convinced I'm not CIA, convince me that you aren't KGB?"

Adamyants was completely taken aback by the question,especially since Phil asked it aggressively. He responded in kind—"You shouldn't ask me a question like that."

"Are you kidding? After the conversation that just took place a few moments ago?"

There was a sudden tension between them that was new to their relationship. Phil regretted that he had raised the question almost as soon as he had asked it, but he had become irritated with the thought that he was being manipulated like a marionette. When he saw the impact on Adamyants, he softened immediately, reached out and touched his arm—"Krikor *jon* "—an Armenian term of endearment—"I didn't mean to offend you, but I've had it up to here," drawing a forefinger across his throat. "Surely, you can understand that? I've been looking for a manuscript by Ludwig van Beethoven that I have reason to believe may exist, and if it does, may or may not be genuine, and whether it is or not, may or may not be in Hungary. That's all. Quite simple. But what happens? Suddenly, there is interest from unexpected quarters, largely from you guys, who are no longer mystery men but embodied by a very real, and I might add, imposing person who was standing right over there just a few minutes ago. So, please understand."

Adamyants took several drags on his cigarette, then leaned back in the large chair in which Andropov had sat, stared at Phil, and said—"Perhaps it is I who should apologize, Phil. Of course I understand your irritation. It's just that, well, it might be better if you didn't ask that kind of question. Agreed?"

"Allright, agreed. Tell me more about Andropov. He seems most intriguing. Does he ever open up to you about . . . anything?"

"He does, Phil, he does. I have become very close to him. If the reaction to him in our Embassy reflects the reaction in Moscow, you can be sure there are a lot of worried people around. My guess is that the only senior official who doesn't fear him is Suslov."

"Because they became good friends after the Hungarian Revolt?"

"Oh no, not at all. Suslov is a scary kind of guy himself—the Grey Eminence of Soviet Ideology. I've seen him often and to me, there is something menacing, threatening in his very presence. They seem to have a relationship based on mutual fear, but don't kid yourself, when you're the head of the KGB, you surely have the upper hand. The essential thing about Suslov is that he is an absolute puritan in every aspect of his life. That aspect of Suslov has won him Comrade Andropov's respect.

"Comrade Andropov told me last night—we stayed up until three in the morning—that in his travels throughout the Soviet Union, he searches for people who will some day make up his cadre. These are people who, like him, are ideological communists who want to transform the system by ridding it of corruption. He has mentioned a few to me. I don't know them, have never even heard of them. He seemed particularly impressed by someone named, I think, Shevardnadze, a police chief in Georgia. In

Azerbaijan, he likes the KGB chief, someone named Aliyev. Then there is Stavropol, the place that I mentioned to you once, where he was born. In Stavropol, he has a special fondness for the Party chief, whose name is Gorbachev.

"Some day, I wouldn't be surprised if he brings all of them to Moscow. He told me that in 1956, when he was in Stavropol for treatment of his diabetes, Gorbachev gave him a first-hand account of the Twentieth Party Congress in Moscow at which Khrushchev had exposed Stalin's crimes. Yuri Vladimirovich said that when Gorbachev described the speech, he seemed to be on fire with enthusiasm.

"Yuri Vladimirovich then said a curious thing, which might help you understand him. He said that while most of what Stalin did was sheer savagery and that many innocent and harmless people were killed, some dangerous people deserved their fate, but a few others did not. I asked him if he could clarify the difference between these two kinds of victims, and he replied—'They were all out and out criminals—rapists, thieves, murderers. And why did I think they didn't deserve to die? Because the ripples that they make in the great Soviet lake are nothing compared to those who subvert all we have built up over these many years—those who would undermine our entire society. It is not crime that destroys a state, but subversive ideas.'"

Adamyants concluded his recital—"I guess that tells you something about the future fate of dissidence under Comrade Andropov's KGB."

"That is ominous, very ominous, Krikor. Some of it, I suppose, makes sense. But that is all domestic. Does he ever talk about Intelligence, I mean like espionage?"

"No, not in so many words. But after a few drinks—he likes whiskey, by the way—he said an interesting thing, which I can tell you, if the pledge still holds."

"It does."

"He told me about meeting Kim Philby, the British Soviet agent who escaped from Lebanon four years ago to—did you know?—Armenia. Yuri Vladimirovich said he didn't like Philby from the first moment, developed a cool relationship with him and never fully trusted him. He gave two reasons for that: anyone who betrayed the country of his birth could more readily betray the country of his adoption, and second, Philby did not do it for money but for ideology, and Yuri Vladimirovich said he did not trust ideological spies."

It was getting late. Phil took a long breath, slapped his thighs and arose to go, as Adamyants said—"Phil, I made you a promise, and now I'd like to keep it. I've made all the arrangements for your trip to Berlin to talk to your Beethoven scholar. It needed lots of telephoning between here and our Embassy in Berlin and it wasn't easy. But . . ." he smirked, ". . . dropping Comrade Andropov's name these days works like magic. It will be a one-day trip. That should be enough. This document here—please take it—provides you with special authorization. Under no circumstances will you have to show your passport for stamping.. You will be met by someone there just before Passport Control. He will be your escort and your guide."

"Uh, Krikor, I think you know my Russian is virtually non-existent."

Adamyants gave him a sly smile—"Once you are met, you won't need Russian. Or German. Or even English."

EAST BERLIN–LEIPZIG–DRESDEN

EAST GERMANY

1967

Twenty-Nine

Phil made two quick decisions: first, that he would not inform even the DCM of his whereabouts on the day he would be absent, and second, that he would make his phone call to Keilbert from an outside line. His reasoning on the first decision was that even if he faked a trip to some outlying place in Hungary, the DCM would want a phone number where he could be reached. On the second, he wanted no record in the Embassy logs of a phone call to the German Democratic Republic.

He entered the Budapest Central Post Office, and went into a booth. Adamyants had gotten the phone number of the East Berlin *Staatsbibliothek* for him.

"*Guten Tag. Ich möchte mit Herr Doktor Keilberth sprechen, bitte.*"

"*Ein Moment, bitte.*" A long pause, then—"Keilberth."

"*Doktor* Keilberth, *mein Name ist* Faljian. *Ich bin Amerikaner.*"

"You can speak English, if you like," came the accented reply.

"Thank you, sir. I am sorry to trouble you, but I have . . ."

"Where are you calling from?"

"From Budapest."

"Hungary? And you are an American?" Keilberth's voice reflected surprise.

"Dr. Keilbert, I do not have much time, so I would like to make an appointment with you for this Friday."

"Here in Berlin?"

"Yes, I have something very important to discuss with you."

"How do you even have my name?"

"Sir, anyone who is interested in Beethoven knows your name."

"Ah, so it is Beethoven that brings you here. Good. I shall expect you sometime Friday morning."

Phil was very pleased. He returned to the Embassy and looked again at the special document of authorization Adamyants had given him. It covered the time period of three days beginning Thursday and was in German, with all kinds of rubber stamps and initials on it, and dominated by one huge hammer and sickle. He felt his nerves tingle. Was he doing the right thing by keeping this all secret even from the DCM, his close friend, Jim Garland? No, he wasn't, he convinced himself but for the time being it had to remain secret.

On Thursday morning, at the crack of dawn, he quietly rolled his car down the steep hill of his residence to avoid making any sounds and drove to *Ferihegy* Airport. The airport was almost empty, but an Interflug flight to East Berlin was scheduled and Phil got on it. He was one of only ten people.

Just under two hours later, the flimsy Soviet-made plane landed at *Schoenefeld* Airport on the outskirts of East Berlin. As he stepped down from the plane onto the tarmac, Phil felt a sense of guilty excitement. He was in the German Democratic Republic, he was illegally there, but he was also nearer, he felt, to revelations about the Beethoven manuscript.

Having had nothing to check, he strode with his attaché case into the Arrival Hall and looked around. His eye caught a young man of clearly German features who had been reading *Neues Deutschland,* the East German party newspaper, but who looked up, folded his newspaper and watched him. This could not be my contact, Phil thought, or is it? He walked slowly through the glass doors towards Passport Control, but remembered what Adamyants had told him and stopped. The German, who had risen meanwhile and was following him, also stopped. Phil was in a quandary as to his next move, when suddenly a heavy-set, dark-complexioned male rushed through Passport Control and called out—

"*Herr* Faljian?"

He felt that relief one experiences on foreign soil when suddenly recognized. He replied happily—"*Jawohl, ich bin* Faljian," as the man walked quickly up to him, extended his hand and exclaimed—"*Parev, Hayrenagits!*""

Phil stared at him dumbfounded. The last thing he had expected to hear in the GDR was Armenian, yet here was a total stranger greeting him and addressing him as compatriot.

"*Parev,*" he replied, returning the greeting but otherwise speechless, realizing what Krikor meant about Russian or German.

"My name is Sahak," the stranger said, continuing in Armenian,"and I will be your escort, driver, guide and anything else I can do for you while you are here today. Let me have your Document of Authorization so we can go through Passport Control."

They did and were waved on through when the GDR officials saw Sahak. Outside on the sidewalk he told Phil to wait while he retrieved his car. As he walked towards the diplomatic parking area, Phil observed the German standing just inside the airport doors, still watching him. When Sahak drove up in a black Mercedes and got out, Phil said—"Sahak, I'm being watched by that fellow at the door. Is that part of today's program?"

"No, it isn't. Wait a moment."

Sahak entered the door and talked to the German, then took out his wallet and showed him something. Phil observed the German come to attention with a slight bow of his head. Sahak emerged, smiled and said—"He won't bother us again."

They drove off towards Berlin, at first in silence, until Phil asked—"Sahak, you don't have to answer if you don't want to, but, that guy wasn't one of *your* people, was he?"

Sahak looked at him quickly in the rearview mirror and said—"*Our* people aren't as obvious as *these* people, compatriot. The *Stasi* has much to learn."

Phil hadn't heard that word for years—short for

Staatssicherheitsdienst, State Security Service—and he felt a warmth towards Sahak for revealing the source of the surveillance on such short acquaintance. 'That old Armenian . . . something" he asked himself? They drove on an uncrowded highway towards the GDR capital, which the Western Allies occupying it did not recognize as the capital because they did not recognize the state which claimed it to be its capital. The German proletariat had long since arrived at their work places and, Phil thought, if he remembered his earlier German experiences correctly, were probably having their *zweites Frühstück*—second breakfast—at this hour.

From afar he beheld the high rise apartment buildings of the city and eventually the wide avenue known as *Karl Marx Allee*, a name with more staying power than its predecessor, *Stalin Allee*. Sahak turned onto *Unter den Linden*, lined with lovely small trees, slowed down and then parked in front of a grandiose grey stone building.

"This is the *Staatsbibliothek,* compatriot. Take as long as you want."

Phil got out but couldn't resist looking up and down the famed street: the State Opera, the Tomb of the Unknown Soldier, now dedicated to the 'Victims of Fascism,' Humboldt University, the towering Protestant Cathedral, still damaged by bombs, Bebelplatz, where the Nazis had staged their book-burnings, the huge Soviet Embassy up the street, and in the distance, separating the Soviet Occupied part of Berlin from the three Western sectors, the massive Brandenburg Gate. For a few moments, Phil felt overcome with the thrill of place and time. Just the history alone of this city, he thought, is enough to be overwhelming.

Sahak, leaning against the car, was watching him with a small grin, as though he understood what was going through Phil's mind. Phil waved to him and entered the great library. The Music Division was on the second floor and within minutes he had climbed the winding staircase and entered Dr. Keilbert's office and was shaking hands with the eminent musicologist.

Keilbert was a large man with a modest manner but eager to discuss any aspect of music—"I am especially pleased to meet an American musicologist. We do not have such opportunities often, you know."

Phil did not broach the subject of his special interest just yet and allowed Keilbert to talk about his valuable collection of original manuscripts and scores. When he brought out several from the vaults and proudly spread them out, Phil asked why some were in better condition than others. Keilbert seemed uncomfortable at the question initially, but soon warmed up, after talking about climate, humidity and human carelessness—"Let me be quite frank, Mr. Faljian. Between the Nazis and the Russians, I'm afraid these treasures have not fared so well. The Nazis had little understanding for such things, and as for the Russians, well, at the end of the war, so-called 'cultural officers' collected large amounts of our treasures and carted them off to the Soviet Union. Whatever we got back we can thank Khrushchev for. That is only part of the story, however, and while I am not sympathetic to the Soviets, I must say that the larger blame goes to the Poles."

"But there were no Polish troops in Berlin, as far as I know."

"Yes, you are quite right. Let me explain. During the war, many of our most valuable treasures were taken to Middle Silesia and stored in salt mines. We recorded thirty-six sites. But when the war was over and Silesia was ceded to Poland, the Poles transferred them all to Krakow, where they still are today. Would you like to know the names of some of the scores?"

"I have an idea I am about to be stunned."

"You are. How about: Beethoven's Seventh and Ninth Symphonies, Mozart's entire *Magic Flute,* his *Jupiter* Symphony and all of the Piano and Violin Concertos, plus string quartets by all the masters. And that, my dear colleague, is only a part. Do you know how many scores I am talking about altogether? Over 2000."

Phil was speechless and sat in silence as a secretary brought two cups of coffee. He noted to himself that they were not *feketes,* which brought him around to his subject. But first he asked—

"Tell me, Dr. Keilbert, with all these manuscripts still missing from your vaults, what *do* you have that is of value?"

Keilbert went out of the office for five minutes and when he returned, his arms were full. Laying down a large manuscript on the table, he said—"This is my greatest treasure—Johann Sebastian Bach's *St.Matthew Passion*. Pick it up, Mr. Faljian, touch it, feel it, and appreciate that Bach himself held this in his very own hands."

Phil felt the hairs rise on the nape of his neck. He had never seen an original manuscript by Bach. The marvelously symmetrical notes, especially the gracefully drawn sixteenth notes, were in themselves works of art, and reminded him of the Bach poster on his office wall. When he had perused its pages, Dr.Keilbert showed him original letters and notes written by Beethoven, and some piano scores, the contrast of which with Bach were almost shocking.

"Here is the *Appassionata* Sonata, for instance. Look at the crossed-out sections, the smudge marks, the general image of carelessness and rapid composition. Beethoven to the core. I'd like to give you a facsimile of it, if I may."

Phil said he would be flattered and delighted to receive it.

"The very last Piano Sonata, opus 111, is even worse. Let me give you a facsimile of that too."

Phil accepted both facsimiles and thanked his host profusely. He felt perhaps the time had come, since Beethoven had surfaced in the conversation, to make his query.

"Dr. Keilbert, as you are surely aware, I did not come here to admire your musical treasures. Although, let me say, that was a experience I did not anticipate."

"I have assumed, Mr. Faljian, that you had something else in mind. An American does not come to me, in defiance of his government's ban on travel to the GDR, just to examine my manuscripts. On the telephone, you mentioned Beethoven. What specifically do you have in mind?"

Phil felt a certain hesitation in asking his question. He was in some awe in the presence of this enormously knowledgeable and gifted musical scientist and wondered if he would not be risking ridicule. But in view of the effort he and others had obviously made to make this trip a reality, he went ahead.

"If you will indulge me, Dr. Keilbert, I have come all this way, illegallly as you noted, to inquire of you about one particular aspect of Beethoven's musical creativity, and to ask you some specific questions."

Keilbert nodded and waved his hand for Phil to proceed.

"As I most certainly needn't tell *you,* from his earliest compositions, Beethoven employed the cello in his chamber music, never centrally but always in concert with other instruments. His sole concentration on the instrument produced his five sonatas for cello and piano. But never a full work for cello and orchestra. I discount the Triple Concerto as negligible.

"I have reason to believe that Beethoven did in fact write a piece, possibly a Concerto for Cello and Orchestra, which for reasons not known, he did not complete as a three-movement work, nor did he publish what he had completed. I also have some grounds, though not as firm, for believing that he may have worked on such a concerto in the year 1817, which, as you more than most of us know, was for him a relatively barren year. I would appreciate any comment you would care to make."

Dr. Keilbert sat statue-like, looking at Phil for a full minute, and then, clearing his throat, said—"What you have been describing has been rumored for some time in German musicological circles. It *is* a mystery why the Master chose not to write a major work for cello and orchestra. In his sixteen string quartets, he created some of the most beautifully crafted parts for the cello. And, as you undoubtedly know, for you have obviously done much research already, a number of his closest friends were cellists. In fact, strikingly, as I am sure you have also become aware, they were all *Hungarian* cellists. But may I ask how an *American* musicologist would know of it?"

Phil repeated the bare outlines of his meeting with von Hase, to which Keilbert responded—"Ah, I see. So, now, you want my opinion, I assume, on two things: first, whether Beethoven did compose such a work, and second, when. Well, unfortunately, I am sad to say that I have no direct knowledge of either to pass on to you. Despite the rumors, I myself have never seen any indication that Beethoven even planned such a work."

"Nothing at all in his Conversation Books?" Phil hoped to draw on Keilbert's vast knowledge of Beethoven's final years of deafness when he could only respond to questions written in his notebooks.

"Nothing, dear colleague. I see you are very disappointed. Do not be. None of us has all the answers, which is my way of conveying to you that it is by no means out of the question. And I add—why should it be? There are a number of lost manuscripts. We know from a letter by Haydn that Beethoven wrote a complete Oboe Concerto, which was lost. Also lost, a fragment of a Violin Concerto. Then there are fragments which still exist because they were in his Sketch Books, such as a Duet for Viola and Cello, which you can see in the British Museum. You surely also know the famous 24-measure fragment of a Quintet, which is the very last music he ever wrote.

"However, the most important of all of these is the fragment which is to be found in his Sketch Books of a Piano Concerto. Think of that! A Piano Concerto, which would have been his sixth. Can you imagine a sixth concerto, coming after the magnificent fourth and the grand fifth?"

Keilbert became silent, his attention now inward, apparently focused on the notion he had just advanced. But as Phil was about to comment on his own expectation of what new trails such a concerto might have blazed, Keilbert returned to the matter at hand.

"Well, why not a Cello Concerto? But since *I* cannot respond to your satisfaction, I'm going to do the next best thing. Can you go to Leipzig? If you are in the GDR for only one day, your time is very limited. I understand that. But allow me to say that, in the question you are trying to resolve, you may find Leipzig more rewarding than Berlin."

Phil became visibly distressed. The plans laid out by Adamyants did not include any travel beyond Berlin. Even if he agreed to go, would Sahak agree to take him there? Keilbert saw Phil's concern and asked if transportation was the problem. Phil begged to be excused for a few moments and ran downstairs to the street.

"Sahak, something urgent requires me to go to Leipzig. Would you be willing to drive me, and if so, how long would that take?"

The reaction on Sahak's face told Phil that the suggestion, while unexpected, was not outlandish.

"Normally three hours, compatriot, but I can make it in less. Is it absolutely necessary that you go there? Well, if you have to go, let's go. My instructions are to take you wherever you want to go."

Phil almost embraced him for joy, hurried upstairs and told Keilbert the trip was on.

"Now, please tell me where to go and whom to see in Leipzig."

"You want to go to this address that I am writing down for you. The man you will want to see is a quite elderly musicologist named Dr.Werner Scheidemann."

Phil knitted his brow at mention of the name. Scheidemann. Why was that name so familiar? Of course! Von Hase had mentioned him—his personal aide at *Breitkopf und Härtel.*

"I know about Scheidemann. He was Hellmuth von Hase's assistant. He's still alive?"

"Very much alive, and alert. I'll phone him you are coming."

Phil thanked Dr. Keilbert enthusiastically and clutching his two Beethoven facsimiles hurried down the stairs and out to the car. Sahak was waiting and opened the rear door for him.

"Some sightseeing will broaden your horizons, compatriot, although I have an idea that is not why we are going to Leipzig."

"No, it isn't," Phil laughed as he entered the Mercedes.

"Well, whatever the reason, we begin now the Armenian invasion of Leipzig," Sahak exclaimed.

"Sahak," Phil called out good-naturedly, "you are mad!"

"Like all Armenians!" he shouted, looking back at Phil with a big grin as he made an illegal U-turn, barely missed two irate pedestrians, and rammed the accelerator pedal to the floor, racing down *Unter den Linden* at reckless speed.

Thirty

Once on the outskirts of East Berlin, they approached the major checkpoint where a number of cars had stopped, waiting for their papers to be approved by the border guards at the six stations. Sahak drove to one that was free, slowed down temporarily, waved his hand and drove on. Phil turned and saw the guards watching helplessly, hands on hips, as they receded in the distance. Sahak now picked up speed and they sailed down the *Autobahn*, a four-lane highway, Phil reminded himself, that Hitler had built to facilitate the rapid travel of his tanks. He saw on the speedometer that Sahak was doing 120 kms per hour, but the Mercedes was comfortable and the ride smooth. The countryside, he observed, was flat and uninteresting, and one could see for miles without any topographical hindrances.

Phil leaned forward—

"Sahak, how about some lunch?"

"My stomach is asking me the same question."

They stopped at a small eatery and Sahak suggested that they order a *Bauernfrühstück*—a large omelette with potatoes.

"German food can do things to your gut but you can never go wrong with a farmer's breakfast."

Phil looked at Sahak closely. He had good features and might even be considered handsome. His hair was black and thick and low on his brow. When he smiled, he displayed several gold teeth in front. In some respects, Phil thought, he looks more Armenian than I. Phil liked him, for his cheerful manner, his willingness to please, and his sense of humor.

He was about to ask Sahak a question when Sahak asked him first—"Tell me, compatriot, how come someone born in America speaks such good Armenian?"

"I am the product of a strict father, Sahak. He insisted I always speak Armenian and never interrupt my elders. Once, when I was five, some of his friends were over and one of them told a joke that I must have found funny. I burst out laughing. My father frowned severely and was about to rebuke me when, according to my mother, I cried out—'But Father, I laughed in Armenian!' Apparently, even he thought that was funny and I was saved."

"Your father was right. It is funny," Sahak said with a generous display of gold teeth.

"How about you, Sahak? Where are you from?"

"Most of my family was killed by the Turks in the 1915 massacres but I was able to get to Armenia and grew up in a town called Dilijan, where the air is so clean and healthy that many Armenians go there for a cure. It is where I attended school, after which I went to Yerevan to work. I joined the Party and . . . did other things, rising in the ranks."

Phil was on the verge of asking which 'other things' and 'ranks' those were, but thought better of it.

"From Yerevan, I was transferred to Moscow, but every Summer, I returned to Dilijan. To the extent I can say it, my roots are there—my older brother, who saved my life in Turkey, some cousins, distant relatives. Maybe one of these days, I'll find a nice Armenian girl. Meanwhile, I have been transferred here to Germany. The Germans don't like us—of course, they think I'm Russian—and I don't like them. How can I, after what they did to our homeland. Otherwise though, it is a very good assignment. For instance, I have met you, and that is wonderful. I really mean it. This is most enjoyable, meeting an Armenian from America who is a diplomat and who speaks our native language. Would you mind my asking about *you*?"

"Not at all, Sahak. My parents were very young when the Turkish massacres took place, and miraculously survived. They escaped to America where they later met, married and produced me. I grew up in New York in a very Armenian household in which my father never allowed me to forget my heritage."

Phil paused for a moment and decided to skip over the punishments he suffered as an Armenian child at the hands of neighborhood toughs in his street. He continued—"I developed a deep interest in music and wanted to be a music critic. I would probably have spent my life in that field either writing or teaching at a university if the war hadn't taken me."

Phil paused again, this time aware that he was being untruthful, for without the aggressive harassment of Eric Peter Kurz, he might indeed have followed a musicological career.

"After the war," he continued, "I was attracted to diplomacy"—no mention again of the problems he encountered in *that* career—"and, well, here I am, talking to a fellow Armenian in East Germany."

Sahak listened to this with intense interest, never taking his eyes off of Phil's. He reached across and touched Phil's arm—"No Armenian in the Soviet Union has ever spoken to me like this and I thank you for it. This is the very first time I consider something good having come out of the war, compatriot." Then, looking quickly at the clock on the wall, he arose—"Come, we mustn't lose any time."

They entered the car and drove on, and soon Phil spotted the smog and soot of the city. The suburbs of Leipzig were dismal, the buildings old and dirty. As Sahak slowed down, Phil looked at his watch. It had taken Sahak exactly two hours and five minutes.

He gave the address to Sahak who, after consulting with several policemen, drove to an old apartment house. Phil told him he would be at least one hour, maybe more, in case he had something else to do.

"You can always look up an old girl friend, Sahak."

"I'm not much for *Fräuleins* but who knows, maybe I'll find an Armenian damsel somewhere. The question is—can she make a good *pilaf*?"

Phil entered a courtyard, walked up three flights of stairs, found the name on a door and rang the bell. The door was opened by a wizened, bent figure. His voice was creaky but distinct—

"You must be Mr. Faljian, the American. Keilbert phoned two hours ago that you were coming," and signaled Phil to follow him into the musty rooms. The walls were lined with shelves sagging under the weight of many, many books, and a Bechstein grand piano hugged the wall near the windows. Phil was directed to a seat facing the windows opposite Scheidemann, who was almost in silhouette. His German was slow, precise and very academic—

"Keilbert told me you were a musicologist, although now a diplomat. According to him, you are interested in a manuscript by Beethoven. More specifically, concerning a possible Cello Concerto, and that you are searching for this manuscript. Is that correct?"

"Absolutely correct, Dr. Scheidemann. Can you help me?"

"I may perhaps, young man. You will have to determine that for yourself, after our conversation. But first, may I ask when you last saw my chief for whom I have the highest regard. I mean Hellmuth von Hase."

"I first saw him in 1945 when he came to me for assistance, which I gave. In gratitude, he told me about the Beethoven manuscript. I was very saddened to learn of his death. I can understand your esteem for him. I liked and respected him and everything I have learned about him has only reinforced my view."

"I am pleased to hear you speak like that about him. He phoned me from Wiesbaden a few times to inquire after my health. Can you believe that? I was so pleased to know that he re-opened our firm in West Germany. Allright, young man. I have a story to tell you, if you have the patience and the time."

"Dear Dr. Scheidemann, I have not come this long way,

illegally I might add, to spend only a few minutes with you and then run off. Please take all the time you need."

Scheidemann looked pleased, sat back in the large, overstuffed chair, brought his hands together, his fingertips touching, looked up at the high ceiling, and began—

"My young American friend, how much do you know about the *Widerstandsbewegung* during the Third Reich?"

"The German Resistance to Hitler? Not very much, Dr. Scheidemann. Since the end of the war, I have been preoccupied with my diplomatic career in various countries. The German Resistance is a subject largely unknown to me, although I have read a little about it."

"No matter. I will explain its essential features, that is, those features essential to my story. Let me begin with a question: Does the name Carl Goerdeler mean anything to you?"

Phil felt a strange current go through him. It was the same question put to him by von Hase twenty years earlier.

"Yes, it does, and whatever I know about Goerdeler, I know from von Hase."

"That is good, because then your information will be accurate. Let me continue. Goerdeler, as you know, was the *Oberbürgermeister* of Leipzig from 1930 to 1937. I'll tell you later why he resigned, if you don't know. But now, I'm jumping ahead of myself. Let me return to the *Widerstandsbewegung*."

Scheidemann began a lengthy, detailed description of the various groups which comprised the underground opposition to Hitler. Although the opposition began loosely in the late 1930s when many senior officers of the professional *Wehrmacht* realized that the *Führer* was a vastly unprofessional military leader, by the time the war was fully underway, the opposition had hardened and distilled to four essential groups.

First, there was the military resistance to the Hitler regime, headed by General Ludwig Beck, Chief of the Army General Staff.

Then came a group from the Foreign Office, which, although

at times performing heroic diplomatic deeds, did not, according to Scheidemann, play a major role in his narrative.

Third, there was the *Kreisau* Circle, named after the Silesian estate of its leader, Graf Helmut von Moltke, possibly the most far-seeing—in terms of a post-war Germany—of all the resistance leaders.

Scheidemann paused for a moment—"Of course, we all know the name of the most famous member of this group, Claus Schenk von Stauffenberg, who will go down in history for the failed plot to kill Hitler on July 20,1944."

He then leaned forward as though to lend emphasis to what followed. The fourth resistance group, he continued, was the *Abwehr,* German Counter-Intelligence, the very center of the entire opposition to Hitler. Its leader was Admiral Wilhelm Canaris, a fascinating individual, Scheidemann stressed, who was always involved in some kind of conspiracy, such as in 1920, for instance, when he sought with arms and money to restore the Kaiser to power. In 1933, he welcomed the advent of Hitler, and as his reward, this naval officer, still in his forties, was appointed head of the *Abwehr.*

Canaris realized early on that his arch rival was Heinrich Himmler, head of the *Reichssicherheitsamt,* the Federal Security Service, into which were incorporated the *Geheimestaatspolizei,* better known as the *Gestapo,* which was responsible for internal security, and the *Sicherheitsdienst* or *SD,* responsible for external security. Its chief, serving also as Himmler's deputy, was the dreaded Reinhard Heydrich, the 'Hangman of Europe.'

Canaris befriended Heydrich, hoping somehow to neutralize any danger to the *Abwehr* because by 1939, when war began, Canaris' antipathy to Hitler had grown immeasurably. Meanwhile, the resistance cell of the *Abwehr* had become what might be termed 'the fulcrum of the opposition.' Scheidemann recited a dizzying list of names, beginning with Colonel Hans Oster, and continuing with Ernst von Dohnanyi and many others of whom Phil had never heard. He smiled gently at Scheidemann's display of the famous German 'thoroughness' in his recounting of the anti-Hitler resistance movement.

Scheidemann stopped for a moment to explain, with visible amusement, that the official view of the German Democratic Republic towards the Resistance was that it was nothing less than an attempt 'to save the foundations of the capitalistic hegemony of the monopolies,' he said, underlining the quote with a change of emphasis.

"Let me now return to Carl Goerdeler. He was, I suppose, what you would call a conservative German. In the beginning, he didn't entertain any ideas of resistance. But he did things which irritated the Nazis. As early as 1933, for instance, he refused to raise the swastika flag over the Leipzig Town Hall.

"But his antipathy towards them deepened when they began waging their anti-Semitic campaigns. For him, the last straw occurred in 1936, when the Nazis ordered the removal of Felix Mendelssohn's statue from the front of the Leipzig *Gewandhaus*. I assume you know what I am talking about."

"Absolutely. Mendelssohn was a Jew and the *Gewandhaus*, where he had conducted its great orchestra, was the most famous concert hall in all of Germany."

"Excellent! I see you are well-informed," the old man exclaimed, rubbing his bony hands together. "Now we come to the nucleus of our story. During his tenure as Lord Mayor, Goerdeler was very friendly with my old chief, *Herr Doktor* von Hase, whom he visited often. I remember so well when the Mendelssohn statue was removed because von Hase, who was the President of the *Gewandhaus*, was up in arms. My God, none of us could believe it. Mendelssohn, one of our greatest men of music.

"Beyond all that, however, Goerdeler had a far more personal reason to hate the Nazis. He had lost two sons on the Russian front and was a deeply embittered man. His hatred of Hitler became an obsession, but even so, and this is curious, he never favored assassination, only overthrow. Why? A matter of honor, of obedience, of conscience, maybe even *Führerprinzip*—respect for the leader?"

Scheidemann suddenly seemed tired and paused for a full minute to gather his strength. Phil rose, asking if he could get him some water, but was waved down. The old man took a long breath and resumed—"Then, one day well into the war, *Doktor* von Hase called me to his office and said the Lord Mayor was coming and that under no circumstances should I allow any interruptions. When he told me this, his safe was open and I distinctly recall seeing several pages of a musical manuscript spread out on his desk. He obviously had been examining it closely."

Phil's heart began to beat faster, and he asked—"A manuscript of what, Dr. Scheidemann, and by whom?"

"It was something by Beethoven, something *Doktor* von Hase had once told me he had discovered by chance, and at the time he had described it as a musical fragment. I could tell it was Beethoven from the notation. Beethoven's musical handwriting, as you well know, is very distinctive. The manuscript was upside down, but I made out the word *Konzert* at the top of the page.

"Well, Goerdeler arrived, quite excited, and they closed the door. I sensed that something was wrong."

"What was the date, do you recall?"

"I believe it was sometime towards the middle of 1943, maybe in May or June."

He fell silent for a few seconds, then added, wistfully—"You know, my field has always been music, but politics permeated everything we did in those days. Maybe even now, too. What do the French say—'Everything changes, but everything remains the same.'

"I had already heard enough around *Breitkopf und Härtel* to realize that our country was being led to its doom by a madman, and I also suspected, more than suspected I should say, that Carl Goerdeler was deeply involved in something quite dangerous. So, feeling slightly disloyal to my chief, I put my ear to the keyhole and listened.

"He was saying something about the safety of our firm and employees, and that he could not get involved.

"Goerdeler replied that he would not get him involved, but that my chief could help in a very indirect way. Now comes the most important part of what I heard that day. Goerdeler said that he had just learned something which was absolutely astonishing, and that his source was unimpeachable. He then lowered his voice, and I remember his words so distinctly—'My source is one of us—Canaris.' Do you remember when, a few moments ago, I told you of the four major groups in the Resistance? Canaris was the head of one of them, the *Abwehr.*

"Goerdeler had lowered his voice and I had to listen hard but I heard most of it. Canaris, he said, had sent him a private message to the effect that an officer on his, Canaris' staff, someone whom he trusted and who bore a name which evoked our deepest military traditions, might be an agent working for the Nazis. This could only mean, Goerdeler maintained, that the Gestapo had penetrated the ranks of the Resistance and was using this officer to build dossiers on everyone.

"I then heard Goerdeler say that it had to be the one single explanation why every plot to date had failed, and that while future plots were being planned, he was wary of putting so many lives at risk. At that moment, I was overcome with fear because I realized that what I was hearing was information whose danger potential was beyond measure. I was about to withdraw when my chief spoke and I simply had to hear his reaction to all this.

"He asked how he could help and still stay out of danger. There was a long silence, after which Goerdeler replied that he didn't know if Canaris had informed any of the others—those were his words—but that if, in the perilous days ahead, he, that is Goerdeler, should be arrested, disappear or lose his life, he wanted at least one other person, preferably an old and trusted friend, to know the identity of this traitor. He said he guessed that Canaris had given him the name as a warning to be careful if Goerdeler ever met up with the officer.

"By now, a thousand horses could not have dragged me from that keyhole, and I listened so intently that the rest of the conversation is engraved in my memory, and I can repeat it word for word.

"Goerdeler said—'If I am eliminated, let it be you, dear Hellmuth, who can warn the others. I will write the name down for you on something. What is that lying on your desk? Here give it to me.' I heard the shuffling of some papers, then Goerdeler said—'You needn't look at it now if you don't want to, but you'd better put that scrap of paper away in your private safe.'

"*Doktor* von Hase then said, and, my American friend, this will mean much to you—'That *scrap of paper*, Carl, happens to be a manuscript by Beethoven that the music world doesn't even know exists.'

"And the patriotic fervor of Goerdeler's reply is etched still in my mind—'My dear friend, let us not equate a piece of music, even by Beethoven, with the fate of our beloved Fatherland.'"

Thirty-One

A thousand thoughts and images were racing through Phil's mind as he tried to digest the significance of this new information. The saga of the Beethoven manuscript had taken an astonishing turn. That was obvious, but its ramifications were not all that clear. For one thing, the intriguing displays of Soviet interest in the manuscript and in Phil's efforts to locate it remained obscure. There was no way Scheidemann could throw any light on that. One other possibility did exist, however, and Phil decided he had nothing to lose by exploring it. He had come a long way, a way he would probably never come again, especially with so much protection, so he took the plunge.

"Dr. Scheidemann, what can you tell me about a Hungarian musicologist who was visiting around that time?"

The elderly musicologist looked up at him—"Ah, so you know about him too. Yes, the infamous Fekete, the Hungarian fascist, that reeking scum. I assume that my old chief must have told you about him. Oh God, how the *Herr Doktor* resented him, hated him. Yes, young man, you ask the right question, for Fekete may be a vital link. Let me see how much of all that I can recall.

"Fekete was always hanging around in his oily manner, flirting with the secretaries. Some, the lonely ones, were taken in by his Old World *Küss-die-Hand* style, their husbands at the front, or with no husbands at all. If you knew him, you would wonder what they saw in him, but those that found him charming were, if I may say so, not the most attractive of women.

"But what most of us recall were not these office encounters but the scandals which followed. Not with the married secretaries but their small daughters. Yes, dear colleague, that startles you, but in wartime, all kinds of things happen. That scoundrel who bore the name of Fekete apparently had a penchant for little girls. An example. My secretary was Christa Weber. A wonderful, caring woman whose husband was later killed in the defense of Berlin. Christa felt sorry for Fekete and invited him home one evening. Then several times more. But one morning when she came to work, her eyes were red from weeping. She never invited him again and forbade her daughter, a lovely child of ten, to ever visit the office when Fekete would be there.

"I apologize for the digression, young man. More relevant to our story was the fact that Fekete was always asking questions about the private safe *Doktor* von Hase had in his office and its contents. He either knew or sensed something.

"Then came that terrible night in December. Even though the Nazis had closed us down three months earlier so we could not conduct any business, some of us went in every day just out of habit. *Breitkopf und Härtel* was our lives. On the first day of December—that is in 1943—Doktor von Hase went to Dresden for a week. Three nights later, the bombers came. That night . . ."

Scheidemann stopped and wiped his brow. It was evident he was having difficulty recounting the events of the air raid, but he made the effort—"It was the most shattering experience of my life. Leipzig had been saved from bombings for more than a year, but you Allies wanted to punish us, and it was understandable. For one thing, Leipzig was the main railway junction in Central Germany, and besides, the city was massed with refugees from Berlin. It was the fiercest of all air raids, surpassed later only by Dresden.

"Around four in the morning, I was awakened by the approaching roar of planes, a truly terrifying sound for us. Then closer and closer until, minutes later, flares encircled the entire city, illuminating Leipzig as though it were noon. At 4:30 in the morning, please believe me, that is very frightening. And then, the bombs, the terrible bombs."

Scheidemann stopped, arose and walked around the dimly-lit room. Phil could see that he was overwrought and unable to speak for a few moments. But he settled down again, as before, and continued—

"Later that morning, I went to *Nürnberger Strasse* and couldn't believe my eyes. As I stood in front of the ruins, I felt as though a close member of my family had been killed. I have since read that columns of smoke from the fires rose 15,000 kilometers. I came home and phoned *Doktor* von Hase in Dresden.

"When he arrived toward evening, we went directly to the building. His initial shock was unforgettable to behold, but, do you know, his first comments were about the employees. He was happy to know that no one had been injured.

"Together, we went through the still smoking devastation in his office, and then, when he suddenly remembered the Beethoven manuscript, we began searching for it. He also told me at the time that there was a letter written by Beethoven to his great-grandfather, but that was also never found. Both it and the manuscript were no more.

"However, also missing was Fekete. The day after the raid, Fekete vanished completely. He had originally told us that he would be staying in Leipzig until Christmas, but now, three weeks before, he was gone. Presumably back to Hungary. He disappeared and so did the letter and manuscript. We could only put two and two together. That is all I can tell you, dear colleague."

"You have told me a great deal, Dr. Scheidemann, even though I am a total stranger to you."

"Not quite, Mr. Faljian. Keilbert told me how you were helpful to *Doktor* von Hase, which means you have recognized what a civilized person he is. I am grateful to you for that. And second, you are one of us, a member of the little-recognized profession of musicology. You are engaged in a noble undertaking. But besides us, and a cellist here and there, who in the world really cares whether Beethoven ever wrote a Cello Concerto?"

Phil looked with affection at the aging German, a man so steeped in the music of the past, Phil thought to himself, that when the building in which he had worked all his life was destroyed, the flame of his life must have flickered out and died as well. In the gentlest tones he could muster, Phil asked—

"Would you permit one final question, Dr. Scheidemann? Can you confirm that there was, in fact, a Beethoven manuscript in von Hase's safe at that time, and that it is highly likely that Fekete stole it?"

The old man brushed back a wisp of hair from his forehead, looked pensively at Phil, and replied—"I think I can answer in the positive to both questions. I must remind you, however, that I myself never examined the manuscript, but *Doktor* von Hase did mention it to me. Also, I did overhear him tell Lord Mayor Goerdeler that it was music by Beethoven. Nothing further."

Phil arose and Scheidemann escorted him to the door. There, Phil felt overwhelmed with gratitude and embraced the short, stooped figure, telling him—"When I arrived in Berlin this morning, I knew I might learn something from Keilbert, but I never expected to be in Leipzig, talking to you. Because of you, Dr. Scheidemann, this entire trip has been enormously gratifying. I will always remember you."

Once downstairs, he saw Sahak waiting by the Mercedes, a cigarette dangling from his mouth. Sahak brightened when he saw Phil and asked if he had had success.

"More than I expected, Sahak. Let me see, it is now two in the afternoon. My return flight to Budapest is at nine tonight."

Sahak looked suspiciously at him and said—"I have the feeling there is another bizarre request coming. So, you have seven hours yet before your flight. I can get you to *Schoenefeld* Airport in under two hours. That leaves you five hours. What is that special request that I can read in your eyes?"

Phil gave Sahak a mock punch in the chest, accompanied

by a laugh. Sahak had read him correctly and apparently was not begrudging him a little deviation here and there.

"Actually two, Sahak, but the first is easy, because it is right here in Leipzig. Can we go to the *Thomaskirche*? A policeman can direct us. It is Bach's church and for me, a very sacred place."

"That does sound easy. But what is the second request?"

"I'll tell you after we visit St. Thomas's."

Finding the church was not difficult and when Phil stood before Bach's statue and then entered the church, he felt an inner glow. The great cantor of St. Thomas was buried here and an epitaph on the crypt in the choir space identified his burial site with the simple inscription—

"Johann Sebastian Bach"

Phil walked through the church, reconstructed in the neo-Gothic style, looked at the large pipe organ, and though aware that it had long since replaced the original instrument, tried to imagine the great musician performing on it. Mozart too, Phil reminded himself, had once played on the organ in this church. A plaque on one wall noted that another great composer, Richard Wagner, had been baptised in this church, and that Martin Luther had once preached there. Perhaps most important of all, he mused, on Good Friday in the year 1729, Bach's *St. Matthew Passion*—the same great work whose manuscript score Dr. Keilbert so treasured—was performed for the very first time in this hallowed church. Phil didn't want to leave and sat in a pew and meditated for ten minutes.

He remembered Sahak waiting outside, and also that he did have another request which would certainly take much longer to fill. He walked reluctantly out of the *Thomaskirche* and went to the car. Sahak looked at him with curiosity—"Are you a religious person, compatriot? You seem overcome."

"No, Sahak, it is not so much that I am religious. But in music, Bach is for me the supreme master. You know, we bombed Leipzig in 1943 and fortunately, we damaged this church very little. This was his church, Sahak, Bach's church for twenty-seven years, where he worked as a cantor, performed and composed absolutely glorious music. On top of which, Bach is buried here."

Sahak nodded as though in understanding of Phil's emotions.

"I can see why it would affect you. But now, it is time to tell me what else you want to do . . ." he looked at his watch . . ."in the four hours you have left."

They got into the car and Phil leaned forward and said—"Sahak, I wanted to visit that church because I may never come to this country again. For that same reason, I want very much to see something else. It is not in Leipzig . . ." he hesitated, because Sahak was eyeing him in the mirror ". . . but in Dresden."

Sahak spun around, his eyes wide open, but he was grinning—

"Dear compatriot, after Dresden, will it be the moon? Do you know that Dresden is even further from Berlin? I also don't know how far that would be from here."

"Can we make an arrangement, Sahak? If we find out that it is near enough so that you can get me to the airport on time, will you take me?"

Sahak shook his head, smiled at Phil and said—

"I don't know what it is about you, compatriot, but I have difficulty saying No. Besides, being with you is much more stimulating than my normal duties. Let's find out about Dresden."

A Leipzig policeman directed them to the right road and figured it would take no more than an hour. Within ten minutes Sahak was sailing on a narrow two-lane road toward Dresden.

"Is it proper for me to ask what this very important thing is that you are going to see?"

"Certainly, Sahak. I had no intention of keeping it secret.This has nothing to do with my mission here. I happen to like art very much, but very specially, the paintings of Vermeer, a Dutch artist of the seventeenth century. In Dresden, there is one of the world's great museums, the *Zwinger*, where there are two paintings by him. I want to run in, look at them for maybe twenty or so minutes, and then we can take off for *Schoenefeld*. Why don't you come in with me?"

"Maybe I will, compatriot. Art, and music too for that matter, are not normally in my sphere of activity."

Within an hour, Phil saw the spires of the once beautiful city of Dresden, the fire-bombing of which in February 1945 had left much of the city in ruins. As they crossed the Elbe River, Phil saw how much the massive air raid had damaged some of the churches, as well as the *Semper* Opera House and the *Zwinger* Museum. The Allied raid on Dresden had clearly been far more destructive than the raid on Leipzig.

Sahak drove to the *Zwinger* parking area near the entrance. They walked to the grandly ornate entry and went through the low central arch of the reconstructed baroque building. Phil borrowed five East Marks from Sahak and bought a guide to the Gallery of Old Masters. They ascended a winding flight of stairs to the first floor where he had no difficulty locating the two Vermeers. One, *The Matchmaker,* seemed out-of-character and was almost ribald. The second, *Girl Reading A Letter,* was more characteristic and immediately recognizable as a work by the Dutch master.

Phil saw Sahak peering closely at the second.

"You prefer that one, Sahak? That shows good taste. Why?"

"I don't know why. Maybe its the way her face is lit up."

"That's because of his subtlety, his attention to shading and light. Allright. Now, how would you like to see a work that some experts consider to be the greatest painting in the history of art? It happens to be here in this very museum. Come with me."

Phil looked through his guide and found what he was looking for, and taking Sahak's arm walked with him across to the other end of the floor. He then told Sahak to turn around, and they both looked up. Hanging on the wall above their heads was *The Sistine Madonna* of Raphael. The large painting was illuminated by a skylight overhead which gave to its greenish-blue hues an ethereal aura. Phil stood in awe of its serenity and grandeur. Sahak tugged at his sleeve and whispered—"Tell me, compatriot, why is this considered so great?"

"Well, let me explain it as best *I* can. The expression on the faces of the Madonna and the Christ child, the elegance of the two figures on either side, the two mischievous cherubs below, the draperies, the balance, the symmetry—all these things add up to greatness, Sahak. Let me tell you—I wouldn't know if this *was* the greatest painting. There are so many others that I might pick. But some people, who have studied art all their lives, think it is. As someone said—"It is in the eye of the beholder.' You are a beholder now, Sahak, so make up your own mind."

"Dear compatriot, when I stand in a place such as this, with someone like you, I feel ignorant and humble. But I am flattered that you ask my opinion. Allow me to say that I am very pleased that you brought me here."

Phil looked into the insecure eyes of his escort—or guide or whatever you are, he thought—and said with feeling—

"You know, Sahak, so am I."

They walked back to the Dutch section again where Phil pointed out all the Rembrandts in the gallery.

"Can you believe that? Twelve in one museum in East Germany!"

"I had never heard of Vermeer, but Rembrandt is a familiar name. He is one of the great ones, isn't he?"

"One of the very great ones, Sahak. For me, he is to painting what Beethoven is to music—all drama and passion."

Sahak pointed to his wristwatch, Phil nodded and they left. As he held the door for Phil to enter the car, he said—"May I ask a great favor? Would you consent to sit up front with me?"

Phil beheld an anxious look in his eyes, as though fearful that the request would be rejected. He nodded, walked around the car and sat next to the driver's seat. They drove for twenty minutes before Sahak broke the silence—"I am not well educated, compatriot, and much of what you have shown me today is beyond my understanding. But something is very troubling. Just today alone, you have been talking with German experts in music, you have visited a church where the great German composer Bach worked, and you have shown me works of art which, while over my head, were collected by Germans over the centuries. These are all signs of a highly civilized people.

"But less than thirty years ago, Germans went crazy. They butchered people everywhere, invaded the Soviet Union, and almost reached *our* country, Armenia. These fascists turned my world upside down, uprooted whole nations and destroyed others. You are clearly an educated man, so please, explain to me how this could have happened?"

Phil nodded at the question to which there was no ready answer, but he made an attempt—"You are asking me something that troubles many intelligent people, Sahak. They want to know how the same people who produced Bach, Beethoven, Goethe, Schiller, Heine, Dürer, Einstein and so many others, could also build concentration camps, gas millions, slaughter children. The only answer I can give you, Sahak, is the word you used just now, *fascists*. Every country has its fascist-minded elements. There are people like that in America and, no offense, Sahak, but in your country too. And in 1933, Germany was whipped into a frenzy and *elected* the top fascist into power by an overwhelming majority. The German people were in some kind of hypnotic state, and they made Hitler and the Nazis legitimate. That is what troubles you and me.

"But as the war progressed, they began to wake up and realize their folly. Some brave souls resisted, tried to take action. Tell me, Sahak, do you know any bad Armenians?"

"Plenty, compatriot. I wouldn't give you one kopeck for some of them. Out and out criminals. Why do you ask?"

"Because there were also bad Germans, evil Germans, the fascist Germans, such as the SS and the *Gestapo*. The worst crimes in the war were committed by them. And today, Sahak, maybe other crimes are being committed by other Germans, here in the German Democratic Republic."

Sahak did not respond, his eyes straight ahead. Finally, he said—"I understand, and yet I do not understand. Maybe that's why I cannot warm up to Germans."

The drive to *Schoenefeld* was largely in darkness and Phil felt drowsy and said little. Finally, they arrived at the airport. It was a quarter past eight. Phil suggested a cup of coffee and they repaired to a small cafe in the airport.

Sahak sat silently, stirring his coffee, apparently uninterested in drinking it. After minutes of silence, during which Phil looked at him often, wondering what was going on in his mind, Sahak said—"If you will not be embarrassed, compatriot, I would like to explain something. You are a very cultured man. I am not, and the difference between us has become evident today in the few hours we have spent together. I hope you will understand that in the Soviet Union, especially Armenia, we have no time for such luxuries."

"I *do* understand that, Sahak, and you needn't feel inferior about your background, but thank you for saying it. Let me ask *you* something: Do you have any idea what I am doing here?"

Sahak shrugged his shoulders—"Yes, maybe not the whole story, but some of it. You are looking for some music. Frankly, I don't know why an American diplomat, although an Armenian in his heart, I have discovered, would be searching for music in East Germany, but I have my orders."

"Your *orders*? That strong, Sahak?"

"Yes, that strong. And what is more, from high up."

Phil peered into Sahak's eyes, trying to read something in them, and met a blank. But Sahak then did an unusual thing. He leaned over and lowering his voice, even though speaking the language no one in that airport could understand, cautioned—

"Dear compatriot, be very careful. I don't know everything, but something about my orders suggest to me that there is danger ahead, and I would not want any harm to come to you."

As they stood up, he handed Phil the Document of

Authorization, embraced him warmly, then watched as Phil walked through Passport Control and Customs, turned and they waved to each other for the last time.

Phil walked across the tarmac for his Malev return flight feeling a pang of regret at leaving his new-found friend. But as he buckled himself into his seat, his regret was replaced by a growing sense of insecurity at Sahak's parting words and what faced him in Budapest. He was tired and tried to sleep but the images and faces of this crowded, intense day kept his mind in turmoil. Additionally, throughout the return flight, he was troubled by an image he couldn't readily comprehend: a montage of Vermeer paintings and Beethoven manuscripts.

One thing above all had become clear, however: the Beethoven manuscript was no longer in itself just a rare piece of music but the carrier of some kind of information, so vital that it was being sought at a very high level in Moscow.

Further, if Sahak's warning were to be heeded, continuing the search for the manuscript could lead to consequences he had never even suspected.

"Krikor *jon*, you'd better have *all* the answers for me this time," he mumbled as the demanding activities of the long day finally took their toll and he succumbed to a troubled sleep.

BUDAPEST—FERTÖD

Hungary

Thirty-Two

Phil arrived at *Ferihegy* Airport close to midnight, got into his car in the diplomatic parking area, and drove home. Erzsébet had left a hall light on for his late arrival. He showered and collapsed into bed.

The next morning, driving down the Buda hills through *Zugliget,* past the bakery, grocery and dairy stores he knew so well, over the *Margit híd*, and even in front of Central Committee headquarters overlooking the Danube, he was overcome with the cozy feeling of being at home. In German, he thought to himself, the two words *fremd* meaning strange, and *Fremde* meaning foreigner, expressed it very well: in East Germany, he had been a foreigner in a strange country. But here in Hungary, with its muted Marxism, its intellectually intoxicating atmosphere, and—he couldn't resist the thought—its beguilingly exotic, although for him untouchable, women—he felt almost native.

When Phil entered the Embassy, Annie said that the DCM wanted to know the minute he arrived, and began phoning upstairs even before he had passed the Reception Desk.

Jim Garland was pacing up and down in his office as Phil entered.

"Phil! Where the hell have you been? What's going on that you can't even tell *me*? The Ambassador was looking for you all day yesterday, and I couldn't tell him where you were. Do you realize how stupid that makes me look? I'm supposed to know everything that goes on in this Embassy, but *you* are something else. If you were in my shoes, what would you do right now?"

"Kick me in the ass, Jim. That's what I'd do in your place."

Garland glared at him. "Where the hell were you yesterday?"

Phil decided he could no longer withhold anything from Garland, the only colleague in the Embassy who had an understanding for his operating style and objectives. He beckoned in the direction of the tank and saw the DCM mouth a silent 'Oh.' Phil obtained the key to the Secure Room, turned on the noisemaker, and they entered. The DCM leaned forward eagerly, aware he was about to hear something far beyond the routine diplomatic work he supervised in the Embassy.

Inasmuch as Garland had been previously made aware of the von Hase-Fekete-Szabolcsi connection, Phil decided to start his narrative with the initial contact he had made with Adamov. At mention of the name, Garland showed dismay.

"You've been dealing with a member of the Soviet Embassy? Are you out of your mind? What's gotten into you?"

On observing Garland's concern at mere mention of Adamov, Phil decided to eliminate all reference to Andropov. He had been uncertain as to what lengths he would go to keep his pledge to Adamyants, but his reticence now had nothing to do with the pledge and everything to do with protecting himself from abuse—and the DCM from a fit of apoplexy.

"Please let me continue, Jim, and perhaps it will not seem as sinister as you are imagining. Besides, there is a lot more that you might find equally disturbing."

Garland buried his face in his hands, shook his head, and muttered—"Allright, give me the worst. Give me everything. And please don't tell me you've been negotiating with the Politburo in Moscow about your God-damned Beethoven manuscript."

Phil shot back—"That's preposterous, Jim" but thought, 'If you only knew.'

He took a deep breath, looked at Garland, who was watching him as though expecting the Apocalypse, and began—"Through the good offices of Adamov, I was able to do something yesterday which would otherwise have been impossible, and which also opened up an entire new page in this whole story."

"I'm afraid to ask what it was."

"Not *what* it was, Jim, but *where* it was."

"Don't tell me I was close to the mark just now!"

"Not quite. Jim, I spent all of yesterday . . . in the GDR."

Had he struck the DCM with a baseball bat, the impact would have been no less forceful. Garland rose halfway from his chair, opened his mouth, and barked—"I don't believe you! Phil, tell me you're blowing bubbles."

Phil tried to remain calm. He gestured with his open hands for Garland to sit down, and continued—"There's nothing stamped in my passport, Jim. I am well aware we have no diplomatic relations with East Germany. That is where Adamov was most helpful."

"And why, may I ask, the GDR?"

Phil explained first about Dr. Keilbert in Berlin and his recommendation that Phil see Dr. Scheidemann in Leipzig.

"*You were in Leipzig too*?" The DCM had indeed become apoplectic.

"It turned out to be more important than Berlin, Jim. I originally thought that Keilbert, as an authority on Beethoven, and especially the Conversation Books, would be able to throw some light on all this. He couldn't, but suggested that Scheidemann, von Hase's former aide, might. As it was, Scheidemann told me some remarkable things which I am now going to check out with Adamov."

"With Adamov," Garland mimicked, his voice heavy with sarcasm, "your new buddy. And what interest do our Soviet friends have in all this? I am amazed, Phil, that someone with your experience doesn't smell a rat."

"Quite honestly, Jim, I don't know. It's part of the growing mystery about this entire thing. I began by looking for a musical score I first learned about some twenty years ago, and now I seem to be embroiled in some kind of cabal. All I can tell you is that, apparently, on a page of that score is a name, the name of someone who may have been a Gestapo agent whose mission it was to expose the underground resistance movement in the Third Reich."

Garland threw his hands up in despair and fell back in his chair with a heavy thud. He stared fixedly at Faljian, waiting for the next explosive revelation.

"There isn't much left to tell, Jim. I have to pick it up from there."

Garland was silent for a few moments, then said—"Phil, when you first told me about your search for this manuscript, you may recall that I told you it was not to interfere with Embassy business. But now I see that you've got some other agenda going which has *nothing*, I repeat, *nothing* to do with the U.S. national interest. How in hell do you think Washington would feel if they knew about your doings? You travel secretly to the GDR not only with the approval but the overt assistance of a Soviet Embassy officer . . ." he paused for a moment, then nodded quickly—" . . . ah, so *that's* why you invited him to our Fourth of July party. I see. Well . . . you visit with prominent people in the GDR, and travel to two cities in a country . . ."

"Excuse me, Jim, but to be truthful, it was *three* cities. The third was Dresden."

"What! Why Dresden?"

"To look at the Vermeers. Sorry, Jim."

"Three cities in a country with which we have no diplomatic relations! If I remember correctly, Berlin, Leipzig and Dresden are not all that near each other."

"I had a driver."

"A driver? Arranged by whom?"

"I guess by Adamov."

"And he agreed to take you everywhere? Who was he?"

"His name was Sahak."

"What kind of a name is that?"

"It's an Armenian name, Jim. He's Armenian, just like Adamov."

"*And just like you!*" Garland cast his eyes imploringly toward the ceiling, and called out—"Sweet mother of Jesus, spare me all these fucking Armenians!"

"Oh, Jim! Please don't ever, ever, *ever* say that. I beg you. It's so unjust. It's because we are all Armenians that this could have happened. I do owe you an apology for all this, and you can penalize me any way you want. But could you, please, for a moment look at it my way? What if I had asked your permission? Would you have allowed me to travel to the GDR? Under Soviet auspices?"

"Only if I were out of my mind."

"That's what I mean. I took a chance, a very big chance, but it worked."

"You don't really know if it worked. Right now, you're in debt to a Soviet diplomat, maybe someone who is not all what he seems. Have you thought of that? Time will tell what consequences you must bear."

"I understand your point, Jim, and promise, from here on in, no more illegal travel, and no more clandestine activity—without your knowledge. Am I forgiven?"

The DCM, his eyes steely, looked for a full half minute at Phil, then lowering and shaking his head, but his voice calm, he said—"You really are an incorrigible son of a bitch. Why do you do this to me, Phil? I thought we were friends, good friends. Allright, you leave me little choice, but you ought to know that if I do forgive you, it's against my better judgment and with reluctance. Now, go in and tell the Old Man you were at Debrecen University all day and got back too late to come to the Embassy. Incidentally, you were lucky to have missed his better half. She wandered into the Embassy around noon and happened to look into your office. I got the impression she was disappointed you were not there. You might have spent yesterday more fruitfully driving a stake through her heart than motoring around the East German countryside courtesy of the KGB."

He continued to look disapprovingly at Phil as they walked out of the tank. Phil chatted with Ambassador Quigley, who made no mention of the previous day. He seemed more interested in knowing whether Phil had made any plans for Leopold Stokowski's two days in Budapest the following month.

After Phil explained that conducting the Budapest Philharmonic was a distinct possibility, George Quigley said—"By the way, Phil, Grace wanted to know if you could take her to a few museums. Ever since Mrs. Portland praised you so much, Grace has realized she was missing out on your considerable knowledge of Hungarian culture."

"With your permission, Sir, I'll give her a call."

"Of course, my boy, do that."

'I'd rather not,' Phil mused, as he went to his office and phoned Adamyants at the Soviet Embassy.

"Hello, Krikor, I'm back and very anxious to see you. *Hüvös Völgy* tomorrow at one?"

"See you there, Phil, and I'm glad you're back because I'm just as anxious to see you."

Thirty-Three

Phil drove to the luncheon appointment in a truculent mood. It was exhilarating to hear the revelations of Scheidemann—suspecting that Adamyants had known it all along—but quite another to be dressed down by the Deputy Chief of Mission.

Jim Garland was his friend, Phil told himself, and he had not behaved as a friend should. In fact, he had displayed a degree of disloyalty which went beyond friendship and duty. Were Washington to find out, his career would be in jeopardy. He fully deserved the verbal lashing he had been given, and he was more angry with himself than at the DCM. But most of all, he was angry at Adamyants, who, he now saw, had arrived early and was talking to the waiter.

"Hello, Phil. I've already ordered for both of us to save time. I have the impression that from your trip, you learned a great deal. Which means that you have questions to ask. But I'm going to take the leap and tell you just about everything I know. So, hold your questions until I'm finished."

The food and drink came quickly. Adamyants said he would talk while they ate because he had a long story to tell. He began—

"What I am about to tell you is so classified that only one person in our Embassy knows it, namely myself. Then, of course, there is Yuri Vladimirovich who, when he was Ambassador, was involved, and besides, because of his new post, now knows just about everything too. So, listen carefully as I give you the whole truth. In other words, what you have always wanted to know.

"Early in 1956, Yuri Vladimirovich, then Ambassador, called me into his office and said he wanted me to put a check on someone named Ferenc Fekete. Our KGB *Rezident* had apparently told Yuri Vladimirovich that there was something strange going on concerning Fekete, rumors of which had reached the *Rezident* from AVO associates. Employing my own AVO liaison, I did what had been asked of me, without knowing who this Fekete might be. I learned rather quickly that he was a musicologist who was totally disliked by the Hungarian musical community. The late Zoltán Kodály, a noble human being whom we respected, had nothing but contempt for him, and musicologists such as Bence Szabolcsi—I know you know him also—could not hide their antipathy when questioned about him.

"I learned that Fekete had been a fascist, an ardent Nazi-minded Hungarian, going back to the mid-thirties. He had joined the Party of the National Will when it was formed in 1935 by a certain Major Ferencz Szálasi, who had been dishonorably discharged from the Hungarian Army. You look puzzled. Because you think you recognize the name? How about if I jump ahead ten years and tell you that this was the same Szálasi who in 1944 was named Hungarian premier and head of state."

"You mean the leader of the Fascist Arrow Cross Party?"

"The same. The Arrow Cross Party. It even has a swastika-like emblem, doesn't it? Well, that was the fascist party which the Nazis installed in Budapest. To return to my story: Fekete was a charter member, my AVO liaison told me, and could do as he pleased. Thus, it was easy for him to travel to Leipzig in 1943, at the height of the war. Why he chose to go, we don't know. But we *do* know that after he returned in December of that year, he stayed out of sight. Perhaps he was too obnoxious even for Szálasi. But after we liberated Hungary, he vanished completely.

"I reported all this to Yuri Vladimirovich, who explained that

Fekete had requested a meeting with him, and him alone, but the Ambassador had refused because, as he said to me—'The Hungarian intellectuals are stirring things up and I have no time for musicologists, especially fascist musicologists.'

"By then, it was the Summer of 1956. Comrade Khrushchev had made his famous speech exposing Stalin's crimes, which had caught fire, first in Poland, then Hungary, and once the Counter-Revolution started here in Budapest, it turned everything upside down, so, of course, I forgot the matter."

"Did the meeting with Fekete ever take place?"

"Yes, in July of last year. In other words, ten years later."

"*Ten years later?* You mean in all that time, Fekete made no attempt to contact your embassy?"

"Oh, he did. We have a file on him, of course, and when I looked into it last year, I saw that during those ten years he had attempted to see our Ambassador almost annually, but had been turned down every time. Last year, however, he specifically asked for Comrade Andropov. Of course, it was no longer *Ambassador* Andropov, but *Central Committee member* Andropov, who was visiting Hungary for discussions with János Kádár. As I've told you, Kádár was made party chief after the Counter-Revolution largely on Comrade Andropov's recommendation."

"But I was under the impression that Andropov's visits to Hungary were secret." Then, recalling what Ilona had discovered from Szirmai, he warily asked—"Do you have a clue as to how Fekete would know?"

"We have been aware that Fekete had some connection to upper ranks of the Party and figured that was how he knew that Comrade Andropov was here. This time, Comrade Andropov agreed to the meeting, because, as he said to me—'Anyone who persists for ten years must have something valuable to tell us.' You know, he has a remarkable instinct for such things, and as it turned out, he was right. I welcomed Fekete into the Embassy, but left them alone. On Yuri Vladimirovich's instructions, however, I recorded the entire conversation."

Adamyants paused for a brief rest, ordered another bottle of beer, and resumed.

"Briefly, Fekete said he had the Beethoven manuscript. No, Phil, don't get excited, not yet anyway. Just hold on. Fekete said he had been unaware that the manuscript had any value beyond its being a musical rarity—he even called it a treasure—until by chance, one day he happened to discover on the back of the last page, a name scrawled in a corner. It was a German name, a very distinguished-sounding name.

"Fekete said his curiosity was aroused and he decided to do some investigating. He said he communicated with German contacts and asked them to trace the name. It is astonishing that this vermin, this Fekete, could extract the information he did. He learned that this German was an officer with the rank of Major, that he had been in the *Abwehr* on the personal staff of Admiral Canaris, and that he had suddenly disappeared in late July 1944. You have a question?"

Phil had raised a finger indicating Adamyants should halt for a moment—"Yes. Something just occurs to me. You said that Fekete's meeting with Andropov took place in July of last year. My *first* lunch with you took place two months later. What I'm saying is that at that time, you already knew from Fekete about my search, but you gave me the impression that what I was telling you was news to you."

Adamyants looked sheepishly at Phil and replied—"Yes, Phil. Of course I knew it, although not why. But it was one thing to hear Fekete talk about it, and something else to have you confirm it. Quite honestly, it set me back. I wasn't being disingenuous with you. I just couldn't tell you more at the time. Let's get back to Fekete now."

"I see." Phil said. "Allright, let me ask one more thing, about Fekete. How can someone like this obnoxious character find out things about people and events that took place over twenty years ago in the Third Reich?"

"Good question. My guess is that his so-called 'contacts' were former members of the SS, with whom he had kept in touch. So now, Fekete, with his conspiratorial turn of mind, dug deeper, this time probably with the help of his Politburo ally and East German ties, and was able to establish that the Major had been under suspicion by Canaris for some time. Canaris, it seems, had become increasingly aware that the Major had always been around whenever there was a plot to kill Hitler. As we know, the plots always failed. But mere presence was not hard evidence and that, combined with the mitigating factor of the Major's German military lineage, had made Canaris reluctant to act."

Phil's mind was churning as Adamyants unraveled the facts which had so recently been recounted in another scenario by Scheidemann in Leipzig. For the very first time, he felt as though something tangible was taking shape which, with much manipulation of his mind, he might understand. But there were still gaps. First and foremost—who was this bizarre Major who had suddenly appeared on the scene, like some *deus ex machina* who would explain away all the mystery?

Adamyants observed Phil's demeanor and said—"Don't try so hard to decipher what I've told you. It will make sense shortly. Back now to Canaris. Fearful of *Gestapo* retribution, for the Major was clearly a *Gestapo* plant, Canaris decided not to take drastic action but to isolate the suspect.This was now about to take place when, as Fate would have it, Canaris himself was arrested by the *Gestapo* just prior to the July 20 plot to assassinate Hitler at his East Prussian Wolf's Lair. But in the confusion that followed July 20—mass arrests, suicides by conspirators, executions—the Major vanished.

"When our Red Army attacked Berlin in 1945, German *Abwehr* officers loyal to Hitler and who had known the Major claimed to have seen him atop a Soviet tank in Red Army uniform. This could not be confirmed, but it was enough for the ever-suspicious Fekete to draw only one conclusion: the Major had defected to the Soviet Union."

Phil sat in silence, somewhat overwhelmed by this parade of information, but finally said—"Krikor, this doesn't make any sense to me. A pro-Soviet German officer preventing the German Resistance from killing Hitler? Come on."

"Don't rush so quickly to judgment, Phil. The fact is, Fekete was not far off the mark. He said this was why he had wanted to see Comrade Andropov when he was the Ambassador, but now that he had moved up to a new echelon in the Soviet hierarchy, the offer Fekete said he wished to make might have even greater potential for success. Further, now listen to this, Phil, Fekete said he had been visited by an American diplomat about the manuscript—now I can tell you that—which had convinced him that the CIA was involved, and he could wait no longer."

"Are you agreeing with that bastard that I'm CIA?"

"Just a minute, Phil, it was not *I* who said that but Fekete."

"OK. Now tell me, what was Fekete's offer that my visit, it seems, forced him into making?"

"Simply this: if the Soviet Embassy did not want this information to leak out, Comrade Andropov had to accede to Fekete's demands, namely—safe exit to West Germany with the Beethoven manuscript; the Major's name erased from the back page; and no dispute when he, Fekete, laid sole claim to the discovery of the manuscript in a long-forgotten closet somewhere in Hungary."

"Martonvásár."

"I have no idea. That is something you would know better. In any case, he had one final demand: he wanted his name expunged from all Arrow Cross records now in AVO files. As for the manuscript, Fekete said it was in safe keeping. How do you like that, Phil? Some nerve, wouldn't you say? I can see from the expression on your face that this is all news to you."

"Hold it a moment, Krikor, before we return to Fekete. You're telling me that a German *Abwehr* officer who was working for the *Gestapo* defected to the Red Army?"

"No, I'm telling you that *that* was what Fekete believed, and was threatening to expose. I don't mind admitting to you at this point—before I get to what will surely astonish you—that what we don't know is how the Major's name came to be written on the manuscript."

"Well, Krikor, for once, perhaps it is *I* who can enlighten *you*. My trip to the GDR also took me to Leipzig, about which you certainly know, and provided me with your missing information. By the way, your man Sahak is one terrific guy."

"I'm glad you liked him. He liked you too. Said he learned alot about culture from you."

"OK. Late in 1943, Carl Goerdeler—you know who he was . . ."

"The Mayor of Leipzig."

"Exactly. Well, in late Spring of 1943, Goerdeler visited his close friend, Hellmuth von Hase, about whom I've told you."

"Yes, the man who first told you in Bad Nauheim about the Beethoven manuscript."

"Precisely. A short time earlier, my guess is a few days, Goerdeler had received a secret message from Canaris telling him that the *Gestapo* had penetrated the *Abwehr* and that he, Canaris, strongly suspected one officer because he seemed to be present at every foiled assassination attempt on Hitler's life. Goerdeler wrote the name down on the back page of the Beethoven manuscript in case he were killed."

"Goerdeler! So that's who it was. Thank you, Phil. Your trip has helped us all. Allright. Let *me* now fill in some gaps. You said that visit took place in late Spring, let us say in May or June of 1943, which places this information *after* two of the major attempts to get rid of Hitler. Both occurred in March of that year."

"Two attempts? In one month?"

"That's right, in fact within days of one another. Most people know only about July 20. They don't realize there were other attempts. Get comfortable and I'll review them for you. I'm something of an expert on this.

"Until late 1942, things were going great for Hitler and the *Wehrmacht* was rolling along deep into the Soviet Union. You may not have known this, Phil, but in August 1942, the swastika was flying atop Mt. Elbrus, the highest mountain in the Caucasus, higher than Mt. Ararat. But then came the notorious Russian winter and with it a series of defeats, climaxed by the massive defeat at Stalingrad—the turning point of the war.

"Many elements of the German General Staff had nothing but contempt for the Austrian corporal's military strategies, and after Stalingrad, this contempt turned into active resistance, with one objective—to assassinate Hitler.

"There is something within the German character that demands obedience to constituted authority. It is an ethos that some historians identify as the psychological basis for the many failures to eliminate Hitler. Oh yes, don't look so surprised, I did say *many.* This brings us now to the crux of the matter: why did the July 20 plot, and all the other plots, fail?"

"Before you continue, tell me—were there really genuine attempts before July 20 to kill the bastard?"

"At least ten that we know of. One popularly accepted explanation for their failure, but not the real explanation, was that Hitler, aware of the growing opposition in the military, and even in the country, displayed what has been called 'intuition.' He would not appear at a scheduled appointment, would cancel a meeting, shorten a visit or change his itinerary—all at the last moment. Want a few examples?

"In the middle of March 1943, Generals Henning von Tresckow and Fabian von Schlabrendorff wrapped two bombs into a package resembling cognac bottles, which were put on a plane carrying Hitler from Smolensk to his headquarters in Rastenburg. The bombs, although armed to explode in half an hour, inexplicably failed to do so.

"A few days later, Hitler was to visit the Berlin Arsenal to inspect Russian battlefield trophies. Colonel Rudolf von Gerstdorff was in charge of this operation and the bomb was intended to kill not only Hitler, but Goering, Himmler and, incidentally, von Gerstdorff too. But, strangely, Hitler left early before the bomb could even be armed. Another failure.

"I can tell you about Colonel Stieff, who planted a bomb in

Hitler's headquarters that went off prematurely, injuring no one. Or a younger officer named Axel von der Bussche who pledged to give his life to save Germany from the madman. Using hand grenades, he made two attempts, in November and December of 1943, both failures."

Phil waved to the waiter, held up Adamyants' empty beer bottle and two fingers, and asked—"I'm very impressed, Krikor. You really do know your stuff on all this. So all these attempts were prior to the big one in July 1944, you say?"

"I'm coming to that. One day after Christmas in 1943, there appeared a Colonel by the name of Claus Schenk von Stauffenberg. He was 37 years old, with no right arm, two fingers gone from his left hand, and blind in one eye—all mementos of the North African campaign. His plan was to carry a bomb into Hitler's headquarters, but again, at the very last moment, Hitler decided to go to Berchtesgaden.

"One failure after the other. Was it really intuition, or fate, or chance, including even the last great attempt, which was only inches away from success? The answer to all this is the name on the back of your Beethoven manuscript: the name Canaris sent to Goerdeler, the name that Goerdeler wrote on the manuscript that Fekete stole and whose secret he discovered and with which he has threatened us. The name is the key to all of the failures to kill Hitler.

"This now is where you want to be, Phil, for this is the answer to it all. Let me now reveal to you this name, and much, much more. The name is Ulrich von Manteuffel. Any reaction?"

"It's a very impressive name, although I don't know why."

"It is impressive because Manteuffel was a Field Marshal in the 1870s, in other words, in Bismarck's time, a distinguished name which to military ears may not have sounded immediately identifiable but which had an aura of tradition, commanding respect. Names such as that have a certain resonance in Germany."

"You're not going to tell me that Manteuffel was instrumental in all the failed attempts to assassinate Hitler, are you?"

"I am indeed, but you still have more to learn, so listen. Incidentally, if Yuri Vladimirovich hadn't authorized me to tell you all this, I never could or would. He seems to have taken a liking to you."

He poured his beer when it came, took a long drag on his cigarette, and said with a mischievous smile—"The importance of being Armenian, Phil."

Thirty-Four

Phil suddenly remembered that he hadn't told Jim Garland where he would be, and asked to be excused while he made a phone call. Adamyants looked at him questioningly but Phil assured him it was only to let his DCM know he would be back at the Embassy in an hour.

Garland appreciated the call—"Nice to know that you're at least in Hungary. Nothing urgent going on that concerns *you.* We've got a group of Iowa farmers here and Watson and Hager are giving them an economic and political backgrounder in the library. I don't think you'll be needed but don't be too late, just in case."

Phil returned to his seat and asked Adamyants to continue.

"I hope you're not in a hurry to get back, Phil, because this will take some time. No? Good. Allright, let me begin. Late in 1941, after the Nazis invaded the Soviet Union, Stalin, furious at Hitler's betrayal of the pact between them, held a very private meeting with the head of the NKVD, the precursor of the KGB. At this meeting, Stalin ordered that Hitler be taken alive so that he could be put on trial, exhibited throughout the Soviet Union, and finally executed in full view of the whole world.

"The wider purpose of such a capture was two-fold: first, to embarrass the western Allies—whom Stalin never trusted anyway—with possibly the single most brilliant exploit of the war, an exploit they couldn't, and didn't perform, and second, to bolster the morale of a severely shaken people who had not only suffered massive losses but whose faith in the Soviet system was at rock-bottom.

"Hitler in the prisoner's dock, Hitler paraded around the country in a cage, Hitler hanged on the gallows—for the whole world to witness. That was Stalin's goal."

"This is absolutely incredible, Krikor. I had no idea. How well-known is all this?"

"Not well-known at all, except perhaps to some intimates, and who knows if they have survived. After all, Phil, we are talking about events that occurred twenty-five years ago."

"You just said 'intimates.' May I ask, 'intimates' of whom?"

"Yes you may, but I was coming to that anyway. The NKVD chief with whom Stalin met was his loyal Georgian compatriot, Lavrenti Beria. Beria considered this idea totally unrealistic because, at the time, the *Wehrmacht,* as I mentioned before, was going through our country like a knife through butter. But Beria could not dissuade Stalin and had to find someone whose mission it was to keep Hitler alive. Any German attempt to kill Hitler had to be scotched because it would ruin Stalin's plan."

"But initially, only Beria knew of Stalin's plan."

"Initially, yes, only Beria. It had been a two-man meeting, but, needless to say, Beria had to take others into his confidence in order to accomplish a task fraught with so much challenge and danger. Eventually, I think only five other NKVD officers were cut in on it. And now, of course, you will want to know how this was done. Right?"

Phil nodded, oblivious of the time.

Adamyants flicked the ash from his cigarette, and continued—"I assume that you have heard of the *Rote Kapelle?*"

"The Red Orchestra. Yes, of course. The 'Red' part is obvious, but I never understood 'Orchestra'."

"I can explain it. In our intelligence jargon, a short-wave radio is known as a 'music box,' and radio operators as 'musicians.' Hence, Red Orchestra, because its members were sending vital information back to us by coded short-wave messages."

"Those members being German communists."

"Look, Phil, they were a tightly-knit organization of very courageous Germans, admittedly with strong pro-Soviet sympathies, sending invaluable information to Moscow. Let's not be so judgmental. After all, we were allies then. Besides, as late as the end of 1943, even so conservative a German as Carl Goerdeler was in touch with German communists. You look surprised, but that is the truth.

"Well, when the Red Orchestra informed us after the Nazi invasion in 1941 that the German Resistance, led by senior armed forces officers, including even one top Gestapo official, was conspiring to rid Germany of Hitler, Beria and his aides searched through the NKVD files for an intelligence officer to foil these plots. It was then that the NKVD activated a sleeper whom it had dispatched to Germany fifteen years earlier.

"He had been sent as an 'illegal' into the Germany of the Weimar Republic in the mid-twenties to live under deep cover and learn to speak the language like a native. Seven years later, he joined the Hitler Youth, then the National Socialist Party, and finally, through forged papers, the *Wehrmacht* where his name alone had other officers virtually clicking their heels.

"Late in 1941, upon activation by the NKVD, when he was already a Captain, he requested transfer to the *Abwehr* figuring that in counter-intelligence he could be closer to information which would help him accomplish his mission. Admiral Canaris took a liking to the eager and seemingly well-connected officer, whose knowledge of Russian—which neither Canaris nor anyone else found suspicious and served to enhance his prestige—made him unique. Soon after his transfer, he was promoted to Major and assigned to Canaris' personal staff.

"Just think of that, Phil. Our own man working under Admiral Canaris, one of the senior officers plotting to kill Hitler. In time, the Major discovered to his utter joy—and ours as well, I was told—that he was now at the very center of the German Resistance. Can you imagine a more brilliant Intelligence coup?

He could work in the Resistance but, of course, towards a quite opposite end."

Phil opened his mouth in astonishment—"Are you telling me that this Major was . . . Ulrich von Manteuffel?"

Adamyants grinned—"Exactly, Phil. So now you know that Major von Manteuffel was *not* a German Army officer, as your friend Fekete and his SS confederates believe, but a *Soviet Intelligence officer.*"

"A double agent?"

"No, no. A Soviet Intelligence officer in the guise of a German Counter-Intelligence officer, who worked exclusively for us, not for *both* sides. What he accomplished may be the greatest, to use an American phrase, cloak-and-dagger exploit of the war, and one which, ironically, we cannot publicize, for the reason I will shortly explain. What Kim Philby did was impressive, but most of Philby's contributions came *after* the war, and further, he was operating out of his own country."

It took Phil some moments to digest Adamyants' electrifying account. He sat in silence, staring at his half-filled glass, still unaware of the relevance of all this to his mission. Perhaps that was coming. He looked up at Adamyants—"This Manteuffel had a formidable task. He must have been a man of great courage and ingenuity to carry out an operation like that for so long."

"He certainly was. Just imagine: here was an *Abwehr* officer who was forever advising Hitler's aides on when and where the *Führer* should be and for how long. The aides, long since aware that there was ceaseless plotting against the *Führer*, found the Major's advice faultless. He always seemed to be right. For all they knew, he was a super-secret agent known only to Himmler. No one dared question his credentials, not with a name like von Manteuffel. Meanwhile, Canaris and his anti-Hitler clique in the *Abwehr* and the rest of the Resistance wondered how their carefully-laid plans always went awry.

"Think of it, Phil: the Major became a confidante of Canaris, possibly the foremost leader of the Resistance. He was at the center of the conspiracy and was in on all the plots targeting Hitler, and therefore, until Canaris' distrust of him, was above suspicion. He succeeded in every mission. Every failure of the Resistance was a success for the Major. As for the very last mission of July 20, 1944, just think what it would have meant had Hitler been killed: not only would it have ruined Stalin's plans, but it would have engineered a major *coup d'etat,* led to a separate peace with the West, with a very different war's end and a very different post-war Europe. Ironically, Hitler had the last laugh on Stalin when he committed suicide and shattered Stalin's plan altogether."

"He could not have known of Stalin's scheme, could he?" Phil asked, thoroughly intrigued by Adamyants' revelations.

"I am certain he did not, else it would not still be secret."

Both quietly sipped their beer.

"Oh, and one more thing," Adamyants suddenly added, "You, by which I mean the Americans, made it all the easier when Eisenhower decided to stop at the Elbe and leave Berlin to the Red Army. Stalin, I have been told, danced for joy, because now his great goal of capturing Hitler alive could be realized."

"I'm sure glad his joy was short-lived, Krikor. But I do have a question."

"Only one?" Phil exclaimed.

"Yes, but a troubling one. By thwarting all those plots, wasn't the war prolonged? I mean, didn't Stalin realize that with Hitler alive and still at the helm, countless lives would be lost on the battlefield?"

Adamyants' manner changed, and his features became grim.

"No argument there, Phil. The carnage was horrendous and you are absolutely right." Adamyants raised his eyes and looked at Phil. "I sometimes cannot forget that I am a Soviet officer, and you are an American officer. That poses a problem for me."

"Allright. I understand that. But why can't we talk to each other as we always have—Armenian to Armenian?"

Adamyants apparently felt more comfortable with this approach, for he bent closer as though for secrecy, and said—

"In that context, Phil, it is morally easier for me. You asked—by keeping Hitler alive, didn't Stalin realize that countless lives would be lost on the battlefield? Phil, Armenian to Armenian, I can say to you now—Stalin was a monster, responsible for the loss of millions of lives—Russian lives, Armenian lives, Ukrainians, Georgians, Azeris, every nation in the Soviet Union. And on the German side, after July 20, 1944, more Germans died in the remaining nine months of the war than in all of the previous 59 months. As far as I'm concerned, they deserved it, but the statistics tell a brutal story. Answer your question?"

"Sure does. But let's get back to the Major. You've explained that he was a Soviet Intelligence officer who masqueraded as a German officer working through Counter-intelligence to foil the plots to kill Hitler because Stalin wanted Hitler kept alive. Wild as all that sounds, in my ignorance, I accept it. But let me ask you something: what difference does it make anymore if Fekete or anyone else has the name of a non-existent German officer who, as far as he knows, defected to the Soviet Union? I mean, so what? And why is this complicating *my* life when all I'm doing is merely looking for a manuscript on which, it happens, this name is written? And most of all, Krikor, why the hell are *you* guys so damned interested?"

"Phil, I see you are irritated, and believe me, I can understand why. A Soviet Embassy officer takes a deep interest in your search for a piece of music, and suddenly you are confronted by the head of the KGB. Well, I guess the time has now come for me to get to the core of this whole story.

"Yuri Vladimirovich said an interesting thing to you, as you will certainly recall. He said that being Armenian is very relevant to this matter. I will now explain that remark to you.

"First of all, I have told you that he was born in the Transcaucasus, in Stavropol, which means, he knew many Armenians as a child. So, when I told him *you* were Armenian, he was immediately intrigued. I remember that he stopped smiling, and I could almost see the wheels turning in his head. It was clear to me that, from his standpoint, your interest in this matter could have many angles."

"All because I was *Armenian?*"

"Let me continue, Phil. It will become clear to you. You see, the Major who had been a Soviet operative in the *Abwehr* whose false German name was on the back of your Beethoven manuscript, was *himself* an Armenian who, since the end of the war, had returned to the NKVD."

"*Another Armenian*?"

"Yes, but not the last. Today, the KGB, has a number of Directorates, each responsible for some aspect of Intelligence activity. The First Directorate, which handles foreign intelligence, like sending agents abroad and analyzing their input, has three departments, one of which is headed by Major General Ivan Aghayants. Yes, I knew that would get a rise out of you. Another Armenian. He is responsible for Disinformation, disseminating false information. I believe you have the same kind of activity. Well, Aghayants . . ."

"You aren't going to tell me that Aghayants was the Soviet agent in the *Abwehr* who spiked all those attempts on Hitler's life, are you?"

"No, Phil, I'm not. Not Aghayants. His deputy, whose name may ring a bell for you. And that, Phil, is what this whole thing is all about. His *real* name."

There was a dramatic pause as both men looked fixedly at each other—Adamyants dead serious, Faljian feeling he was on the edge of a precipice.

"The Major's real name is—Mikoyan."

Phil's eyes opened wide in amazement—"The President of the Soviet Union? What in hell are you talking about, Krikor?"

Adamyants laughed mirthlessly, but which seemed to ease the tension—"No, Phil, not the Old Man. Certainly not Anastas Mikoyan. No, no. It is his nephew, Alexander, or 'Sasha', as he is widely known in the KGB, where he is a living legend. You can perhaps now understand why there is so much concern about this matter: how the Beethoven manuscript is linked to protecting Mikoyan's name, and about preserving the secret of the failed Hitler assassination attempts.

"In fact, Fekete's threat was not only to expose the German officer as a defector to the Red Army, but also to embarrass the Soviet Union by charging that we were primitive and uncultured for preventing the publication of a newly-discovered Beethoven composition.

"Can you explain something to me, Phil? When someone attempts to blackmail a senior Soviet official, who in the meantime happened to become the head of the KGB, does he have an ace up his sleeve, or is he just plain stupid?"

Thirty-Five

The luncheon crowd at the *Hüvös Völgy* had begun thinning out and as Phil sneaked a look at his wrist-watch he saw that it was already half-past two. He knew returning to the Embassy in the time he had promised the DCM was no longer possible, but in any case Garland knew where he was if he were needed.

Adamyants was looking at Phil as though expecting him to say something, and Phil realized that those last comments were not rhetorical but direct questions, to which Adamyants was awaiting a reply.

"In my view, Krikor, I don't think Fekete is stupid. On the other hand, what can he be holding in reserve as protection from . . . what shall I call it . . . KGB antics? All I can think of is a secret hiding place for the manuscript, or—and this is likely too—if anything happens to him, an accomplice to deal with the manuscript on instructions left by Fekete. If that is the scenario, then who might the accomplice be? Someone in the AVO? An old Arrow Cross confederate? Maybe one of those former SS characters? Hard to say. Maybe we should settle for his being stupid."

Adamyants wagged his head dubiously.

Phil continued—"Question for you: Fekete's blackmail, as you put it, is a year old. I presume he knows when Andropov is making one of his routine visits here and expects that in time he'll be getting an answer. Of course, by now he knows Andropov's new position, and if you haven't heard a peep out of him in all this time, is it, do you think, because he's wary of whom he is dealing with, or just hoping and waiting?"

"We too have pondered this question. It's true that we haven't heard from Fekete and *I* have no intention of contacting *him* The fact is that Yuri Vladimirovich and I aren't at all sure about this fascist. Sometimes I think that he could be stupid, but still have lots of nerve. I mean what in Yiddish is called *chutzpah.* Of the various possibilities you raised, I find the AVO connection the most plausible."

"You do? That is surprising to hear. I would have imagined your Intelligence services and Hungary's to be pretty much under the same roof. Working together, common aims, and all that. Are you saying that isn't so?"

Adamyants became edgy, shuffled his feet, and said—"Phil, the AVO hates us. They don't show it openly, of course, but we know they think we are always interfering."

"Aren't you? You know, Krikor, soon after I arrived in Budapest, it was discovered that the bars on my office windows had been cut, but with such delicacy that the eye could not detect it. Our analysis of that, plus other things I prefer not to mention, was that it had Soviet know-how behind it. Are you telling me that the AVO resents all that?"

"I'd rather not get any further into that, Phil."

"No problem. It's not why we are meeting today, anyway. Can we return to the German Resistance, your Major, and Beethoven?"

Adamyants looked relieved. "What more can I tell you? What exactly do you want to know?"

"Well, needless to say, the story of that final famous attempt on Hitler's life on July 20 raises some questions in my mind as it pertains to the Major. There is a generally accepted version , but you apparently have a different one. So, tell me what *really* happened at the Wolf's Lair in Rastenburg? I know Colonel Stauffenberg was the central figure, but I want to hear about the Major. What did he do?"

"A fair question, my reply to which will give you some insight as to the kind of person we are talking about.

"By the time of the July 20 plot, a number of critical developments had brought the Resistance to such a crisis that the attempt at the Wolf's Lair had become a 'now or never' proposition for Stauffenberg. For instance, the *Kreisau* Circle . . . do you know what that is?"

"Yes, thanks to a wonderful old man in Leipzig named Dr. Scheidemann."

"Good. The *Kreisau* Circle, to which Stauffenberg had belonged, had been exposed by the *Gestapo*; the *Abwehr* leadership had been neutralized, and Canaris shipped off to a concentration camp; and Goerdeler, the Resistance's candidate to be the new Chancellor of Germany, was in flight from the *Gestapo*. But the Major was actively involved in learning of new plots to kill Hitler.

"What happened on that fateful day in Rastenburg, as we later learned from the Major, was as follows: Stauffenberg expected to brief Hitler in the underground bunker whose tight concrete construction guaranteed that the explosion would kill everyone in the room. To the Major, who had arrived earlier, representing the *Abwehr*, this would have meant a total success for the plotters and a total failure for him.

"Therefore, just prior to Hitler's arrival, the Major spoke urgently to Field Marshal Keitel, the *Wehrmacht* Chief of Staff, recommending that the briefing take place instead in the loosely-constructed wooden barracks, which were closer and therefore made for quicker and easier access. Keitel, impatient that the briefing begin, concurred."

"And no one suspected anything?"

"Apparently not. Stauffenberg, although dismayed at the change, brought in his briefcase with the bomb and the Major saw him place it under the table near Hitler. The *Führer* paid no heed because he was already deeply absorbed in the bad news from the Russian Front. The Major knew that because it would take ten minutes for the acid to dissolve the metal strip holding back the firing pin, the bomb had to have already been armed. Since some minutes had already passed, he was down to about five, and had to act fast."

"And throughout all of this, he had to avoid behaving in a suspicious manner," Phil interjected.

"Precisely. Then, his nerves taut but his mind razor sharp, he saw an aide accidentally kick the briefcase and try to stand it upright. In his most casual and relaxed manner, as he later described the entire episode, the Major murmured that he would take care of it and carried the briefcase down to the opposite end of the long table. He then cooly returned to his original place between Hitler and Keitel, closed his eyes and, as he later said, silently spoke the words—'Long live the Soviet Fatherland'—as the bomb exploded.

"The blast ripped the table, the building and the clothing of everyone to shreds. Four were killed, everyone else was seriously injured. And Hitler? With his clothes in tatters and he in partial shock, changed into a fresh uniform and met Mussolini at the train station."

Phil listened to this dramatic recital with rapt attention. He had, after all, requested it, and now, with the details fleshed out for him, he was speechless, as his mind transformed Adamyants' narrative into vivid imagery. He felt almost as though the events were something he had personally experienced and he was deeply affected by them. Adamyants had stopped speaking but was ready for Phil's questions—

"If, as you have said, the Major is now in Moscow . . ."

"Where, I can assure you, he holds a rank much higher than Major . . ."

"I don't doubt that. But if he is in Moscow, working with Aghayants, he obviously survived. Without a scratch?"

"Far from it. With *many* scratches, plus one burst ear drum, half an arm, a shattered leg and, while temporarily blinded in his left eye by the flash and smoke, the complete loss of his right eye. He wears an eye-patch."

"But he obviously got away. How?"

"You see, when it was discovered that Stauffenberg had left the compound before the explosion, ostensibly to take a phone call, Hitler sensed that he must have been the guilty party. The order was issued to arrest every member of the Stauffenberg family. Do you know the ancient German word *Sippenhaft?*"

"Not off-hand, but it explains itself."

"Then you know it means imprisonment of all kin. It was invoked by Himmler who vowed to exterminate all the Stauffenbergs. He arrested the entire clan, from the age of three to eighty-five. To jump ahead a little, it is strange that despite Himmler's pledge, only Colonel Stauffenberg and his brother Claus were killed. His wife and children were sent to Dachau and, as you must know, were liberated by your troops."

"I remember that."

"Hitler was so insanely fanatical about revenge that he executed more than 10,000 people, some barely connected with the plot. And you may know that some of them were executed just days before the end of the war. We don't know exactly how many civilians, or even senior diplomats, but we do know of twenty-one generals and thirty-three colonels."

"What about Canaris? Do we know what finally happened to him?"

"Ah yes, Canaris. You know, Phil, from that stuff you learned in Leipzig, it is obvious that in sending the Major's name to Goerdeler, Canaris may have begun to have doubts about his fellow *military* conspirators, so he turned to the one *civilian* Resistance leader whose credentials were impeccable. The Major had an ambivalent attitude toward the conspirators. It was his mission to keep Hitler alive, but at the same time, he secretly admired their heroism.

"He truly liked and respected Canaris. When, early in 1944, the *Gestapo* seized Canaris and dispatched him to the Flössenburg concentration camp, the Major felt a deep sense of personal loss. As for what happened to Canaris, well, he was strangled by piano wire to a slow and tortuous death just weeks before the war's end. It is sad, even tragic, to realize that he died probably thinking he had been betrayed by someone who, in actuality, admired him."

"So, are you saying that there were also some good Nazis?"

"No, never, but there were many good Germans, and we shouldn't overlook what they did, or tried to do."

"That reminds me of something else I've wanted to ask you. Do you know anything about a General Paul von Hase? He was apparently a cousin of the von Hase who headed *Breitkopf und Härtel.*"

"I remember *that* von Hase from what you've told me, but about *Paul,* very little. I know that he was in charge of the Berlin garrison and if Project *Walküre* had succeeded, he would have been in command of Berlin. Of course, he too was executed."

"I see. Can you tell me anything more about Sasha . . . Oh, excuse me, I mean the Major of course. What happened to him?"

"As I've told you, his innocence was established by the fact of his presence in the barracks when the explosion occurred. But he became convinced that his luck might be running out, so after receiving treatment from German medics at Rastenburg, and a brief hospitalization where, if you can believe this, Hitler himself came to thank him, he quietly slipped away and eventually contacted advancing Red Army units, and disappeared. He was never seen again in Germany. That story of Fekete's about the Major riding a Soviet tank into Berlin is sheer nonsense."

"All of this is quite unbelievable," Phil said, shaking his head, "I've been trying to enter the mind of someone like the Major whose mission it was to save the life of his country's bitterest enemy, and I just simply can't. He seems like a one-of-a-kind patriot. Quite remarkable. Krikor, I hesitate to ask, but ask I will anyway. Have you ever met him?"

"Yes, I have, Phil. In the upper echelons of Moscow,

Armenians pretty well know each other. The first time I saw him, it was without knowing who he was. I saw a limping man with a cane, in his sixties, with one arm and an eye-patch. I later learned that in the KGB where he lectures to the younger officers, he is idolized by them, for everyone knows of his heroic exploits as an undercover agent in the Third Reich."

"And I suppose his real name is not exactly a handicap either."

Adamyants laughed at Phil's irony. "Not at all. You can imagine with what pride the Old Man—I mean of course the Comrade President—speaks of Sasha. I know because he has spoken about him to me. It also worked the other way, too."

"I don't understand."

"I mean, even though the project to capture Hitler alive failed, it didn't hurt Comrade Mikoyan's standing with Stalin that a bearer of his family name carried out Stalin's orders until almost the very end. To this day, the President takes enormous pride in speaking of his nephew."

The restaurant was now completely empty but for the two diplomats. The waiters kept eyeing them with hostility and pointedly looking at their watches. Phil arose and Krikor followed suit as both walked to their cars. Standing by his, Krikor said—

"I've given you as much as I know, which may be more than I was authorized to tell you, Phil. But I felt I had to so that you would understand why our interest in this is so great. You are an American, I am a Soviet, but, as you observed earlier, we are both Armenians, and, as Yuri Vladimirovich said, being Armenian is not irrelevant. Remember? Put quite simply—we must protect Sasha by not exposing his real name. By now, his false German name is well-known in some quarters. But if his true name became known, it would bring disaster to him and disgrace to his uncle, our President. And to top it all off, Phil, I remind you that they are both Armenians.

"Protect them from whom? Rodents like Fekete?"

"The Feketes are inconsequential, Phil. They can be . . . swatted away. But there are others who are far, far worse, because they are cunning, audacious, dauntless. They are the ones to fear."

Phil opened the door of his car but didn't enter. He was watching Adamyants' car kicking up dust on the rural hillside road as it drove off. The mystery which had hung over his head at the beginning of the luncheon had slowly evaporated and up to a moment ago, Phil felt as though he understood everything. But now with his final comments, Adamyants had confronted him with yet another enigma. Who were the "others . . . the one's to fear?"

Phil wondered when he would ever really know the whole truth.

Thirty-Six

"Remember me? Your next-door neighbor?"

Her voice was high-pitched, hostile, and on the very edge of hysteria.

"Grace, I don't know what to say. I know it's been some time, and I'm full of apologies. You must know how busy I've been."

"Oh yes, I know that very well. George keeps me informed. He also told me that he asked you to phone me weeks ago. You know why? Because I asked him to. That seemed about the only way I could get through to you. Ironical, isn't it, reaching you through my husband. That wretch of a housekeeper you have . . . every time I call, her manner is so nasty."

"She's got her own problems, Grace."

"Well, she makes me feel as though I'm one of them."

Phil saw that it was eleven in the morning, and since it was a rainy Saturday, he asked if she wanted to visit a few museums. She laughed sardonically—"You mean, just like that? Today? Well, I can't today."

Just as well, he thought, because Sunday would be better if the Ambassador would also be with them.

"How about tomorrow?" he asked, hopeful she would accept.

"Tomorrow's fine, because George is spending the day with the French Ambassador and I'll be free."

He cursed silently. Walking through barren galleries in

museums with Grace wasn't the most pleasurable way to pass a Sunday, but caught in his own snare, he accepted.

After lunch on Sunday, he walked over to the Residence in time to catch Ambassador Quigley departing. Grace was not in sight.

"It's mighty nice of you to do this on an off-day, Phil. Grace and I appreciate it."

Phil waved to Imre as the Lincoln rolled down the driveway and out through the gate onto *Zugligeti út*. When he turned around and looked up into the entrance, he beheld Grace standing barefoot in the hallway in a robe. He stared at her, wondering why she was obviously in no state of dress to visit museums. He walked up the stoop slowly, his eyes anxiously on her, her eyes catlike on him. When he entered he closed the door, and as he did, she opened the robe and let it slither to the floor. Grace stood before him stark naked.

He opened his mouth to reproach her but, his throat bone dry, couldn't find his voice. When he finally did, he rasped—"No, Grace, no, no, no," and walked out to the driveway.

Half an hour later she emerged from the Residence, a half-smile on her lips and a mocking expression in her eyes.—"Did I frighten you, darling?"

Determined at first not to react to her behaviour, as though it had not happened, Phil looked sternly at her, the anger beginning to well up in him. "If you intend to persist in this, Grace, I'm not sure I'll even take you to museums today or any day. And I mean it."

"Sure you do," she said cooly and got into his car.

They drove to the Museum of Fine Arts on Heroes' Square and spent the next ninety minutes walking through the various galleries. Phil pointed out the exquisite paintings of the Italian Renaissance, of the Dutch School, of the Romantics and the Impressionists. But Grace hardly looked at the paintings, her eyes always on Phil, and once, in an isolated corner when she rubbed against him, he pulled away in irritation, with the admonition—

"I guess you just haven't gotten the message, Grace, have you?"

It was the boldest thing he had ever said to her and she seemed stunned by it. But only for a moment, for she retorted—"Have you gotten mine?" which he ignored.

They drove back to the Residence without speaking, Phil staring straight ahead and counting the minutes until they arrived. The Ambassador was already there, having returned close to five. He greeted both of them with great cheer and asked Grace how the visit had gone.

"George, you were right," she said, her voice dripping with boredom. "Phil could write a book about art. I'm going up to rest. My feet are killing me."

When they were alone, the Ambassador asked Phil to stay for a drink. They sat in the porch and for the first time Phil felt no twinges of guilt in talking with the Ambassador in the Residence.

"Did you meet with the Iowa farmers, Phil?"

"No, Sir. I was out of the Embassy at the time. How did it go?"

"From what Jim tells me, it went well. I had no desire to meet with them, being a New Englander myself with no farming experience. But apparently one of them interrupted Watson while he was describing the economic shortcomings of the collectivization program and asked the damnedest question, something that only a farmer would ask—'How much for a pound of tomatoes here?' Watson didn't know and was about to admit it but was saved when another farmer, who apparently had his hand up at the same time, asked about the presence of commissars on the farms, like in the Soviet Union, and Hager jumped in and rescued his colleague."

He laughed softly and sipped his drink. Phil looked at him with some affection and thought—this decent, well-meaning man deserves better than Grace. Phil felt a certain pleasure in having spoken to her so sharply. She was probably taking it hard, but at least the pressure on him would ease up, he and Kiki could be more independent with each other, and, Phil smiled inwardly, Garland would be very relieved.

His thoughts were interrupted by the Ambassador—

"I think the time is nearing for the Stokowski visit, isn't it, Phil?"

"Yes, Sir, it is. I've made some arrangements and I do hope things work out. This damned Hungarian *Interconcert* Agency is dreadful in booking and arranging programs. I think I'll have to go around them, as I've had to before."

"Well, my boy, if you have the same success with this one as you did with Stern and Douglas, everyone should be pleased. Do you think I should host a dinner at the Residence for him?"

"From what I've learned, Sir, Stokowski does not like to party. But I'll find out for you."

"Whatever you say, Phil. And thanks again for looking after Grace."

"My pleasure, Sir," he replied as he walked back to his residence, his spirits higher than they had ever been since Grace first set eyes on him.

Thirty-Seven

A week later, the phone rang in his office. It was Annie, to say that Imre Kun, head of *Interconcert,* was phoning.

"Faljian *úr,* I must speak with you urgently. Can you give me a few minutes?"

"Please proceed, Kun *úr.* What's the problem?"

"Simply this. We had engaged David Oistrakh for a concert but he has just cabled us that he is ill and must cancel."

"And the Soviet Embassy cannot get you a substitute? Richter or someone else of that calibre?"

"Apparently impossible because everyone is booked. However, I know that one of your great conductors is coming soon and I wondered if you could advance his dates."

"If you mean Leopold Stokowski, yes, he will be coming, but the plans are not yet final. What are you proposing?"

Kun said that if Stokowski could arrive a week earlier, *Interconcert* would immediately arrange for him to conduct the Budapest Philharmonic Orchestra and to also make a recording of anything he wished, in return for which *Interconcert* would double his fee.

Phil said he would have to check this out with the Bureau of Cultural Affairs in Washington and with Stokowski himself. Kun expressed his appreciation for Phil's assistance, adding that he was in a serious bind. When Phil noted that he wished there had been this kind of cooperation when Isaac Stern had been booked, Kun immediately replied that the director of *Interconcert* at that time had so mismanaged affairs that he had been fired.

Phil dashed off a cable to Washington with Kun's proposal. He then dug out the various messages on Stokowski from Washington and saw that scheduling adjustments with other posts were possible.

Three days later, a cable arrived confirming that changes were in progress and that Stokowski had agreed to the Hungarian proposal. He would be in neighboring Romania just prior to coming to Hungary.

Phil and Kun were at the train station to meet the legendary conductor when he arrived as scheduled from Bucharest. Stokowski, dapper and agile for his 85 years, his white hair full and flowing, thanked him for coming and added urgently—"Can you find Philip Faljian for me? I must speak to him immediately."

"Maestro, *I* am Faljian."

Stokowski put his arm possessively around Phil's shoulders and followed him to the Lincoln which Ambassador Quigley had placed at their disposal. He asked why the schedule had been changed and what was planned for him. Phil explained everything in detail and by the time they reached the Gellért Hotel, Stokowski seemed satisfied. He asked not to be disturbed for two hours, after which he wanted to see Phil again.

Reporting back to the Embassy, Phil informed the Ambassador and DCM of Stokowski's arrival and said he foresaw no problems. Moments later, Kun phoned and said he wanted Phil to approve the program the Budapest Philharmonic would ask Stokowski to conduct. Phil smiled when he heard that; this degree of cooperation from a Hungarian agency was unprecedented.

In the days that followed, Phil arranged for Stokowski to meet prominent members of the musical community, and on one afternoon, had a lunch at his residence for just two guests—Stokowski and Bence Szabolcsi. It was an exhilarating two hours which could have gone on much longer as the two musical legends took to each other, discussing many aspects of music—style, performance, virtuosity, orchestration, and especially conducting.

As he was leaving, Szabolcsi whispered to Phil—"Why don't you ask the Maestro if he has any ideas or theories about our missing Concerto? Surely he will be able to give us some insights."

"I intend to, Dr. Szabolcsi, after his concert, when he will be completely relaxed."

The next morning, led by Szabolcsi, the three of them went to the Bartók Archives where Stokowski studied the various exhibits, as large photographs of Bartók looked down on the display cases. The famous conductor paused longer at displays of some original scores that he had conducted and knew by heart.

Phil was struck by Stokowski's avoidance of all matters political, even though attempts were made to draw him out. This was most evident at the press conference Phil arranged at the hotel. Some 40 media representatives showed up and after some questions about young musical talent in the United States—one of Stokowski's favorite themes, a reporter asked him if he were forced to play certain music as a demonstration of American culture.

Banging his fist on the table, Stokowski declared—"No one can dictate to me what I do. I despise dictators, all kinds, wherever they are. I know what dictators are because I am one myself, but that is because conductors *must* be dictators."

The media assemblage laughed and applauded his obviously political statement with its final humorous twist.

A capacity audience attended his concert with the Budapest Philharmonic Orchestra, applauding rhythmically after every piece, as was the custom in East Europe.

When the concert was finally over, the audience reluctant to leave, Stokowski consented to a brief late-night supper. Phil had booked a table at the *Mátyás Pince* in a quiet corner. In fact, the normally noisy restaurant was uncharacteristically subdued. Lakatos must be ill, Phil thought.

He and Stokowski sat down and ordered *gyulás,* some of the heavy dark bread called *barna kenyér,* and mineral water.

When they had finished, Phil asked if he could briefly explore a musical problem. Stokowski looked up and waited.

"Maestro, you of course know that Beethoven never wrote a Cello Concerto, although he wrote a great Violin Concerto and five wonderful piano concertos. It is surely not because he didn't understand the cello, After all, there are those five cello sonatas. So, how do you explain that?"

"I can't," Stokowski replied. "Look at Mozart. Has any composer written concertos for a greater variety of instruments? Yet, nothing for the cello. Brahms wrote a Double Concerto for Cello and Violin and Beethoven *did* write a Triple Concerto for Cello, Piano and Violin. But I take your point—nothing for cello and orchestra. Why do you ask this of me?"

"Because, Maestro, there is good reason to believe that he *did* write such a concerto. A very small number of people have seen the manuscript."

"Really? Who?"

"A director of *Breitkopf und Härtel* in Leipzig, a Hungarian charlatan here in Budapest, and your new friend Szabolcsi, although he saw only the first page."

"This is astonishing news. Where is the score now?"

"That, Maestro, is the key question. We don't know, but I am trying to track it down. In other words, you agree with me, and therefore with Szabolcsi too, that it is not out of the question that Beethoven did try at some time to write such a concerto?"

"I have no reason to disagree, although I've never seen any evidence. It would be a phenomenal find. I hope I live long enough to see it. Good luck."

They left the restaurant and Phil drove the aged conductor to his hotel. In the lobby, Phil said—"Maestro, you have earned a long and restful sleep."

"I appreciate the sentiment, my friend, but it will be a long time before I get to sleep."

"You have other plans?" Phil asked, startled at the thought, inasmuch as it was already well past midnight.

"I do, indeed. After every concert, alone in the privacy of my room, I conduct the entire program all over again. It is a habit of many years with me."

The following afternoon, Stokowski recorded Zoltan Kodály's *Háry János* Suite with the orchestra of Hungarian Radio and Television, and departed the next day for Paris.

As Phil drove back from the airport, his thoughts reverted, as they increasingly did, to the missing manuscript, and Stokowski's words echoed in his mind—"It would be a phenomenal find. I hope to live long enough to see it."

'So do I, Maestro, so do I,' he said to himself.

EX

Thirty-Eight

The DCM walked across the hall and stood in front of the Public Affairs Officer.

"Phil, I've got a special request. I know that you and Eric Hager aren't the closest of buddies in this Embassy, but his time has come. He's leaving in two weeks and I'm giving him a farewell dinner. Because he's a bachelor, it'll be stag. I want you to come."

"Nothing could keep me away, Jim, you know that."

"Sarcasm will get you nowhere, my good man, so I assume you are accepting. I'll hand you an invitation shortly."

"Anyone interesting coming?"

"You mean, besides you?" he said with an impish smile. "Well, let's see, I'll have the Ambassador, the political officers from the British, French, Italian, Greek and Turkish embassies, the U.S. desk officer from the Foreign Ministry, with whom Eric deals. . . ." He paused, wrinkling his brow. "Whom have I left out? I remember counting ten in all."

He repeated the guests by title again, looked at the ceiling in thought for a moment, then suddenly exclaimed—"Of course! The West German political officer."

"Not the Soviet?"

"Oh, I tried but he was tied up that evening, so I called on the German. I met him only once. Don't really know him, do you?"

"Is that someone named Christian Sommer?"

"Yes, I believe that is his name. So, you *do* know him?"

"No, I don't. But Helga Kirsch mentioned him to me."

On Friday, Kiki stood flirtatiously at his door, and said in a seductive voice—"I've been waiting for a tennis invitation."

"Kiki, this is a busy time for me."

"It always is. Ten o'clock at the Club? After which . . ." she pursed her lips and looked at him coyly.

He smiled affectionately, shaking his head, and exclaimed—"Oh, you Greek, you! What healthy male in his right mind could resist such a tempting offer!"

They met the next morning, played three sets with the British DCM and his wife, and had a picnic lunch. Towards mid-afternoon, Phil said it was time to leave and that he would drive her to her apartment, but Kiki insisted on going to his residence. It was eight o'clock before they showered together, dressed and he drove her home. She snuggled up to him in front of the apartment and kissed him several times, to the amusement of the policeman.

Phil returned home, put on his pajamas and robe, made a tall drink and relaxed in bed with three volumes of Beethoven's letters. Beethoven had lived only half his life when the symptoms of his deafness first became apparent, and therefore he began to depend on his Conversation Books when he was barely 30. But he also wrote many letters, at least 1600 that have been collated.

Phil continued reading the letters and came upon one in which Beethoven wrote that he had 'several compositions in my writing desk;' also that he had sent two movements of his *Hammerklavier* Sonata, which he had begun two years earlier—in 1818—to Archduke Rudolph, a benefactor. In another letter, to a publisher in Paris, he revealed that he had given some compositions to his brother Johann for delivery. All of this added up in Phil's mind to nothing more than possibilities: Beethoven *could* have kept the Concerto in his writing desk; he *could* have sent the second and third movements, if they had been completed, to someone else; he *could* have entrusted his brother with the Concerto.

There were also the possibilities that Beethoven could have sent the first movement of the score to Gottfried Härtel, Hellmuth von Hase's great-grandfather, because he feared thievery by his man-servant, of which he had a number and always complained about. Perhaps he wanted it to be in safe-keeping until he was ready to continue with the second and third movements.

Further, in that same letter, which apparently no longer existed, he might have asked Härtel to keep the matter a secret between them, which was something he had already requested in letters to the firm of *Peters* in Leipzig concerning other compositions in progress. All of these posed too many improbables, he concluded. But, he had to admit, they were tantalizing to contemplate.

Finally, he came across a letter written in 1816 again to Gottfried Härtel, which conveyed Beethoven's displeasure with the offer Härtel had made to him for a Trio. If nothing else, it proved that Beethoven *did* communicate with Härtel around the time he may have been working on the Concerto. But Phil could find no evidence in any letter which confirmed the existence of even a fragment of a Cello Concerto. *That* letter had remained in the *Breitkopf und Härtel* safe until 1943 when the great RAF raid must have blown it to pieces.

Phil fell asleep, his bed covered with volumes about Beethoven in German, English and Hungarian.

The farewell dinner for Eric Hager took place on a cool evening at the DCM's residence. Sarah Garland remained discreetly out of sight, supervising in the kitchen. Phil was among the last to arrive and was greeted warmly by Ambassador Quigley and Jim Garland, who took him over to the Greek and the Turk, both of whom were relatively new to Budapest and already heavily engaged in a discussion of the Cyprus issue. When Garland introduced Phil to Mehmet Orsel, the Turk's smile disappeared as he extended his arm in a limp handshake. Stavros Papadakis on the other hand was very cordial and said he had learned from Kiki Boutos that Phil had vacationed in Crete. As they ended their brief conversation, Orsel, who had been standing by silently, began looking around for someone to talk to. Phil sensed a coolness in his manner, turned and joined the British and French guests who broke away from Hager, with whom they had been chatting, and greeted Phil warmly. Neither had much more than rudimentary Hungarian and had frequently depended on Phil, much as their ambassadors did, to assist them in analysing events reported in the media.

After a few banal moments with them, he turned to the Foreign Ministry's American Desk officer, a nervous, mouse-like Hungarian unable to express a single view about anything, and decided to give up on him just as the doorbell rang. The DCM's butler opened the door to let in a man in his thirties whom Phil did not recognize. Garland greeted him and took him around to the others. Phil was the last to be introduced and heard Garland say—

"And this is our First Secretary for Press and Culture, Phil Faljian. Phil, this is Christian Sommer of the West German Permanent Mission."

Sommer extended his hand and jerked his head forward in a quick nod of acknowledgment. Phil was struck by the man's formality. He shook the extended hand and felt a firm grip.

"Knowing you speak excellent German, *Herr* Faljian, may I say in my native tongue that I have been looking forward very much to meeting you."

Phil looked into a pair of very blue, alert eyes. Sommer was blonde and as superb a specimen of the German race as could be imagined.

"I am delighted to meet you also, *Herr* Sommer," he replied in German. "May I welcome you to our small diplomatic community. My Embassy has cordial relations with your Mission and I hope you and I will as well."

"That is something I look forward to with great anticipation,"

Sommer replied with a zeal which made Phil wonder whether he had overdone his welcome.

After two rounds of drinks, everyone sat at the table and engaged in polite and inconsequential conversation about where they had been, where they were going, how they had spent leave, what their wives were doing, and how their children were adapting to the British school in the British Embassy.

Phil viewed these preliminary stages of diplomatic dinner parties as a sheer waste of time. It was rare that he ever learned anything interesting, such as once when he had conversed with the Finnish Ambassador. During Phil's study of Hungarian in Garmisch, the instructor had said that there were about 200 Finnish words in use in Hungarian, it being a strain of Finno-Ugrian. When Phil mentioned this to the Finn, he turned in astonishment and said—

"If that is so, why don't I understand one single word of this bloody language?"

On most other occasions, however, the conversation was superficial and painfully insipid. Phil didn't expect anything more on this evening, for he was seated between Hager and the Frenchman. Directly across from him was the Turk who occasionally eyed Phil and when Phil looked at him, would avert his eyes at the very last second. But the guest whose eyes seldom looked anywhere but at Phil was Sommer, seated diagonally opposite near the other end of the table, and whenever their eyes met, Sommer would smile and nod. Phil felt an uneasiness in the German's demeanor. He remembered Helga Kirsch's comment that the new officer had inquired about him. What was Sommer all about anyway, he wondered?

The traditional toast and encomiums, led by Ambassador Quigley, followed on dessert. As the praise was showered on Hager, who seemed to enjoy it, Phil and Jim Garland exchanged looks which conveyed their utter revulsion at the glowing words coming from the other guests around the table. Phil signaled to Garland that he didn't want to be tapped and he wasn't, the panegyrics concluding with Garland himself, in cliched phrases such as 'protecting the U.S. national interest.'

As they arose and went into the large living room, Phil whispered to Garland—"Thanks for skipping me, and I didn't know you loved Hager so much."

Garland muttered—"I had no choice, and up yours, too," as they joined in small groups for further inconsequential small talk. Phil found himself face-to-face with the Turk, who realizing he could no longer avoid Phil, said in English—"So *you* are Mr. Faljian."

"You make it sound almost as though I enjoy some notoriety."

"In my Embassy, you do."

"That sounds ominous. Is that view shared by your Ambassador, with whom I play tennis?"

"Partly, although he says you never discuss politics with him. Or . . . other things."

When speaking with Turkish diplomats at the several posts where he had served, Phil was always wary of those "other things," the most sensitive issue between Armenians and Turks—the 1915 Turkish massacres of the Armenians. On some occasions, when *they* introduced the topic, he would take them on, but ordinarily he would let it slide. He tried usually to steer the conversation in a very different direction, but was convinced that Turkish diplomats were permeated with so much guilt about their cruelty towards Armenians that they were constantly seeking some form of catharsis by talking about it. Their position was always one of total denial and whenever Phil heard that, he would reply contemptuously "I'd like you to say that to my orphaned father," at which point, unerringly, the Turk would abruptly walk away.

In Budapest, he learned in time from other diplomats that the Turks knew how he bristled at mention of *the problem* and consequently avoided it. For his part, Phil had become convinced that argument was pointless: the Turks were guilty of a massive war crime, the evidence in the archives of the United States,

Germany, Britain, Austria, France and Italy was overwhelming, and in time, history would correct the record and impale the guilty. Phil ignored the reference to "... other things" and asked the traditional question of all newcomers—"Where were you posted before you came to Budapest?"

The Turk sipped his cognac, and said—"In Istanbul."

"Oh, the Foreign Ministry has an office there?"

When Orsel didn't respond immediately, Phil looked at him questioningly, and to his astonishment heard the Turk reply—"Well, actually, I was not. I was . . . in a band in a night club. By profession, I am a musician. I play the saxophone." He added, sheepishly—"You probably won't believe that."

"You're right, I won't believe it. You mean you went from playing sax in a band into the Turkish Foreign Service?"

"That is what happened. I saw no future in music, and besides, after listening to the recordings of Coleman Hawkins and Ben Webster, I knew my playing had no future. You probably don't know who they are."

"I know very well who they are. I grew up with their records, but in later years, I became an ardent admirer of Lester Young. Would you know who *he* is?"

"Of course, of course! He is also great," the Turk replied animatedly.

They spent another ten minutes discussing Young's work with Count Basie, at the end of which Phil sensed a more enlightened attitude towards him from the former Turkish musician. Phil wondered how many other Turkish diplomats had such curious tales to tell. He remembered once at a reception how a Turkish Ambassador had regaled him with stories about an earlier assignment as Foreign Ministry Protocol Chief and describing in lascivious detail the perversions of President Sukarno of Indonesia which he practised on Turkish girls procured for him.

Moments later he broke away and found himself inches from Sommer, whom he addressed again in German—"*Herr* Sommer,

I cannot suppress the thought that you want very much to speak to me."

"That is very perceptive of you, *Herr* Faljian, because I do indeed. Can we perhaps have dinner soon?"

"Whenever you wish. Please give me a ring at the Embassy."

He saw Ambassador Quigley look at his pocket watch and knew that the party was almost over. As Quigley departed, followed by the foreign guests, Phil proposed dropping Hager off. After final farewells, Hager accompanied Phil to his car and they drove towards another part of Buda where Hager lived.

On arrival, Phil switched off the motor, turned to Hager, and said—"Eric, this might be our only time to talk candidly with each other, and I don't want us to part on . . . unfriendly terms. It's no secret to me that you've resented my role in the Embassy, my inroads into this society and my reporting on it. Agree?"

Hager was startled by Phil's directness but apparently understood that it might well be the time for total candor.

"I've had some difficult moments, I must admit."

"Now look, we're both Foreign Service officers, both deeply interested in the political affairs of this country. Sometimes I discovered things, sometimes you did. But what puzzles me, Eric, is why you didn't make more of your insights. You know, when I have been Duty Officer at night, in making security checks of the various offices, I have looked in on yours and found countless magazines, journals and books, opened to pages where you have underlined things, made marginal comments."

Hager looked sharply at Faljian, startled that something very private about him had been discovered, but remained silent.

"I read some of those passages and realized that you had uncovered ideological discrepancies in Hungary's approach to classical Marxism. Good stuff, Eric, I mean *real good analysis.* Why didn't you report such things?"

Hager was looking straight ahead through the windshield. After moments of silence, he turned and said—"I wasn't aware that you knew this. I should have realized that if anyone in the

EX

Embassy would have appreciated what I had come up with, it would be you. The Ambassador or DCM would have thought it too philosophical, too esoteric. As for Washington . . ." his voice trailed off.

"I understand, Eric. I'm truly sorry we were on different wavelengths. People in the Foreign Service such as you and I should be working *with*, not *against* each other. Maybe next time."

Hager looked at Phil, his gaunt features almost spectral in the shadows, and extended his hand—"Thank you, Phil. Yes, maybe next time."

As he drove home, Phil mused over the events of the evening. The Turk had been a surprise and Phil couldn't imagine that he would be playing tenor saxophone in a night club one night and then reporting on political developments in a communist country months later.

The Greek had the same sunny disposition as the country of his birth and would be enjoyable to cultivate as a diplomatic colleague.

Eric Hager had proven to be human, and Phil, as a fellow bachelor, realized that the Political Officer's life must have been very lonely, and that the antipathy towards him in the Embassy had probably contributed to his envy of Phil—a poacher on his territory.

Finally, there was Christian Sommer, pleasant, agreeable but puzzling. Why would a Political Officer from the German Mission be showing such unusual interest in him—inquiring about him, watching him, displaying such inordinate affability? Was there more to Sommer than appeared on the surface? If a dinner invitation did materialize, Phil guessed, it might peel away a few layers of *that* mystery.

Thirty-Nine

When the phone rang, Phil saw on the radium dial of his wristwatch that it was 2:45 AM. Sal Frascatti, the Security Officer, was very apologetic.

"Hello, Phil? I'm *really* sorry to disturb you at this hour but I'm Duty Officer tonight and the Hungarian Police just phoned. Someone asked me for your home number, but I didn't give it out. Has anyone called you there?"

"Not yet, Sal. What's going on? What have I got to do with the police?"

"I'm not sure. I asked and somebody with pretty good English said that your name had been found in someone's apartment."

"Any idea who that was?"

"No idea, Phil, and even if they had told me, it wouldn't mean anything to me. I don't know that many Hungarians. Did I do the right thing by not giving out your private number?"

"Yes, you did, Sal, and thank you. Look, if they call again, tell them to phone me at the Embassy around nine."

Falling asleep again was difficult. He arose, went down to the kitchen and made himself some hot cocoa. Thirty minutes later, the phone rang again. This time it was the DCM.

"Phil, something strange has happened and the police want to talk to you. They just phoned me. Be sure you come to the Embassy early."

It was close to five and still dark before he fell asleep again.

At eight he arose, showered, ate a quick breakfast prepared by Erzsébet and drove to the Embassy. The DCM arrived, looked in on him, shrugged his shoulders, his face a puzzle, and without saying a word went to his office.

At nine sharp, Annie called up to him with the message that the Hungarian Police were on the line.

"Faljian *úr*," a cultured voice said in Hungarian, "My name is Timar. I am a detective with the Hungarian Police. Because your Embassy is extra-territorial, we may not enter it without special permission, as you know. So would you be so kind as to allow us to come in and speak with you?"

"Only the Ambassador can make that decision. If he agrees, I will expect you here at the Embassy. Please call back at ten when he will be here."

At 9:45, Ambassador Quigley arrived, was briefed by the DCM and PAO, and asked—"Any idea what this is about?"

"None, Sir, but we'll know very shortly."

At ten, the same detective called and was told permission was granted. An hour later, Annie called up to say a Detective Timar was waiting in the lobby. Phil immediately went down and greeted him. He was a tall, very polite gentleman who apologized for the late-night calls but said the matter was urgent. Phil took him into the library, which was empty, and looked expectantly at Timar.

"Faljian *úr*, I can conduct this in Hungarian or in English. Please decide."

"Normally it would be irrelevant to me, Timar *úr*, but since it is a police matter, perhaps my native tongue might be the better choice. Please proceed."

"Very well, Mr. Faljian. May I ask first, when was the last time you saw someone named Ferenc Fekete?"

"Ferenc Fekete? Has something happened to him?"

"Please answer the question, Mr. Faljian."

"Well, the answer is easy. I have seen him only once and that was sometime last year. It was an unpleasant encounter."

"How so?" Timar asked, leaning forward.

"Well, it's something of a long story, Mr. Timar, but in brief: I have been searching for a manuscript, a piece of music, that my information told me Fekete stole from East Germany and had in his possession. I went to see him about it. When I raised the subject, he became violently angry and just about threw me out of his apartment."

Timar took out a notebook and began writing things down.

"And you say you saw him only that one time?"

"That is correct. After that, never again. Incidentally, I have two sources that can vouch for all this."

"Who are they, Mr. Faljian?"

"One is your famous musicologist, Dr. Bence Szabolcsi, and the other is the Soviet Embassy's Cultural Officer, Gregor Adamov."

At mention of the second name, Timar stopped writing and looked up, a frown on his face.

"From the Soviet Embassy, you say?"

"Yes, Mr. Timar. I think you should check that out."

The detective appeared strained, took out a handkerchief and wiped his brow. He wrote something down and looked up—"You must understand that there are certain difficulties. For one, he enjoys diplomatic immunity."

"And don't I, Mr. Timar?"

"Of course, of course. Just that . . . well, never mind."

"Mr. Timar, don't you think it's time you told me what this is all about."

Timar pressed his lips tightly together, closed his notebook, and his manner now even more official, said—"At 11:45 last night, the body of Ferenc Fekete was found floating in the Duna." Even when speaking English, Hungarians still referred to the Danube by its local name. "It had been washed close to the embankment where an elderly pensioner was fishing. He immediately phoned the police. When we arrived, the body was dragged out of the river. The corpse was fully clothed but we could see that his hands and neck bore severe bruise marks.

When the medical examiner arrived, he determined that Fekete—we identified him from papers in his wallet—had been badly beaten and his neck broken and that although his lungs were filled with water, he was already dead when he had been thrown into the river."

Phil sat immobile and silent, stunned by the news. For one thing, Fekete's death took a key player out of the game. For another, it made it all the more difficult to find the manuscript. Who else beside Fekete knew where it was?

"I still think you should contact the two gentlemen I mentioned. They may be able to throw some light on all this. By the way, how exactly did you find my name?"

"Once we knew whose corpse it was, we went to his flat, and looking through his papers we found a notebook, actually in the form of a diary, and we saw, as you told me, that you had indeed visited him last year."

Phil looked resentfully at Timar—"So, you were really checking up to see if I would lie?"

"Please do not jump to conclusions, Mr. Faljian. A detective's work is not always agreeable. I hope it will not be necessary to trouble you again. Please accept my apologies for this intrusion."

Phil returned to the third floor, went in to the DCM, and told him about the visit.

"I imagine this complicates matters for you, Phil. I mean, what with a missing manuscript and a dead musicologist who knew where it was . . . or is."

Phil merely nodded, asked Garland to tell the Ambassador, went back to his office and called Adamyants.

"Yes, I know about Fekete, Phil."

"Oh, the police have called you already?"

"Well, actually, no, but I knew about it. Phil, excuse me, I'm in the middle of something urgent. I'll get back to you."

For the first time in their relationship, Phil sensed that he was being rebuffed. He hung up feeling irritated. He phoned Szabolcsi and invited him to lunch at the *Száz Éves.*

The reputedly hundred year-old restaurant—hence its name—was only half full when he arrived, followed moments later by Szabolcsi. The elderly musicologist greeted him solemnly and said—"The police called me as I was leaving and said that a fellow member of the Academy of Sciences had been found in the river. When I asked his identity, they said it was Fekete. I was shocked. How much do you know about all this, dear colleague?"

Phil described all that had happened since discovery of the body and what he knew. Szabolcsi was just as mystified as Phil and they tried comparing notes but soon discovered they had very little to work with. Phil left the restaurant and walked back to the Embassy. There was a message to call Adamyants, and he did.

"Phil, apologies for my abruptness before. The police were just here and told me how the body had been discovered and that they had questioned you. That's apparently how they got my name. I told them that you were completely in the clear, that your interest in Fekete was academic, and that they should drop the investigation. I have reason to believe they will."

There was a long silence.

"Phil, are you there? Did you hear what I said?"

"Yes, Krikor, I heard you. Let's leave it for another time."

He hung up, sat back, and felt an uneasiness in his stomach. Something foul had occurred and he had absolutely no doubt that Adamyants knew all about it.

Forty

It took the Soviet Embassy switchboard ten minutes to locate Adamyants and when he got on the line, his tone was jovial and friendly.

"Hello, Phil. Glad you called. I'm sorry about yesterday. My manner in these last two conversations may have seemed brusque to you, but believe me, I've been under lots of pressure. I need to tell you about it, if you have the time."

"When have I not had time for you, Krikor? If it's something that concerns me, let's get together."

"I think you'll discover that it concerns you very much. One o'clock tomorrow?"

"See you at the *Hüvös Völgy*."

When Phil arrived at the heavily shaded area in which the restaurant nestled, he saw through the trees that Adamyants was at an outdoor table, and that he was not alone. Phil couldn't see who the other person was, and a fleeting thought suggested possibly Andropov again. As he neared, he knew it was not Andropov—certainly he wouldn't dare being seen publicly with an American diplomat, Phil thought—and after approaching a few feet more, he also knew that it was not a man.

He approached the table from behind the woman and greeted Adamyants, who stood up, extended his hand, and then said in German—"Phil, may I present to you *Fräulein* Hannelore Weber. *Fräulein* Weber, this is Philip Faljian of the American Embassy."

A blonde German woman in her mid-thirties with a creamy white complexion, blue-gray eyes and delicate features looked up at him, smiled, revealing perfect teeth, and extended a white unmanicured hand to him. Phil took her hand and pressed it gently. She was smiling, and although cordial, there was an anxiety in her eyes. Phil thought her attractive, even though she wore absolutely no makeup. In a sense, she didn't have to, for her face was naturally arresting, and Phil was already quite taken with her.

"Now, Phil, you must behave yourself," Adamyants said in English with a taunting grin. "*Fräulein* Weber speaks only German, and Russian of course, so we'll have to converse in German, if you have no objection."

Phil finally took his eyes way from the woman, who, self-conscious at his attentions, seemed to be blushing slightly, and let her eyes drop. Phil silently berated himself for having embarrassed her and looked at Adamyants, who was looking at the woman with equal admiration.

The waiter interrupted their general reverie and they ordered, Adamyants confirming his order with the German woman. Then he settled back, looked with some self-satisfaction at Phil and said in German—

"My impression, Phil, is that you have absolutely no idea who *Fräulein* Weber is."

"Your impression is correct."

"In that case, may I suggest a name that might ring a bell? A name like . . . Scheidemann?"

Phil started, looked at the faces of his two luncheon companions for a clue, saw nothing but expectation in both, and then shook his head—"I am drawing a complete blank. Dr. Scheidemann was the musicologist with whom I had a long discussion in Leipzig a few months ago. I haven't the faintest clue how *Fräulein* Weber—forgive my obtuseness, *Fräulein*—connects with Scheidemann."

"Did the good Dr. Scheidemann not tell you about his secretary?"

"Yes, I believe he mentioned her, but quite frankly, I've forgotten her name."

"It was Christa Weber."

At mention of the name, the woman shifted in her chair. Phil merely looked at Adamyants, waiting for some clarification.

"Phil, you are not your usual sharp self today. *Fräulein* Weber is the *daughter* of Christa Weber."

Phil's eyes went from Adamyants to the woman. She was staring at him, her features taut.

"Please continue, Krikor. I'm beginning to sense some relevance, but speaking candidly, I don't quite know what it is."

"*That* I can understand, because now the story takes a turn which to you, Phil, is familiar, but to me, is not, just as it is obnoxious to both of us. *Fräulein* Weber, would you be so good as to proceed, if you feel you can."

Hannelore Weber drew herself up, sipped some water, and began her narrative in a lovely, soft German which, when spoken by a cultivated woman, made that ofttimes gutteral-sounding language a thing of beauty.

"My mother worked for Dr. Scheidemann, who was always *Onkel* Werner to me. But she often worked for Dr. von Hase as well. I believe you know him also, from what *Herr* Adamov has told me. I would frequently go into the office of my mother after school so we could go home together. The *Wehrmacht* had taken my father and he was somewhere on the Russian front, so we were alone, just the two of us. *Mutti* missed my father very much and was very lonely and although we sometimes entertained friends, even *Onkel* Werner a few times, it was not quite the same as someone—this I now realize—who might have been, what shall I say? 'interested' in her.

"I should mention at this time that often when I was in the office, studying my lessons, Dr. von Hase, who was a serious but not unfriendly man, would call me into his office and chat with me. One day, I saw on his desk, some handwritten music which he had been looking at. I asked him what it was. You know,

Breitkopf und Härtel had published so many masterpieces that it would not have surprised me if he had said it was Bach's this or Brahms' that or Mozart's something else. Instead, he said in a rather mysterious way—'My darling Hannelore, this is an unknown piece by Beethoven. The world has no idea it exists.'

"I was intrigued, even at the age of ten. I went to his desk and sat on his lap, and he turned the pages of the score. I didn't know music then, but I remember that it added up to something like ten pages."

Adamyants interrupted—"No question, Phil, what it was that *Fräulein* Weber saw. Not *one* page, as Szabolcsi said, but the entire first movement. I don't believe you still need confirmation that such a score exists. However, that is not why I have brought you here. *Fräulein* Weber, please continue."

"About a year later, I believe it was . . . no, I *know* it was 1943, when I went to the office in late afternoon, *Mutti* said a man was visiting from Hungary."

Phil, who was already in thrall to her story, now looked quickly at Adamyants, who smiled and signaled with his hands for Phil to be patient.

"I met him and disliked him immensely from the beginning. I didn't like the way he looked at me. I'm afraid I'm going to be somewhat . . . indiscreet. I hope you don't mind."

Phil had long since been accustomed to the candor with which European women discussed intimate matters, and waved his hand for her to proceed.

"You can imagine my dismay when, one evening, *Mutti* told me she was bringing this person home for dinner. After they had arrived and I had taken his coat, I realized how repulsive he was to me. He was always touching me, his hands on my hair, my arms, my waist, and once, when *Mutti* was out of the room, on my legs. I was raised very strictly, *Herr* Faljian, and had no experience with boys, but my intuition told me that this person had evil intentions. The second time he came, I pretended to have much homework and stayed in my room. But the third time was a catastrophe.

"*Mutti* had prepared a lavish meal and was in such good spirits. She insisted I not be rude like last time and that I entertain him while she worked in the kitchen. It was then that it happened. He asked me to show him my room. I felt strange about doing that but, remembering *Mutti's* admonition, I did. Once we were inside, he sat on a chair, pulled me to him, turned me around with my back to him, and I felt his hands under my dress. He held me tight, I could feel his foul breath on my neck, he began to groan and then . . . I felt his . . . please excuse me if I don't describe it in detail, except to say that he had opened his trousers."

The woman's eyes filled with tears and Admayants bent close and offered her his handkerchief. Phil sat motionless, totally in sympathy with the German woman's distress, anger welling up inside of him. He thought of Ilona and her recital of a similar experience with Fekete, and for the first time since learning of the musicologist's fate, he experienced gratification that Fekete was dead.

Phil leaned over and consolingly patted her arm, saying—

"*Fräulein* Weber, it is not necessary for you to continue. I just want you to know that I feel deeply about your agony."

He sat back and looked questioningly at Adamyants. He wanted his look to convey his perplexity as to why Adamyants was having this poor woman go through all this. Adamyants seemed to understand, for now he picked up the narrative, but in English.

"Four days ago, Phil, I was called on by the GDR Political Counselor, whom you don't know, of course, because you have no relations with his government. He told me that a German woman from Leipzig had visited the GDR Embassy and spoken with him. She was asking the whereabouts of a Hungarian musicologist named Ferenc Fekete, and said he was an old friend and she wished to visit him. My GDR colleague told me there was something abnormal about her. She was very tense and fidgety and her general demeanor aroused his suspicion."

"Why did he come to you?"

"Because, as it turned out, *Fräulein* Weber said she might contact the Soviet Embassy as well, and he wanted me to be prepared. I decided not to receive her and told him to keep her away, but that I would give him Fekete's address, which I did. The next day, he phoned me and said—'She is going there this afternoon at three.'

"I pondered this, and I don't mind telling you, you figured in my thoughts. I knew nothing about her, except that she wanted to visit Fekete, and, according to my GDR colleague, she was acting strangely. I therefore made up my mind to go there also. Waiting until three-fifteen, I approached his door and was about to ring the bell when I heard shouting. First a man's voice, then a woman's, both shouting in German. I heard the crash of falling furniture, then the shattering of glass. They were running around the flat, although I couldn't determine who was chasing whom. I decided to find out, and pushed hard against the door. To my amazement, it was unlocked. I entered, hurried through a corridor into a large living room—you must know it, Phil, you've been there—and beheld an astonishing sight. Fekete had fallen across the sofa and was lying helplessly, and *Fräulein* Weber here was standing over him, shouting hysterically and brandishing a large knife.

"I seized her arm and took the knife away. She began to sob, looked at me wild-eyed, her face contorted in agony, and then started to run to the door. I caught her and said I was a friend and would not harm her. I sat her down near the door and asked her to wait. I returned to the large room. Fekete was trembling wih fear, his face wet with perspiration, his chest heaving. 'Who are you?' he asked, his voice cracking, and not waiting for an answer, cried out—'This crazy bitch tried to kill me!'

"You know, since that one time he came to our Embassy to see . . . my colleague, I had not laid eyes on him. He was a miserable wretch and I had no pity for him. Besides, I also knew your experience with him, and his entire fascist background.

"There was one other thing—the manuscript. I asked myself

whether I was standing in the room where it might be hidden. I looked around, not knowing exactly at what. Then, on a sudden impulse, I bent low and said in my most villainous manner—'You scum, where is the manuscript?' He cried out and I saw his eyes look past me. In his terror, he had impetuously given his secret away, for I knew that behind me was his bookcase. I went to *Fräulein* Weber, who had calmed down, and escorted her out of the apartment and to a cafe. There, she told me the same story she has just told you—I mean about Fekete, not the part about von Hase and the manuscript. She has no interest in that and, of course, is unaware that we do. But that part of her story was a bonus for you. Any questions?"

Phil looked sympathetically at the woman and in his gentlest manner asked in German if he might put a question to her. She nodded.

"After the great air raid of December 1943, when the building was destroyed, did you ever hear von Hase or Scheidemann or even your Mother ever say that Fekete had stolen the manuscript?"

"Absolutely. *Herr Doktor* von Hase definitely, and *Onkel* Werner too. Of course, *Mutti* only repeated what she had heard."

Phil turned to Adamyants—"Krikor, I have some questions for you, too, if I may?"

"I was expecting a few."

"When you asked Fekete about the manuscript and he seemed to give its location away, why didn't you follow through? Your interest in finding it is as great as mine."

"I didn't have to, Phil," he said, now suddenly solemn, "it was taken care of for me. Next question?"

Phil looked for a full half minute at Adamyants, who was smoking thoughtfully, and then said in measured tones—"I think you just answered it."

He had been right. Adamyants not only knew what had happened to Fekete, he had, in all probability, engineered it. The arrival of this German woman had only accelerated what was, in all probability, inevitable. There was only one question left.

"Krikor, can you tell me where the manuscript is?"

Adamyants snuffed out his cigarette and replied—"You will learn that when the time comes."

The woman suddenly shuddered, for it had turned cool. Adamyants said he would fetch her coat from the car and left them for several minutes. To Phil's surprise, she bent forward and began speaking quickly—"*Herr* Faljian, you are as much a stranger to me as he, but you are American, and he is Russian. I have always felt good about Americans, and as you surely know, we Germans intensely dislike the Russians. Therefore, you will understand why I can speak more openly with you. Can you tell me what all this is about, I mean, the manuscript, and so forth? The two of you seem to get along well. Do you trust him? Should I?"

"*Fräulein* Weber, he is Soviet but not Russian. He and I are both Armenian and, therefore, share a common ethnic heritage. Yes, I trust him. You can too. As for Fekete, what has been done to Fekete is not something I can condone, but I believe he deserved it."

The young woman became misty-eyed, wiped her eyes and said in a controlled, subdued voice—"*Herr* Faljian, I have explained how this monster mishandled me. It was traumatic for me and shocking to my mother, who happened to walk into my room and saw everything. She screamed at him to leave. From that day on, she was never the same. Then, when we got the news that my father had been killed in the defense of Berlin, my mother collapsed. She might have survived the news about my father, many other German women did, but the shattering experience with that fiend had already reduced her to a pitiful state. In late 1945, she died, leaving me an orphan. My despair soon grew into anger and a powerful urge to avenge my mother and myself. I will only say that, close as I came to accomplishing my purpose, I am grateful it happened otherwise."

Phil listened with deep compassion to her narrative, and

observing that Adamyants was approaching, said hastily—"In any case, you needn't trouble yourself about manuscripts or anything else any more. You have been avenged and destiny has worked in your favor."

'But for me,' he said to himself, 'destiny has yet to reveal itself.'

Forty-One

"Have you seen this, Phil?"

Jim Garland thrust a cable into his hands. It announced that Zsa Zsa Gabor was visiting Hungary for three days and that the Embassy should accommodate her as it deemed appropriate.

"The Ambassador wants you to be the escort on this one," Garland added and seeing Phil's frown, continued brusquely—"Sure, I know, it interrupts your more important private mission. Listen Phil, I told you once before that Embassy business comes before everything, and Zsa Zsa Gabor's visit is Embassy business. Is that clear?"

Phil nodded glumly.

On the day of her arrival, Phil phoned the film star at the Gellért Hotel. "Welcome to Budapest, Ms. Gabor. The Ambassador is inviting you to a small reception at the Residence. His car will pick you up at seven. I hope you can make it."

"But of course I can, darling. How sweet of you."

The reception was indeed small, no more than twenty-five people, but everyone was fawning over the blonde star.

For the next two days, Phil always seemed several paces behind her. She went to the *Divatszalon*—the Budapest Dressmaker's Showroom—and ordered coats, blouses, skirts, a Givenchy dress, hats, belts and silk shoes. The press quoted her as insisting that "it be delivered free as Dior does in the States," which she denied as having said. The *Divatszalon* asked for the Embassy's intervention as mediator but the DCM instructed everyone to refrain from any involvement.

She informed Phil she had bought a horse at the *Babolna* Stud Farm and needed the Embassy's help in getting it out of Hungary, but the Ambassador rejected her request. Later, she bought two dogs that mangled the rugs and drapes of her suite, for which she reimbursed the hotel.

When finally she departed Hungary, *Népszabadság*, the Party newspaper, ran a lengthy critical article recounting her short stay, which evoked the comment from her—"I don't ever want to come back to a Hungary run by communists," as she emplaned for London.

It had been a difficult three days and Phil took a day off and slept, played some golf by himself at the Club's four-hole course, and read a prolix German article Bence Szabolcsi had sent him about Beethoven's hearing problems as discussed in a medical journal filled with scientific terms unfamiliar to Phil.

That night, as he was falling asleep, the Duty Officer phoned to say that someone named István Varga was asking Phil to phone him in the morning. Phil was too tired to even speculate on Varga's identity.

At ten the next morning, Phil called the number left by Varga and discovered he was the new Director of *Interconcert*. Varga apologized for the short notice but thought Phil should know he had just succeeded in squeezing in Ella Fitzgerald who had a few free days while in Germany.

"Well, *you've* booked her and will be handling the arrangements. I appreciate your telling me, but what am *I* expected to do?"

"Perhaps nothing, Faljian *úr*, but I think she would be pleased to know that the American Embassy is aware of her engagement."

"I understand. And *I* would be pleased to call on her."

The jazz vocalist's stay was so brief that Phil decided not to disturb her at the hotel and called on her just before the concert. She appreciated his visit and invited him to a party after the concert.

The Erkel Theatre was so packed that the orchestra pit was cleared for additional chairs, and the large number of standees in the rear overflowed into the aisles. The audience of 3000 was star-studded with Hungarian stage and screen artists, eminent intellectuals and journalists, while the official government box was occupied prominently by the Prime Minister.

Ella Fitzgerald performed for almost three hours, and after she sang the last of four encores and stepped back behind the falling curtain, the audience thundered its appreciation

Ella's party was a quiet affair. She and the Keter Betts Trio were all tired and the occasion consisted of a few welcoming remarks and a dinner. Ella was very gracious and thanked Phil for his presence.

When Phil retired that night, he felt grateful for the two episodes with visiting Americans which had diverted him from the sobering events of the previous week. But now they were gone and his burdens, official and personal, paradeded before his closed eyes, and he fell asleep troubled by a melange of phantomlike images of Grace, Kiki, Fekete, Adamyants and his *Fräulein*, Andropov, Christian Sommer, and above all—the missing manuscript. There could be no question any more, after what Hannelore Weber had said, that it was a more extended composition than the one page Szabolcsi had been permitted by Fekete to see. But where was it and why was Adamyants being so secretive?

Towards noon the next morning, the DCM looked in on him and said—"I'm taking Hager to the airport. Want to come along?"

Phil nodded. 'Why not? he thought, 'these were Hager's final hours here and after the conversation the other night, it would be a conciliatory gesture Hager might appreciate.

They went in the DCM's car—Garland, Hager and Phil—and at *Ferihegy*, Hager checked in, they had a final *fekete* together, and after shaking hands with the DCM, did the same with Phil, who wished him Good Luck, went through Passport Control and, as they watched from the observation platform, boarded with a final wave of his hand.

"Well, so much for our Political Officer. Not really a bad guy. He had a few personal problems, but hell, who doesn't? Don't you think?"

"I've seen worse, Jim. He'll be allright. But definitely not DCM material."

"That's for sure. Say, isn't that the new German guy over there?"

Phil looked across the huge reception lounge and saw Christian Sommer shaking hands with Helga Kirsch, who had three pieces of luggage near her. Phil walked over and greeted them in German.

"Oh, Phil, how nice to see you. I believe you've met my colleague. Christian, you know Phil Faljian of the American Embassy."

"I do indeed," Sommer beamed. "But I hope to know him better."

Helga explained that she was going for consultation to Bonn but would be back in three weeks. Phil wished her a good stay in Germany, and as he was walking away, Sommer asked if they could have dinner the following day. Phil agreed and departed with Garland.

In the car he told the DCM about Sommer's curious attention to him.

"You must realize, Phil, that you've got quite a following here among your fellow dips. You speak the local language, you've got contacts galore, more than anyone in any Embassy, and, from what they all tell me, you're generous with your information. So, it makes sense that Sommer wants to cultivate you."

"Maybe," Phil said softly, deep in meditation as they drove back to the Embassy. "But I just wonder."

There was something unquestionably different about Sommer.

Forty-Two

Around ten the next morning, Phil received a call from Sommer suggesting that they meet that evening at the *Alabárdos* Restaurant in Buda. Phil agreed. He knew the restaurant to be one of the most elegant and expensive in Budapest and rarely went there. The last time had been with Kirk Douglas, where the film star had been lionized by swarms of tourists.

At seven fifty-five, he parked and entered the castle-like interior of the *Alabárdos*. Its candle-lit tables and white walls with their displays of medieval weapons—*Alabárdos* meant halberd—exuded an atmosphere, he thought, reminiscent of pre-war Budapest.

He looked around and saw Sommer wave to him from a dimly-lit corner. The German arose as Phil approached and shook hands warmly.

"I am truly delighted you could come."

"It was kind of you to invite me," Phil responded, still curious about this new member of the diplomatic community.

Sommer signaled to a waiter who took both their orders. When they settled back, Phil was completely relaxed but observed that Sommer was not.

"Are you very busy, *Herr* Faljian?"

"Since we're going to be colleagues and I am an informal person, I would prefer it if you called me Phil, if I may also call you Christian."

"Agreed, Phil. Thank you."

"To answer your question, yes, I have been very busy, but in the last few weeks, busy with visitors who are really very tangential to my work. A movie star and a jazz singer do not mean very much in our overall relations with this country."

"They can create a pleasant atmosphere, can they not?"

Phil laughed—"Do you know of the *Népszabadság* article after our movie star departed? It didn't help much towards creating a pleasant atmosphere. The jazz singer was the opposite. She was featured on the cover of *Muzsika,* which is a real coup, considering the coolness of US-Hungarian relations. But in the long run, it means very little because events such as these are ephemeral. Not so, I might point out, as a visit by your wonderful novelist, Günter Grass."

"Yes, I know he was here last year. It's too bad I hadn't arrived yet. Did you attend his lecture?"

"Most certainly. The Hungarian PEN Club was jammed. Every one of note in literature was there, and he spoke in German, without an interpreter because everyone present understood him. Now *that* was a cultural event. Some of my intellectual contacts still talk about it."

"But you had Isaac Stern and more recently Leopold Stokowski. I would certainly characterize those as true cultural events. Unfortunately, Phil, cultural affairs are not my field, although because we are still a small Mission and not yet an Embassy, we don't have a full-time Cultural Officer. But from what I've heard of you, your interests are widespread, going far beyond cultural matters."

Phil shrugged his shoulders and smiled self-effacingly.

"Because of the people I deal with, information falls into my lap which frequently seems outside of culture," he explained. "But as you will learn, Christian, *everything,* and I do mean *everything*, in a Marxist society is political. I assume this is your first tour in a communist country?"

"It is. Previously, I was stationed in Bonn."

Their orders came and they ate for a few minutes in silence.

Phil wondered if Sommer wanted to probe his mind about the Hungarian political scene. But when the German spoke again, he seemed more anxious to talk about the latest German film playing in Budapest, or noting that West Germany had become Hungary's foremost Western trading partner, or observing that he had absolutely no contact with the East German Embassy.

Throughout these meanderings, Phil had a deep suspicion that this was not why Sommer had invited him to dinner; not why he had wanted to 'know you better,' as Sommer had put it. But Sommer continued in an almost babbling vein, after which dessert was ordered and then coffee. Dinner would be over within five minutes, Phil thought to himself, and so far it had been a total waste of time. Sommer was more on Eric Hager's wavelength than his own.

And then, just after they had had coffee refills, Sommer dropped his first bombshell.

"Tell me, Phil, what success are you having in your search for the Beethoven?"

Phil was just sipping his coffee and when he heard the question, he choked and began coughing. Recovering quickly, he saw that the German was calmly eyeing him. Sommer said—"I didn't mean to startle you like that. My apologies."

"I *was* startled, but it is I who should apologize. Let me understand your question. You are asking me about Beethoven?"

"Not exactly, Phil. I'm asking you about *the* Beethoven. I do not intend to play games, nor to waste your time. I am essentially a straightforward person. So, to be more specific, I am asking about the Beethoven *manuscript*."

Phil looked Sommer directly in the eye and said—"I am no different than you, Christian. I too am candid and ingenuous, so I will have to know some things before I reply."

"Please ask whatever you wish."

"Well, it seems you know that I am searching for a manuscript score by Beethoven."

"I do."

"Do you know what it is exactly?"

"I know that, too. It is the first movement of a Cello Concerto which has been unknown for over 150 years."

"And how did its existence become known?"

"Through the underground machinations of a Hungarian musicologist named Ferenc Fekete who contacted former members of the SS in Germany for some information about it."

Phil was astonished to hear information recited so glibly that he had obtained with so much difficulty. It immediately became clear to him that this was no ordinary dinner between fellow diplomats, and that Christian Sommer was no ordinary Political Officer.

"Now that you've told me this much, can you also tell me why *you* are so interested in this manuscript. I mean, am I going to have competition in searching for it?"

Sommer smiled, spread his hands on the table, and leaned forward—"It all depends on *why* you or I want that manuscript, doesn't it?"

"For its inherent musical value?"

"Come, come, Phil, let us not be naive. Where is your candor now?"

Feeling slightly stung, Phil cleared his throat and said—

"Allright, let me direct the question differently. The manuscript obviously has inherent musical value. But does it have something else that we can discuss openly?"

"Now we are making progress, Phil. *That* is genuine candor. Thank you. Rather than continue this fencing match, let me get right to the crux of the problem. The Beethoven manuscript is the carrier of information which is of the utmost interest to us. More specifically, it has on the back of one of its pages the name of a German officer who defected to the Soviet Union towards the end of the war.

"The defection took place immediately after the July 20 attempt on Hitler's life. The officer was a Major Ulrich von Manteuffel. Our *Wehrmacht* archives contain no background about him, and indicate simply that he existed. By that I mean that although he went by that name, there is no family line, no family tree, and no living relatives which lead to him. This is impossible because there *was* a Manteuffel family, in a famous military tradition, but there was never an Ulrich.

"Since the defection, we have concluded that if he is still alive, this same Manteuffel, obviously a fraud, has to be living in Moscow. The problem is that he has changed his name, and we do not know what it is, or where he is, or what he does. However, you are having frequent contact with a member of the Soviet Embassy which suggests that there must be some kind of rapport between you. We are hopeful that perhaps this may be a channel through which we too can make some headway."

Sommer now sat back, his eyes fixed on Phil, who said—"I see. And may I ask why it is so important that you find this man who was Ulrich von Manteuffel."

"You can most certainly ask, because you must realize how important a role you are playing—and will continue to play. This man is being sought because we know from the files of the *Abwehr* that he may have been instrumental in foiling every plot to kill Hitler, especially the last one, which would have changed the course of history—at least in Europe."

Phil now realized that Christian Sommer was as deeply implicated in the intrigue as he and Adamyants. Further attempts to pretend ignorance would be transparent, as well as useless. But revealing Manteuffel's real name and his whereabouts . . . that was something else again. It was not a matter of honor, for he had made no promise. But he did feel that in revealing so much to him, Adamyants, with the tacit approval of Andropov, had taken him into his confidence, and until the situation left him no alternative, he would respect that trust.

Phil wanted to establish one more thing before the dinner ended. "Christian, you have several times used 'we,' and I have no idea who 'we' represents. Are you at liberty to tell me?"

The German drew himself up to an erect position in his chair.

His face became solemn, and when he spoke, his voice was tense—"First, I must confess to you that my name is not Christian Sommer. Christian yes, but Sommer no. My real name is Christian . . . von Hase."

This time, Phil's cup almost fell from his hand, spilling some coffee on the tablecloth. He pushed his chair back, dried his cuffs with a napkin, apologized for the second time, and looked at Sommer in utter consternation.

"Did you say *von Hase*? I mean, like *Hellmuth von Hase?*"

"Yes, Phil, that is what I said. But *that* von Hase is a distant relative. Much closer to me was another member of our family. Does the name *Paul* von Hase mean anything to you?"

"The general who would have taken over the Berlin Command in Operation *Walküre* if Hitler had been killed . . ."

"Exactly."

". . . and who was executed."

"Also correct. So now, Phil, I will answer your question as to who I mean when I continually say 'we.' *We* are the sons of Hitler's victims. My name is von Hase, but it might just as well be Stauffenberg, Canaris, Goerdeler, Oster, Dohnanyi . . . need I go on?"

Phil listened in a near state of hypnosis at this recital of the most famous names in the German resistance to Hitler—all of them, and thousands more, executed after the July 20 plot. Sommer continued—"Whoever Manteuffel really is, remains for us a matter of the most urgent priority. We have studied every piece of evidence and every detail of every assassination attempt, and we have concluded that this traitor intervened in every instance to foil the plans of all the heroes of the German Resistance. Every one of these courageous and patriotic men died because of this man's treachery and we shall not rest until we have seen to it that justice is done—our way."

Sommer concluded this dramatic account of his mission. His hands were trembling and Phil realized that the earlier coolness of his manner was but a facade hiding a soul in turmoil. Phil had an urge to lean forward and shake his hand. He liked Sommer. He recognized a certain nobility in this German, and he respected his mission.

There was something else Phil pondered. The German kept referring to Manteuffel as a 'traitor' and ' a 'defector,' which revealed that those who were seeking vengeance thought of him as a German. Obviously, they did not know the truth, namely that Manteuffel had really been a Soviet Intelligence officer who had executed a remarkable strategy, right under the noses of Adolf Hitler, the German General Staff, German Counterintelligence and even the German Resistance.

How long he could keep, or wanted to keep, Sasha's identity a secret had in the last moments become a burning moral issue which he knew would trouble him. It was obvious that he had to discuss this further with Adamyants, with perhaps even the possibility of having to disclose the German's mission. But in speculating on what Adamyants' reaction would be, Phil had a suspicion that his Soviet colleague knew more than he had let on.

When they left the *Alabárdos* together and shook hands, Sommer thanked Phil for his time, apologized for having drawn him into what he called 'our intrigue,' and requested that Phil continue to address him, at least in front of others, as Sommer.

His final words stayed with Phil for some days—"I know what you did for Hellmuth von Hase at the end of the war when he fled Leipzig and came to Bad Nauheim. Our entire family is grateful to you. And now, it seems almost like destiny that another von Hase is soliciting your help, this time here in Hungary. Therefore, please try and understand what we are seeking to do, why we are doing it, and, most important of all, that we need *your* help to accomplish it."

Forty-Three

Phil was working quietly on his In-Basket, trying to empty its contents consisting mostly of requests from Washington for information he considered largely superfluous, when a knock on his door made him look up. It was Frascatti.

"Yes, Sal. What's up?"

"Sorry to bother you, Phil, but there 's been a change in the Duty Schedule because of Hager's departure. I wonder if you're free, and wouldn't mind taking duty tomorrow night. I know you're one helluva busy guy and this is very short notice, but, to tell you the truth, it would really help me out."

Phil liked Frascatti for his directness and unaffected ways. The ex-Marine knew what his job was in the Embassy and didn't put on any airs about it. His mission was to safeguard the Embassy against every kind of penetration and to protect the staff. He was aware that his was a twenty-four hour a day responsibility and he carried it out with dedication. He had acquitted himself extremely well in the demonstration against the Embassy the previous year and had been commended by the DCM.

"Sure, Sal, I'll be happy to fill in, if it will help you out. Tomorrow night, right?"

"Right, Phil. Many thanks. It *does* help me out. I owe you one."

"No you don't."

Phil did not really want to take duty. He had hoped to spend that night at home catching up on his reading of several articles in Hungarian literary quarterlies. There seemed to be an ideological feud going on between Hungarian and East German communist theoreticians about the views of György Lukács, which interested Phil very much. That would not be possible now, not with the various requirements of Night Duty: taking the Cardinal for his walk, bringing him his food, taking the tray away, checking the offices of every staff member for openly displayed classified documents, and finally, the dreaded excursion into the fourth floor and attic.

He suddenly had an idea. Why hadn't he thought of this before? Why hadn't *anyone* thought of it? He went down to the second floor where the military attaché offices were and asked for the list of films which had just come in—Hollywood feature films circulated by the Department of Defense for the morale of staffs in the Soviet Union and East Europe. In the previous week's circular he had noticed one particular film for this week and when he ran his eyes down the list of eight films, he beamed. It had come in. He wrote his name down reserving it for the following night, and returned to his office.

Towards noon, he went to Cardinal Mindszenty's door and knocked. On hearing a dim response from within, Phil entered.

"Your Eminence, please forgive this disturbance."

"You are not disturbing me, Mr. Secretary."

"Tomorrow night, Your Eminence, I shall be on duty."

"Ah, that is good. We can have a good talk. I've been wanting to continue our discussion on certain aspects of Armenian Christianity, specifically about the dual nature of Christ."

Accustomed to the Cardinal's probing curiosity about the divergent tenets of the Armenian Church, about which Phil felt largely ignorant, he was pleased that he could divert the Cardinal's attention with an alternative.

"Your Eminence, have you ever had the desire to watch a film, here in the Embassy?"

The Cardinal adjusted the small red cap on his head, and said with a smile—"You know, Mr. Secretary, I cannot imagine there is a film whose theme would be of sufficient interest to hold my attention for an hour or two."

Phil approached the table at which the Cardinal was seated, poring over Viennese newspapers, and said—"I can fully understand that, Your Eminence. But let me try something out on you. You know of Michaelangelo's work in the Vatican."

"Of course. He painted the Sistine Chapel."

"At the request of Pope Julius the Second, with whom he also had a running dispute about his work. Would you be interested in seeing a film of about two hours depicting their relationship, Michaelangelo's life and this huge undertaking?"

The Cardinal's eyes sparkled—"*Is* there such a film?"

"There is. It is called *The Agony and the Ecstasy* and if you wish, tomorrow night, I can show it to you. I saw it a few years ago and enjoyed it very much. I know you will too."

"I already have the feeling that I will, especially if you recommend it. Please make the arrangements."

Phil informed the Ambassador who commended him for thinking up ways to entertain the eminent guest of the Embassy. The following evening, after the courtyard walk, the Cardinal's tray was left at the third floor entrance and Phil took it in to him, with the suggestion that the screening begin around eight-thirty. The Cardinal agreed.

At eight-twenty, the Cardinal emerged from his quarters and sat in a large easy chair Phil had placed at a convenient distance from the screen, switched off the lights and started the film.

Phil enjoyed the Cardinal's reactions as Charleton Heston and Rex Harrison quarreled and quibbled until finally the masterpiece was completed. The Cardinal sat enthralled, especially when the interior of the Sistine Chapel was on the screen, and when finally it ended, he applauded, turned to Phil and said it had been one of the most enjoyable nights of his asylum.

Later, alone in the Communications Room where he was trying to sleep, Phil's mind was a phantasmagoria of scenes from the film and scenes from the obsessive features of his recent life. The question of authenticity loomed large, mostly because of the chance remark by AVO Colonel Polgár repeated to him by Ilona. These doubts were further fueled by his own preoccupation with the Van Meegeren forgeries of Vermeer. A sudden thought made him smile: could anyone forge the Sistine Chapel? Because of its site and dimension, Michelangelo's masterpiece was unfakable. Vermeer, on the other hand, was not. Those small jewels of art were measured only in inches. As for music, why couldn't a Beethoven manuscript be forged, too? Why not, indeed!

He mused about the nature of his assignment. This was certainly not in the line of normal diplomatic work—entertaining a Cardinal of the Roman Catholic Church, a recluse for eleven years in the Embassy, wanted by the Hungarian Government should he dare to set foot outside the Embassy, urged by papal emissaries from Rome and Vienna to vacate the Embassy and go to the Vatican.

That was one strange component of his Hungarian assignment, Phil mused. There was also the other, not one imposed by his government, but by himself—the search for a Beethoven score which might be apocryphal. In either case, its inherent worth appeared to lie not in its cultural value but in something which by sheer chance had been scribbled on the back of one of its pages. That, plus the inclusion of Christian Sommer in the enigmatic equation, put a twist on events which were confounding.

Suddenly, out of nowhere, a phrase insinuated itself into his thoughts: 'There is something else as well . . . but perhaps it is no longer important.' Phil sat up, his eyes narrowed. Those words 'There is something else as well . . . ' His mind slowly focused on an interview, twenty years earlier, in Bad Nauheim. It was coming back now . . . with the elegant German, yes, with Hellmuth von Hase! And after all these years and all that had transpired, that 'something else' was *indeed* important. Von Hase had clearly been thinking of the name Goerdeler had scribbled on the back page of the manuscript. For him, at that time, in Bad Nauheim, it had no longer had any importance.

For Phil, now, in Budapest, it had become the core of his problem.

Forty-Four

A week later, Phil was called by the Secretary of the Hungarian PEN Club, inviting him to a Conference of European Poets that would take place the coming weekend. Phil was aware that no American poets had been invited, and said so, but the Secretary observed that the American Embassy's Cultural Officer would certainly not wish to be absent from a Conference that included Louis Aragon of France, Salvadore Quasimodo of Italy, Stephen Spender of Great Britain and Alexander Twardowsky, the liberal editor of the Soviet periodical *Novy Mir.* Phil agreed that because of such a distinguished assemblage, he could not stay away. As it turned out, none of the four came. Nevertheless, some 86 poets from 17 countries showed up and, in the long run, Phil did not regret attending.

The key speaker was Hungary's Gyula Illyés, the most respected of Hungarian writers and, after the death of Zoltán Kodály, the most esteemed Hungarian patriot whom not even the regime could touch. Phil spoke with Illyés at the opening of the Conference and the poet complained that while none of the major figures who had initially accepted were in evidence, those who did come were 'a strange assortment of birds.'

As Phil discovered, two of these 'strange birds' came from Great Britain and provided some of the most memorable and entertaining moments of the Conference. One was Edwin Morgan, who was an exponent of what he called Concrete Poetry, in which the arrangement and typography of words formed striking visual images. An arresting example was Morgan's "Siesta of a Hungarian Snake," which consisted entirely of the following—

s sz sz SZ sz SZ sz ZS zs ZS zs zs z

Morgan was generous in including mention of Karl Shapiro and William Carlos Williams in a lecture he delivered, noting that without these two American poets, any survey of world poetry would be incomplete.

But the most sensational moment of an otherwise uneventful Conference arrived when another British poet, George Macbeth, recited what he termed a love poem dedicated to the only two pandas outside of Asia: An-An and Chi-Chi. The Hungarian press had been lavish in its attention to the attempted mating of these two pandas from the London and Moscow zoos, and the audience sat enthralled as Macbeth began his recital.

The poem consisted of the dual syllables of each panda's name. Employing every possible combination of the two basic sounds, Macbeth cleverly conveyed the situation of a coy lover and the reluctant beloved, ranging from the gently-spoken "An . . . An?" and "Chi . . . Chi?" to the more determined "Anchi-anchi . . . Chian-chian," eventually reaching a peak of primordial passion with the staccato repetition of "Anananan . . . Chichichichi," which had the audience clapping and cheering. It was an astonishing demonstration of what Illyés in his speech had called "the universality of poetry," and the audience of poets devoured it with enormous gusto.

As Phil left the PEN Club and drove back to the Embassy, his mind turned to the more immediate problems at hand. His dinner with Sommer, or von Hase, as he turned out to be, had given him yet another jolt in a sequence of astonishing revelations. It compounded the problems that he himself faced in what had initially begun as a straightforward search for a missing manuscript, but had since evolved into the intrigues of the German Resistance, the charmed life of Hitler, the involvement of the Intelligence Services of two, perhaps three countries, the murder of a Hungarian intriguer, the high-level interest of a prominent

Kremlin official, and the overriding issue of protecting the identity of a mystery figure in Moscow who seemed to be the focus of everyone's attention.

Phil brooded over the many facets of the dilemma. There was the KGB on the one hand, exemplified by the enigmatic person of Andropov, which, if Adamyants was to be believed, was working to protect one of its own as part of the larger scheme of protecting the good name of the President. There was the AVO, resentful of the KGB, motivated perhaps by questions of turf, but also—because of the Soviet hold on Hungary—possibly by the dormant goadings of nationalism. If Ilona were here, he mused, she could have learned something from her AVO friend.

He realized suddenly that he was caught in Budapest traffic and unable to drive on. It gave him time for a bit of self-pity. How did I ever get into this mess, he thought, when all I wanted was to find a piece of music? Sheer fate had put someone's name on the manuscript that had no bearing whatsoever on the document's cultural value, and yet, it had turned his world upside down and gotten him caught in a web of intrigue involving elements alien to his interests and irrelevant to his objective.

The traffic began to move again and Phil reached the Embassy and parked on the side street. It was very late in the afternoon but he decided to look in for messages. There was one, from Ambassador Quigley, asking Phil to phone the Residence around eight that evening. Phil walked over to the DCM, who was still working, and asked if he knew anything about the message. Garland looked up briefly, shrugged and shook his head.

At home, he dined, Erzsébet cleaned up and left, and at eight he phoned next door, It was the Ambassador himself who answered the call.

"Thanks for phoning, Phil. Can you come over for a few minutes? Grace and I have a special request."

In the two minutes it took to walk over to the Residence, Phil tried to fathom what kind of request this would be, the source being "Grace and I." He knocked on the side-porch door and entered the living room where Ambassador Quigley was reading the Paris Herald-Tribune. He arose on seeing Phil, shook his hand and asked if he would like a drink, just as Grace joined them. Once served by the butler, they all three relaxed and engaged in idle conversation about the weather.

Within minutes, however, Ambassador Quigley came to the point. "Phil, Grace and I would like to get out of Budapest for an overnight excursion. We'd like to go somewhere in Hungary, someplace special, where something cultural is happening. I know we can count on you to come up with an unusual suggestion If you know of something like that soon, perhaps you can work it out for all of us. Of course, we'd like you to come along too."

Phil shot a fast look at Grace, who hid a smile behind her large whiskey. The source of this proposal was no longer a mystery. He cleared his throat and said it was a good idea because it was not only relaxing but would show the Hungarians the interest of the Ambassador in their country and the broadness of his horizons.

"May I chat with you about it tomorrow in the Embassy, Sir?"

"Of course, my boy. I'll be delighted."

Phil drained his glass and arose to go. Grace said she would show him out. She walked behind him to the side porch door and when they were alone, he whispered—

" Grace. What's this all about?"

"I just want you to be with me—with us—away from everyone else."

The next morning, he went in to the DCM. "Jim, something of a problem has popped up. The Quigleys want to spend two days away from Budapest but inside Hungary. They've asked me to arrange an outing to a cultural event . . . and to go along. Ordinarily, that might not be so unpleasant. But . . ."

"But what, Phil?" Garland asked, leaning back in his chair, his eyes locked with Phil's. "Isn't that the function of a Cultural Officer?"

"Jim, you of all people in this Embassy should realize what the hell is going on."

"Yes, but he'll be there too, won't he?"

Phil rotated completely around in disbelief, his palms against his head, and said—"Come on, Jim, be realistic. You know what's on her mind. Besides, aren't you the one who's been pressing me to tell her off? Well, for your information, I have."

Garland arose from his chair—"I don't believe you. You actually . . . did?"

"More or less, yes," Phil replied, his eyes downcast.

"What does that mean—more or less?"

"Well, I told her that she apparently hasn't gotten my message that . . . I'm not interested."

"I see what you mean by 'more or less,'" Garland said, "but it's meaning is clear."

"Yeah, so clear that now she wants me to join them in an excursion. And if we do what I originally had in mind only for Kiki and myself, it'll be an overnighter."

"Which was?"

"You know the Eszterházy estate in western Hungary?"

"I've heard of it, but was never there."

"Well, in ten days, the Tatrai String Quartet is going to give a recital in the Eszterházy Castle and I was going to ask the Foreign Ministry's permission to attend. It's well beyond the 40-kilometers we are restricted to, as you know."

"Not a bad idea. I don't know how the Quigleys feel about string quartets, but it's worth a try."

"Jim, I don't want to be alone with them."

"What can I do about that?" Garland's voice had suddenly become tart.

Phil squinted at his colleague, "You and Sarah can join us."

Garland remained silent for a few moments. His eyes had narrowed into what seemed to Phil to be an almost hostile stare. "Let's get something straight here. You're not interested in Sarah and me enjoying an excursion and concert. What you want is protection."

Sheepishly, Phil conceeded that it was, but he persisted—"OK, maybe that is part of it, but don't you think we might convert the occasion into some fun in Haydn's back yard?"

Garland considered that for a moment. "I don't know." Another pause. "It depends also on the dates." Phil named them and said it would be a weekend. Garland checked his calendar and murmured—it seemed to Phil with reluctance—that it was clear.

Looking up at Phil, he added—"I'll check with Sarah but I'm sure she'll agree. OK. We'll come along. It's only for an overnight and it is in-country. "But," he continued with emphasis on the word and looking intently at Phil, "I've got a condition."

"Sure, Jim, anything," Phil said, his hopes rising.

"Don't look so pleased. You won't like it, but it's a condition from which I won't back down. Here it is: this trip is the watershed, Phil. Somehow, you're going to find the moment to tell her—Grace, lay off, stay away from me, I am absolutely not interested. And you're going to do that in the next 48 hours."

Phil had never heard the DCM speak to him with such firmness and determination, and he knew there was no alternative.

Garland watched as Phil clenched his fists, his face a grim mask, and concluded—"Otherwise, Sarah and I stay home."

Reluctant to meet Garland's gaze, Phil merely nodded with castdown eyes, his jaw set.

As though feeling compassion for the tension his friend was undergoing, Garland said gently—"I'm aware of your concerns if you do this, Phil, but you have two things going for you—the Old Man's respect, and mine. Neither of us will let you down."

Phil finally met Garland's gaze and thanked him. He went up to Kiki and said he'd like to talk to the Ambassador. Kiki, seeing no one was within view, blew him a kiss, arose and went in to the Ambassador's office. She emerged with a smile and waved him in.

"What have you come up with, Phil?"

"Sir, how do you feel about going on a car trip to Western Hungary, a ride of about two hours or so, to see a castle and attend a very exclusive concert?"

Ambassador Quigley arose from his chair, opened his arms wide and exclaimed—"You never fail me. That is a great idea and I know Grace too will be delighted. Now, you *are* coming with us, aren't you?"

"Yes, Sir, with pleasure. May I make a suggestion? How would you feel if the Garlands joined us?"

"Excellent! Why not? Set it up and I'll tell Grace. And listen, Phil, while you're at it, why not bring someone yourself."

At that moment, Kiki entered the office with a batch of cables from Washington and other East European posts. She overheard Quigley's final comment and said—"Going somewhere, Mr. Ambassador?"

"In fact, yes, Kiki. Say Phil, what do you think?"

Quigley tilted his head in Kiki's direction. Phil responded—

"Kiki, the Ambassador is inviting you and me to a two-day excursion together with the Garlands. Can you join us?"

"It's an overnight somewhere?"

"Yes, we go on a Saturday morning and return Sunday evening."

"Count me in. With great pleasure."

When Phil got home that night, Erzsébet told him the Rabbit had called, and that she sounded upset. Phil did not return the call.

As that weekend approached, Phil wrote a memo to the Ambassador and DCM explaining that the car trip would be partly on side roads and might last as much as three hours; that the Esterházy Castle was located in the town of Fertöd, and that there were rustic but comfortable sleeping accommodations which he had already reserved—four rooms in all.

On the evening before the trip, Phil saw Imre standing by the Lincoln waiting to drive the Ambassador home.

"I'll see you tomorrow morning, Imre," he said, but Imre shook his head dourly—

"No, Faljian *úr*. I am not driving to Fertöd. The Ambassador decided he wanted to drive his own car."

Phil was surprised to hear that. There had been occasions when Quigley had driven his Chrysler, but that was on short trips, to the Club, or just in the nearby countryside. Fertöd was more than two hours away and seemed to him a strenuous experience for the Ambassador.

The next morning, Phil walked over to the Residence at ten. Grace met him at the porch, and muttered—"I know we're *behind* the Iron Curtain, but you didn't have to draw one *between* us. While you were at it, why didn't you invite the whole God-damned Embassy? Any way you do it, I'll have my eyes on you."

Her words catapulted Phil into despair and he bemoaned the loss of a much-anticipated weekend with Kiki which had included the further treat of attending a chamber music concert. He looked coldly at Grace as she fussed with her hair.

She had put on too much makeup, wore a garish green scarf around her head and was in red pants. She was dressed for a picnic, not a cultural event. He walked into the Residence where Ambassador Quigley greeted him warmly, dressed also in sport clothes. Moments later Imre arrived, bringing Kiki, as the Ambassador had instructed. Grace's reaction to her husband's secretary was visibly frigid. She made the seating arrangements after the Garlands arrived, having Kiki drive with them while Phil sat in the back of the Chrysler with her,

As they drove down through *Zugligeti út* and towards the Northwest, George Quigley called back over his shoulder—"Phil, I'm counting on you for directions. Perhaps you should sit up front with me."

"No, he can't," Grace called back. "I'm not sitting all by myself. Phil can direct you from here."

They drove on the usual highway out of Budapest, the Garlands following close behind. When they arrived at Györ, where the road took them normally to the border at Hegyeshálom and then on to Vienna, Phil directed the Ambassador to take a left towards Sopron. Some thirty minutes later, after taking a side road off the highway, they arrived at Fertöd. All disembarked and Phil directed everyone to the accomodations for the night, even though it was only two in the afternoon. The building housing their rooms was behind the mustard-colored castle, and when they were all together, to everyone's surprise, Grace took it upon herself to assign the quarters. Jim and Sarah Garland watched with amusement as Grace designated one double for herself and her husband, another for the Garlands; for Phil and Kiki, she pointed to rooms at opposite ends of the floor. George Quigley slapped his hands together and said—"Well, Grace, we're all grateful to you. Now, why don't we get settled, and then re-assemble for lunch."

Kiki shot venomous looks at Grace and withdrew into her room at the far end of the corridor, as Phil did into his. Grace appeared to be in better spirits and was humming a tune as she opened the door and ordered her husband to bring in the luggage.

In his room, Phil sat on the edge of the bed, his head in his hands and thought—'How am I ever going to get through this?'

Forty-Five

Because the concert was to be given at four o'clock that afternoon, everyone freshened up quickly, drove to a nearby inn where the chef, excited at having his small establishment visited by American diplomats, and the United States Ambassador no less, recommended a sumptuous Hungarian lunch, followed by a chestnut *purée* with whipped cream for dessert, and ending with a cup of *fekete*. Phil winced on hearing the name that had ugly connotations for him.

The concert by the Tatrai Quartet took place in a large ornate room of the castle with 20-foot high mirrors on all sides, and a ceiling depicting a celestial scene filled with cherubs and clouds.

The program included, as it had to in view of Haydn's thirty-year residence at the Eszterházy estate, a Haydn quartet, followed by chamber works of Kodály and Schubert. When the concert was over, it was five-thirty and quite dark.

At Phil's suggestion, they dined in Sopron, returned to their small overnight quarters, Grace bade everyone "Sweet dreams!" and waited at her door until Phil had gone to his room and Kiki had retreated sourly to hers at the very opposite end. The next morning, they assembled at nine for breakfast at the inn and then made a tour of the castle.

Phil was conversant with the castle's history and served as tour guide, describing how it had been built in the mid-eighteenth century by Miklós Eszterházy on the model of Versailles. Its gardens, known as the "French Park," were in fact almost a duplicate of the beautiful gardens of its model, but much shabbier. It was where Joseph Haydn had spent almost three decades of his life in composition and conducting the court orchestra.

As they toured the many rooms, Phil overheard a guide tell another group of visitors from Austria—the border was only minutes away—that Beethoven had once conducted at Fertöd. He lowered his head and suppressed a smile. Tour guides were notorious for mixing fact with fiction. Phil knew from his readings that Schubert had been to Fertöd twice as a music teacher, but Beethoven never, although he had once composed a Mass at the request of Prince Nikolaus Eszterházy to be performed in the chapel. But the mere mention of Beethoven was enough to set his mind to churning. He had hoped to temporarily escape the mysteries of his obsession on this Eszterházy weekend, but knew that his and the Beethoven manuscript's destinies were inextricably intertwined.

The tour of the castle could have lasted all day but the Quigleys began to show signs of fatigue—in Grace's case, boredom—and the Ambassador said it was a long drive back and he wanted to get home before dark. Phil proposed a quick lunch, after which they all returned to their rooms, packed, and by three o'clock were ready to board the two cars. By pre-arrangement with Phil, the DCM informed the Ambassador that he and Phil had some work to prepare for the following morning and wanted to discuss it on the return drive. The Ambassador agreed, and with a glowering Grace sitting beside him, they drove off.

As Sarah and Kiki chatted out of earshot, Garland looked pointedly at Phil, who, understanding its meaning, pleaded—"Jim, I never had an opportunity to talk to her."

"Well, your 48 hours aren't up yet," Garland observed as Phil, nodding sullenly, joined Kiki in the back seat of the Garlands' car. The drive home was relaxed, largely because of Garland's attempts to lighten the atmosphere.

"Sarah and Kiki, I think you both have heard one way or the

other that Phil is searching for a manuscript by Beethoven. He is becoming a Beethoven scholar in the process. So, Phil, tell us some of the more interesting things you have learned about the great man. Anything that'll kill a couple of hours."

Phil was pleased with the suggestion and went into a long discourse on Beethoven's manners, habits, the impact on him of his growing deafness, which began when he was only 28 and was the cause of his occasional distemper, the messiness of his quarters—socks, shirts, papers strewn all over the floor—which extended even to his person—not shaving daily because he always cut himself, his awkwardness, such as the inability to keep time when dancing.

Garland interrupted to ask—"What's your prime source for all this?"

"An excellent biography by a man named Thayer who spoke to people who had actually known Beethoven personally. But a few years ago, another scholar named Emily Anderson collected some 1570 letters Beethoven wrote to over 230 people all over the world. How she was able to decipher his atrocious handwriting is a miracle in itself. Most of my reading is in Thayer and Anderson. But there are still large numbers of letters and manuscripts yet to be discovered. There are also forgeries. Anderson tells us that his impossible handwriting, especially in the final years, was not difficult to forge."

He stared out the window, his mind not on the letters but on the missing manuscript and said abstractedly—"Forgery is an on-going problem, in all of art," and continued: Beethoven's letters were filled with concern over money—commissions, sales, personal,expenses, rent, servants' wages, repairs of clothing—but he was not a pauper. Phil described Beethoven's fame while he was still alive when musicians would come to kiss his hands and how the public idolized him as 'the greatest composer in the world.'

"So, Thayer and Anderson are your main sources of information?" Sarah asked.

"Primarily, yes, but there are also his Conversation Books. You know, in his last nine years, when he was totally deaf, he always kept sheets of paper or a notebook with him in which people would write down something to which he would respond. Altogether there were over 400 of these, but one of his friends burned most of them thinking they were unimportant—can you imagine!—so we now have only 138."

"Could you clear up something for me, Phil?" Garland asked, half turning around. "I read once that on his death bed, there was a clap of thunder and he raised his fist in defiance and then died. Is that true?"

"Yes, it is, and no wonder that it has mythic overtones. Can you believe that in late March, when Vienna was still covered with snow, there would be a thunder storm? Beethoven lay comatose for two days, with some of his friends present. Then, as the final hour approached, there was a flash of lightning and a violent clap of thunder. Since he was stone-deaf, it couldn't have been the *sound* of the thunder that awakened him, but possibly the vibration, or maybe the lightning. In any case, Beethoven opened his eyes, lifted his right hand, fist clenched—some have interpreted that as defiance—and fell back dead."

"Can I ask something" Kiki piped up? "I haven't heard you say anything about his love life. Didn't he like women or was he . . . different?"

"No, Kiki, he emphatically wasn't what you not so subtly imply. He adored women, fell in love with every female pupil he had, and he had many. Then there is the great enigma of the Immortal Beloved. When he died, a letter was found in his desk, never sent, addressed to an unknown woman. Who she was has preoccupied scholars for a century and a half. The best guess had been Therese von Brunsvik, whom he got to know when he visited Martonvásár, here in Hungary. But a few years ago, thirteen letters were discovered, addressed to Therese's sister Josephine. But doubts still continue. We may never know who the mystery woman was."

With less than an hour left, Garland asked Phil to recapitulate for the two women exactly how he had first learned of the manuscript, where his search had led him, and how matters now stood. Phil did, making certain to omit all the details he had kept from his friend. Those, he thought to himself, will have to wait until I know more myself.

Now everyone became silent, pondering the various facets of Beethoven's personality, and the complexity of Phil's hunt for the manuscript. He, on the other hand, brooded over the frustration of not knowing where, in all the materials he had researched, there might be a clear-cut clue to illuminate the mystery surrounding that manuscript.

He looked blankly at the passing landscape on the highway back to Budapest, which was less interesting now that it was getting dark. More demanding of his attention was a very content Kiki who snuggled up to him in the shadows. As he put his arm around her, Phil caught Garland's approving eyes in the mirror but, at the same time, the DCM's glance served to remind him of his pledge to confront Grace once and for all. When would he be free of that burden, Phil asked himself, feeling the desperation spread within him like an all-consuming disease?

Forty-Six

The Garlands dropped Kiki off at her apartment, then drove Phil to his residence.

The DCM accompanied Phil to the door and said—"You're not going to let me down, are you, buddy? I realize you couldn't have spoken at length with Grace yesterday or today. But we did make a deal. I'm expecting you to keep your word, just as I've kept mine by coming along on this trip."

Phil knew deep in his heart that his moment of truth was near. Once inside, Phil made himself a drink, took a shower and lay back on his bed, staring at the ceiling. The drink did little to quiet his nerves as he began to visualize the scene he knew could no longer be avoided: the words that would knife into her heart, her shock, then her rage, her accusations of cowardice, attacks on his manhood, all of this delivered with rising hysteria . . . the outcry of a scorned woman!

Phil sighed, poured himself another drink and decided to divert himself. On his nighttable he spotted the German volume by Dr. Keilberth on Beethoven's Conversation Books. He picked it up, nestled in bed and transported himself into the world of the deaf genius, the singularity of the books underlined by the fact that they contained only what others had written, a one-way conversation consisting largely of questions on which the reader could only speculate as to Beethoven's responses.

The tiring day and the emotional pressure on him began to

take their toll as the rising fatigue overcome him. He fell into a half-sleep and was on the edge of total slumber when the ringing of his phone jarred him back to consciousness. He looked at his watch and saw that it was barely nine o'clock.

Garland's voice was choked with emotion. "Phil, can you get over here right away. Something terrible has happened. Fast as you can."

Phil pulled on whatever clothes were within reach and ran out the door to his car. As he wound his way up the DCM's driveway, he saw that Sal Frascatti's Chevvy was there also. "What's the Security Officer doing here at this hour on a Sunday night," he muttered as he rang the bell.

A dishevelled Garland opened the door and waved him in. Frascatti was standing in the middle of the living room and Sarah was just coming in from the kitchen with a tray of coffee. Uncharacteristically, she didn't smile when she saw Phil.

He turned to the DCM with a questioning look and waited for him to speak.

"Sorry about this, Phil, but . . . but . . . oh shit! Sal *you* tell him."

"At about six o'clock, the Ambassador got lost trying to find the highway back from where you all were today and went down some country road and . . ." Frascatti paused, seeming unable to get the words out.

"Well, tell him, Sal, tell him!"

"He went down a country road and, I guess, couldn't see where he was going, and . . . hit a woman who was walking with a cow. The cow is badly mangled, but the woman is dead."

"My God!" Phil exclaimed. "And he wanted to get back before dark. How do you know all this? Where is he now? I didn't hear them come home."

"They should be home by now," Frascatti said. "I got a call about seven-thirty from the Foreign Ministry saying the Ambassador had been held by the police at a town called Tata something."

"Tatabanya," Phil said. "That's on the way back, not too far from Budapest. So, you went there and brought him home? What shape is he in?"

"He's a wreck, and his wife is going batty."

Phil felt the blood rush to his head. He knew Grace would take her anguish out on him. He looked at Garland, who was staring intently at the floor, clenching and unclenching his fists.

"What now, Jim? Sounds to me like we've got to inform the Department right away and ask for advice. This has some nasty ramifications."

"*Very* nasty ramifications. I think I'd better phone Washington rather than lose time with cables. But first, let's the three of us go to the Residence and see how the Old Man is doing."

The Residence lights were on when they arrived and Ambassador Quigley opened the door himself. His hair was askew, his eyes bloodshot and he was unsteady. Clearly, he had been drinking. Grace was not in sight.

The four of them conferred and agreed to the Washington phone call. The Ambassador, slurred in his speech but still able to think, insisted that the DCM do it from the Residence. Garland went into the study and put the call through as Phil tried to console the Ambassador, who seemed on the verge of tears every time he would mention the accident—"My God, Phil, I hit her so hard, she broke my windshield . . . flew up into the air . . . out of my headlights . . . came down about twenty feet ahead. I braked hard . . . the God-damned cow got in my way. It was badly chewed up. Oh, Christ, why did this have to happen?"

Another drink began to stupefy him, which, Phil decided, was merciful, for now he became sleepy. Jim returned from the study, saw that the Ambassador was almost out, beckoned Phil to a corner, and said in a whisper—"The Department Duty Officer will notify the Secretary in the morning, which means in about three hours. Until we hear further, we have nothing to say to the press. Keep them away from the Ambassador, Phil. We'll get our instructions soon. Why don't I go to the Embassy and wait. Sal, you can go home. Thanks for all you've done. And Phil, can you get the Ambassador into bed? Sort of look after him?"

Phil nodded, but was not pleased with the assignment. After Garland and Frascatti left, he helped the Ambassador out of his chair, held him firmly by the waist and walked him to the stairs. When they had reached the first floor landing, Phil guided him to the bedroom.

As he slowly opened the door, facing him in the middle of the bedroom stood Grace. Her hair was almost on end, her eyes blazing, and her mouth distorted. 'This is what Medusa must have looked like,' Phil thought, experiencing, for the first time ever in her presence, the sensation of fear.

"Throw the son of a bitch into bed, and don't expect any help from me," she barked in a voice filled with contempt.

Phil guided the semi-conscious Ambassador to the bed, took off his shoes and covered him with a blanket. He turned now to Grace, who was swallowing the last of her drink, and asked if there was anything he could do.

"Look, kid, don't feed me any bullshit! My idiot of a husband just killed a woman and I know we're in trouble. I told the stupid son of a bitch to slow down. It's dark, we don't know the roads, he's doing sixty-five. Can you imagine that? Sixty-five, and I'm yelling at him to slow down, when all of a sudden, out of the dark, we see this peasant with her cow. Crash! The whole God-damned windshield smashes into a million pieces, the woman is out of sight, up in the air, and we're covered with blood. I don't know when we hit her God-damned cow. But he braked, we got out, and then a car drove up and two men got out."

"You were under surveillance. Maybe for once it was a good thing."

"Yeah, sure. They drove us to the police station. The Chrysler is a wreck. The cow saw to that. So, tell me, what happens now?"

"Jim Garland has informed the Department and he's at the Embassy waiting for instructions. Meanwhile, Grace, why don't you get some sleep."

She looked at him for a long moment, unkempt, slovenly, on the edge of a breakdown. She was pitiful. He led her to the chaise and sat beside her. He had no qualms any longer by displaying sympathy for he sensed that the end of *his* problem was near—without any intervention from him.

"Phil, what's going to happen?" she whimpered in a voice that was childlike.

"I don't know for sure, Grace, but we should know something in a few hours."

His mind raced through the various possibilities: certainly the Hungarian Government's outrage at the killing, even if accidental, of one of its citizens by the American Ambassador; a demand for restitution by the woman's family, and for the cow as well; putting on hold every aspect of US-Hungarian relations; and finally, the possible immediate recall of Ambassador George Quigley. This last he knew would be the worst thing he could tell Grace.

Grace was quietly crying in his arms, George Quigley was snoring nearby, and Phil's world, he observed to himself, had suddenly been very much transformed. He decided to put Grace to bed and join the DCM at the Embassy. She resisted leaving the chaise but he finally forced her up, and suggested she take a shower and then retire.

It was now close to two o'clock in the morning. Washington would be coming to life in another hour or two. He arrived at the Embassy, parked, and greeted the Security Police standing at the door. They seemed astonished to see him and after he rang and the Duty Officer, who was Fillmore that night, let him in, he saw them still staring as he entered the Embassy. Upstairs, Garland was pouring some coffee from a thermos.

"We've got a few hours yet, Phil, so relax and have a cup. How did it go at the Residence?"

"Well, Jim, I think that the tapes that were made tonight might be close to Number One on the KGB Hit Parade this week."

Garland displayed a humorless smile—"The Foreign Service is always toughest on the wives. By the way, if this evolves the way I suspect it will, you're off the hook, and your days and nights—and mine too—will be less stressful."

Garland looked at his watch and said they had still some four or five hours to go before Washington could make a decision. They both took a nap in their offices and were awakened by the morning sounds of the staff arriving, accompanied by banging doors, loud chatter and laughter.

At nine o'clock, the Communications Officer entered the DCM's office with a long cable marked FLASH—EYES ONLY for Garland. He read it and buzzed Phil to come over to his office. He closed the door and handed the cable to the Public Affairs Officer.

It was a personal message from the Secretary of State to the DCM and was in three parts: the first asked that the DCM or whomever he designated express the profound regrets of the United States to the Government of Hungary for the tragic incident, and determine the extent of monetary restitution for the loss to the surviving farmer, which would be paid forthwith; the second informed Ambassador George Quigley of his immediate recall to Washington 'for the good of U.S.-Hungarian relations' and that a suitable assignment would be found for him; the third contained talking points for the PAO and would apply to press inquiries in both Washington and Budapest, the two themes being that: Ambassador Quigley had already completed two years of a normal three-year tour, but because of ill health, had requested re-assignment to Washington. Finally, any further press inquiries concerning the accident were to be deflected and the accident itself be played down as minor and inconsequential.

The Secretary instructed the DCM, or his designee, to inform the Hungarian Government of these talking points as well and gain its concurrence.

The cable concluded with the following comment: "The foregoing has been discussed with the responsible authorities at the National Security Council and approved by the President."

Phil sensed immediately that the NSC authority was Garrison Portland and wondered how much input Ilona had had in the decision.

Whether she had or not, Phil had understood all along that George Quigley could not remain in Budapest as Ambassador. His position had become untenable and he could no longer discuss vital issues with the Hungarian Government with any semblance of moral authority, as long as this accident and the death hung over his head.

But how would he take it? How would Grace?

Forty-Seven

As the DCM related it to Phil at noon the next day, one hour after the cable was decoded, he had taken it to the Ambassador that morning and found George Quigley philosophical about his recall: He had read the message carefully twice and then, like the true professional that he had become, asked dispassionately if Garland had taken care of its instructions. Garland said he was dispatching Phil to the Foreign Ministry explaining that the United States' regrets would sound more sincere if conveyed in Hungarian, to which Quigley had agreed.

He said he did not think there should be the usual round of diplomatic good-byes—"largely tributes that are hogwash," he labelled them—and that adhering to the cover story of ill-health necessitated a quick exit from Hungary. He had also surmised that packing immediate things might take two days, with household effects to follow later, so that departure could be set for mid-week.

"I told the Ambassador that Sarah, you and I were available at all hours of the day or night to facilitate matters, and then drove here to the Embassy.

"So, Phil, the Ambassador agrees that it should be you who makes our apologies to the Hungarians. Get an immediate appointment with Kovács and . . . well, you know what to say."

Phil did and called the Foreign Ministry. The snippy switchboard operators with their flippant "*Külügy*," meaning Foreign Affairs, always reminded him of the same superior attitude of Foreign Ministry operators everywhere. He asked for Deputy Foreign Minister Kovács' office, and when connected, informed the secretary that it was urgent business requiring that he see Kovács as soon as possible. After a brief consultation at the other end, the secretary informed him that an appointment would be made for three that afternoon.

Phil drove on to the *Margit híd* across the angry waters of the Danube and parked at the Foreign Ministry. Inside, he was escorted upstairs to the office of the Deputy Foreign Minister responsible for American and Western Affairs. Tivadar Kovács was waiting for him.

"I know what this is about, Faljian *úr*," he said in Hungarian, "and so, I shall not beat about the bush. Please sit down. May I serve you a *fekete*?"

Phil nodded, and began, expressing the deep regrets of the United States over the incident and hoping that the Hungarian Government would display understanding and magnanimity. The United States was prepared to indemnify the family of the deceased woman, as well as for the cow, and saw no other recourse but to recall Ambassador Quigley from Hungary. The United States also hoped that this incident would not cloud relations between the two countries and that on-going exchange programs in the arts, sciences and education would continue, unencumbered by this tragedy.

Kovács displayed understanding for the United States' position and was amenable to the remaining talking points which Phil ticked off, especially the point stressing that ill health was the reason for Ambassador Quigley's return to Washington. He observed that Hungary wished to minimize any problems with the United States, that the entire incident was highly regrettable, and that he and his colleagues had enjoyed working with Ambassador Quigley and were sorry to see him go. Then, to Phil's surprise, he asked if a new Ambassador was under consideration.

"*Miniszter úr*, you must understand that it is entirely too soon. The accident was only last night. Can you truly believe that the

State Department has had a nominee waiting in the wings for an emergency such as this? We don't operate that way."

"I don't know how you operate in Washington, Faljian *úr*, but let me use this unhappy opportunity to make a point. When Washington decides to send us another Ambassador, he should have one of two qualifications: either he is a close friend of the President, which means he has authority, or, second, he is allied to business interests. Quigley was neither, so, regrettable as his departure is, we hope for an appointment that will move us forward in every way."

Phil sensed that the meeting was over and arose to go just as the secretary brought in two cups of coffee. Discourtesy prevented him from declining, so he remained for another twenty minutes, which was taken up largely with questions from Kovács about the imbalance in the United States between quality and wealth. He failed to understand, for instance, how somewhat as 'trite' as Elvis Presley could make millions while serious opera singers had to work in Europe to make a living.

At the Embassy, Phil reported the substance of the meeting to the DCM, who thanked him and said it appeared everything was as Washington wanted it. "What we do now, Phil, is ward off the press. That's *your* beat."

He then handed Phil a cable which had been received only an hour before. As though oblivious of the bizarre event which had just occurred, it announced the arrival of the Alwin Nikolais Dance Theatre in two weeks. It was an engagement that had apparently been booked some time ago by *Interconcert*, and asked that the Embassy Cultural Officer get further details from the Hungarian agency directly.

"I'll do that after the Quigleys have left," Phil said to Garland. "I think that right now, they must remain our first priority."

The Ambassador spoke with Garland four times on that Monday and twice on Tuesday, announcing that they would depart on Wednesday morning on an Austrian Airlines flight to Vienna, overnight there with the Ambassador, an old friend, and then fly to Washington on Thursday at noon. He also phoned Phil once to ask him to inform his counterpart in Vienna of Washington's talking points for the press.

Phil dreaded the ringing of his phone that first night, and it didn't. But on Tuesday night, towards eleven o'clock, after he had retired, its shrill jangle inches away from his pillow made him start.

"I hope I woke you up," Grace said bitterly. "I'm coming over," and hung up.

Phil leaped out of bed and put on slacks and a shirt in time to descend the stairs and open the door for her. She was unkempt again, as she had been Sunday night, but because of the chill had wrapped herself in her mink coat. She pushed him aside, walked to the liquor cabinet and poured herself a long whiskey, which she downed. in one gulp. Looking at him, she growled—

"Just a final toast to what might-have-been. You failed me, sonny, especially after that blonde bitch came here. And I blame you for the accident. Anyway, in that now famous toast—'Here's lookin' at you, kid,' and I do mean *kid,*" whereupon she threw the remnants of her drink in his face and exited, shouting—"*I don't want to see you at the airport!*"

Phil watched stupefied as she walked out, and although still stung by her final words, felt a sense of liberation that she would soon be out of his life.

He recounted the scene to Garland the next morning and both agreed that it would be unseemly for him not to see the Quigleys off at the airport, no matter what Grace had said.

"You know, Phil, as a good Catholic, I often observe life's sometimes inexplicable vagaries as the ways of the Lord. This may be one of those times."

"Well, Jim, as you know I am not a Catholic, but I am an Armenian, and in our faith, we trust just as much in the Lord's judgment. An old Armenian saying has it that there is good even in evil. I am deeply sorry for the Old Man's misery, but as for Grace leaving, well, it does simplify my life."

"And mine," Garland muttered, with a long sigh of relief.

The next day, he and the Garlands followed the Lincoln as Imre drove the Ambassador and his wife for the last time in Hungary. At the airport, Phil avoided Grace, which was not difficult since she never looked his way, but chatted privately with the Ambassador. Phil thanked him for his support and said he would always hold him in the highest regard.

As the Ambassador shook his hand, he looked Phil squarely in his eyes and said in his gentlest manner—"It is *I* who should be thanking *you,* Phil, because you have been discreet and most considerate in a delicate matter which we have never discussed, but which has not escaped my attention. I have never blamed you. It is an old story, and one to which I have become accustomed. Let me leave you with the thought that you have behaved more prudently and gentlemanly than the others, for which you have a secure place in my esteem."

Phil was stunned as the humbled diplomat turned and walked slowly to the gate. Grace never turned to look back. Sarah accompanied her to the gate and then both Quigleys walked out to the plane as a small group of Hungarian officials—some of them no doubt AVO, Phil speculated—watched with particular interest.

Phil walked with the DCM back to the car, the Ambassador's parting words filling him with equal parts of awe and shame. He turned to his friend and said in a trembling voice—

"Jim, for Christ's sake, the Old Man knew! And he never held it against me."

Forty-Eight

It was one week later that the DCM walked across the hall and looked in on the PAO. "If I'm not mistaken, Phil, we're going to the same dinner party tonight."

"Yes, Jim, at the Brits. Thank Heavens you and Sarah will be there. Do you know if there's a special occasion?"

"Yes. My British counterpart told me that the Mandrakes are putting up a visitor from London, a novelist named Fiona something, and you will be her escort. Lucky single guy. Gets all the women."

"My irresistible Armenian charm."

"Sure as hell couldn't be your mind," Garland grinned.

The Quigleys' departure had greatly reduced the tension between the two friends and Phil welcomed the jocular teasing.

It was an uneventful day in which he busied himself with paperwork and didn't leave the Embassy. Young Fillmore came up from the Consular Section to tell him about a visa request from Miklós Jancso, the famed movie director, to visit New York during a showing of some of his films.

"He wants to go tomorrow, if you can believe it," Fillmore said, "but I told him it would take at least a week. He's very upset and asked for you."

"Well, I certainly can't change the rules, Hal. I'll see him if you think it will do any good."

They both went down to the Consular Section, and learned that Jancso had left in a huff. Phil shrugged, thanked Fillmore and said if Jancso returned, he would talk to him.

By late afternoon, Phil felt drowsy and went home. He told Erzsébet he wanted to take a nap because he would be up late, and that she could leave. She was in high spirits, singing as she worked, a rarity for her. He knew the reason, of course. Only yesterday, just as the phone had rang, she had said as she lifted the receiver—"I know it is not The Rabbit, because she will hop no more in Hungary."

At six, he showered, put on his tuxedo, had a drink and arrived at the British Ambassador's residence punctually at seven-thirty. Although he liked the Mandrakes, he didn't care for black-tie affairs, which was obligatory with the British Ambassador. It also tacitly announced that no Hungarians would be present, simply because Hungarians did not dress up for these diplomatic dinners. Consequently, Phil never looked forward to such occasions where the guests were all diplomats, except, of course, for the occasional out-of-town guest.

In this case, it was Fiona. He never got her last name, which was largely her fault. A reticent, shy woman, she was dressed simply, wore no makeup, had straight, short hair and maintained her mousy demeanor the entire evening. She seemed overwhelmed by the grandiose residence with its crystal chandeliers, richly costumed guests and formally-attired waiters. After several attempts to communicate, Phil gave up trying to decipher the whispered incoherence of her replies.

The Mandrakes had invited ten guests: the Garlands, Phil and Fiona, the French Ambassador and Mrs. Fauquier, the British Embassy's DCM, Derek Thomas and his wife, and the Military Attache, Colonel Broxburn and his wife. The Colonel was resplendent in his striking dress uniform with great splashes of crimson to match his hair. As Phil nursed a drink, he scanned the room and mumbled to Garland—"Do you see any purpose to this dinner?"

"Sure. To entertain your friend Fiona. I think Mandrake is counting on you mostly for that."

"Well, he can forget it."

EX

After dessert, the women left the dining table, as was the British custom, and the ritual of the port wine followed. Ambassador Mandrake poured himself a glass of port and passed the carafe to his attaché, who did the same and extended it to his DCM until the bottle had made the circuit of all six males. Cigars were lit and casual conversation began. Phil had a deep loathing for these moments. In the absence of any Hungarians from whom to learn something, the diplomats turned to each other for information on what was happening in the political life of the country. Ignorance breeding on ignorance, he thought. He saw Garland give him a visual reprimand, having most certainly read his mind.

The time has come, Phil said to himself, for the Ambassador to hold court. Now he will go around the table with his feeble attempts to draw us out and manufacture meaningless dialogue. On cue, Ambassador Mandrake cleared his throat, as though he were rapping a gavel, and said solemnly—

"May I say to our American guests this evening how deeply we regret the absence from Budapest of my close and trusted colleague, George Quigley. I am certain Pierre joins me in this. George and I had developed an excellent relationship which I for one shall miss. A toast to Ambassador Quigley."

Everyone drained his glass in this somber tribute. Phil had resigned himself to an evening of tedium and was just reaching for the wine again when he heard Mandrake address him directly—"I say, Phil, what's all this we've been hearing about some obscure manuscript you're looking for?"

Startled, he looked quickly at Mandrake, then at Garland, who seemed equally surprised by the question. Recovering, he said in temperate tones—"Oh, nothing that will change the course of history, Roger. It's a music score, actually a fragment of a score, that Beethoven *may* have composed. It's authenticity has not as yet been proven."

"I see. Where is this score now?"

"That's part of the problem. I don't know. It could be in Hungary, and it could not. The way things stand right now, I may never know."

"Really? But you are pursuing the problem assiduously, are you not?"

"To the degree my leads and time permit."

"Time? Surely the Embassy gives you considerable leeway in this search. I understand that certain other . . . quarters—if you catch my meaning—are deeply interested as well, which makes me wonder whether we too shouldn't be, let us say, included."

Mandrake's eyes never left Phil's as he fingered his empty wine glass. Phil felt the tug of tension in his chest as he speculated that the British Embassy must have learned of his close association, even collaboration, with the Soviet Embassy and Adamyants. The intrusion of the British Secret Intelligence Service would muddy already murky waters even more. Mandrake's SIS officer was a seasoned though gruff operative who would surely question everyone concerned thoroughly and aggressively. Besides, how could SIS be invited in when Squibb and the CIA had been frozen out?

Phil's eyes darted to Garland who, sensing his concern, turned to Mandrake and said—"Roger, this is not at all what you perhaps suspect it to be. Believe me that it is not a matter of major concern. Some years back, in fact at the end of the war in Germany, Phil was told that there *might* be a piece of music by Beethoven that had hitherto been unknown. He had reason to believe that a musicologist had absconded with the score to Hungary. Hardly any of this has been confirmed, but it has become a kind of preoccupation of Phil's to find it. If I were to tell you that neither Washington nor Ambassador Quigley knew of Phil's search, would that convince you of its lack of relevance to our joint interests here in Hungary?"

Mandrake nodded slowly and deliberatively, as though only partially convinced, but he said—"Yes, I imagine it would. But one never knows how small, seemingly irrelevant things suddenly loom large on our horizons. In any case, it is most intriguing, I must say.

"Derek," he said, addressing his DCM, but with a quick

sidelong glance at Garland, "you will, of course, be kept informed by our good friend Jim here if events warrant our involvement."

Then, turning to Faljian—"I wish you luck, Phil. My own Cultural Officer from the British Council, who is unfortunately on leave in London, is primarily a specialist in literature, as you know. Taught at Oxford. But you are mostly into music. Tell me, is Bartók all that he is cracked up to be? I have difficulty with his music."

Phil swallowed a tart reply to what he considered an inane question, and said instead—"I think, Roger, that if you give him a number of hearings, you will begin to understand why he is surely one of the top composers of the century. You know, in some circless, where they talk of the three B's of music, they are considering adding Bartók to the list."

"Fascinating!" Mandrake said in a way that Phil thought truly expressive of his essential fatuousness. "I understand he left Hungary before the war. Did he have any family here?"

"Yes, his second wife, and a son by his first wife."

"He had a wife here? She must have died since then."

"On the contrary. I visited her last month. Her name is Ditta Pásztory. She was a very good pianist and recorded a number of Bartók's works."

"You called on her?"

"I had just received an album of records by the Juilliard String Quartet in which they performed all six of Bartók's quartets. Presenting the album gave me a good reason to visit her. But it made me quite sad."

Ambassador Fauquier was apparently very interested and anxious to know the details of Phil's visit.

"She lives near the center of town in a dark second-story apartment cluttered with two Börsendorfer grand pianos, piles of furniture, photographs, Bartók memorabilia and God-knows-what. She lives virtually in another world. Birdlike and delicate, she barely understood what I was saying to her. I had studied music with Bartók at Columbia University in 1941 and tried to tell her that. She didn't know what I was talking about. It made me very melancholy."

"I see what you mean," Fauquier said, as the others nodded, all having listened sympathetically to Phil's account.

"Well, that was very unfortunate," Mandrake said. "But I wish you good luck with your search for Beethoven. Wouldn't the AVO enjoy knowing about that?" He laughed, looking for everyone to join in, but no one did.

After an awkward silence, the British Ambassador said—

"Jim, did any of you at the Embassy happen to catch that Hungarian Television program on the Kennedy assassination? I happened to turn it on sometime during the middle, I guess, and wasn't able to understand the narrator. Hungarian is so infernally difficult, don't you know. What did you all think of it?"

Because not everyone at the dinner had seen the program, Garland and Phil spent forty minutes describing its content, which played up the conspiracy theory, pointing fingers at the CIA and FBI. Phil concluded by saying—"The program had one clever angle—the titles. The opening title was 'Who Killed Kennedy?' but at the conclusion, the title was altered by one letter so that the 'Who' of the opening title was not singular, *Ki*, but plural, *Kik*."

"That's quite clever," Fauquier said.

"Yes it is. We can't do that in English."

"So, Phil, will the Hungarians give you the film?"

"They already have and I've shipped it to Washington."

There was a general silence for a few moments, then Mandrake turned to his DCM and said—"Derek, keep in close touch with our American colleagues about that too so we can report everything to the Foreign Office when I get back."

"Are you going on leave, Roger?" Garland asked

"Just my annual trip to Switzerland. I'll be back in a fortnight. Shall we join the ladies?"

EX

In the larger room where they all mingled, Phil observed Thomas and Garland chatting somewhat privately, and relieved that Fiona was preoccupied with Sarah Garland, joined the two DCMs. As Phil approached, Garland turned and said—"Come listen to this, Phil. You won't believe it. I just asked where Mandrake goes in Switzerland. Derek, why don't you repeat what you told me."

Derek Thomas was clearly uncomfortable, and seemed reluctant to continue the discussion, but confronted as he was, there was no way out.

"Ambassador Mandrake has been going to Switzerland for the last twenty-five years. He told me he always lodges at the same place, a small Alpine village called Meiringen. Between Meiringen and the next town, is the spot to which he is drawn."

He stopped talking for a moment and glanced furtively across the room at his Ambassador. Phil looked from Garland to Thomas and said—"What is so remarkable about that? Or is there more?"

"There is," Thomas said, lowering his voice, "and it will surely sound improbable to you, but believe me, it is the truth. Have you ever heard of the Reichenbach Falls?"

Phil shook his head and noticed the amused smile on Garland's face.

"Reichenbach Falls is the place where Sherlock Holmes and Professor Moriarity struggled on the brink and then fell in the abyss to their deaths. Of course, as we later learned from Conan Doyle, Holmes did not die."

Phil's bafflement continued, and he asked—"What has that fabricated event involving two fictitious character s got to do with Mandrake?"

"Remember, I warned you that it would sound improbable. The fact is that for Roger Mandrake, Sherlock Holmes is not fictitious but quite real. He has always believed that Holmes existed, and the Reichenbach Falls, where Holmes ended

Moriarity's career in crime, is for him a sacred shrine to which he returns year after year."

Garland beckoned to one of the waiters and asked for three large whiskies. When he turned to look at Phil, he observed a torturous effort to suppress laughter.

Once the French Ambassador, the senior diplomat attending, prepared to leave, the others, in observance of protocol, knew they could as well. Phil and the Garlands bade farewell to everyone, in the process Phil spending more time in conversation with Fiona than he had all evening. Once outside, they walked to their cars and as Phil held the door for Sarah, Garland said—

"Phil, why don't you follow us home for a nightcap. I've got something to ask you."

At the DCM's residence, Sarah excused herself and retired, whereupon Garland fixed two drinks and plunked himself down in an easy chair.

"That was hilarious, that final bit about Sherlock Holmes and Professor Moriarity," Garland said, chuckling.

"It certainly was. Mandrake sometimes appears to be an odd-ball, but on occasion, I find substance behind that facade. "

"Yes, there is. He's no fool. Roger is very proper in his own way. Likes everything clean-cut, above board, no secrets, especially between his Embassy and ours."

"Well, he certainly proved that with his questions about my musical search. It made me uncomfortable. How do you suppose he knows about it?"

"Oh, I'm sure he overheard some chance remark here or there. After all, your British counterpart sees some of the same people you do and one of them may have said something. I don't think anyone else knows very much. Look at our Embassy. Out-side of me, and very recently Sarah and Kiki, who else knows anything about it? Why are you concerned?"

"Well, the fewer who know, the better. The whole thing has gotten so incredibly convoluted, so complex."

He observed Garland watching him closely.

x

"Phil, is there more that you haven't told me?"

"Not yet. But I promise you that when there is, you will be the first to know." Phil sipped his drink and asked—"Tell me, Jim, what was it you wanted to raise with me?"

Garland cleared his throat, and said—"You seem to have *two* obsessions, Phil, and I've been meaning to ask you about the second one. I'm talking about Vermeer. What's *that* all about?"

"Of course. No mystery there. I saw my first Vermeers, three of them, at the Frick Collection in New York and fell in love with his work. After I read about him, I discovered that although in the forty-three years of his life he painted some 70 canvases, only about thirty-five survived, and I vowed that some day I would get to see them all. You know, in New York alone there are eight Vermeers, and another four in Washington, and I've seen seven in Holland, two in Berlin, and one in Vienna. And that's the reason I simply had to go to Dresden, which adds up to twenty-four."

"Yet, you don't have a single reproduction in your office."

"That's true. The reason is that every Vermeer is small and I wanted something really vivid and large, like the Matisse I have there. Which, by the way, Grace liked very much."

Garland ignored the last observation. "I assume, however, that the Beethoven project takes precedence over seeing the remaining eleven Vermeers?"

"You're not chiding me, are you Jim? Of course Beethoven comes first. It's simply that with this doubt about the authenticity of the manuscript, I say to myself—Forging a manuscript by Beethoven is child's play compared to what Van Meegeren did."

"Who's Van Meegeren?"

"A master forger, Jim, who created paintings so much like Vermeer that, at first, even the experts were fooled."

"I see. Well, I certainly understand your concern. You *will* keep me informed, though, I hope."

"That's a promise, Jim."

As he drove home through the backstreets of Buda and

negotiated his steep driveway, he looked at the Ambassador's Residence and felt near elation that it was dark. The Quigleys' dramatic departure from Hungary had brought relief on two counts—from Grace's relentless and often indiscreet pursuit of him, and, the need for Garland to cover for him during his many absences because of the manuscript search.

The temporary Chief of Mission was his friend to whom he told just about everything. "But even *I* don't know everything," Phil mumbled as he turned off the ignition. He had just promised Garland to keep him informed, and he hoped fervently that he could keep his word. Except that that too was a problem, because the next move was up to Adamyants, and Phil knew what misgivings Garland had about consorting with a Soviet Embassy officer.

EX

Forty-Nine

The intellectual elite of Budapest was abuzz with excitement as the two-day engagement of the Alwin Nikolais Dance Theatre approached. Since the Hungarians had made all the arrangements, the Embassy had little to concern itself with, except that Phil kept tabs on the engagement with regular calls to *Interconcert*, and on the day before the first performance, dropped by the theatre to watch the rehearsal.

Jim Garland had been designated *chargé d'affaires ad interim* by Washington, but because of his innate modesty, had not moved into the Ambassador's office. Phil always kidded him about it and Garland always smiled with embarrassment and waved him away. But he was beginning to show the weight of the burden which George Quigley's recall had placed on him.

"Phil, are you sure Nikolais has everything he needs? What if he isn't getting full cooperation? A complaint to Washington . . . you know . . ."

"Relax, Jim, for Heaven's sake. I've got things under control. Nikolais is satisfied with everything. His manager had some beefs, and I don't blame him. Hungarian Customs held him up for two hours while they examined all forty-two pieces of luggage he brought in for the company. Other than that, everything is fine."

"Any word on sales? You know, Alwin Nikolais is pretty far-out stuff for a conservative country like Hungary."

Phil sat on the edge of Garland's desk and said—"Look, the Opera House seats almost 1500 people, and it's been sold out ever since the first announcements appeared. For both nights. And from what my literary and artistic friends tell me, everybody, and I mean *everybody* will be there. This should outdo even Ella's concert."

With the Residence next door empty, Phil now felt totally free to have Kiki visit him and to frequently stay overnight. Since Grace's departure, Kiki had become so regular a guest that even Erzsébet became accustomed to preparing dinner for two.

On the first night of the engagement, Kiki arrived by taxi in time for dinner and then she and Phil dressed and drove to the Opera House. Phil was gratified to see the official personages milling about in the lobby—government and party figures, newspaper and magazine editors, heads of the various unions representing writers, composers, painters and dancers, as well as the many artists themselves. He was greeted by many and saw his informative friend Tibor Hegedus wave to him as he chatted with Iván Boldizsár, Hungary's Intellectual Ambassador At Large.

It was at that moment that Phil suddenly had an urge to turn his head and look to his left. His eyes met those of the same stranger he had first beheld at the Film Actors Club reception for Kirk Douglas. The stranger, his powerful visage still a standout in the otherwise regular features of the Hungarian crowd, stared back at Phil without any expression, as Phil, uneasy at the attention, took Kiki's arm and guided her to their third-row seats and then went backstage.

Nikolais was in high spirits and said that the company was particularly excited about the engagement. "I know that this isn't exactly normal fare for Hungary, but other communist countries liked us. I hope this audience will too."

The audience did, although it took almost an hour for the fascinated spectators, amazed at what was happening on stage, to react.

Phil looked across the aisle at his friends from the Hungarian Ballet Corps, especially at Hungary's Prima Ballerina, Zsuzsa Kun, who was sitting on the edge of her seat, wide-eyed at the miracles taking place on the staid Opera House stage.

x

The applause was thunderous as the curtain fell for the Intermission. Walking up the aisle, Phil bumped into Deputy Foreign Minister Kovács, who, wagging a finger teasingly, joked—

"So, Faljian *úr*, now you are using dance to corrupt our minds. To tell you the truth, innovative as it looks, I really don't understand it."

"Give it a chance, Kovács *úr*. Maybe by the second half . . ."

As he brought Kiki a juice in the lobby, someone touched his arm. It was Bence Szabolcsi, who said, his voice rising above the din—"I haven't heard from you in some time, dear colleague. Anything new?"

"Unfortunately, no. But we should see each other. I'll call you at the Archives."

"Please do. By the way, this is absolutely exhilarating. I think it must be an entirely new art form."

Phil was about to ask Kiki if she knew anything about Nikolais' Greek connection when a warm Armenian voice said in his ear—"Good evening, Phil. This is a remarkable event for the United States. I am envious."

Phil turned and looked into the smiling countenance of Adamyants. "Krikor! Wonderful to see you."

As he spoke, he realized that Adamyants was not alone. "*Fräulein* Weber. Forgive me. I didn't see you right away. Are you enjoying the program?"

"Tremendously," she replied, continuing in German. "In the GDR, we never see such artistically innovative things such as this. It only confirms what I have always felt about the United States."

She blushed suddenly, turned to her Soviet escort, and said—"I meant no offense, *Herr* Adamov."

He laughed and assured her he took no umbrage. After Phil introduced her to Kiki, Adamyants led him aside and said—"I was looking forward to seeing you tonight. Things are beginning to move and we have to talk. And while I have you alone, perhaps you've noticed the uncommon attention we are getting from across the lobby."

Phil looked into Adamyants' eyes, only inches from his—"No, I haven't noticed. I'll have to look later to see who you mean. I assume it is someone you know."

"It would be more correct to say that it is someone *you* know. *Hüvös Völgy* next Monday?"

"One o'clock. By the way, Krikor, if you haven't already noticed, I find *Fräulein* Weber very attractive."

Adamyants beamed—"So do I, Phil."

Phil turned his attention to Kiki, and as he did, he casually looked in the direction indicated by Adamyants. Standing in a corner smoking a cigarette was Christian von Hase, in the company of Helga Kirsch. Both bowed their heads in greeting as he acknowledged them, and when he escorted Kiki back into the auditorium, he felt the German diplomat's eyes on him all the way to his seat.

Even though the curtain went up to reveal yet another Nikolais conceit, in which the dancers addressed the audience with parts of meaningless conversations spoken simultaneously—an allusion to the Tower of Babel, Phil's mind was preoccupied with the various motifs which his encounters this night with Adamyants and von Hase had evoked.

The Soviet diplomat knew where the manuscript was, wanted to protect his compatriot in Moscow even as he wanted to help his compatriot in Budapest, but was apparently not beyond employing extreme means—the KGB term was 'wet affairs'—to do so.

The German, for his part, was out for revenge, a revenge sought by an entire generation of survivors of Hitler's terror, but didn't know on whom to wreak this revenge. Was Sommer/von Hase in the business of 'wet affairs' as well?

And my role in all this, Phil asked himself, what should it be: to help Adamyants protect the good name of the Soviet President, an Armenian to boot, or to help von Hase avenge the heroes of the German Resistance?

Kiki leaned close and whispered—"What's wrong, darling? You're shaking your head."

Phil had been so immersed in his own thoughts as to be unaware of his demeanor. He apologized to Kiki and sought to become involved in the performance, but it was in vain. The curtain fell, the audience roared its final approval, stomping with its feet until the walls trembled and the lights finally came up.

"Kiki, I'm dropping you off. I'm no good to you tonight. Forgive me."

She was very disappointed and murmured complaints all the way to her apartment. He kissed her in the car and said he loved her.

"And this is one Greek who loves one Armenian," she murmured.

"Don't get ideas," he warned, tweaking her nose.

Driving up the winding road leading to his house, Phil looked over at the silhouetted Residence and wondered what was happening to the Quigleys in Washington. Their departure was already three weeks old, and he and Garland had speculated as to the Ambassador's future in the Foreign Service.

In the morning, there was a note from Consul Fillmore informing him that he had been to the Gorki Book Store on *Váci utca* and seen some books from Armenia. Phil called down to him on the first floor and thanked him.

At noon, Phil walked to *Váci utca*. It was Budapest's most fashionable street—the *Divatszalon* of ZsaZsa fame was also there—and after perusing the music shops with their recordings of East European jazz and rock groups, reached the Gorki Book Store.

There were about a dozen people in the store which was the outlet for Soviet books and artifacts. Phil went to the foreign language section and next to books in Russian, Uzbek and several other Central Asian languages, he saw three books in Armenian. One was a school book teaching the alphabet with pictures, the second was a collection of poetry by Kevork Emin, and the third was a travel guide to Armenia. Phil decided to buy the Emin. He took the slender volume from the shelf and opened it. As he did, a deep male voice speaking in Hungarian sounded close by—"A rare book to be found in Budapest, I am sure."

Phil turned politely to face the speaker. He had discovered that no matter where he went, his apparently obvious identity as an American often prompted total strangers to address him.

But this time he froze as he stared into the same fierce countenance of the stranger who had observed him intensely on two previous occasions—at the Film Actors Club and during the Opera House intermission the previous evening. Despite the bony structure of his face, the heavy nose and deeply cleft chin, Phil continued to find him coarsely handsome. Since the stranger had initiated the conversation, Phil decided to engage him and thereby possibly learn his identity.

"Yes, it is rare. Emin is a contemporary Armenian poet and a rather good one. I would have to travel to Yerevan to find a copy. Yerevan, you know, is the capital of Soviet Armenia."

The stranger smiled and said—"I am well aware of that, Faljian *úr*."

"Do we know each other?"

"In a manner of speaking," the stranger replied.

"Well, since *you* seem to know *me*, may I ask *who* you are?"

"My name may not mean anything to you, Faljian *úr*. It is Polgár Jenö."

Hungarian names, as in many East European countries, were reversed, and for a split second, the name was meaningless. But an instant later. he suddenly realized who the stranger was, and Phil's eyes opened wide—this was Ilona's friend in the AVO!

"I'll be damned!. You are . . . *Colonel* Polgár, aren't you?"

A quick smile parted Polgár's thick lips—"I see that a mutual friend has talked about me. She shouldn't have."

"But only, I assure you, in the best of terms. You told her some things which she repeated to me. Maybe that's why you did. I appreciated that. Can we talk somewhere?"

"No, I regret to say. It will not be wise to be seen with you, but in the few moments we have, just some words of advice. Why, you might ask, is an AVO officer giving advice to an American diplomat? I will tell you why. Ilona phoned me last week and said I should be of help to you. I follow closely what you do, Faljian *úr*, and I know that you mean well. Ilona has confirmed that Hungary has few friends in Washington, but when someone does come to us and displays genuine good feeling, we are grateful."

"When you say 'we,' do you speak on behalf of the AVO, Colonel? In our view, the AVO is no better than the KGB. I hope you will forgive my bluntness."

"You have good cause to think so. But let me assure you that the AVO, like any organization, has its good and bad elements. So does the KGB. So does the CIA. There are colleagues of mine who would find speaking with you utterly deplorable. I feel differently."

"Possibly also because of Ilona?"

Polgár sighed—"Ilona. My life and her life would have been so different if it hadn't been for her father. Isn't she a beautiful woman? She was even fifteen years ago. Well, that is neither here nor there, Faljian *úr*, but listen to me. I do not know everything about this business you are involved in. But I do know that some of my colleagues in . . . another organization play rough. They sometimes stop at nothing. Ilona does not want you to get hurt. This manuscript you are looking for seems to have some secret that . . . my . . . colleagues want to remain a secret."

"You do not know what it is?"

"No, and they won't tell us. That should say something to you about fraternal socialist cooperation. I cannot imagine that I would ever be saying things like this to a class enemy, but, well, according to Ilona, you are different."

"Think of me more as being discreet. Let us also agree that because we have both loved the same woman, we have common ground. As a token of my respect, may I display it by asking you a frank question?"

"You certainly may, but as for answering it . . ."

"Ilona told me you are responsible for Western Intelligence gleaned from diplomatic sources."

"She should not have told you that, but since she already has, please continue."

"Would you be willing to tell me, from the information you already have, whether the German diplomat Christian Sommer is an Intelligence officer?"

Polgár coughed, looked around at the sparsely visited store, turned to Phil and said—"If I answer that, will you also answer a question?"

"I will try to."

"Yes, Sommer is an operative of the *Bundesnachrichtendienst*, the West German Intelligence Agency, Now it is my turn. Tell me—what does he have to do with all this?"

Polgár's face had become rigid, his manner no longer congenial. Phil bit his lip. My God, he thought, what am I getting into: first I deal directly with the head of the KGB and now with an Intelligence officer of the AVO.

"Colonel Polgár, I don't know how much you really know. Doesn't the KGB tell you *anything*?"

Polgár laughed sardonically—"As little as possible, as I implied before. But they demand everything of us. I infer from what you say that they know a great deal."

"To tell you the absolute truth, I don't know how much they know. But this much I can tell you. There is someone in Moscow they are protecting and it is vaguely possible, I stress *vaguely*, that they are protecting him from this man Sommer. How much do you know about him?"

"Sommer? I assume you mean whether I know that his real name is von Hase. Frankly, that means nothing to me. Should it?"

Polgár was watching Phil like a cat, studying his every facial expression. Phil decided not to cross the line any further than he already had.

EX

"Colonel, there are some things which you really must get from your KGB friends. I have been simply searching for a manuscript, I have discussed it with one of your most eminent citizens . . ."

"We know about that. Bence Szabolcsi is a decent man."

". . . and in pursuing it with one of your less eminent citizens . . ."

"Fekete was pure filth. I regret you had anything to do with him. Incidentally, if you can believe me, *we*, and I assume you know who I mean, had nothing to do with his death. But there were severe repercussions in my organization. Somehow, there seems to have been high-level interest in him, but I don't know exactly from what quarter, nor do I understand why."

"Thank you for telling me that, Colonel. Well, in my search, I have also become involved with a Soviet diplomat, which . . ."

". . . has not escaped our attention," Polgár interrupted with a smile. "The triumph of blood over ideology?"

"However you wish to characterize it, Colonel," Phil said, disconcerted momentarily by Polgár's comment, and continued—"Now, I have reached an impasse because of complications which, I might add, the KGB is in a better position to discuss with you. Frankly, I don't know what to do next."

"Tell me, Faljian *úr*, why is this fellow Sommer, or von Hase, so preoccupied with you? We saw him eyeing you last night at the performance. He spends most of his time talking to that Kirsch woman about *you*."

"I can't really answer that, Colonel."

"Well, I wish that I could tell you to turn to me for help, but under the circumstances, that is really impossible. An American diplomat seeking the help of the AVO!"

They both chuckled at the incongruity of the thought, shook hands, and Phil watched as Polgár exited the book store. He purchased the book of poetry and briskly walked back to the Embassy, exhilarated by the contact with an AVO officer.

'Yet another thing I cannot tell Jim, or anyone,' he thought.

How fascinating that the AVO and KGB worked on opposite sides of the street. How equally intriguing, as a consequence, that the AVO, despite its sophisticated listening techniques, didn't know what the German diplomat was really up to, or the importance of his true name. To Phil, this suggested supreme caution on the part of Sommer, that is, speaking only when absolutely certain of not being overheard, or, using a Secure Room. Why? What were the Germans up to?

Krikor Adamyants might shed some light on that as well.

Fifty

"You know, Phil, I used to come here to the *Hüvös Völgy* often with Hungarian friends, and once even with Yuri Vladimirovich when he was Ambassador. But in the last two years, you have been my only luncheon companion here."

"Except for a certain German beauty."

Adamyants laughed—"She *is* lovely, isn't she? I like her very much, Phil. Maybe I've been a bachelor too long. An Armenian-German union is not so very bad, don't you think?"

"In fact, it is quite good. Our great novelist, Khatchadoor Abovian, was married to a German, and the tradition has continued for many years. You're in good company."

"Thank you, Phil, but that is not why we are here today. I have something to tell you. But first, I think you have something to tell me."

"Give me a hint, Krikor, so I'll know what we are talking about."

"The German diplomat, Christian Sommer. What do you know about him?"

Phil became very uncomfortable, stalled, emptied his beer, looked around at the surrounding woods, but finally brought his gaze around to Adamyants, who had been quietly watching him.

"My question gives you that much difficulty?"

"Maybe, Krikor, maybe. I don't know. This whole thing has gotten so out of hand, so devilishly complicated, that I sit here with very mixed feelings about your request."

"Well, I must say, Phil, that is *really* very disappointing. When you first mentioned the manuscript to me, I was taken aback because after the Fekete-Andropov meeting, we realized its huge importance to us. Our paths crossed, our objectives coincided, and I decided, with the approval of Yuri Vladimirovich, to pull you in, make you, as it were, a fellow conspirator. You, an American, part of a Soviet mission! I told you just about everything, took you completely into my confidence. And now, when we may be on the verge of a breakthrough, I find you reluctant to do the same with me. Look at me, Phil. Is that fair?"

Phil became embarrassed, then nodded and finally sighed—"You're right, Krikor, you're right. Yes, you *have* confided a remarkable amount of information, slowly, to be sure, but I am grateful for the trust you have placed in me. Allright. Let me see what I can tell you."

Adamyants sat back in relief, ordered more beer, and said "Now just relax and let's talk about this as two friends. I have no tricks up my sleeve, but there are some things I must know. And let me say this now—when I know them, your mission will be facilitated as well. Tell me about Christian Sommer."

When the beer came, Phil took a long sip, wiped the foam from his lips and began—"Do you remember my telling you about *Breitkopf und Härtel* in Leipzig and how I first met its fleeing director, Hellmuth von Hase, in Bad Nauheim at the end of the war?"

"I remember every word of it."

"Do you also remember my asking you about a General *Paul* von Hase? That was when you told me about the events leading up to the July 20 plot against Hitler."

"Yes, the German officer who would have assumed the Berlin Command if *Walküre* had been successful?"

"The same. But as things turned out, when the plot failed and Hitler sought out the conspirators, General von Hase was caught and executed."

Adamyants was hunched over in total concentration, his eyes

blinking with impatience—"So, what has this got to do with Sommer?"

"Just that Sommer is not his real name. His real name is von Hase. Christian von Hase."

Adamyants' reaction was immediate. He turned pale, straightened up in his chair, lit a cigarette, inhaled deeply, and, with the words and smoke emerging together, said—"So, that's the game, is it?"

"What game, Krikor? What are you talking about?"

"You don't really know, do you? Allright, now I'll tell *you* something. Look, for some time now, our Intelligence has picked up talk in bits and pieces about revenge from various sources. We haven't known exactly what that meant, I mean revenge on whose behalf and against whom? The only thing we have known about this Sommer fellow is that he is BND—*Bundesnachrichtendienst.*"

"You've *known* that he was an Intelligence officer?"

"Yes, that we have known. But now, from you, I have learned who he really is. By the way, what was he to General von Hase?"

"I don't know precisely. Maybe a son. But in any case, certainly closely related."

"And your friend Hellmuth von Hase?"

"Christian referred to him as a distant relative. I might as well tell you everything he said, Krikor, and God help me for it. Sommer, or von Hase, and the BND are convinced that Major Manteuffel was a German and a traitor. They have no idea that he was a Soviet plant. Their objective is to find and kill a German traitor, whose success in foiling the plots to kill Hitler resulted eventually in the execution of countless members of the German Resistance. My anguish, Krikor, is that these Germans were heroes, and your Major may have been responsible for their deaths. Don't you understand that?"

Adamyants' reaction showed that he did. He took a long drag on his cigarette, peered long into the ashtray, then said—"I have no argument with that, Phil. But war is war. War is unreasonable, illogical, irrational. The Nazis were out to destroy us, and we were out to destroy them. Wild, insane impulses to annihilate each other. We wanted to punish the author of this madness. You may say that the author of *our* plan was just as mad as Hitler. I will not dispute that—certainly not anymore. What I *will* say, however, is that the objective of our side was not ignoble, and in the process of reaching that objective, tragically, good people died. I regret that. You do too. But let's be realistic, because that was *then* and this is *now*. Can we agree? And if we can, there is much in it for you."

"You can make me a promise such as that?"

"Yes, but it requires your agreement to do something, well, how can I put it, something that you will find unusual."

Phil held his breath. It sounded so ominous "What exactly must I do?"

Adamyants exhaled a long cloud of smoke, looked unblinkingly into Phil's eyes, and said quietly—"Go to Moscow."

Phil sat rigidly in his chair without batting an eye, and when finally his pulse had slowed, he said—"It was bad enough for me, personally I can assure you, going to the GDR, but the Soviet Union? I don't know, Krikor."

"I thought you wanted to bring this whole thing to a conclusion?"

"I do, I do. But my God—Moscow!"

He fidgeted uncomfortably in his chair and asked—"When is this supposed to happen?"

"Do you have anything on your agenda in the next two weeks? I know how active you are in promoting cultural affairs in Hungary."

"Nothing for a month or so."

"What happens then?

"A very talented American film director named John Frankenheimer is coming to do a movie called *The Fixer,* and I'd like to be around for the filming. Other than that, my slate is clean."

x

"That's fine. I can have you in and out of the Soviet Union in two, at the very most three days, without any stamps in your passport, no one the wiser, and you'll be back here in Budapest as though nothing had happened."

"Somehow, Krikor, I sense that Christian Sommer is to be involved in your plan. Your interest in him and—now that you know his true name—his mission, tells me that there may be some unpleasantness ahead."

"You need have no fear of problems for you, my Armenian brother."

That mode of address gave Phil a degree of comfort. It told him that blood, indeed, talked, as the old Armenian saying ran—a concept that Colonel Polgár had seemed to understand. Adamyants was unlikely to create a situation, Phil told himself, that would bring him harm or disgrace. But one thing remained outstanding.

"I have to know something, Krikor, because it poses a dilemma for me. If this plan of yours is to succeed, and Sommer is to be implicated, how is he going to find out? Am *I* to be the informant?"

"No, Phil, not you. *I* will resolve your dilemma. And when I do, and this whole thing is over, you will be a happy man."

"Krikor, I haven't been a happy man for a very long time."

Driving back to the Embassy, Phil wondered what ace Adamyants would have up his sleeve in Moscow in the drama whose cast seemed to be constantly expanding. He also pondered the harsh reality that, from here on in, he could no longer keep Jim Garland out of any part of the picture.

Fifty-One

"Jim, can we talk..?" Phil gestured toward the tank.

The *chargé* looked up from his papers and nodded. Phil led the way to the Secure Room. Once seated, Jim stared austerely at his PAO and asked—"What is it now, Phil?"

"There's a thorniness in your voice that tells me you're slightly exasperated. Is it me or, I hope, something else?"

"It's not entirely you, Phil. The Foreign Ministry has been pressing me about Most Favored Nation status and I happen to know Washington is totally against granting it, neither now nor in the distant future. This country is economically on the rocks, it is politically just about bankrupt, and socially it is becoming more shredded every day. That leaves nothing but culture. How would you evaluate that?"

"Actually, there's a tolerant climate in the air. Kádár has given the intellectuals some breathing space and writers like Tibor Déry are taking advantage of it."

"Well, I'm really happy for them," Garland observed sardonically. "Now, why are we talking in here?"

Phil took a deep breath, aware of the reaction his opening comments would evoke, and said in as calm a manner as he could muster—"Yesterday, I lunched with Adamov again. No, Jim! Don't get excited, please, and just listen. We talked about the matter which has preoccupied him and me for some time. The focus of our conversation this time was a fellow diplomat. You surely remember a German named Christian Sommer."

"Of course. I invited him to the farewell stag dinner for Eric Hager. Actually, I met him again last week. The Swedish Ambassador had me and Sarah over and Sommer was there, in fact, with your one-time companion Helga Kirsch."

"They seem to be inseparable these days."

"What about Sommer? What interest does the Soviet Embassy have in him?"

"Not the Soviet Embassy, Jim, just Adamov."

"By the way, was your Soviet friend gloating about our Ambassador's hasty departure?"

"No, actually he never even raised the subject. Now, about Sommer. There is something I must tell you, Jim, because it is a terribly vital part of the whole."

Garland recrossed his legs impatiently in anticipation of a another startling revelation. Phil smiled—"I know, Jim. With me it's never easy. But here goes anyway. I vowed to keep you informed and I'm going to. The first thing you should know is that Sommer's real name is von Hase."

He waited for a reaction, but there was none immediately. Just as he began to continue, however, Garland interrupted—"Von Hase? Why is that name vaguely familiar? I have a suspicion, however, that you're going to tell me."

"Actually, Jim, you have a good memory if the name is even vaguely familiar. It is the name of the man who first put me onto the Beethoven manuscript, Hellmuth von Hase."

"*Breitkopf und Härtel*. Leipzig. Yes, now I remember. It was at the end of the war."

Phil went on to define exactly who Christian von Hase was and his involvement in the search for the manuscript. When Phil described his dinner with the German diplomat and then reeled off the names of the chief July 20 conspirators whose deaths he wished to avenge, Garland displayed alarm—"My God, Phil! Do you realize what a mess you've gotten yourself into? And—I tremble at the thought—maybe this whole Embassy?"

"It is exclusively *my* affair, Jim. The Embassy will not be contaminated." Phil's reply was controlled and low-key.

He brought Garland completely up to date on events since the trip to Berlin and Leipzig, but he omitted the meetings with Andropov and the encounter with Polgár. Garland certainly would not believe him. *No one* would believe him, and he couldn't blame anyone for that. An American diplomat in private conversations with the KGB and AVO would surely strain anyone's credulity. Finally, he arrived at Adamyants' proposal for the trip to Moscow.

Garland's reacted immediately. He arose, walked impatiently back and forth in the small area of the tank, turned and pointing a finger at Phil, his voice shaking, said—"This thing has now gotten completely out of hand. Phil, *under no circumstances* can I allow you to go to the Soviet Union. Especially on government time."

"But surely, Jim, you won't restrain me from going to Moscow on my own time, will you?" Phil ventured warily.

On seeing Garland's responding glare, Phil reacted, his voice stronger but defensive in tone—"Jim, for Heaven's sake. Two decades ago I stumbled upon a startling piece of information which I tried to pursue from afar. In the last year, here in Hungary, I've gotten closer and closer, largely, I must add, because of a Soviet colleague. Yes, you can shake your head all you want, Jim, but that is the gospel truth, and you know it. You never discouraged me from seeing him. You only disapproved. And now, thanks to him, when I'm on the verge, maybe, of a remarkable discovery, you're slamming the gate shut. Allright. We agreed that my search should never take precedence over Embassy business. Can we now agree that this trip will be unofficial, off-the-record, and very private?"

Garland studied him for half a minute and Phil observed that his face was no longer flushed. When next he spoke, his manner was calm—"This whole thing has never meant as much to me as it obviously has to you. I can appreciate the importance of your mission but I'm not sure that it's worth the risk. OK. If you are so absolutely intent on going, take some leave and disappear. I can't stop you. but don't tell me about it. I don't want to know where you are, or why. Is that clear?"

Phil nodded with relief—"Yes it is, Jim, and I want to apologize if I've caused you any grief. I regret most that with your new responsibilities you've got to concern yourself with me. But all I ask is that you carry your understanding just one more inch out on the limb and realize that I can't give up now. It's reached a point where I must see it through to the end."

Garland looked steadily at him and, as though having resolved an inner conflict, said calmly—"Let's agree right now that this discussion never took place. If ever asked, I will deny it. Understood?"

"Absolutely, Jim," Phil said, confident now that Garland's resistance to the trip had fully collapsed.

"OK. After settling that, let me get your promise on one other thing. There must be no contact with our Embassy in Moscow."

"Have no fear. I won't go within a mile of the Embassy."

"Good. Now, is it as clear to you as it is to me that you're being set up as some kind of patsy?"

"I could be a dupe, Jim, I know, but I trust him."

"However you want to label it, are you going to inform Sommer, or whatever his name is, of your trip to Moscow?"

"I don't think plans have reached that stage yet."

"Well, someone will have to, otherwise what's the point? You're going to Moscow for a purpose, which is—if all these so-called friends of yours keep their word—to get the manuscript. Sommer and the BND are interested in another part of the same project. He's got to know. So, what happens next?"

"That's what I don't know. We haven't gotten that far. I know that Sommer and his buddies want revenge, but what that entails, where and how, I just don't know."

"Perhaps there's a way that *we* can find out."

Phil eyed the *chargé* with dismay—"Am I anticipating what you have in mind?"

"What do I have in mind, Phil?"

"Squibb and Company?"

Garland nodded.

"Jim, you can't! For one thing, he's a lamebrain. You and I both know that Langley has some brilliant operatives—intelligent, clever, resourceful, aware of the bigger picture. But Squibb, Christ, once he's in on it, he'll louse up this whole thing, bring in a crew from Langley and they'll put me through the ringer and want to know everything."

Garland suddenly lost his benign demeanor—"Well, much of what you've told me already is pretty much CIA business and well within its parameters. But, I'm beginning to wonder if you've really told me *everything*. Well, Phil, have you? Why are you so jumpy?"

Now it was Phil's turn to pace up and down. Garland looked at his wristwatch and said—"We've been here already thirty minutes, Phil, and I've got lots of work waiting for me. Can we wrap this up quickly? What more do you have to tell me?"

Phil realized that he now had to lay it all out, not only because it would relieve his conscience with Garland, his friend, but also in the hope that by doing so, he could dissuade Garland from pulling in the Station Chief.

"Allright, Jim. No holds barred. No secrets. Everything on the table."

He began with Ilona Portland, her involvement with the manuscript, her call on Fekete, her friendship with AVO Colonel Polgár and what she had gleaned from him, the two clandestine meetings with Yuri Andropov—Garland half arose from his chair when Phil mentioned Andropov—and concluded with the encounter with Polgár in the Gorki Book Store.

"That's it, that's everything, Jim. I've told you the rest of it."

Garland gripped the arms of his chair, his knuckles white, and at first, seemed unable to speak, but when he did, his voice was so strained that the words barely came out—"*M-i-s-t-e-r F-a-l-j-i-a-n,* I can't believe this!—*twice*, with the head of the

KGB, and as though that weren't bad enough, you've held a long and friendly conversation with an AVO officer. The KGB! The AVO! Are you out of your mind? How an intelligent, savvy officer like you can allow all this to happen is sheer insanity. Tell me—How can I be sure that this Embassy hasn't been compromised *already*? You realize, I hope, that when Washington finds out, it will be the end—not just for you, but for me too."

Although chastened by Garland's outburst, Phil refused to be cowed. "Jim, please listen to me. I promised no secrets and I kept my word. Perhaps now you can understand why I just simply can't get our own people involved in this. The questions, the doubts, the pressures, would be unbearable. I truly believe that I can handle all this. Strange as it may sound to you, I have a degree of confidence in Adamov. We are both Armenian, and while that may sound incredibly naive to you, it carries much weight with both of us. How could I possibly explain that to Squibb's boys?"

"Even *I* have trouble with that," was Garland's bitter reply.

He sat silently, playing with his pen. His eyes, his face, the restlessness of his hands all reflected his deep anxiety. The silence continued for a full minute and as Phil was about to break it with an apology, troubled that he had so disturbed his friend, Garland said—"It's clear to me that you can't be dissuaded. Therefore, I return to what I said earlier—go and do what you feel you must, but don't tell me when or where, and if something goes wrong, I don't know anything about it. How could I if this meeting never took place? Right?"

"Right, Jim. I'm sorry, truly sorry, for all this. But thank you."

They shook hands and the *chargé* wished him a gruff "Good Luck."

"I'll need every bit of it," Phil muttered as they walked out.

Fifty-Two

Bence Szabolcsi had invited Phil to an obscure little restaurant up on the *Vár* in Buda and when they had both settled in and ordered, the Hungarian musicologist informed Phil of further research he had conducted on the missing manuscript. Phil listened respectfully, reluctant to inform his aging and gentle friend that the existence of the manuscript was no longer in question. The challenge now was to locate it, and the resolution of that problem lay far away to the East—a drama in whose *dénouement* he was about to be embroiled all the more.

They were seated in a corner of the restaurant in the shadows and Phil had not paid much attention to the twenty or so patrons already there when, as Szabolcsi lumbered on about vague hints in Beethoven's letters to works not yet completed, out of the corner of his eye, Phil saw a couple enter the restaurant. They were directed to a table at the opposite end and for a few seconds he gave it no thought. But then, suddenly, as though a light had flashed in his head, he turned and looked at the couple, and gasped.

Facing each other at the table were Christian Sommer and Hannelore Weber.

"Is something wrong, dear colleague?"

"No, no, Dr. Szabolcsi," Phil said hastily as he turned back and pretended to be listening with renewed interest to Szabolcsi's discoveries.

Sommer and Weber, or, more provocatively, von Hase and Weber!

The West German Intelligence Officer and avenger of the July 20 plotters lunching with the East German victim of Fekete's depravity and now Krikor Adamyants' girl friend. What was going on here?

Phil deliberately ate slowly and dragged out the discussion with Szabolcsi until he saw that the German couple was leaving. He thanked Szabolcsi, who wondered about the sudden abruptness of his friend, and drove to a nearby hotel and phoned the Soviet Embassy. Adamyants came to the phone shortly.

"Can we have a beer?"

"Yes we can."

Some time back, both had agreed that were a quick meeting necessary, it would be signalled by the word 'beer' and scheduled for nine o'clock the same night at what the Germans called a *Kneipe*—which in Budapest meant a small bar off *Rákóczi út*.

Phil arrived first and occupied a small table, the only one available, and by the time Adamyants entered, the place had filled up and was buzzing with the sounds of loud discourse.

"Something obviously urgent, Phil. What's up?"

"*You* tell me, Krikor. Today, I saw something that was hard to believe."

"Can I guess? You saw Hannelore lunching with Sommer. May I ask what the hell you were doing in such an out-of-the-way restaurant?"

"You may. I was invited there by Szabolcsi, who knows every little dining place on the *Vár*. He works there at the Bartók Archives, as you know."

Adamyants nodded, lit a cigarette, and asked—"Is that what has you so worked up?"

"Naturally I'm worked up. I'm hoping you're going to tell me why they were meeting and what's going on."

"Well, I guess you have a right to know. I certainly can't expect you to go through the plans we've made without knowing the answers to some of the questions that must have arisen in your mind.

"Acting on my instructions, Hannelore walked into the West German Permanent Mission and asked to see Sommer. She told him that she was from Leipzig, had vacationed in Hungary, but wanted to escape to West Germany. In return for his help, she was willing to pass him inside information on the personnel of the GDR Embassy. You know what I mean—personality clashes between officers, conflicts among the wives, the nature of relations between the Ambassador and his DCM, things like that."

"I thought the East Germans were your allies. Doesn't it bother you, selling them down the river like that?"

"Of course not. Passing that kind of information to the West Germans doesn't bother us at all. *West* Germans, *East* Germans, to us they are just Germans and we couldn't care less how they treat each other. By the way, I do not include Hannelore in that equation. She is special. But as you imply, there was more to the meeting than that. I told you last time that I would spare you the dilemma of wanting to assist Sommer but not wanting to expose . . . our countryman."

"I begin to see. So, *Fräulein* Weber's mission in that lunch . . ."

". . . was to inform Sommer of some of our plans. I told her not to raise anything related to those plans until Sommer did. And that is exactly what happened."

"Did Sommer ask about our compatriot in Moscow?"

"Not exactly. He was quite subtle, according to Hannelore. He apparently was curious about our relationship, I mean Hannelore's and mine. Sommer had observed us together at the Nikolais performance, and he also had seen you and me talking during the intermission. That was good because it lent credence to what Hannelore eventually told him."

"Which was?"

"Sommer asked why Hannelore was so friendly with a Soviet diplomat, and she said that I had met her at an East German Embassy reception and had followed up with several invitations to dinner and the performance and that she was a virtual slave to my wishes until she could escape. Sommer asked if she could give him any enlightening details about me as well, and she said she would when she got to know me better. At that point, she let drop a small tidbit of information which Sommer leaped upon."

"About me and Moscow?"

"No, no, Phil, not so fast, You've got to handle these things with care and caution, otherwise they arouse suspicion. The subject was still me. Hannelore said that she knew I was planning a trip but she didn't know when and where, or even if it were for me. Then, almost as an aside, she said the plans had seemed to firm up after you and I talked at the performance intermission. That got Sommer's attention right away."

"Did he pursue it?"

"Oh yes, he certainly did. He asked a number of questions about you, such as, how friendly you and I were, whether she knew of any reference to music or missing manuscripts. Hannelore kept a straight face and replied negatively. Actually, *I've* never talked to her about the secret of the manuscript. Have *you?*"

"For God's sake, Krikor, when have I ever been alone with her long enough to talk about anything so complicated?"

"You have a point. Well, the scene has been set, most of the players are on stage now. I think you can expect some West German surveillance, Phil, because Sommer will watch you like a hawk."

"How many services have me under surveillance, Krikor? Outside of those I do not know, there is the AVO, the KGB, and now the BND."

"Correction, Phil. *We* do not have you under surveillance. Please disabuse yourself of that. The AVO, yes, I am sure. Are you certain of your own people?"

Phil was startled by the question. Squibb and his unknown minions watching him? The thought seemed ludicrous.

"I don't think so, not a chance. Somehow, I'd know. Incidentally, Krikor, I have a request. If I am now going to Moscow, I might as well squeeze everything I can out of it. In all those wonderful art galleries you have in Moscow, are there any paintings by Vermeer? I think you know of my special regard for him."

"Not my field, dear friend, but I suppose I could find out for you. Who knows, maybe we've got a forgery or two."

The word gave Phil a start. It always troubled him to hear it.

"I had planned to meet with you in a day or two, but since we are here, let me try and firm things up. Can you take leave next week? For instance, Thursday? If you can, I'll have you on a plane to Moscow Thursday morning. You can take care of our business in the next two days, and be back in Budapest by the the very latest Saturday night. But only two days of actual leave. I need to know as soon as possible. What do you think?"

"I think that can be managed."

"With your Ambassador no longer there, how do you get on with your *chargé*?"

"In almost every respect, Krikor, that's none of your damned business. But the truth is that we get on famously, as we always have. We understand each other."

"Good. I'll let you know the specific plans early next week."

"I don't understand something. How will Sommer know our plans just by putting me under surveillance?"

"He won't. He'll find out from another source."

It didn't take Phil very long to guess who that source would be.

MOSCOW—YEREVAN

U.S.S.R.

EX

Fifty-Three

On the following Thursday, Phil drove himself to *Ferihegy* at eight in the morning. He parked and entered the large reception hall where he reported in at the Aeroflot counter. He kept his one piece of luggage with him. He had thirty minutes before his flight and decided to brace himself with a strong *fekete.* As he sat in the small cafe sipping the bitter brew, he reviewed the events of the last few days.

Most troubling was Jim Garland's irritated reaction to Phil's request for two days of leave. The *chargé* knew the reason for the request and had let Phil know that he knew. Next was Sommer's constant observing of him from afar at diplomatic receptions, and the conniving smile when his greetings, transmitted by a nod, were acknowledged. But compounding everything was the hovering figure of Adamyants, accompanied always by Hannelore Weber, lately seeking him out at functions for a conspiratorial word or two of encouragement. At the most recent of them, just two nights before, Phil had asked what was supposed to happen after he landed in Moscow? Would he be met? If he were, how would he know if it was a legitimate part of Adamyants' plan? Was there a code word? Wasn't he to be given some instructions even before arriving in Moscow? Adamyants had responded with that same enigmatic Andropov-like smile to all these questions, declaring that everything would soon become clear.

Then, last night, his doorbell had rung at ten, and a driver from the Soviet Embassy had handed him a large envelope. He had opened it and found inside a smaller envelope, with an attached note in Armenian—"Phil, open this envelope once you are on the plane. Good luck. Krikor."

The envelope was in his breast pocket and he was itching to tear it open. As he emptied his cup, he looked around the hall. There were few people at that hour, but certainly no sign of Sommer. Had Adamyants' carefully-laid plans failed?

At 9:45 he boarded the Aeroflot flight to Moscow and sat in the narrow uncomfortable seat of the Soviet Ilyushin-62 four-engine jet. Twenty minutes later, the plane was airborne and Phil reached into his jacket pocket and extracted the envelope. He looked around, saw that none of the other passengers were watching him, ripped open the envelope and began reading.

It was a brief message which instructed him not to speak to anyone on the plane, even the stewardess; to disembark the Aeroflot flight when it arrived in Moscow, walk to the main building, enter and approach Passport Control, where he would be met by someone who would know him.

The "someone" would take care of him and then provide further instructions. He read it again, then sat back and closed his eyes, thinking that this had to be madness. If this whole escapade didn't work, it would mean the end of his career and, perhaps, even his life. Phil was suddenly seized by an anxiety which persisted for the next three hours until he landed at *Sheremetyevo* Airport.

Phil left the plane and walked towards Passport Control, his hand clutching his passport still in his pocket. Adamyants had promised there would be no evidence of this trip and Phil wondered, as he approached the stern, determined-looking Soviet Customs guards, how this would be managed. As he entered the gate, a voice called out in Armenian—"Hey, compatriot, over here."

Phil looked to the side and with a sudden big smile and a sense of relief, he saw the familiar figure. He rushed over to Sahak, his driver and guide in East Germany and embraced him warmly. Sahak, his big smile displaying his gold-capped teeth, appeared genuinely happy to see Phil, while Phil was enormously grateful that he would once again be in Sahak's capable hands.

"Sahak, you old rascal, what are you doing here in Moscow?"

"Waiting for my capitalist countryman!" he replied jovially, embracing Phil again, and continued—"I'm sure the food they served you on the plane was abominable, so first of all, we're going to have a decent breakfast. We can do that outside the airport. Second, you have two hours before your next flight. Ah, I see you are surprised. Yes, there is another leg to your trip. Third, after we get to the restaurant, I will give you another letter, which you will take to the rest room, read very carefully, memorize everything, then return to the table and give it back to me, together with the first letter. You will not see either of them again. Agreed? Good. Now, just follow me and say nothing."

Sahak led the way to Passport Control where he flashed something in his wallet. When the guard examined it closely, he stood up in the glass booth, looked quickly at Phil, then back again at Sahak, mumbled something in Russian and, with a quick motion, waved them both through. The same maneuver took place at the Customs gate. Outside, Sahak beckoned to a Volga limousine which drew up, the driver got out and held the door for both of them, and after some instructions from Sahak, began a long drive away from the airport in what appeared to be a great swing around it. After thirty minutes, they arrived at a village where they stopped in front of a small cafe.

Once inside and seated, Phil did as Sahak had told him to, eventually returning from the rest room to the table and handing over both letters. Sahak put them in his breast pocket, tapped them, and said—"For safe-keeping."

"Why are they safer with you than with me, Sahak?"

"Because in an hour I will give them to my driver who will know what to do with them. Answer your question?"

Phil laughed. It was a rumbling, genuine laugh, without

innuendos or misgivings or nervousness, because with Sahak, he felt safe and secure. He wasn't entirely sure why, but it was so.

"Oh, I almost forgot. I have a message for you, in answer, apparently, to something you asked Krikor."

Phil was drinking the last of his tea, stopped, and looked up quizzically.

"There are no Vermeers in Moscow," Sahak said sorrowfully.

Phil put his glass down and said admiringly—"You guys sure work together—and thoroughly!"

Sahak enjoyed Phil's comment and said—"I hope you realize what a huge distance it is from Moscow to Dresden, dear compatriot, so please, I beg you, don't ask to be driven there."

Both laughed as Sahak paid the bill and they got back in the limousine.

"I assume we are returning to the airport."

"Not to the same airport, compatriot. We are going now to *Vnukovo*."

"I don't understand. Why?"

"Because *Sheremetyevo* is Moscow's international airport and *Vnúkovo* is for domestic flights."

Phil said he still didn't understand.

At *Vnukovo* Airport, Sahak spoke in a low voice to the driver, gave him the two letters and dismissed him. As Phil watched the limousine pull away, he turned to Sahak, filled with curiosity about the mysterious 'next flight.' "Sahak, can't you tell me anything about my next destination?"

"*Our* next destination, compatriot. Just follow me."

He checked in at one of the desks and told Phil to sit down until boarding time. The boarding area was filled not only with people but also with shouts, which Phil discovered to be the same word over and over again. It was the Russian word *delegatsia* and Sahak explained that that these were groups from unions of writers, artists, parliamentarians, workers, farmers, miners students and other segments of society, who were representing the Soviet Union at conferences being held in East European socialist countries. Delegations always carried a high priority in Soviet flights, he observed.

"I am relieved that you are coming with me, Sahak."

"I will be with you most of the time. Not every minute, but always near enough for you not to be concerned."

He had no sooner spoken when a boisterous group of men rushed to the check-in counter and slapped down their tickets. They were laughing and exchanging comments loudly and raucously and Phil looked at them with distaste. Sahak noticed his displeasure, leaned over and said—"Journalists, dear compatriot. Some of them yours."

Indeed, Phil heard the clear American lilts of the South and Mid-West, along with New York and Boston. He was annoyed and a bit embarrassed, noticing the reproachful looks they were getting from Soviet passengers awaiting the flight.

Ten minutes later, an amplified voice very close to them announced the flight three times and Phil was startled to hear "Yerevan" mentioned in each announcement. Sahak was watching him with amusement and when he saw Phil's reaction, he nudged him with his elbow—"Tell the truth, compatriot, are you really surprised to be going to Armenia?"

"Believe me, Sahak, I am indeed. I am genuinely surprised, but just as I am elated, I am also disappointed."

"I don't understand. Elated but disappointed?"

"Yes. Elated because I have always wanted to visit Armenia, and disappointed because I couldn't prepare for it. Had I known in Budapest, I could have gotten travel books and guides and prepared properly for this trip."

Sahak nodded and said—"Have no concern. I will be your guide in Armenia."

"Will there be time to see anything? I don't know yet what happens in Armenia, all planned for only one day."

"We'll see."

Sahak and he boarded the Soviet plane. It was a TU-154

two-engine turbo-jet but not much different inside than the plane from Budapest to Moscow. They settled in their seats side by side and buckled up as Sahak said that the flight would last two hours, but because of the time difference, it would be one hour later in Yerevan. Once in the air, they relaxed, unbuckled and just as Sahak started to get up, a stewardess with flowing black hair, long lashes and sparkling dark eyes greeted him warmly in Armenian and said it had been some time since they had run into one another. She looked questioningly at Phil, apparently waiting for an introduction.

"Ah, you want to meet my friend? He is one of us, but from far beyond our borders. Compatriot, meet Anoush, the best stewardess in the entire Soviet Union."

Phil smiled admiringly at the stunning woman, aware that Sahak had not mentioned him by name. After she had walked on, he said—

"With those eyes, she couldn't be anything but Armenian. Tell me, is it common for Armenian women to be stewardesses?"

"Mostly on these flights to Armenia. Some go elsewhere too, but from Leningrad and Moscow to Yerevan, you will find a largely Armenian crew. For instance, on this flight, the captain, his co-pilot, the purser and Anoush are all Armenians. That other stewardess over there is Russian."

"You know them all?"

"Of course, dear friend. In the Soviet Union, at certain levels, all Armenians know one another." He laughed and walked to the rear of the plane to chat with Anoush. When he returned he whispered—"I just arranged for special food for us. But we'll have to go back to the crew's quarters so no one will be the wiser. Especially those journalists. Poor Anoush. They are giving her a hard time."

"How?"

"Some want a date, others are saying lewd things—she knows a little English, and one even grabbed her leg. She doesn't deserve that. Anoush is a very decent girl. Besides, she's happily married."

After lunch, Sahak drew the window curtain and suggested a nap. The drone and vibration combined to lull Phil into a turbulent sleep. It was over an hour later that he felt a slight tug at his sleeve. It was Sahak informing him that they were flying over the Caucasus Mountains.

"Look there, compatriot. That is Mt. Elbrus, the highest peak, even higher than Mt. Ararat."

Phil felt an excitement as he opened the curtain and looked down at the snow-capped peak, remembering what Adamyants had told him of a swastika having flown from the summit. He was no less excited when Sahak prodded him again and pointed to the unmistakable slopes of Mt. Ararat, adding—"We are now over Armenia. See there, that is Lake Sevan."

Phil looked down at the azure surface of Sevan, a mountain lake much like an inland sea.

"If we are lucky, tonight we will dine on *ishkhan,*" Sahak said. "The lake has four kinds, you know, and they are all very tasty."

Phil had heard that Armenians considered their Sevan trout as something quite special and hoped he could find out for himself.

They buckled up and prepared to land. Anoush came by to check, bent down and whispered into Sahak's ear. He smiled and patted her cheek. Phil pretended not to have noticed and when he heard the landing gear grind down and lock into position beneath them, he closed his eyes again and braced himself for the descent. Fifteen minutes later, they were on the ground.

Sahak led the way across the tarmac, through the airport reception hall, which was teeming with people, and out onto the street, where he hailed a taxi.

"Take us to the Hotel Armenia," he told the driver.

Some thirty minutes later they arrived at Lenin Square and entered the hotel. Sahak went to the Reception Desk, asked for the manager who, when he saw Sahak, became obsequious and insisted on personally accompanying the two guests to their rooms on the fifth floor.

Phil unpacked his one piece of luggage and waited for Sahak to contact him. That happened a quarter of an hour later, with a knock on the door.

"Are you settled, compatriot? Good. I see you have a clear view of Mt. Ararat from here. It's far away but one of these days we'll get it back from Turkey. It belongs to us, to Armenia."

Phil had not heard such nationalist sentiments from Sahak before. He was warmed by Sahak's comments, but said with a tinge of sarcasm—"Why Sahak, I thought the Soviet Union and Turkey had a good working relationship."

"Oh, they do, dear compatriot. But you have a saying in the West: politics makes strange bed-fellows. In this case, it is economics that has us cohabitating with Turkey. But who knows what the future will bring? Now, tell me. It is four in the afternoon. You have an appointment at eleven tonight."

"I do? Why don't I know about that?"

"Because that is in your final instructions, which I will give you later. Now, in the seven hours between, two of which will be taken up with dining, you have five free hours. Do you want to stay in your room?"

"For the first time in my life, Sahak, I am in Armenia, something I have dreamt of for years, and even with only five hours, you want me to spend it in this dreary room?"

"I knew you would say that. Good, let's go. I'll try and show you a few of our more memorable sites."

For the next four and a half hours, with the help of a taxi, Sahak took Phil to *Geghard*, the 13th century church carved out of a rockcliff, to *Dzidzernagaberd*, the monumental memorial to the 1915 victims of the Turkish genocide, to *Etchmiadzin*, the fifth century cathedral and seat of the Armenian Patriarch, and a very hasty tour through the National Gallery—at Phil's insistence.

"No Vermeers here either, compatriot. Sorry."

"I didn't expect any, Sahak, and I don't mind. The Gallery has other riches."

They returned to the hotel at seven, freshened up and went down to eat. As they neared the dining hall, Sahak said—"I'll come to your room around nine. Have a good dinner, and remember to ask for the *ishkhan*."

"I was expecting us to have dinner together."

"Enjoy your dinner, compatriot, without me."

Non-plussed, Phil walked to an empty table and sat down. Ten minutes later, a waiter came to the table and Phil asked if there was any *ishkhan* to be had. There was, so he ordered it, together with some local wine and a salad.

Seated next to a large window, Phil looked out into the city, where street lights had come on, but with few pedestrians and even fewer vehicles. As he sat, trying to accustom himself to the fact that he was actually in Armenia, the land of his forefathers, a roar of voices made him turn in time to observe the journalists enter the dining room. Phil cursed under his breath, hoping that the clientele would not recognize some of them as Americans.

The group numbered ten and after studying them for awhile, Phil concluded that only five were Americans. Although all were speaking English, the others had foreign accents, and he thought he heard rhythms and inflections which indicated Swedish, Italian, French and German. No matter where they were from, he said to himself, their behaviour had been shameful—at the airport, on the plane, and now here.

He finished his meal, drank some coffee and arose. He saw Sahak at the other end of the dining room, sitting alone at a table. Their eyes met for a few seconds, then Sahak looked down at his plate. Clearly, he didn't want any contact or public association with Phil.

Walking out into the lobby, Phil saw a number of elderly Armenians loitering around a circular bench, and as he walked past, one, an aged male, looked up at him with watery eyes and said in a faltering voice—"You are from America, aren't you?

Do you happen to know my sister in Los Angeles," and gave Phil her name. It was very saddening, and became even more so as others came up to him with similar questions about relatives in cities across the entire American continent. Phil extricated himself from the growing throng and just as he was about to enter the elevator, he heard footsteps approaching briskly. He turned, hoping it might be Sahak, but beheld instead a bright-faced male of about thirty-five, who, grinning broadly, said—"Excuse me. My name is Jürgen Schiller. I understand you are an American diplomat of Armenian heritage. Is that true?"

Phil was annoyed. He was not supposed to speak to anyone, but he saw no way out of this situation.

"That is correct."

"Well, the only reason I trouble you is that I, in fact all of us, are here to do stories and I thought perhaps, with your fluency in the language, you might have some angle that would make my coming to Armenia worthwhile. I am stationed in Moscow and don't get down this far very often. If you can't, perhaps we could meet later and walk around the city, maybe find something to write about."

The smile had left his face and he was eyeing Phil closely. There seemed to be only one way to disengage himself, and Phil employed it—"I'm sorry, but my visit is for the sole purpose of visiting a terminally ill relative. In fact, I have little time for anything else. Sorry I cannot help you. Good night."

He went up to his room, annoyed with himself that he had communicated with the journalist. 'Arrogant and intrusive fellow,' he muttered to himself. Inspecting the room carefully, he looked at the faded curtains, the worn carpets, the sagging overstuffed chairs, and reminded himself that this was considered the best hotel in Armenia.

At nine, the knock announced Sahak, whom he let in. Sahak looked untypically stern. "You were speaking to one of the journalists."

"I know, Sahak, I wasn't supposed to talk to anyone, but he came up to me and requested my help for a story."

"What story?"

"Any story. He seemed to know who I was, although he didn't mention my name. I told him I was here to visit a dying relative."

"Fast thinking. Very good."

Sahak sat down and asked quietly—"Did he identify himself?"

"Yes. He said his name was Schiller."

Sahak displayed a half smile. "Allright. Now listen to me. The time has come for your final instructions. No letters this time, just me. I'm going to convey them to you orally, here and now."

Phil was struck by the imperiousness of Sahak's manner. Gone was the easy joviality and carefree manner of before. This was a man in command.

"I want you to listen to me very, very carefully. Do not interrupt me, but if you have any questions after I have finished, ask them. Understood? Now, sit over here."

Phil nodded and sat in a chair opposite Sahak, who began a slow detailed description of what Phil was expected to do in the next few hours. Phil remained silent during the run-through, but asked a few questions immediately thereafter. Sahak answered everything patiently. Actually, the instructions were not complicated, but Phil had the distinct feeling that something was being left out, like the missing part of an equation. He was troubled not so much by what Sahak had said as by what he had left unsaid. Sahak's recital appeared to have a beginning and a middle, but an end that seemed to be dangling loosely. What was he omitting?

"Now, I want you to repeat everything I said, just to be sure," Sahak ordered, watching him closely, a lit cigarette between his fingers filling the room with pungent smoke. When Phil had finished, appearing to be in something of a daze, Sahak's earlier jauntiness returned. He became merry, grinned his gold-toothed, reassuring smile, stood up and said—"Yes, compatriot. We are now at the climax. You certainly never thought that your search would bring you to the Fatherland. Have no fear. You are in good hands. *My* hands."

Sahak spoke with a firmness that reassured Phil. "In five minutes, I will go down and out of the hotel alone. You will follow minutes later. We should not be seen leaving together. I shall be waiting for you to the left of Lenin's statue, as you face him. Meet me there in ten minutes."

Sahak put his hands on Phil's shoulders and gave him a reassuring smile—"You have waited a long time for this, compatriot. Take heart. You are almost there."

Sahak left the room, his footsteps echoing in the empty corridor as he walked towards the elevator.

Alone now, Phil fell on the lumpy bed and stared at the cracked ceiling. He felt the exhilaration within him of the knowledge that his search was nearing an end. How that was going to happen he did not know. What he did know was that this mission was so secret that, outside of Garland, neither his Embassy nor Washington knew of it, and as that thought began to loom large in his mind, his exhilaration began to diminish.

The mission was not only secret but was also fraught with danger, he reminded himself, for he was in the southernmost republic of the Soviet Union, far out of reach of the Embassy in Moscow. And as the enormity of the gigantic risk he was taking grew on him, his entire being was permeated with fear.

For while it was true that he was about to embark on the final stage of his adventure, it was also glaringly true that he had become a pawn not only of his country's arch enemy, but also of its arch organ of terror.

Fifty-Four

Phil waited another five minutes and then went down in the elevator to the main floor. It was almost nine-thirty and the crowd in the lobby had thinned out. He walked to the entrance and as he reached the doors, he took a final look behind.

Was it his imagination, he wondered, or did he see a blonde head duck out of sight behind the dining room door? Blonde heads in Armenia were a rare sight. In fact, the only one he had seen since arriving belonged not to an Armenian but to the journalist who had asked for help on a story. Phil shook his head and walked out into the crisp Armenian night.

Walking very slowly, in the five minutes it took him to reach Lenin's statue, he reviewed the final instructions Sahak had given him and wondered about his own capability to carry them out. He was in the capital of Soviet Armenia, with the conspiratorial support of Soviet authorities to carry out a mission from which, he had been told, he would benefit. Or would he? Or would Christian von Hase benefit from *his* mission?

Plagued by these doubts, Phil approached the larger-than-life statue outlined against the night sky to meet the only person he knew in the entire country.

Lenin towered above him and when he looked to the left, he saw the dim contour of a man standing there. He hesitated until he heard Sahak call out softly to him, and even then he approached timidly. Sahak's voice was soothing—"Have no fear, compatriot. It is only I. Come closer and stand here in the shadows with me."

Phil was now close enough to see Sahak's features in the reflected light from the street lamps. "Thank God it's you, Sahak."

"Who else should it be? Come now, relax. Here, let me help you unwind. I'll show you something foreigners in Armenia never see. We are now completely to the right of Lenin, correct? Now, look up at him, not all the way, just as far as his waist, and what do you see?"

Phil didn't comprehend what Sahak was talking about and tried to locate whatever it was without knowing exactly what he was looking for. Sahak laughed quietly, and then, whispered—"If you look carefully, because of the outline of his extended finger, it looks like Vladimir Ilyich, who is in the act of making a speech, was aroused in another way as well."

Sahak's attempt to break the tension succeeded, for as Phil looked, he saw, indeed, what Sahak meant, and shook with muffled laughter. It was a highly incongruous protuberance from the Founder of Soviet Communism. Sahak slapped him cordially on the back, put his lips to Phil's ear and said—"A Yerevan secret that we Armenians don't want the Russians to know that we know, or that we laugh at."

"A rather bawdy view of the father of your country, isn't it,?"

Sahak snickered—"Not the father of *my* country, dear compatriot."

The moment of levity had worked its effect, and Phil felt more at ease as he listened to Sahak's instructions—"From here to where you are going is about an hour's walk. I shall be with you only for the first fifteen minutes. From this point where we are standing, which is Lenin Square, we will proceed together, as my instructions to you made clear, turning sharply to the left on *Amiryan* Street, which will take us to Lenin Boulevard. After we have arrived there, you will proceed alone. You cannot miss your rendezvous point because it will be directly ahead of you. Now, let's go."

Sahak stepped out of the shadows and after scrutinizing the area, beckoned to Phil to follow. At that hour of the night, there were few people in the streets. They walked together across the square to *Amiryan* Street, Sahak occasionally turning to look back. Once they arrived at the corner of *Amiryan* and Lenin Boulevard, Sahak touched Phil on the shoulder—"From here, you are on your own. Have no fear. Your mission is soon to be completed. Good luck, compatriot."

Sahak smiled and disappeared into a nearby doorway.

Phil was now alone, and he felt very much alone as he began walking up Lenin Boulevard. The broad street was lined with apartment houses, sycamore trees and shrubbery. After several blocks, and to confirm that he was not in error, he looked for the landmarks that Sahak had mentioned to him. Sure enough, there on the right was a large building which was the Spendiarian Opera and Ballet Theatre, and just before it, the memorial to Sayat-Nova with a larger-than-life bust of the famed Armenian nineteenth century troubador.

He noticed now that he was gradually walking uphill because of the avenue's incline. He was becoming tired. It had already been a very tiring day, he reminded himself, beginning at six that morning in Budapest, but there could be no hesitation now. Within ten minutes, he found himself at the end of Lenin Boulevard where, just as Sahak had said, he would see a narrower cobble-stoned road lined with hemlocks. There was no one in sight, and only distant muffled sounds from the city. He walked onto the uneven stones and approached a steep flight of steps. He stopped for a moment to catch his breath, then, his pulse beating faster—was it fatigue or fear?—he began the ascent.

As Phil reached the top of the first flight, he stopped and looked up. Looming against the starry sky was the silhuouette of a monumental building which, as Sahak had described it, was the *Matenadaran.* If *Etchmiadzin* was the spiritual center of the Armenian nation, the *Matenadaran* was its intellectual core—the repository of thousands of ancient manuscripts, many of them translations from Greek, Syriac, Persian, Latin and Hebrew of documents long since lost in the original. Phil stood in awe of the most revered of all Armenian secular institutions, one he had read much about but never dreamed he would ever see.

He quickly reminded himself that this was not why he was there nor the time even for wonderment. He continued his ascent until he stood at the top of the uppermost flight of steps. Facing him was a huge seated statue of Mesrob Mashtots, creator of the Armenian alphabet.

Now, according to Sahak's instructions, he was to turn to his right and proceed along a walkway toward a dark area shielded by a few trees. At this point, he was to stop and look around to make certain there were no late-night strollers or, as Sahak had put it, "love-birds looking for privacy." When he was absolutely certain that the place was empty, according to Sahak's briefing, he walked out of the shadows into the open, and waited.

The only sound that reached Phil's ears was the beating of his heart. A thousand thoughts raced through his muddled mind, two especially: how did he find himself in this predicament, and, who was he to meet? His instructions ended at this particular point, without identifying whomever he was awaiting. He pulled his coat collar tighter around his neck as the Armenian winter penetrated his clothing and his bones. Five minutes went by, and still no sign of anyone. Could something have gone wrong? Signals mixed? Why couldn't this have been done in Moscow? Why did he have to travel all the way to Armenia, and fly out the next morning?

It was while he was in the midst of these ruminations that Phil heard a new sound nearby. It was a footstep, followed by a very low, muffled cough. He tensed up and turned toward the shadows. When his eyes had accustomed themselves to the dark, he made out the dim outline of a human figure. He hesitated for a moment, then took several steps toward it. The figure didn't move away, indicating to Phil that he was expected. But Phil decided not to speak and to allow the other to make the initial move. He didn't have to wait any longer.

"Are you the American who knows about me?"

The words were barely audible and tinged with a regional Armenian accent.

"Perhaps," Phil replied warily. "How can I know you are the one I am to meet?"

There was a long silence, then Phil saw the figure move toward him in slight, shuffling steps and within ten seconds, standing before him, illuminated partly by the reflected light from the city, was a stooped male with graying hair who seemed to be in his sixties. But what struck Phil the most were two other aspects of the stranger: he was leaning on a cane, and he wore a dark patch over one eye.

"My God!" Phil gasped. "You are . . . Sasha!"

There was a low chuckle, as though of appreciation at having been recognized. Then, abruptly—"This is why you came here. Take it."

He handed Phil a packet in a manila envelope. In something of a trance, Phil took the envelope but stared at the legendary Soviet Intelligence officer. The envelope was securely in his hands, and it probably was what he had come for, but he didn't want the meeting to end like this. He hoped for some conversation, an attempt to reach out and make contact, even if superficially. The man before him was an extraordinary human being, whose wartime exploits, as recounted by Adamyants, were incredible.

It was while he was in the midst of formulating a question that he heard the sharp breaking of a twig, the rustle of parted bushes, and saw a man emerge quickly out of the shadows under the tree, extend his arm over which was draped a jacket, and fire three quick muffled shots at Sasha. All three bullets entered the chest of the bent figure, who groaned and fell to the ground, his crumpled body twisted awkwardly, the cane lying across his legs. It happened so quickly that Phil stood petrified, but aware that as the stranger fired, he had shouted in German—"Traitor! Son of a bitch!"

The sharp smell of gunsmoke hung in the still air as Phil looked down with horror at the body buckled at his feet. He turned and recognized the gunman.

"You!" he cried out hoarsely. "The journalist who wanted my help!"

"Yes, and you *have* helped me. Now, I must do one more thing."

Phil took a step back, fear filling his heart. This German was going to kill him too, so that there would be no witness. He extended his arm, his palm out as though to prevent being struck, and shouted—"You can't do this! You simply can't!"

"What are you talking about? What can't I do? All I want is the manuscript. We know why you are here. I'm not going to harm you. Just hand me that envelope."

Phil clutched it closer to his chest, momentarily relieved that his life was not in danger. "Haven't you done enough already? You've killed the man you sought. You have your revenge. I do not condone murder, yet I sympathise with your cause. But what has this manuscript got to do with you?"

"Beethoven was a son of the German people, and his music belongs to us, not to these dirty Bolsheviks."

"Beethoven belongs to all mankind, not just to the Germans."

"I have no time for argument," the journalist retorted, snatching the envelope from Phil's hands.

Phil was now overcome with despair. He had not been alerted to any of this by his Soviet accomplices: he had not been told he would be followed; nor that he would be meeting Sasha; nor that Sasha's life might be in peril; nor that the manuscript might be taken from him. He had assumed that he was to be a decoy, but not to abet in such violence, or in such a totally bankrupt outcome. He stood now empty-handed, his mission a failure. Phil's despair turned quickly into outrage. He saw that the German had put his gun away, so he decided to attack him and retrieve the envelope.

He had no sooner made the decision than he saw a figure emerge quickly out of the shadows, leap at the journalist and strike him on the head with an object. The German collapsed and fell alonsgide the bloody corpse.

"Sahak! Thank God! What is this all about? Is it what you expected?"

"Mostly, yes, compatriot." Sahak's voice was calm and comforting. "But most important of all—are you allright? He didn't harm you, did he?"

"Somewhat shaken, but I'm allright," Phil said, as Sahak returned the envelope to him. "What happens now?"

"Are you sure you want to know?"

"I leave that up to you, Sahak, but you know I can't afford to get involved in any of this." He looked down at Sasha. "In murder," he almost whispered.

"Of course not, and you won't. You know the way back to the hotel. Leave now, go to bed and come down for breakfast at eight o'clock. I'll be at a table and, this time, you can join me."

Phil felt gratitude at being dismissed from the crime scene.. He walked back to the hotel, got his key from the sleepy *dezhurnaya* at the fifth floor desk and fell on his bed troubled and exhausted by the events in which he had been a major performer.

It was then that he suddenly remembered the envelope. He arose and retrieved it from the breast pocket of his overcoat. The astonishing events of the day, which had taken him from Budapest to Moscow to Yerevan, evaporated and his thoughts now focused on the packet he held in his hands. With trembling fingers he ripped open the envelope, out of which tumbled a sheaf of papers. They were of a brownish hue and in the poor light of his room difficult to decipher. He went to a lamp, switched it on, and peered closely at them.

At the sight of the top page, Phil held his breath. It was a photostat reproduction of a sheet of music paper, across the top of which was handwritten—

Konzert
für Violoncello

but because the bottom half of the sheet had been torn, the rest of the title was missing. Obviously it would have included the words

und Orchester

but what else? Possibly

Erster Satz

for surely, these few pages could not have been an entire concerto but merely the First Movement.

Phil turned the page, consumed with the hunger to see and to hear what, until this moment, had only been described to him by Bence Szabolcsi: a solo cello introduction which, after eighteen measures, blended into a mellow, introspective entrance by the full orchestra, picking up the cello's opening theme and merging it with a new second theme which the composer treated contrapuntally, gradually intertwining cello and orchestra to a soaring climax towards the coda, but then, diminishing in sound from the fortissimo of before to a gentle pianissimo conclusion.

Phil fell back in the armchair and closed his eyes, in awe of what he had heard in his head. It made sense to him. This music was clearly in the style of his third period, the period which abandoned the conflict and passion of Beethoven's middle years and found him pensive, meditative. Phil thought of those before him who had actually seen this music, held it in their hands: Hellmuth von Hase and the intellectual excitement he must have experienced; Bence Szabolcsi, who had pursued the search with a musicologist's zeal, leavened with an academic detachment; and for a fleeting moment, Phil even felt a certain rappport with Ferenc Fekete, who in his own corrupt way, had also appreciated the remarkable find.

He gathered up the flimsy pages, looking at each one as he

stacked them. How could there be any doubt about their authenticity, he wondered: the smudge marks, the coffee stains, the almost indecipherable notes, scrawled in lightning-like haste on the staves. On the other hand, if Vermeer could be faked, why not a manuscript of Beethoven?.

Phil stuffed the sheets back into the envelope, refusing to give the matter any more thought. His mind was numb from fatigue and the image of a pathetic figure who, having survived so many hair-raising moments in the Third Reich, now lay dead in the shadow of the *Matenadaran.* Although it did not prevent him from eventually falling asleep, Phil's final shattering thought was that Sasha had died for something that was now safely under his pillow.

x

Fifty-Five

Phil awoke at seven on Friday morning, walked past the empty refrigerator in the outer room and entered the bathroom for a shower. There was no trough and no shower curtain, and when he had finished, the entire area was flooded with water, emptying very slowly down the drain in the center of the bathroom floor.

At eight, he entered the dining room and spotted Sahak, who waved to him ostentatiously, in contrast to the discretion he had practised the previous night.

"Slept well, I hope," he said with a broad grin.

"Considering what happened last night, I didn't sleep badly."

"What happened last night?" Sahak said with feigned surprise.

"Oh, cut it out, Sahak. Every time I think about it, my stomach turns."

Sahak chose to ignore Phil's complaints and ordered breakfast, then asked if Phil wanted a cognac—"Like those fellows overthere." He seemed to be in a bantering mood.

Phil saw that they were indeed drinking cognac at eight in the morning.

"The night shift just getting out," Sahak explained.

They ate in silence, Phil anxious to ask questions but unable to find the right words. They checked out and took a taxi to the airport, where Sahak guided Phil through Passport Control. Half an hour later they were airborne to Moscow. Unlike last time, there was no joking with the crew, which was the same as on

Thursday's flight. Phil sat glumly for the first hour, except for occasional moments of elation as he felt the envelope in his breast pocket, but then he would remember the shocking events of the previous night and become distressed again.

None of this escaped Sahak, who watched his ward carefully. Finally, he leaned over from his seat on the aisle and asked—"You are troubled, compatriot. I can understand that incidents such as the one last night are disturbing. Much as I try, even I sometimes cannot get accustomed to them, but . . . well, one does what he must do. Ask me whatever you want."

Phil had been looking out the window at nothing in particular since there was a total cloud cover below, but now he turned and saw that Sahak had become serious. There were no smiles, no jokes, no twinkle in the eyes.

"I'm certain you won't answer all my questions, or, if you do, not truthfully. Am I right?"

Sahak reached for a cigarette, lit it, took a long drag, exhaled with a long whoosh and said—"Let me put it this way. Those that I will answer, I will try to answer truthfully. Others, I will not answer, not because I don't know the answers but because I am not at liberty to. Save them . . . for later."

The last phrase had an ominous undertone which Phil inferred to mean he should save those questions for Adamyants once he arrived back in Budapest.

"Allright, Sahak. First question: why did I have to come all this way, down to Armenia, for this," touching his breast pocket.

"Because the man who gave it to you was vacationing in Armenia with his family."

"I see. Can't we call him by his name? I mean, Sasha?"

"As you wish. Sasha."

"I take it you are aware of his exploits during the war."

"Many of us are. He is a living legend."

"Correction, Sahak. He *was* a living legend, which brings me to my next question. Why was it necessary to sacrifice a war hero in order for me to end my search for a manuscript? And, I should add, gratify a German desire for vengeance?"

"If you got what you came for, you shouldn't be particular about the circumstances."

"The end justifying the means? Oh no, Sahak. Don't pull that one on me. We're not breaking eggs here to make an omelette. We're talking about murder, the death of a man, someone you claim to look up to. Last night, before my very eyes, a man of uncommon ingenuity and valor was shot to death. You could have prevented that, because you came out of the bushes in time to rescue me—and the manuscript. Which brings me to more questions: who was that journalist, if that is what he was? Did you know about him all the time? Was this what back home we call a set-up, in which I was the decoy? And by the way, why was I given a *copy* of the manuscript, and not the original?"

Sahak sighed, looked at Phil dolefully and said—"Well, now we have reached the point where you must save questions like those for later. I do not want to lie to you."

Phil eased back in his uncomfortable seat as a light snack was served. Both men ate in silence, Phil morose, Sahak detached.

The captain announced that seat belts had to be fastened because they were approaching Moscow. Within thirty minutes they were on the ground. Sahak was very solicitous, helping Phil with his overcoat and carrying his one piece of luggage. They walked through the various gates and stood near the outer doors.

"Now to the other airport, Sahak? I return to Budapest within a few hours, don't I?"

"Not just yet, compatriot. There is a car waiting for us. Please be patient, and, if you still can, trust me."

He took Phil's arm and escorted him out to the street where the same Volga limousine and driver as on Thursday were waiting. Sahak handed him his small carrying bag and opened the door.

"Aren't you coming with me, Sahak?"

"Yes he is, Phil, get in," said a voice from inside the car. Phil bent down, incredulous on hearing the familiar voice and looked into the smiling face of Krikor Adamyants.

They shook hands, Phil pleased to see his friend but showing his obvious surprise too. "Krikor! I'll be damned. What in hell are you doing here?"

Adamyants laughed as Sahak got in the front seat next to the driver. "This is my home town, Phil. Remember?"

"Come on, Krikor! I was expecting to see you in Budapest later today or tomorrow. I've got lots of questions for you."

"I'm sure you do, Phil. Didn't Sahak answer some for you?"

"No, not the really important ones. Will you?"

"Yes, if you can keep calm and be patient just a little bit longer. Let me put it another way: when you leave Moscow in a few hours, all your questions will have been answered."

"Fair enough," Phil said and sank down into the luxurious cushions of the limousine.

The car drove at a rapid speed away from the airport toward Moscow. On both sides of the highway, Phil observed large billboards displaying what clearly looked like anti-American images: degenerate-looking men with hooked noses, their hands filled with dollar bills, their hats covered with stars and stripes.

Adamyants saw Phil looking at the large cartoons as they whizzed by and said—"Pay no attention to those. No one else does."

Soon the spires of tall buildings began to appear through the wintry haze and shortly the traffic became congested as they neared the center of the city.

"Unfortunately, there is no time for sightseeing, Phil, any more than there was in Yerevan."

"Oh, Sahak and I found a few hours and he took me to a number of fascinating places."

He noticed that Sahak, sitting up front, was smiling, apparently pleased to know his efforts were appreciated.

Adamyants said—"I'm glad to hear that. Sahak knows Armenia better than I do."

In the distance, Phil recognized the outlines of the Kremlin complex, with its gleaming onion-domed cathedrals and bell towers. As they approached the southern end of Red Square, the driver slowed down. The colorful spiral domes of St. Basil's Cathedral lay directly before them, the grim, forbidding Kremlin Wall on the left, and running parallel to it a seemingly interminable line of people waiting to enter the low, box-like structure of Lenin's Mausoleum.

It was a very brief look, however, for the driver turned sharply to the right, then left, and eventually straight ahead onto October 25 Street where, turning right again, he drove towards another open, though smaller, square and stopped. He and Sahak got out and held the doors on either side as Adamyants and Phil stepped out of the limousine. Phil was looking at a statue some twenty feet away in the center of the square. It was of a solitary figure in a long coat standing on a pedestal, its back to the building. Adamyants looked in the direction of Phil's gaze and said—"Felix Dzerzhinsky, Phil, founder and head of the Cheka."

"The Cheka? You mean the secret police!"

Adamyants laughed—"If you want me to be more precise—the Extraordinary Commission For the Suppression of Counterrevolution and Sabotage."

"That means secret police to me, Krikor. So, if this is Dzerzhinsky Square, then, as I know from my readings about the Soviet Union, that . . ." he turned around and beckoned toward a massive nine-story building—"must be the Lubyanka."

"It *is* the Lubyanka, Phil, and you are about to go inside."

The words, spoken gently, nevertheless sent a current of fear through Phil. Was this, then, what it had all meant? Had he been duped into coming to the Soviet Union by the promise of the manuscript he had so long sought, only to find himself a captive, never to be heard from again? Is that why secrecy was so important to this journey? Not even Jim Garland knew exactly where he was—incredibly, standing in Dzerzhinsky Square in the heart of Moscow, Adamyants on one side of him, Sahak on the other, and he, an American diplomat, about to enter the headquarters of this most dreaded of organizations. He had arrived at the end of his life.

His childhood terrors, the academic insults, the sneers of his haughty colleagues all came tumbling into his mind. He had suffered all those indignities because he was Armenian. Had his Father been wrong to instil in him the pride of his race, which had brought him so much distress in the past, and which now by delusion and subterfuge was to be his complete undoing?

His only hope all these years for liberation from the prison of his ethnic lineage had been finding the Beethoven manuscript, whereby he could soar above the pettiness of his tormentors and transcend once and for all the ignominy of inferiority he had faced for so many years. The curse of being Armenian would be erased and the pride of his Father and of his nation reinstated. Where all had gone so well, thanks perhaps to 'the relevance of being Armenian,' was it all now, in the final moments of the adventure, to suddenly become irrelevant? Phil felt an agony he had never experienced in his life.

An arm went around his shoulders and he heard Adamyants say—"Phil, for Heaven's sake, what's wrong with you? Don't tell me you're afraid of us?"

Sahak was watching from a distance. He approached, gave Phil a pat on the back, and murmured words of assurance. It did little to quiet Phil's fears. His sense of dread mounted as he felt the firmness with which Sahak took his left arm and Adamyants his right.

The three Armenians now began their walk to the front entrance of KGB Headquarters.

It consisted of two buildings, one of seven stories, and attached to it, a newer structure of nine stories, both in imitation of rococo architecture. The austerity of the building's facade and ground-floor barred windows was lessened only slightly by the leafless trees which lined the front length of the buildings, and

x

did nothing to reduce Phil's tension as they entered the large front door.

Phil was struck by the dreariness of the entry hall with its faded rugs and dim lighting. Adamyants and Sahak showed ID cards, said something in Russian to the two guards inside the entrance and then accompanied Phil up a brief flight of stairs to the elevators. Sahak was very business-like and solemn, and Adamyants rocked back and forth on his heels, as they waited for the elevator to arrive. When it came, all three entered in turn. Phil was too confused, his mind in a complete jumble, to note at what floor they got off. He thought it might be the third. His mind was numb as he followed dutifully down a pale green corridor until they stood in front of a large oak door. Adamyants knocked three times, heard a voice inside and opened the door, guiding Phil into an ante room.

A plain-looking woman with no makeup, steel-rimmed glasses and dark hair knotted in a bun arose with a welcoming smile and said they were expected. She led them to another door and opened it. Adamyants, Phil and Sahak, in that order, entered a simply-furnished office, whose windows looked out on Dzerzhinsky Square. There was a desk at one side with some papers on it and three telephones. The shelves had very few books. Phil found the ascetic simplicity of this office even more Spartan than the entry below. He did not move until Adamyants gestured toward a large leather sofa, where all three sat down.

Totally dejected, Phil sensed that the moment of betrayal was near.

After a full minute of total silence, punctuated only by the ticking of a large clock on the mantel, a door opened abruptly and, his face wreathed in that enigmatic smile Phil had come to know so well, Yuri Vladimirovich Andropov entered the room.

Fifty-Six

Adamyants and Sahak leaped to their feet and Phil followed suit, but more slowly, as Andropov approached him with extended hand, which Phil shook weakly. Andropov said something in Russian, then looked at Adamyants and gave a brief nod toward Phil, which Phil understood to mean—translate for me. Adamyants did into Armenian.

"Mr. Faljian, I am delighted to see you again, and this time here in Moscow."

Phil felt a tightness in his throat and for a moment thought he might not be able to speak, but he finally overcame his nervousness. "Thank you, Mr. Andropov. You surely understand that I am overwhelmed by the circumstances of this meeting."

Andropov laughed, adjusted his rimless glasses, and said—"Quite understandable. Being in Moscow, in Lubyanka, with the head of the KGB. No one will ever believe you, and I wouldn't blame them."

Phil smiled nervously at this and the tension in the room decreased as the others joined him and Andropov in an audible display of amusement.

The head of the KGB continued—"I, of course, know what happened in Yerevan. It must have been very disturbing for you."

"It was *very* disturbing, and I cannot erase it from my mind."

"On the other hand, you now have your manuscript."

Phil looked at the bespectacled Director of the KGB for a moment and then asked—"The manuscript and I are both in your power, Mr. Andropov. I am far from home, even far from my diplomatic base, and it is difficult for me to understand everything that has happened."

Andropov looked puzzled—"I do not understand, Mr. Faljian. You seem concerned."

"With all due respect, Mr. Andropov, wouldn't you be? Look at this situation. An American diplomat is sitting in the office of the head of the KGB, in Lubyanka, and being told in very benign terms, that he has successfuly ended his mission."

"Yes," Andropov replied, "I can understand that this might seem curious. Except for the fact that we know that you have acted honorably. Let me explain. You have always maintained that your interest in the manuscript was strictly cultural. At first, we didn't think so, but your assistance has confirmed for us that your objectives were sincere. In Washington, Mr.Faljian, there may be a view that we are a dissolute, criminal body, but believe me, there are some of us—I sometimes think, however, not enough—who respect honor and honesty. That is why we have helped you—and in the process, helped ourselves. I will not deny that we have. Surely you understand that we must operate in the best interest of the Soviet Union, In the present case, fortunately for us all, everyone has come out a winner. Wouldn't you agree?"

As Andropov spoke, Phil's fears gradually diminished, for these were not threatening words. For the first time he realized that he might even look upon Krikor and Sahak unflinchingly as allies, in a venture which had had very divergent purposes, to be sure, but a conclusion which suited everyone. In the end, it had been the Armenian connection, at several levels, which had served as the major force in this international adventure and achieved for him the prestige that would surely come when the discovery was announced.

"Yes, Mr. Andropov. I do agree, and perhaps I even understand." Phil replied. "Could I, nevertheless, ask you some questions?"

Andropov beckoned for him to continue.

"Sahak has explained why I had to travel to Armenia to complete the mission. But there are other questions, and I guess the most important of them is—was it necessary to have a remarkable man killed? Killed for this manuscript, killed to satisfy a German hunger for revenge? I had heard so much about this man, Sasha, and suddenly, there I was, face-to-face with him in Yerevan! It was an awesome experience. Surely, you can understand my state of mind?"

"Of course I do, and you have good cause to ask this question," Andropov responded, turned to Adamyants and said something. He then went to his desk, pressed a button, and looked at Phil, the smile still on his face. The door through which Andropov had entered the room now opened again, but gradually, and as Phil heard its creaking and turned, his eyes opened wide, he stepped back, his face frozen in astonishment. Standing before him was a stooped figure with a cane and an eye-patch who could be no one else than the Sasha he had seen killed before his eyes.

As the figure approached with shuffling steps, the three others in the room watched Phil closely. Sasha rested his cane against his hip to free his one good hand, extended it and said in the purest Armenian—"At last we meet, my friend from America. I owe you my life and I am very happy to thank you in person."

As though in a trance, Phil shook the gnarled hand. He looked into the deeply-lined face, the one eye he could see, the brown teeth visible through the weak smile, and felt an electric impulse surge through him. Standing before him was the legendary Sasha, Intelligence officer extraordinary, instrument of a most remarkable mission, survivor of an act of terror that could have transformed the world. But was he? If this was Sasha, who was the stooped figure with the cane and eye-patch who was killed only a few feet from him in Yerevan?

Recovering, he turned to Andropov—"I don't understand. In Yerevan, before my very eyes . . ."

Andropov picked up the thread of Phil's thought—". . . before your very eyes in Yerevan, what you saw actually did happen, *except* that it was not what you thought. Our intent was not to fool *you*, but to fool the one who *followed* you."

Andropov looked at his wristwatch, frowned, and said—"I regret having to leave this gathering of Armenians. Curiously, I must be at a meeting in fifteen minutes with yet another Armenian—the President. And by the way, Mr. Faljian, he knows of your service to us and appreciates it. Now, if you will excuse me . . ."

He spoke in Russian to Adamyants again, shook Phil's hand firmly and said—"We shall probably not meet again, my American friend, but, in our work, you never know. So, allow me to draw on my very limited Armenian vocabulary and say *Tsudesutyun.*" He then waved peremptorily to the three others in the office and left.

Everyone grinned at hearing Andropov's 'Until we meet again.'

There was no need now to speak anything but Armenian, and Phil looked to Adamyants for guidance. "Krikor, my questions still require answering."

Adamyants, meanwhile, was looking admiringly at Sasha and didn't respond immediately to Phil. When he did, he said—"You must appreciate, Phil, that I have seen our brave countryman only a few times, but never really spoken to him. This is almost as much an occasion for me as it is for you."

Sasha interrupted to say, modestly—"We are all servants of our ideals. What I did, any of you could have done. The difference was that I was there."

"The difference," Adamyants quickly but respectfully disagreed, "was that you had a courage, a skill, a virtuosity, a prowess that we all aspire to. It is an honor to be in your presence."

Both Adamyants and Sahak, who clearly shared his colleague's view, gazed with total wonder at the bent figure. Sasha, meanwhile, seemed to be fumbling for something in his breast pocket, and when he finally found it, turned to his two colleagues, his one visible eye sparkling, and said—"There is something about me, or perhaps better said, about my experience, which neither of you know. In fact, outside of Comrade Andropov, very few know, but which fills me with a special kind of pleasure. I would like to tell you and our Armenian friend from America about it at this time, especially him because he has guaranteed that my final days will be peaceful and secure."

Addressing Phil, he said—"During the Great Patriotic War we were allies, and now, sadly, we are not. An irony, no? Well, let me give you another instance of war's many ironies.

"After the explosion on July 20, I was rushed to a make-shift hospital in Rastenburg. My first day there is a bad dream that I would prefer to forget. But on the second day, my arm half gone, my leg shattered and my right eye blinded and bandaged, despite my partial deafness, I suddenly heard shouts in the corridor which, as it turned out, were loud commands, then many footsteps. I closed my one good eye and just lay there. The sounds stopped near my bed. Someone was touching my hand. I opened my eye and found myself staring into the face of the *Führer* himself—Adolf Hitler!

"I had, of course stood close to Hitler many times, but never with our faces only inches apart. This time, a sudden fear penetrated my heart, because, for all I knew, perhaps it was I who was under suspicion for a seemingly suicidal attempt to kill him. But my fear vanished when I saw that he was smiling sympathetically. Then, I heard him murmur '*Ich danke Dir,*' after which he put something on my chest, and walked out. This is what he gave me."

Sasha took from his pocket a medal on a ribbon and dangled it for all to see.

"The Iron Cross!" Adamyants exclaimed, in astonishment.

"The Iron Cross—First Class, the highest Nazi honor," Sasha underlined. "Can there be anyone else in the world who has been decorated personally by both Hitler and Stalin—and, irony of ironies, for the very same deed! "

All stared at the medal in awed silence. After some moments,

Phil cleared his throat noisily and the others turned their attention to him.

"Krikor, I still have more questions, which in the interest of time, I'll reduce to three. First, who really got killed in Yerevan—if anybody?"

"Someone did get killed, Phil. When we were planning this scheme, it was Yuri Vladimirovich's idea that we recruit someone as a stand-in for Comrade Mikoyan—Sasha. We knew that you would be leading a potential assassin to him, so we selected someone whose loss would be of no concern."

"You deliberately sacrificed the life of an innocent man for all this?"

"An innocent man? If I tell you he was a criminal, would it make a difference?"

"What kind of criminal?"

"A rapist and murderer, responsible for the deaths of three women. Armenian women, Phil. Try and think of what happened to him as an execution. A justified execution for a crime for which he would have been executed anyway. Does that answer your question?"

"It will have to do, I guess. Well, second question. Who was the assassin?"

"He really *is* a German journalist, but he is also a West German Intelligence officer from the BND, on whose orders he was commissioned to execute Comrade Mikoyan. As you know, our German colleague back in Budapest, Christian Sommer, was trying to find out from you the location and new name of the defecting German officer responsible for keeping Hitler alive. He did not know, and must never know, that the officer in question was a *Soviet* Intelligence Officer. I hope you will honor that secret."

"I have no cause not to. But let me understand this. As far as the BND is concerned, Major Manteuffel is dead, shot in Yerevan by one of their intelligence operatives. In other words, the German Resistance has wreaked its revenge, and Sasha is now safe. Correct?"

Sasha spoke up—"Absolutely correct, my friend, that is why

I said I owe you my life. I shall no longer be hunted. At the same time, let me tell you that I was devastated when I learned of the massive Nazi arrests and executions after I foiled the July 20 plot. Most of all, I grieved for Admiral Canaris because I knew him so intimately. Even though I was aware that he suspected I was a Gestapo agent, I admired him for his idealism. When we speak of bravery, my dear compatriots, let us respect the courage even of our enemies."

Phil addressed him—"If I could ask you one more thing, Mr. Mikoyan. The manscript that I was given was a *copy* of the original. That the title page was torn is not so important, because it is the music itself that is."

"About the title page, that is how I received the manuscript when our people delivered it to me. My understanding is that when they procured it from this fellow, what was his name . . . ?"

"Fekete."

"Yes, Fekete, there was a struggle and he tore the title page in two. The bottom half somehow got lost. But I agree with you, that is not important. Why not the original? In view of the great value of this find, it was determined—not by me, I emphasize—that the original Beethoven manuscript be kept in the vaults here in this building."

"For what purpose?" Phil asked in astonishment.

"I have no idea, maybe just insurance. But have no fear that we will exploit it. It is clearly understood that the copy you have is for your use. When you go public with it, you can say that the original was lost. After all, if I understand these things correctly, no matter how many times it is copied, the music stands by itself. Isn't that so?"

Phil nodded a number of times and let out a long sigh.

"Yes it is. Thank you for answering my questions. Finally, Krikor, may I ask Sahak something?"

Adamyants waved his hand in assent.

"Sahak, when I left you last night at the *Matenadaran*, you had two bodies on your hands, one dead and one, I hope, still alive. What did you do with them?"

x

"Compatriot, we have an office in Yerevan and the staff had been alerted to the problem. The criminal was buried that same night without a trace. The German was unconscious from my gun butt and taken to our office. When he came to, we interrogated him. He was terrified and confessed to everything, even to working for the BND. We told him that he had just killed a Soviet citizen for which he could be tried and executed. But because Moscow was seeking to improve relations with Bonn, we wished to avoid discordant incidents and, therefore, would release him, but only on condition that he keep silent on everything except the fact that he had accomplished his mission with the German defector. If he ever broke his silence, we would release his confession of murder, thereby exposing his cover as a journalist and embarrassing both his organization and his government. He will be returned to Moscow tomorrow and request re-assignment. None of this could have been accomplished here in Moscow, only in Yerevan, where we exercise much tighter control. That is why you had to travel to Armenia, not because of vacation plans, as I told you earlier. I apologize for telling you that untruth. Answer your question?"

"Yes, Sahak. That is incredible. In fact, all of this is incredible. A search for a music manuscript led me into the intrigues of several intelligence agencies, a hunt for a mystery figure, two murders, travel to two Soviet capitals, and finally, the climax here in, of all places, KGB headquarters."

He shook hands warmly with Sasha and watched him shuffle off through the door, and when it had closed behind him, Adamyants said that Phil had to go promptly to the airport for his return flight. They descended in the elevator and walked out onto the street where the Volga was waiting nearby. As he bent down to enter the car, Phil took one final long look at the Lubyanka and heard Adamyants ask with amusement—"Can you believe it once housed an insurance company?"

"After all this, Krikor, I can believe just about anything."

Fifty-Seven

The Volga limousine returned to October 25 Street and at Red Square turned right onto Gorki Street, which became Leningrad Prospect and then the airport highway. Phil was far more relaxed than before, chatting amiably with Adamyants, with occasional backward looks from Sahak sitting up front.

"These two days will stay with me always, Krikor. Incredible days. By the way, would you allow me a pointed question?"

Adamyants nodded.

"As far as I can guess, we were on the third floor. Can you tell me what goes on below?"

Outside of a tightening of his lips, Adamyants was expressionless as he replied—"That is not a subject I care to discuss, even with you, Phil. Just believe me when I say that I've never been below."

Phil understood that he would not get a frank reply so he switched to another theme—"Did you ever truly think we would wind up like this, here in Moscow at your headquarters?"

Krikor allowed a small smile to play about his lips. "Life plays strange tricks on us, Phil. No, frankly, I didn't. When Fekete first came to Comrade Andropov with his threats and schemes, it didn't strike me as anything for someone in Yuri Vladimirovich's position to worry about. But then, a short time later, when, if you recall, I asked how you spend your leisure time, and you replied that you were searching for a manuscript, the very same manuscript that Fekete threatened us with, bells started ringing in my head.

"You see, for some time we had known that the BND was playing a peripheral role in all this, but it wasn't until you told me Christian Sommer's real identity that everything fell into place. After that, with my friend's help . . ."—he used the Armenian feminine ending for friend—" . . . we devised this plan, so that, once and for all, the Germans could think that they had achieved their objective, and in gratitude for your help, we could help you achieve yours. Everyone gained."

"Except that poor bastard with three bullets in him."

Adamyants shook his head—"No, Phil. He was condemned to death before he played that role. The agreement with him was that his sentence would be commuted to twenty years. *We* knew, of course, that his life was in danger, but *he* didn't. If he had survived, he too would have gained. The important thing for you is that you found what you had been looking for."

Instinctively, Phil put his hand inside his breast pocket and felt the envelope. The contact filled him with gratification and a degree of anticipation. Something occurred to him—"Tell me, Krikor, as far as you know, have any of your experts been able to verify the authenticity of the manuscript?"

"No one has ever said anything about that to me. Why? Do you have some doubts about it?"

Phil looked out the window at the swiftly passing scene and said softly—"I don't know. I just don't know."

They arrived at the airport and all got out of the car. Then, to Phil's surprise, Adamyants extended his hand and said—"Well, Phil, I guess this is Good-bye—for now anyway. How about if we leave it at *Auf Wiedersehen*?"

"What do you mean? Aren't you returning to Budapest?"

"No I'm not. I've been re-assigned . . . to Moscow Center. Besides, Lori is waiting for me in my apartment."

"Lori?"

"Hannelore Weber, Phil. We're going to be married here, in Moscow. It's the only way I could get Yuri Vladimirovich to be my Best Man. I still believe in some of the old ways and he has no objections."

Phil braced himself against the cold wind, speechless and, he had to admit to himself, disappointed. He had long since come to think of Krikor Adamyants as a friend. Slowly, he took off his glove and offered his hand, but instead of taking it, Adamyants wrapped his arms around Phil in a warm embrace and said in his ear—"Let us not forget each other, my dear friend."

He stood on the sidewalk and watched as Phil walked with Sahak through the doors, responding one last time when Phil turned around for a final wave. They reached the Aeroflot counter where Phil checked in. Sahak then negotiated an effortless passage through all the guards at Customs and Passport Control, flashing his ID and saying something to each of them.

Phil had virtually no time before boarding his flight, and turned to say farewell. Sahak seemed suddenly nervous, fidgeted and tried unsuccessfuly to light a cigarette.

"What's wrong, Sahak?"

Sahak looked at Phil and spoke haltingly, as though uncertain as to what to say—"You know, compatriot, I really have no family, only distant relatives. My father and mother were killed in the massacres of 1915. Only my older brother and I survived. In my life, I have taken to few people. But in the days we have been together, here and in Germany, you have treated me with respect, even though you know what I do. We have been taught that you, I mean *all* of you, are the class enemy. But you have not behaved with me like an enemy. You have spoken to me of music and art and other things of which I am ignorant, and made me feel like an equal. That is why you have become more than a compatriot to me. And . . . I will miss you."

Phil was deeply moved and his eyes filled suddenly. The loudspeaker announced his flight and as he offered his hand again, as he had to Adamyants, Sahak, like Adamyants, embraced him and, to Phil's surprise, kissed him on both cheeks. Phil's lips tightened as he nodded in rapid jerks, turned and without looking back walked out onto the tarmac.

The flight back was turbulent and his seat belt was never unfastened, but the indelible memory of the last two days diverted him from the discomforts of the trip. He relived the scenes, some major, some minor, but all vivid: Sahak again, the frantic delegations at *Sheremetyevo*, the snow-capped peaks of the Caucasus, the lovely stewardess called Anoush, Armenian cathedrals, memorials, art galleries, the ominous walk to the *Matenadaran,* Sasha in the shadows, who turned out not to be Sasha, the three shots, the two bodies on the ground, Krikor in Moscow, Lubyanka, Andropov and finally—the real Sasha!

When Phil resettled himself in the narrow seat, he discovered that he was experiencing an empty feeling. It took him but a few moments to realize that it was the emptiness of loss, the loss of his Armenian friends, Krikor and Sahak. He had come to realize in the last two days that without the ethnic kinship of all three, his mission and their mission could not have been accomplished. Their pride in their lineage had restored his belief in his own—a belief that had been so shaken in the past. He had trusted them and they had trusted him. If they had intrigued, it had not been at his expense, in fact, to his advantage. And their genuinely emotional parting conveyed to him that they too shared his sense of loss.

"Would anyone, anyone at all, ever believe," he muttered under the roar of the plane's engines, "that an American diplomat has two friends in the KGB!"

BUDAPEST

Hungary

Fifty-Eight

He disembarked at *Ferihegy*, retrieved his car from the parking lot and drove back to Budapest. Because it was almost seven, he decided to go directly to his home in *Zugliget*. Erzsébet was waiting for him and on hearing the car coming up the steep driveway, threw the door wide open and beamed.

"Faljian *úr*, I am so happy to see you. Where have you been?"

He had no intention of telling her and said merely that he was called out of town and hadn't the opportunity to inform her. Erzsébet knew that was not true but it did not diminish her joy. She had prepared a good dinner for him which he devoured and finished off half a bottle of *Égri Bikavér*, a wine he knew would put him more easily to sleep.

After Erzsébet had gone, he made three phone calls. The first was to the *chargé*.

"Jim, I'm back."

"Well, thank God for that!" Garland sounded genuinely relieved. I'm sure there's plenty to tell me."

"There is, but it can wait. See you tomorrow at the Embassy?"

"Absolutely. Around ten."

The second was to Bence Szabolcsi, whom he found at home.

"Dr. Szabolcsi, this is Faljian. Can I see you either tomorrow or Sunday?"

"Let us meet at the Archives on Sunday at twelve. I'll be waiting inside."

The third call was to Kiki.

"How is my favorite caryatid today?"

"Phil! For Heaven's sake, you haven't been to the Embassy, you haven't been home. You don't tell me anything. What's going on? Don't I count anymore?"

"If you didn't count, Kiki, I wouldn't be calling. I just returned from an arduous trip, I'm very tired, but I want to see you tomorrow. Can you get to the club by early afternoon?"

"Sure, How about one or two?"

"Two is fine. Make some sandwiches."

She giggled with pleasure and murmured in Greek—"*S'agapo, parapoli.*"

"And I love you too—very much."

He got into bed realizing once again that there was no Krikor Adamyants to call anymore. But within minutes he was sound asleep, oblivious of his emotions, his thoughts and of the whirlwind events of the last two days.

On Saturday morning, Phil drove to the Embassy where the sidewalk guards acknowledged him with brief nods. Upstairs he walked into the *chargé's* office. Garland arose and went quickly to him—"Phil, I am *really* happy to see you. A thousand wild ideas went through my mind yesterday and today. I was even sore at myself for having allowed you to go. As Sarah knows, I've had a restless night, partly out of worry, and partly out of remorse at the way I spoke to you. You know I didn't mean much of it."

"No explanations needed, Jim, and I deserved everything you said. But, well, here I am, safe and sound. The tank?"

Garland nodded quickly, got the key and within minutes they were inside the Secure Room, although Phil couldn't help wonder why, inasmuch as the KGB had engineered everything, so why keep it from the AVO? He began by relating everything that had happened from the moment he set foot on Soviet soil. Garland was hunched forward, eating up every word, and his expression, composed and serious, didn't change, except for a wrinkled brow when Phil described the murder of 'Sasha.'

But when Phil reached the part of his story that began at

Dzerzhinsky Square, Garland sat up erect, his eyes looking steadily at Phil, and said with an incredulous edge to his voice—"I hope you're not going to tell me you went into Lubyanka?"

"I'm afraid, Jim, that I am. Right into KGB Headquarters. But I'm sitting here with you now, which means I got out again."

He attempted a laugh, but Jim's expression continued to be solemn. "Allright, keep talking," although his voice displayed no anger.

It was when Phil arrived at Andropov's entrance into the room that Garland reacted sharply—"Not again! For the *third* time?"

"Cross my heart, Jim. It was Yuri Andropov, again, for the third time."

Phil had decided to hold back nothing from his friend. Washington, he decided, was another matter.

"You're absolutely certain it was Andropov?" Garland persisted. "Not a double?"

"Come on, Jim. Cut it out. I've had enough of forgeries. Shall I continue?"

"I'm so accustomed to your contacts with the uncontactable, that I'm no longer alarmed. Go on."

Phil kept to the facts as they unraveled, wanting Garland to experience all the vagaries of the epic adventure just as he had, so that when he described Sasha's appearance in Andropov's office, Garland was as stunned as he had been.

"In other words, the Sasha in Yerevan was not Sasha at all?"

"Exactly. The whole thing had been a ruse to trick the Germans and the BND into thinking they had struck gold. Of course, as it emerged, they also wanted the manuscript. Sommer, von Hase that is, had never mentioned that to me. It's possible that the BND didn't plan that either, and that it was just the journalist's idea. In any case, I have my Soviet friends to thank for setting it right and getting it to me. Actually, I prefer to think of them as my Armenian friends."

"Can I, at long last, finally see this much-storied, notorious manuscript?"

Phil opened the envelope and spread the top two sheets of music paper on the table.

"This is a photostat," Garland said with surprise.

"I know, Jim, but that is the best I could do. The original is in Moscow, and will remain there for a very long time. They promised me it would not be exploited for any purpose."

"And you believed them?"

Phil sighed, looked down at the brown sheets before him, and nodded—"Do I have a choice?"

Garland picked up the first page of the score and looked at the scribbled dots scattered seemingly haphazardly across it.

"This looks like a mess. But I suppose it makes sense to you."

"It does, Jim, and tomorrow, I'm meeting with Szabolcsi, the musicologist, to show it to him."

Garland pushed his chair back and stood up.

"You know, Phil, if anything had happened to you, it would have been my ass. First the wife of the Ambassador, and now this. You may enjoy playing recklessly with your career but I've still got mine to think about. That's the main reason I'm relieved you're back."

"Not because you were concerned about my well-being, Jim?" he asked with a twinkle in his eye.

Garland smiled impishly—"Not at all. In fact, it would have been good riddance. Speaking of which, I got a phone call from Washington last night alerting me to an EYES ONLY cable on Monday which has something to do with you. I hope that gives you two sleepless nights."

Fifty-Nine

Kiki was just arriving at the club as Phil drove up. When he saw that she had her tennis sweatsuit on, although tennis had not been mentioned, he opened the trunk of his car and took out the tennis gear he always kept there. She ran over and kissed him several times.

"Oh God, how I've missed you," she said breathlessly.

"As a tennis partner?" he teased.

"You know what I mean!" she shot back and kissed him again.

The club was heavily attended on this Saturday by the many diplomatic families eager to enjoy the fresh if chilly air of the Buda hills. Kiki didn't mind the stares from the various foreign diplomats who were surprised to see her with a tennis racquet in such frosty weather. She asked Phil if he were hungry enough for lunch or did he want to play first. He suggested she go on the court while he changed in the clubhouse. They played singles for half an hour when he spotted the Turkish Ambassador and his secretary approaching the court. He knew the invitation to play doubles was pending, so he informed Kiki quietly that it was time for lunch.

"I'll save that gorgeous Greek body from black and blue marks," Phil said, encircling her waist as they walked off the court.

"I don't mind the marks if they're made by an Armenian," she laughed, kissing him on his ear.

The Turkish Ambassador watched disappointedly as they left the court and walked to an isolated corner of the Club. There, they enjoyed their first lunch together in some time as more diplomats and their families gathered.

After lunch and some bland conversation with the just-arrived Roger Mandrake about the beauty of the Swiss Alps—"and waterfalls," Phil added mischievously, a remark the British Ambassador pretended not to hear—Phil and Kiki took a long drive through the hills and toward six, when it was getting very chilly, they arrived at his residence.

Without Erzsébet at home or phone calls to disturb them, Phil and Kiki spent the rest of the night in a darkened house, listening to the Well-Tempered Clavichord and reacting to each other. When at one point hours later, Kiki, cuddling close to Phil in bed, asked—"You won't be angry, I hope, if I ask you, darling, but . . . did Grace Quigley ever mean anything to you?"

Phil cupped her chin and looked affectionately into her olive-dark eyes—"My darling, Grace was nothing but trouble and never, I repeat, *never* meant anything to me. She is a thing of the past, something I want very much to forget. You shouldn't ever have had doubts about me, then or now. I truly thank the Lord she is gone. You, on the other hand, are here with me now. Isn't that enough?"

"Yes, it is," she said, moving even closer and exploring as she did.

'If all Greek women are this insatiable,' he thought, 'God help me if I'm ever assigned to Athens.' But he turned towards her and responded.

On Sunday morning, Kiki made a big breakfast, after which, over her protests of 'just one more,' he drove her to her apartment, kissed her at the door, winked at the watching policeman, and continued on across the Danube over the *Margit híd* to the Bartók Archives.

Bence Szabolcsi was waiting inside as Phil entered. They greeted each other genially and the elderly musicologist said they could use his office. Once there, he asked if Phil had learned anything new.

"I assume you have found some time to do more research. I know how busy you have been with your normal Embassy activities. Is there anything you can tell me?"

Phil looked with affection at the Hungarian scholar and said—

"Dr. Szabolcsi, I cannot tell you with what excitement and joy I come here to see you. Let me say that some things have happened of late which have been highly productive; so much so that, well . . . I don't know how to continue, except to say . . . here, look at what I bring you."

He inserted a hand in his breast pocket, brought out the manila envelope, laid it on the table and looked up triumphantly.

Szabolcsi didn't move. His bald head shone from the bright light overhead and he wet his lips several times. Then, gingerly, he opened the envelope, took out the beige sheets of paper inside, spread the first three pages on the table, and studied them. There wasn't a sound in the small office and no one was visiting the Archives at that hour. Phil sought even to suppress the sound of his own breathing as he watched. It was almost two minutes later that Szabolcsi looked up at Phil through his thick-lenses. His voice, normally gentle and even, was tinged with heavy emotion—

"This is the same score that Fekete showed me. Of course, I saw only the title and the first page, but I recognize the cello introduction, and it is the same. Incidentally, I also note that this is a copy. Do you know where the original is?"

"It is in safe-keeping, Dr. Szabolcsi. I have the word of people I trust that it will remain so."

Szabolcsi nodded his acceptance of Phil's assurance. He studied the second and third and fourth pages again, then began to hum as he went through the rest of it, finally coming to the end.

"There is no cadenza, which, while not conclusive, tells me it is somewhat unfinished. But, nevertheless, I would not call it a fragment. It appears to be an almost complete first movement for a cello concerto."

"Dr. Szabolcsi, for some time now, without myself having seen this manuscript, I have wondered about its authenticity. Someone said something about that once, which put a doubt in my mind. Hellmuth von Hase told me he had found a letter from Beethoven to his great-grandfather, Gottfried Härtel, which reported that the Master was writing this concerto. And of course, there is the score itself. Perhaps you recall that during our trip to Martonvásár, I talked to you about the Vermeer in the National Gallery and wondered about its authenticity. It was in the context of the Van Meegeren forgeries which in recent years have been sold in Europe—masterly imitations of Vermeer by a master forger. We could really call him a master painter too. Therefore, I ask—If Vermeer could be faked, couldn't Beethoven also?"

Szabolcsi looked down at the score once again—"I have spent decades looking at scores, especially Beethoven's. If this were a forgery, then it is by a gifted musician who could almost, and I stress *almost* hold a candle to Beethoven. So, I ask myself, why would he waste his time pretending to be the great composer when he could be composing quite good music himself? No, I have no doubt whatsoever that this is genuine. We have before us most of the first movement of a Cello Concerto by Beethoven, something the world never knew because Beethoven and Gottfried Härtel kept it a secret.

"This quite lengthy solo cello introduction appears to violate the traditional form of the concerto, but Beethoven was always the iconoclast. Take his Violin Concerto, for instance. Would any composer consider beginning a violin concerto with four drum beats? No, this is a product of his third period and it is evident he was reaching out again, as he always did, for something transcending tradition and classical form. My guess is that he began the Concerto, set it aside and never returned to it, writing his last two cello sonatas instead."

He emitted a long sigh, adjusted his glasses, and predicted—

"We'll have to hear this many times before we can judge its place in his music. For the present, however, dear colleague, some questions arise. For instance, in view of the strange circumstances of its discovery and the even more bizarre twists and turns of its history, how do you propose to proceed? In other words, what happens next?"

"I have been thinking of that, Dr. Szabolcsi, especially when it became evident to me that the time had come when the problem had to be resolved. Consequently, I believe I have found the answer.

"I cannot regard myself as anything but a diplomat whose mission it is to pursue the objectives of my government. But *you* are an eminent musicologist, with the mission of revealing music in its social and historical context. Because of that, and the rich experience of knowing and working with you, I wish, in gratitude, to present this manuscript to *you* so that it be you who divulges it to the world, who interprets its meaning and gives it the significance in musical history that it deserves."

The two men looked at each other silently, then Szabolcsi took his glasses off and wiped them with a handkerchief. Phil saw that his eyes were moist. The elderly academician swallowed several times, and responded humbly—"This is an honor I do not deserve, dear colleague."

"On the contrary, no one deserves it more than you. I propose that we go somewhere and celebrate the occasion—the completion of our mission."

Phil helped the aging musicologist up from his chair, folded the manuscript and handed it to him, and both walked out into the cold sunlight of a wintry day. They entered a small cafe and ordered two cognacs. When the waiter said that a shipment of Soviet brandy had just arrived, at which Szabolcsi wrinkled his nose, Phil, brightening, asked the waiter to bring an entire bottle. When it came, Phil laughed triumphantly and said—"Just as I thought. It is Armenian brandy. Here, look at this label—*Ararat.*"

"In that case, it is appropriate that we drink it," Szabolcsi said, but in contrast to Phil's lightheartedness, his demeanor was sombre.

"Something is wrong, Dr. Szabolcsi, and I wish you would share the problem with me. I thought this would be a happy occasion."

"Oh, it is, my dear friend, please do not think I am not highly pleased, and honored too. No, my thoughts are with the manuscript, and its future. Your presenting it to me places a great burden on my shoulders, a moral burden, you understand. But I think I have the solution, if you will give me your permission."

"Whatever it is, Dr. Szabolcsi, it is *your* decision and yours alone."

"Thank you, my dear friend. This is what I shall do. At the earliest opportunity, I shall go to Berlin and see Dr. Karl-Heinz Keilbert at the *Staatsbibliothek*. Because of your visit with him, Keilbert knows about your search, and it is possible Scheidemann in Leipzig has already told him what he told you. I shall have him examine this copy and render a judgment. After all, the world's leading authority on Beethoven should have the final say."

Phil looked with admiration and respect at the great scholar— "It was a corrupt Hungarian musicologist who stole the Beethoven from Germany, and it is an honorable Hungarian musicologist who returns it to Germany. For me, Dr. Szabolcsi, that is very just, and very gratifying."

"I am pleased that you find it so, dear colleague. I address you as such with all my respect for your zeal and obvious talent, even though I am ignorant of all that this search entailed. It is better that I remain in the dark. But be assured of one thing Keilbert is a scholar of such integrity that when he announces the find, he will make certain that credit for its discovery is fully given."

"That will surely include you, Dr. Szabolcsi."

"Perhaps. But most certainly *you.*"

Phil hoped that Szabolcsi would not notice the flush of pleasure which he felt on his cheeks.

They reviewed some of the odd twists and turns of the long search, especially the massive Leipzig air raid of 1943 and Fekete's theft of the musical treasure. Phil made no reference to the more sinister corners of the story—the German resistance, the Soviet espionage, the KGB climax in Yerevan and Moscow, from which he had always spared the elderly scholar. They both agreed it to be a gross musicological aberration that an unknown score by one of music's greatest geniuses should be discovered and revealed to the world because of the corrupt machinations of a degenerate charlatan.

It was after another thirty minutes that Phil asked for the check and they left the cafe. They walked slowly up to the Fisherman's Bastion, engaged in animated conversation, but Phil was aware that with the resolution of the Beethoven problem, Bence Szabolcsi would no longer be a fellow sleuth probing a musicological mystery, but would revert instead to the more traditional role of mere contact for the Embassy's Cultural Officer.

Szabolcsi was perhaps aware of these same thoughts, for when Phil finally said it was time for him to go, Szabolcsi seemed shaken. In addition to the advent of a different relationship, his years of reclusive academic life in a restrictive society had ill-prepared him for the act of magnanimity from which he had just benefited. He simply looked up, wordless, and covered Phil's hand firmly in both of his, his grateful eyes giving expression to all he felt.

During the drive home, Phil wondered at the reaction of the music world when the Szabolcsi-Keilbert investigation results would be made public. The discovery would most assuredly be front-page news, while the musicological journals would search for clues in documents—Phil smiled with amusement—that he had himself explored for so long, coming up with the same fruitless results. One interested reader of all these reports would most assuredly be Eric Peter Kurz, still active as a musicological elder statesman, whose initial reaction might be envy, Phil surmised, until he learned of the role of his former 'lower species' student. Whereupon, Kurz, sneering with contempt, would charge "Fake, hoax, forgery," and exploit the fact that the evidence was not the original manuscript.

Phil was not concerned by the possibility of such questions being raised by other more objective musicologists. They could easily be brushed off with the explanation that the original had been lost. Moscow would certainly remain silent, reluctant to open the Pandora's box of intrigue connected with Sasha and Hitler's miraculous escapes from death. 'Sort of a pact between me and the KGB,' he laughed quietly. As for the right of first performance, Moscow could work that out with its East German and Hungarian allies.

He guided the car around a bend and up his driveway. He changed into jeans, sank into the sofa on his porch and relaxed with some Lester Young. The style of the great tenor saxophonist, his intricate manipulations of melody and ideas, were soothing to his ear.

Phil looked up at the shelf laden with books on Beethoven and smiled sadly. Gone was the excitement of the quest, the burning need to know the When, Where and What. The search was over and everything was now in the capable hands of Bence Szabolcsi.

It was not until he had retired that Phil remembered what the *chargé* had told him about the cable he was expecting the next morning. Garland had said that it would have something to do with him. It was while speculating on its contents that Phil, contrary to Garland's wish, had his first uninterrupted sleep in many months.

Sixty

On Monday morning, eager to read the EYES ONLY from Washington, Phil entered the Embassy at nine, and found a note on his desk from the *chargé*, which said simply—"See me."

Phil walked across the hall and knocked on the *chargé's* door. Garland looked up, snatched a cable off his desk and handed it to Phil, noting—"This is not the cable I mentioned. You can see that one later. This one is for me. Tell me what you think."

Phil read it carefully. It requested the *chargé* to approach the Hungarian Government for approval—in the diplomatic procedure known as *agrément*—of the White House's proposed candidate for Ambassador. When Phil saw the name, he whistled and looked up at Garland.

"The current DCM in Bonn? He's a career officer and big league. Hungary is moving up the NSC's ladder of priorities."

"I agree. Hungary is damned lucky to get him. OK. Now, *this* is for you."

The cable was two pages long, a TOP SECRET—EYES ONLY for the *chargé*, but it asked him to show the cable to PAO Faljian because the bulk of its message was for him. The cable was from Garrison Portland at the National Security Council. Phil sat down, sensing that it could be a reprimand for his recent activities, which, probably through his own miscalculations, had somehow become known to Washington. As his eyes sped across the words, he realized quickly that it was nothing of the kind.

In the introductory paragraphs, Portland was informing the

chargé that the Public Affairs Officer, First Secretary for Press and Culture Philip Faljian, was being transferred from the American Embassy in Budapest to Washington for a senior assignment on Portland's staff at the National Security Council. The rest of the cable was addressed to Phil.

It informed him that he would assume a newly created position on the NSC as Deputy to Portland in dealing with Soviet and East European Affairs. The transfer was to take effect in two weeks, followed by two weeks leave for him before assuming his new duties. A longer leave would be arranged later.

In preparation for his new assignment, the cable continued, he was to prepare a report on the new chairman of the Soviet Committee for State Security, Yuri Vladimirovich Andropov. The request was based on the fact that in 1955 and 1956, Andropov was Soviet Ambassador to Hungary, as a consequence of which, and with the rich variety of contacts enjoyed by Faljian in Budapest, he would be able to extract considerable detail about Andropov's health, habits, proclivities, virtues and vices, from Hungarians who were in close contact with him.

Faljian was to know that this request was being made jointly by the National Security Council and the Central Intelligence Agency, which was in the process of preparing a psychological profile of the new head of the KGB. The CIA was also instructing its Station Chief in Budapest to cooperate fully with Faljian in the compilation of this material. The message concluded by setting a deadline of ten days for the cabled report.

Phil stared disbelievingly at the pages in his hand, closed his eyes, and fell back on the sofa. So George Quigley had been right. Portland had indeed had his eyes on him, and, Phil speculated, perhaps Ilona had played no small role in the appointment.

Garland arose from his desk, sat down beside Phil, and said—

"Do you realize that very soon, *you* will be giving *me* orders?"

"That'll be the day! You've got too much on me to put up with my insolence," Phil retorted as they both laughed.

"On the one hand I'm enormously flattered," Phil continued, sobering quickly. "After all the slights in my career, suddenly I leap over all the smug smart-asses who've made me feel the outsider and, to their chagrin—I'll enjoy that!—become the highest-positioned Armenian in the United States Government. My God, Jim, in the White House, no less! That's awesome. But the problem is the policy, the policy."

"You make it sound like 'the horror, the horror.'"

"Well, in a sense it is. I'm to become an advocate of the convergence of capitalism and communism."

"Which in your view can never happen?"

"Oil and water, Jim, oil and water. What gets me is the idea of even considering it. It's so damned defeatist. As though we've lost confidence in our own system and must turn elsewhere—to communism, for Christ sake!—to find compromise solutions. The appointment does have one positive side, though. I can now deal with the István Szirmais throughout East Europe at a comparable level—White House to Politburo. Convergence Theory or not, talking turkey to those bozos will be highly enjoyable.

"On the personal side, while I think I can handle Ilona, imagine being in the same city as Grace Quigley?"

"Oh, you won't have to worry about that," Garland assured him. "I just received a letter in the pouch from Quigley, with regards for you, by the way. He's been offered something in Southeast Asia and is relieved that he's still in the Service."

They both sat in silence digesting the new developments in Phil's career. Garland was the first to speak—"Phil, there's something about you lately I can't quite put my finger on. I mean in the last few months, but especially since your Soviet trip, I've found you more introverted, almost philosophical, and I don't know if I prefer that to the former Phil Faljian."

Phil nodded pensively and turned to his friend—"As always, Jim, you have the knack to see through me. Yes, I've really been shook up, mostly these last few days, and I'll tell you why. I've been surrounded by deviousness. Nothing has been what it seemed. The only true, genuine thing, I think—and hope!—has been the Beethoven manuscript, but even that has yet to be authenticated. It's been like walking through a jungle filled with mirrors. Mirrors, mirrors everywhere, what T.S.Eliot called 'a wilderness of mirrors,' but all with distorted, false images."

"Sounds to me like you've undergone a kind of epiphany."

"Perhaps I have. It certainly has made me examine myself, my identity, my outlook. Jim, I need something stable in my life, something, someone, to keep me on an even keel. Someone like . . . Kiki."

He looked questioningly at Garland, who said immediately—

"Is that a request for a transfer or a request for advice?"

"Both."

Garland laughed—"For Heaven's sake, Phil, in your new capacity, *you* call the shots. I think it's a splendid idea. Besides, the new Ambassador coming here will most certainly bring his own secretary."

"I knew you'd understand, Jim, and I'm grateful."

"You know, this place is going to be dull without you. Especially after this past year. You've given me some uncomfortable moments, but all in all, we've had a great tour together, and both Sarah and I will miss you very much."

Phil had never heard Garland speak in such benign terms to him. He had always, or almost always, been indulgent and appreciative of Phil, but the intimacy and warmth now were striking.

Garland suddenly adopted a mock business-like manner—

"Now, about your report, I'll exclude you from most Embassy matters—don't forget you're still on my staff—so you can get on with your inquiries . You've got no time to lose, and . . ." looking at Phil with a sly sidelong glance ". . . since the central figure of your report is surely a stranger to you, I suggest you get together immediately with the Station Chief."

Phil rolled his eyes skyward.

"I guess I'll simply have to, for appearance sake, if nothing else."

"Don't be so sure about that, buddy."

Phil looked at Garland, around the corners of whose mouth he detected a latent smile.

"Jim, you don't think . . . ?"

"Is it so unthinkable? Maybe he's already met the guy. Been to Moscow. Even been inside Lubyanka!"

They looked connivingly at each other and broke into laughter. Sobering quickly, Phil mumbled something.

Garland bent forward questioningly—"I didn't catch what you said."

"'*Plaudite, amici, commoedia finita est,*'" Phil repeated. "Beethoven's words on his deathbed," and responding to Garland's puzzled look, translated—"'Applaud, friends, the comedy is over.'"

Garland nodded slowly, absorbing their meaning. "Hmm. From all that I've learned from you, his life was no comedy. So at the end, it sounds like he became cynical."

"No, Jim, not cynical. He loved humanity too much to be a cynic, even in the closing years of his life. Remember that in his last symphony Beethoven shouted to the world 'Embrace, ye millions!' 'The comedy is over' expresses a profoundly tragic irony. Who can blame him? Life dealt him a savage blow and robbed him of his hearing. But look what happened: when total silence imprisoned him, he created those late great works—the sonatas, quartets and symphonies, maybe even a Cello Concerto—which have become monuments of our civilization. That was Beethoven's response to Life's cruel joke—the ultimate irony."

Garland looked inquisitively at his friend—"And you, Phil? Tell me. How would you characterize *your* life?"

Phil walked to the window and somberly watched the first snowflakes of the winter began to float down, rapidly coating the cold streets of Budapest with a white layer of frost.

"Thus far, Jim, it has been mostly good fortune. The demons

x

of my past—my violent childhood, my aborted musicological calling, my troubled diplomatic career—have been vanquished. I have confronted evil more than once and seen its many faces. I have forged new friendships, some unlikely, but yours the most treasured. I have experienced an often disquieting journey of adventure and excitement. And perhaps most of all, I have learned the virtue of, well, virtue.

"The past has been good to me, Jim. But it is the future that causes me concern, for no matter where I am, I know that I shall always be listening for the sound that started all of this—Fate knocking on my door . . . once again."

***

Author's Note

A novel is largely a product of the author's personal and professional experience. My prime sources have been my earlier academic studies in musicology, war-time activities in Psychological Warfare, followed by the de-nazification program, and finally by a career in diplomacy which took me to East and West Germany, Hungary and the former Soviet Union. Additionally, I have drawn on a variety of other sources to supplement—sometimes with only a fact or two, other times with more extensive information—my own experience in the matters pertinent to the novel.

The sources to which I am most indebted are:

"Thayer's Life of Beethoven"—Revised and Edited by Elliott Forbes, Princeton University Press, Princeton, 1964

"The Letters of Beethoven"—Emily Anderson, St. Martin's Press,NY, 1961

"The Interior Beethoven"—Irving Kolodin, Knopf, NY 1975

Historical materials from the *Széchenyi* Library, Therese von Brunsvik's diary, and the Beethoven Museum in Martonvásár, all in Hungary.

"A History of Hungary"—Peter F. Sugár, Editor, Indiana University Press, Bloomington, 1990

"Hitler"—Joachim C. Fest, Transl. by Richard and Clara Winston, Vintage Books, NY, 1975

"The German Opposition to Hitler"—Edited by Hans Adolf Jacobsen, Bonn, 1969

"Berlin Diaries, 1940-1945"—Marie Vassiltchikov, Edited by George Vassiltchikov, Knopf, 1987
"Canaris"—Andre Brissaud, Weidenfeld and Nicolson, London, 1970
"The Andropov File"—Martin Ebon, McGraw Hill, NY, 1983
"Andropov"—Zhores Medvedev, W.W.Norton, NY, 1983
"Behind The Kremlin Walls"—Vladimir Solovyov and Elena Klepikova, Transl. by Guy Daniels, Dodd,Mead & Co., NY, 1986

Printed in the United States
2008